HARMONY HALL

by
Jane Meredith

A SIGNET BOOK
NEW AMERICAN LIBRARY
TIMES MIRROR

NAL BOOKS ARE ALSO AVAILABLE AT DISCOUNTS IN BULK QUANTITY FOR INDUSTRIAL OR SALES-PROMOTIONAL USE. FOR DETAILS, WRITE TO PREMIUM MARKETING DIVISION, NEW AMERICAN LIBRARY, INC., 1301 AVENUE OF THE AMERICAS, NEW YORK, NEW YORK 10019.

This book is fiction based on historical fact. Some of the characters may have had their part in actual history but none are intended to reflect on any person living or dead.

COPYRIGHT © 1971 BY JANE JACKSON MEREDITH

All rights reserved, including the right to reproduce this book or portions thereof in any form whatsoever without the written consent of the author.

Published by arrangement with the author

 SIGNET TRADEMARK REG. U.S. PAT. OFF. AND FOREIGN COUNTRIES
REGISTERED TRADEMARK—MARCA REGISTRADA
HECHO EN CHICAGO, U.S.A.

SIGNET, SIGNET CLASSICS, MENTOR, PLUME AND MERIDIAN BOOKS
are published by The New American Library, Inc.,
1301 Avenue of the Americas, New York, New York 10019

FIRST SIGNET PRINTING, JUNE, 1978

1 2 3 4 5 6 7 8 9

PRINTED IN THE UNITED STATES OF AMERICA

**ON A GREAT PLANTATION—
DIVIDED LOYALTIES AND A WOMAN
TORN BETWEEN DUTY AND PASSION**

Throughout the colonies the American revolution mounted toward its climax—and on the lush Carolina plantation of Harmony Hall the savage struggle was echoed in the heart of beautiful young Elizabeth Richardson.

Two men in turn had saved her life—and now both claimed her love.

One was handsome, mocking James Richardson, fiery rebel leader, whose hand in marriage had snatched her from the gallows. The other was John, his brother, strong, upright, fiercely loyal to the Crown, who had rescued Elizabeth from a fate worse than death in a gruesome slave rebellion.

Iron-bound vows of duty . . . melting ecstasies of desire . . . intertwined as Elizabeth was torn between opposing sides in a war, and between diverging paths of love as different as heaven and hell. . . .

HARMONY HALL

Bestsellers from SIGNET

- [ ] **WOMAN OF FURY** by Constance Gluyas. (#E8075—$2.25)
- [ ] **ROGUE'S MISTRESS** by Constance Gluyas. (#J7533—$1.95)
- [ ] **SAVAGE EDEN** by Constance Gluyas. (#J7681—$1.95)
- [ ] **CRAZY LOVE: An Autobiographical Account of Marriage and Madness** by Phyllis Naylor. (#J8077—$1.95)
- [ ] **EUGENIA** by Clare Darcy. (#E8081—$1.75)
- [ ] **THE INCE AFFAIR** by Joe Morella and Edward Z. Epstein. (#E8177—$1.75)
- [ ] **TWINS** by Bari Wood and Jack Geasland. (#E8015—$2.50)
- [ ] **THE RULING PASSION** by Shaun Herron. (#E8042—$2.25)
- [ ] **THE WHITE KHAN** by Catherine Dillon. (#J8043—$1.95)
- [ ] **CONSTANTINE CAY** by Catherine Dillon. (#E7583—$1.75)
- [ ] **WHITE FIRES BURNING** by Catherine Dillon. (#E7351—$1.75)
- [ ] **KID ANDREW CODY AND JULIE SPARROW** by Tony Curtis. (#E8010—$2.25)
- [ ] **WINTER FIRE** by Susannah Leigh. (#E8011—$2.25)
- [ ] **THE MESSENGER** by Mona Williams. (#J8012—$1.95)
- [ ] **MASTER OF LOVE** by Glenna Finley. (#W8016—$1.50)

If you wish to order these titles, please see the coupon in the back of this book.

To my sons,
CURTIS AND JACK PLUMLY,
and to my husband,
GEORGE MEREDITH,
*for their love
and encouragement* . . .

Foreword

While most of the characters in this story were real people, I have, solely for the purposes of fiction, attributed to some certain loyalties and persuasions which they may not have possessed and placed them in situations in which they actually took no part.

David Fanning is entirely fictitious. He is merely the prototype of the opportunist generally to be found in times of war.

A topographical map once on display in the Public Library in Wilmington, North Carolina, gave me the names and locations of streets and certain buildings in the city at the time of the American Revolution.

HARMONY
HALL

CHAPTER
1

Fine spermaceti candles held their untouched wicks proudly aloft down the length of the table as if awaiting the approval of the young mistress of Land's End. The old silver epergnes, conscious of their superior height over the more utilitarian dishes to come on later, lifted delicately filigreed arms to display burdens of tropical fruits and the small apricot-colored orchids which had that afternoon been brought in from the forest.

Gleaming wineglasses stood ready to receive the rare old Madeira and Burgundy and Oporto, upon which Hugh Purdie prided himself. The lace cover on the table was the color of Devonshire cream.

With the salute of one about to die, the sun broke spears of yellow light against the western windows and shattered them into rainbows across the floor.

At this moment Elizabeth Purdie came into the room, and at her scarlet, clicking heels came Tip-toe. She approached the table, inspecting the appointments minutely. She straightened a serviette here, a fork there. Perfect! Not even Mr. Purdie could find fault with it.

"Tip-toe, have you seen to the cooling of the wine?"

"Yas'm, but he have ax'dent."

Elizabeth turned sharply, lifting one dark eyebrow—a characteristic gesture, and one more to be feared by the house slaves than a whipping.

"Whatever do you mean?"

"Aw, dat silly Dosie walk under de ola jar what's got de wine in it an' hits it wif she head. De rope swings and de jar hits 'gainst de house an' bus'."

"Well, for pity's sake, go and put out more. And tell Dosie that for three mornings Matisse will bring my chocolate."

Tip-toe emitted a sigh of commiseration for the plight of Dosie, and departed toward the winery, lifting his feet gingerly in an earnest endeavor to walk softly.

His peculiar gait had been the subject of much derisive comment in the O'Neal family during the days following his acquisition. Elizabeth smiled remembering her father's booming laugh when, in desperation at the boy's clumping through the room, she had made him walk across the floor behind her a hundred times imitating her steps.

"Tip-toe,"—she would frown—"like this."

"Faith, and ye look like a dancing master in petticoats, lass. Tip-toe, indeed!"

From then on, the slave had been called the ridiculous name, and Mr. O'Neal had chuckled every time he spoke to him.

It had been no laughing matter at first, however, the afternoon she had had to tell Papa she had bought him. She and her mother and her sister Constance, who was soon to be married to a French officer, had driven into Kingston for shopping, and soon Elizabeth had tired of watching her sister petulantly refuse one bit of finery after another. She had stepped outside the shop and, raising her parasol against the slanting sun, stood looking out over the harbor.

The town descended sharply in broad shelves from the street on which she stood, so that the tile-roofed white houses seemed tied to the hillsides by luxuriant vines and braced there by brilliant green shrubs and palm trees. At the bottom of the hill spread the dull gray roofs of warehouses, and the docks. Masts, slashed with white furled sails, stood against the sapphire water like a defoliated forest, their hundred different flags lying limp in the stillness. Beyond, the sea met the sky at the edge of the world.

Elizabeth had never had a nearer view of the wharves. All of her life she had been told that ladies of quality did not go there. But suddenly an unearthly scream tore through the air, followed by another and another. She could see a knot of men gathering. It could mean only one thing: some devil of a slave was getting the hide jerked off him with a cat-o'-nine-tails. Although it was the mildest form of punishment inflicted in Jamaica, God knew, considering what the Spaniards and the French had thought up, her father didn't like it, and more than once had warned his own overseers against more of it than was necessary.

She scooped up her skirts, glanced at the shop door, and

flew down the hill, arriving amid pushing and hauling slaves, seamen, stevedores, and even gentlemen in tricorns with their hair neatly clubbed and tied with swallow-tailed ribbons.

"Stop it!" she cried. "Stop it at once!"

The man's arm froze at the top of his swing, and the slackened ends of rope wrapped themselves around his wrist. His thick-lipped mouth fell open. The years of his life had trained his reflexes to the voice of authority, and he stared at her without moving.

"Put that whip down, you—you—"

The rope was slowly lowered. The motley crew who a moment before had been sadistically enjoying the flogging now stood back in bewildered silence. One bemused seaman crossed himself and murmured, "Madre, Dios!" It was well-known that the sight of a woman on the dock boded no good for the next voyage.

The foreman finally found his tongue. " 'E ain't no bloody good, ma'am. 'E just spilled a barrel o' rice and was on the point o' runnin' when I caught him."

"Take your hat off when you address me," she demanded.

The assembled company clawed off a variety of headgear.

" 'E ain't wuth a pound sterling, ma'am, and I'd take less if I'd a buyer."

Elizabeth unfastened the silk pocket hanging from her belt and tossed it with a clink of coins at the man's feet. Then she turned to the still-crouching slave and motioned him to follow her.

They reached the big barnlike warehouse where the sign said "O'Neal & Son," and marched into her father's office in the rear, the slave clumping along behind her.

Mr. O'Neal was sitting in front of a table piled high with papers and accounts. A jar of quills and a sand sifter stood at one elbow. At the other a grimy black child waved a palmetto fan more or less in his direction. His wig, which had been well-powdered in the morning, had slipped toward the back of his head and little trickles of sweat furrowed down his full cheeks.

Hearing footsteps, he half-turned, then swung around so violently that the little pickaninny left off with the fan and stared, showing the whites of his eyes.

"Elizabeth! By all the saints in hivven! What are ye doin' here?"

"Papa, I have just bought this man—for a pound!"

"Well, have ye now? Holy Mother o' God, and since when

has a daughter of mine felt it necessary to visit the slave market?" he roared.

"I didn't visit the market, Papa. I bought him here on the dock."

"God's whiskers, and that's worse! You've no business here, anyway. Pray explain yourself, ma'am."

Elizabeth's eyes were cast down as she stood respectfully attentive to her father, but now she raised them, he saw her anger.

"Pray explain yourself, ma'am," he repeated in a somewhat modified tone. Elizabeth was his favorite daughter—she had a will to match his own.

A tiny smile quirked the corners of her mouth as she started to tell him what had happened. Mr. O'Neal's face became red and white by turns as he thought of what might have happened to her. Then he began to smile at her daring, and soon they were both laughing so hard that the tears ran down his face and wilted the last traces of starch in his shirt ruffles.

Elizabeth sighed, remembering these things. She turned and wandered out into the patio. Life had changed so suddenly and completely. The smallpox epidemic had carried away her mother and father a year ago, Constance had married her Frenchman and gone to live in Paris. She was alone except for Mr. Purdie, who really didn't count, and Mamba, who had been given to her mother, Maria DeRossett, as a wedding present when she came out to Jamaica from Virginia to marry Kevin O'Neal. Mamba was family. Her skin was very black, but in spite of the mesh of fine wrinkles there was a shine to it like good strong coffee, and there was little that escaped her shoe-button eyes. Regardless of the bonds of slavery, she was the tyrant of her little world.

As Elizabeth dropped into a big peacock chair in the patio, Mamba began to wield the palmetto fan. Her lips pushed out in a stern pout and her voice came cross.

"You is gonna git yo'self so hot fussin' wid dat table you won't look lak nuthin'," she said, accelerating the motion of the fan despite the breeze rattling the banana leaves.

"Well, it's got to look just so or Mr. Purdie will take the roof off."

"You ain't say who comin'."

"Two men from the American colonies. A Mr. Richardson, some trader and shipper Mr. Purdie's done business with a long time. The other one is named Phinney. He is captain of Mr. Richardson's ship, the *Celestine*. Then there's Tim Gregory and Eulalie, the governor and his wife, and Margaret." She grimaced wickedly up at Mamba at mention of the governor's thin, acid daughter. "I do wish the Americans had brought their wives along—if they have wives. I'd like to know about the women in America. They say that the ladies, even the nicest ones, move about with the greatest freedom."

Mamba took a quick look behind her and lowered her voice. "How come Mist' Purdie askin' mens here what ain't got no wives 'long to keep 'em from lookin' at you?"

"Oh, Mamba, he has men here often," she said, making a stab at loyalty.

"He don't have no young ones," she answered firmly, pursuing her point, "an' when he have the ole ones Ah notice you is made scace by bein' sont upstairs while dey pleasures deyselves in de gempmuns' room."

"Oh, I don't know!" Elizabeth burst out, unable longer to put up even a show of propriety. "Sometimes I wish I could—just run away!"

"Naw you ain't. Ain't no DeRossett yit run from nuthin'."

Elizabeth didn't answer. She leaned back and closed her eyes. Maybe Mamba would stop talking. She did not want to hear any more about Mr. Purdie right now, nor the DeRossetts either. She wanted to speculate on what might turn out to be an entertaining evening. Mamba's words had echoed her own surprise when her husband had informed her of his invitation to the Americans, and brought up again her own resentment at the infrequency of her being in the company of anyone younger than the governor or of less kin than her cousin. They must be frightfully important guests! Suppose, oh, just suppose these gentlemen turned out to be young and handsome and . . .

From the distant kitchen came faint sounds of activity, then a muffled crash as of a fallen dish, which Elizabeth knew would be like a battle cry to Mamba. She could move with the swiftness of an old bear despite her weight, and now she dropped the fan and vanished through the loggia at the far side of the patio, her bright yellow turban bobbing ominously and her voluminous skirts aswing. Elizabeth was relieved. Now she could frown if she liked and not be admonished against wrinkles that were sure to come in a scowling face.

And frown she did, thinking that, after all, it was too

much to hope that this evening would be any gayer than others. The guests would probably be no more entertaining than the last had been, and she would go on like this until she was an old, old lady—too old to have any life at all.

But, she brought herself up sharply, it was just a step from this line of thinking to the depths of bitterness she had almost succeeded in avoiding. And certainly she was considered extremely fortunate. She might have anything she wanted so long as it proved Mr. Purdie's success to the world. The great stone house dominating the lush plantation was set high on the hill with terraces overlooking the sea, and was the only dwelling in Jamaica that had water piped into its patio pool. It was beautiful and comfortable, and the finest of everything had been garnered for the grandeur of its furnishings.

Her clothes were the richest and most elegant to be had— though there were few to admire them besides Mr. Purdie and the slaves. But was this all—these mere *things*? Wasn't there something more which should have answered her pent-up longing, the restlessness that boiled inside her? Was this all there was to being married? Was this love she was supposed to feel for Mr. Purdie? If so, those smuggled books were all wrong!

Mr. Purdie had been Papa's friend ever since she could remember. He was always bringing her little presents from far countries. She had liked this, and then Mama and Papa were so delighted when they told her he had asked for her hand in marriage that she, at fifteen, had been obediently delighted, too.

Obediently delighted with a young girl's fairy-tale dream of marriage. She would have her place at the foot of a candle-lighted table; she could swish through the great house in a taffeta morning dress like Mama, a jangling bunch of keys dragging at her waist. All this was mixed in her mind somewhat vaguely with the thought that by the wedding ceremony Mr. Purdie would be transformed into a godlike hero and she into a dignified lady whose only care was the welfare of her household and her husband's happiness—her place in the adult world secure.

Well, now she was seventeen, she had achieved some state of dignity and an outward show of contentment, but it had taken two years of rebellious struggling to do it.

She had never pictured Mr. Purdie stripped of the finery that went such a long way toward making the man. She had not seen him before without the high white stock that held tight and hidden beneath its folds the pendulous, wrinkled flesh swathing his Adam's apple. The first sight of his hairy, red-veined legs sticking out below his nightshirt and the bony chest above it had caused the first awful clutch of fear and dismay she had ever known. This was not the distinguished gentleman she had stood beside at the altar. This was just an old man—in a nightgown.

Only her pride and her promises in the church had kept her in bed, with the covers pulled tight to her chin and her eyes wide.

"Will you only trust me, my dear?" he had said. "You know I would not willingly hurt you."

She had choked out a barely audible "yes," but in the darkness her pulses throbbed in fear and anguish with the first inkling of what was about to happen to her. She would never forgive him for that lie. She could never forget the voracious greed with which he had dealt with her.

She dragged her thoughts back from the dark pit into which they had slipped after all. The scent of jasmine twining around the pillars was almost sickening.

But she had learned at last the trick of detaching herself— of keeping on the surface a calm and serene demeanor so that none but Mamba knew what simmered underneath.

At precisely six of the clock Hugh Purdie came into the patio. His lined face belied the studied agility of his step, which vainly sought to refute his fifty-six birthdays. He wore a fine embroidered waistcoat, yellow satin breeches, a coat of bottle-green velvet, and beneath the immaculate neckcloth a thick gold watch chain did its best to span the amplitude of his belly. He was rich and pompous and overbearing, but he could give no order, nor purchase any ointment that could lift the sagging tissues of his red-rimmed eyelids, nor erase the two fat gray mice that served for eyebrows. Life had etched deep about his mouth lines of selfishness and cruelty and avarice.

He looked at his wife jealously, dreading and fearing to share the sight of her. She was a prize possession, and yet, unlike other of his chattels, he was aware that he would never own her completely. He would have been scornfully incredulous if anyone had suggested that she might be unhappy.

"Damme, Mistress Purdie, you are well-gowned tonight," he said, and drew her onto his lap, his flaccid thighs trembling with the excitement of her nearness.

With adroit diplomacy, Elizabeth pretended to arrange her

skirts while she slid out as far as possible toward his knees, and leaned away from him with a quick question designed to take his mind off making love to her. How many times she had been ready for imminently arriving guests when he had pulled her upstairs, stripped off her clothes, and taken her to bed! His quick pleasure over, she was left frustrated and not understanding why, her face pink with embarrassment and fury. But still she must hurry to dress again, rearrange her tousled hair, and descend the stairs a gracious hostess.

"I've given Tip-toe orders to use more lime in the punch, Mr. Purdie. I didn't think there was quite enough last time."

His favorite subject. "Well, no, p'raps not. I think the darker rum, too, might be more pleasing to the Americans. And by the way"—he pushed her to her feet and walked a few paces—"keep the conversation light tonight. And don't start asking your impertinent questions. The gentlemen all have enough on their minds without talking their troubles at dinner. I want you to center your full attention on the ladies, do you understand?"

"Oh, are the gentlemen in trouble? What kind?"

"No trouble at all," he answered shortly and illogically, "this is strictly business with a danger of war in the background."

"Will your business be affected?" she inquired politely.

But he only lifted his heavy brows, smiling the infuriatingly paternal smile he reserved for occasions when she asked too many questions, and said, "No, no. Don't worry your pretty little head about things that don't concern you."

She was irked by his oft-repeated expression "your pretty little head," as if its sole function were to be admired for its beauty. Her eyes darkened with anger, then brightened with relief at the sound of the entrance bell and guests arriving.

Eulalie came in and threw her arms around her friend, giving her a fond peck on the cheek. "I do declare, Elizabeth darling, when I don't see you for a while I forget how beautiful you are. I do indeed! And isn't this a new frock? La! So soft and filmy, I believe you've been having the spiders spin for you!" It was fortunate that Eulalie's voice was a delight—one heard it so constantly when she was about.

"Dear me, I thought we'd never get here tonight." She smoothed her gown and perked the ruffles of her fichu. "The town is simply full of people. Simply full! Tim says it's because of fresh trouble in the American colonies. England sent some tea over there, and the Americans had already told them they didn't like the tax—pity's sake, who does like taxes!—and so some men from Boston went out to his Majesty's ships and dumped all that tea overboard!" Her laugh bubbled up like a spring.

"Why, that was some time ago," protested Elizabeth.

"Maybe so, but Tim says they are still mad about it. And King George says he is going to close their ports if they don't behave. That's why so many people are in town. The traders are trying to get in all the shipping they can before he does it, and all the planters are in town talking about it!"

Neither chronology nor exactness of information was Eulalie's strong point. Under her telling, world affairs appeared as through the wrong end of a spyglass, they seemed so amusingly unimportant.

Reluctantly, Hugh Purdie introduced Mr. Richardson and Captain Phinney.

"We are delighted to have you gentlemen." Elizabeth smiled, curtsying demurely, and even if she had tried, it would have been impossible to hide the dimple that appeared in her cheek and caused her elderly husband to wince.

It caused John Richardson to stare. Never, anywhere, had he seen so beautiful and appealing a face. Her eyes had lifted slowly as if the weight of the long black lashes was almost too heavy, and there was something in their gentian-blue depths that caught at his heartstrings. Her small white teeth gleaming in the candelight aroused in him a strange, hitherto unknown excitement.

He was quite tall and slightly stooped, as if his habit were to bend for every lintel under which he passed and he found it too tedious to straighten in the interim. His eyes matched the dark-brown hair which he wore unpowdered and clubbed at the nape with black grosgrain. His nose was large and straight, and nicely balanced by a high forehead and a certain jaw. And he couldn't be more than twenty-eight, Elizabeth surmised. Not for a long time had there been anyone so interesting in this house!

"Your humble servant, madam," he said as he recovered himself and bent to her hand, "your husband and I have been friends for years on paper, as it were, trading back and forth, so it is a pleasure to meet at last."

In every line of him it was evident that John Richardson was a chip off the block of stern New England. His solemnity was vast—but he was young!

Captain Phinney, small, wiry, with eyes that reflected the seas he gazed upon, leaned forward on the balls of his feet as if bracing himself against the roll of his ship.

"Servant, ma'am." He jerked a bow from the waist that made the brass buttons of his serge coat twinkle, and started to speak to Elizabeth again when, to Mr. Purdie's relief, the governor's high, nasal twang cut the soft air of the room, drawing her attention from the Americans.

"Elizabeth, m'dear! How is the mistress of Land's End? Gentlemen, gentlemen, how-d'ye-do, how-d'ye-do?" He blew in like a small hurricane, his wife and daughter quite breathless in his wake. For all his genial and effusive manner, he had a cold, sharp eye which he shut conveniently to certain practices of the wealthy traders and planters, and received in return their bountiful taxes, *almost* all of which he duly rendered unto King George. Under his regime both he and England had profited handsomely from rich Jamaica, but the underdog need look for no mercy from Government House. The treatment of slaves and bondsmen under his hand was a scandal even among other countries of the world, themselves not very far advanced in social behavior.

The aperitifs and the rum punch were being served in the drawing room by white-jacketed Negroes. Elizabeth required the serving boys to wear cotton socks in the house. It not only concealed their ugly black feet, but continuously polished the floors.

During dinner she scanned the faces of the other men. There was a tightness, a faint anxiety there that she had not noticed before. The governor alone wore a bland, self-satisfied expression, while he daintily stoked his stomach with great quantities of food. She noted, too, that they were skirting the subject of the American colonies and the crowds of people in town. Later, over cigars and liqueurs, after the ladies had retired to another room, they would put aside polite pretenses and talk. Good male talk. Talk that was fascinating: of ships and seas and cargoes from the world outside their island. She wanted to hear it.

"And what news," she asked with a guileless smile, regardless of Mr. Purdie's command, "do you bring us from America, Mr. Richardson?"

"I fear not very good news, ma'am."

"Pray explain, sir. We have thought your land the proverbial one flowing with milk and honey."

"It's more likely," put in Captain Phinney indelicately, "to be flowing blood before the year is out!"

"Oh, come, come, my good man," said the governor, eager to impress a new ear with the weight of empire behind him, "surely your countrymen can't hope to set themselves against his Majesty's authority to such an extent. These little affairs of Lexington and Concord can't be taken too seriously."

John Richardson looked up. "There's been a deal of talk about that, sir. I fear you don't know the Americans. But from what has been happening in New England, I'd say the chief danger at present, at least, is from the unbridled hostilities among our own people. It is almost civil war, sir. 'Tis bad enough to have our ports closed and embargoes laid down on account of a misunderstanding with our mother country, but far worse to find friends against each other— even families divided."

"You mean your people are not in accord, not solidly against Parliament in its murderous attempt to throttle all your trade?" Tim demanded, his face white with anger.

Hugh Purdie laid a hand on his knee under cover of the table. He regretted now having added the governor to his guest list. When he had invited him, he had thought to draw together a group of repesentative men all of whose views were likely to differ, but which, under the mellowing influence of good wine and a pleasant dinner, might reach a coincidence sufficient to produce some really helpful ideas. But he had, like others not in the midst of it, seen the American crisis in a diffused light, and had failed to allow for such strong feelings. It was not working out at all as he had planned, and to make it worse, this fellow Richardson could not keep his eyes off Elizabeth.

"Certainly not, Mr. O'Neal," answered John. "Opinions in the colonies are as diverse as the stars, but roughly they can be divided into two groups. Many of us hope even now to see the difficulties settled peaceably. We wish to resist the encroachments of Parliament to the limit of British constitutional law—certainly no further. But on the other hand there is a group who clamors for total severance from England. What may result from such a state of affairs is terrible to contemplate."

A supercilious smile twisted the corners of the governor's lips, as he tucked the lace frill into his cuff and began to peel a nectarine. Let the Americans argue over their big, awkward, savage country—old England would claim her own in the end.

"The truth about the matter is," declared the captain as if he had it all figured out, as indeed he had to a great extent, "that the lower classes see in all this a chance to rise and grab for themselves something they never had before and are not willing to work for, and at the same time to settle some old scores with their betters. Naturally nobody is moderate. You can be sure there's bound to be trouble when one of that ilk gets the power of a gun in his hand."

Hugh Purdie sent Elizabeth the age-old scowling demand from husband to wife to change her self-started subject. But she had no such idea. The other ladies were discussing domestic affairs, but Mistress Purdie floated deliciously in the flow of talk from the men, putting her own oar in with a question every now and then designed to keep it moving, and listening absorbed to John Richardson's eagerly offered explanations.

Quickly, her mind received and sorted the facts thrown about by the conversation, and out of it all came the startling knowledge that the trouble in America was likely to affect Jamaica. There was what was worrying Mr. Purdie. Like others, he believed that a good steady profit was to be obtained from importing cheap food for the thousands of slaves on the island—cornmeal, salt pork, rice—and she knew he would have a fortune in these commodities locked up in America by an embargo. Strange as the idea was to her that anyone would dare protest the edict of king and Parliament, yet if the Americans were being financially ruined by them and by having the English run all their bottoms off the sea, one could hardly blame them for protesting. But Mr. Richardson was not protesting much. He must still be on the king's side—though he certainly was far from humble in his attitude toward the crown's Jamaican representative. Imagine speaking so to the governor! And both he and Captain Phinney without a wig before his Excellency!

Though it was startling, she found herself liking the independent spirit of these men. They stood on their own feet and said what they thought, regardless of anybody. It created an impression of vigor and strength in strong contrast to the bowing and scraping and deferring she had been accustomed to before the governor.

The men were all talking louder and louder and getting red in their faces, and the captain had delivered a tirade against the British pawing over his papers and finding excuses to commandeer his men. He said he was as loyal as the Union Jack, but he was American enough to demand his rights as a free shipmaster, by God!

And Tim, emboldened by his words, pounded the table and shouted, "You're right, sir! And as for us, why the whole economic structure of Jamaica is based on our shipping and yours: our copra and hemp, and sugar and coffee and molasses, you've *got* to have in America; we've got to have your cattle and horses and tobacco and cloth and salt pork. Our slaves are starving to death! Already there is trouble in parts of the island. Have you thought what would happen here with our overwhelming percentage of blacks if there is an uprising?" He slammed his fist down on the table so hard that the prisms on the candelabra were set sharply atinkle. "By God, sir, I'll find a way to get my ships through if I have to resort to piracy, and the king be damned!"

The governor's quivering jowls turned purple as if he were about to have a stroke, and his wife fidgeted in her chair.

Eulalie, for once, was silent, her horrified eyes on Tim's face.

Now that she had set this kettle boiling, Elizabeth felt a twinge of fear at the enormity of steam.

"Elizabeth," Hugh Purdie exploded, "ask the ladies to retire!"

CHAPTER 2

The morning was bright with sun. Foliage, rain-washed by a sudden shower during the night, still glittered with emerald drops, and the clean fresh air carried a delicious fragrance of bruised petals and wet young leaves.

Since dawn Elizabeth had flitted about supervising the packing of hampers of food and wines, her laughter alternating with staccato commands. Now she was primped into a frock of flower printed chintz, a bonnet of white straw with chin ties of ribbon and a single pink rose beneath the brim.

From her high window she saw the men arrive and Mr. Purdie go down the steps into the courtyard to meet them.

After dinner the night before, they had succeeded somewhat in smoothing their ruffled feathers. An arrangement had been made for Mr. Purdie to take Mr. Richardson and his captain to the LaRoque plantation, where they would settle on a part of the cargo with which they hoped to reach New England before entrance into their home port became impossible.

News of this had filtered up to Elizabeth through the house slaves, who always overheard conversations and knew everything. To Mamba it was merely a matter of gossip about their master's business—something to talk about among themselves. But to Elizabeth it was another break in dullness. She knew that her incautious behavior the night before had been tolerated only because company was there—company that was financially important. Mr. Purdie couldn't say a word without losing face, and she had enjoyed a delightful evening. Today, while the Americans were still here and she had the chance, she would be even more reckless, but with a little coup designed to please them and herself.

As she entered the courtyard, bonneted and gloved, the

HARMONY HALL

look on Mr. Purdie's face was a sight to see. It was tightened into lines of shocked surprise, fury, and helplessness. He had had no intention of taking her along, but she gave him no time to speak.

"Good morning, gentlemen," she said, dimpling, "we have decided to make this a picnic after your business is finished at M'sieur LaRoque's."

"Splendid!" John exclaimed as he bent over her hand. "I've no doubt that the food in your hampers will match the excellency of your dinner last evening. This is a real pleasure!"

Togo brought the carriage 'round, Tip-toe climbed beside him onto the box, and soon they were rolling along the white crushed coral road between the turquoise sea and the voluptuous verdure of the mountains.

Elizabeth did not enter the conversation for a time. She had decided to be modestly silent awhile, for she knew that even before company Mr. Purdie's patience had its limits. She would pay for this pleasurable day, but it would be worth it.

Presently, she heard Captain Phinney say, "I sometimes wonder why I don't sight myself a little isle down in these waters somewhere and forget the world and its troubles."

"Because you are not made that way, Hosmer," John answered quickly. "You'd die in a month with longing for a ship under you. And even in isolation news would reach you that you might not like. I had a bit myself last night."

"So?" murmured Hugh Purdie politely but not encouragingly, as he caught the focusing of Elizabeth's attention.

"Yes, Captain Smythe brought his schooner into port in the afternoon. He was sailing out of Charleston, but having made several ports of call along the southern coast, he had a deal of news for me."

"Oh, do tell us, Mr. Richardson!" Elizabeth sat forward with bright-eyed interest.

"Well, the South would have been the last place I'd have expected any word that concerned me, ma'am. But this was of my younger brother, James, whom I had last seen at home on our dock. He had been eager for some time to take charge of a trip to the West Indies, but my father considered him too inexperienced to be entrusted with the responsibility of a vessel. Also, he had become interested in this rebel government cause, much to Father's anger. He feared, and rightly so, that James would be led into some hotheaded action, which has proved to be the case." He paused for a moment, and Elizabeth wondered if his tone meant that he was distressed over his brother's behavior or that he would like a little hotheaded action himself.

"One of our other ships, the *Half Moon*," he continued, "sailing under Captain Edmonds for the Bahamas, discovered an unexpected passenger aboard as soon as she was underway. James, always a favorite of Edmonds, and being part-owner of our company, immediately assumed authority of the vessel."

"How daring!" she exclaimed. "Do tell us more!"

"Elizabeth!" came Mr. Purdie's admonishing voice, but she only turned on John a brilliant smile.

"Well, the upshot of the matter was that he put into Nassau, and instead of picking up the intended cargo, he purchased a shipload of medical supplies and gunpowder. He then proceeded toward the Virginia coast, but at Capt Hatteras the ship was driven on the shoals in a squall. Fortunately, the vessel was not totally wrecked and was towed into Port Newberne on the Neuse River by Captain Smythe himself, who stood by and rescued all the men. The cargo was sold to a special agent of Mr. Thomas Jefferson and transshipped overland to Virginia."

"Damned lucky—excuse me, ma'am," growled Captain Phinney. "Those are treacherous seas off Hatteras. But James was always one for luck." Then he laughed. "The year he graduated from Harvard College he'd half the belles of Boston hangin' on his arm."

Elizabeth laughed delightedly. It all sounded frightfully thrilling. She wanted to hear more of this dashing fellow. "And where is he now, Mr. Richardson?"

Mr. Purdie delivered her a sharp nudge, but the smile on her lips remained in expectant waiting for John's answer.

"Captain Smythe left him in Newberne awaiting repairs three months ago, but where he will be by the time I can get there heaven alone knows. Smythe said the Continental Congress was so pleased to receive the supplies he had brought, they had offered him a commission in the American army."

"When do you plan to sail, Captain?" asked Purdie, hoping to draw the subject back to business.

"If the LaRoque stuff gets in on time we'll be loaded by Wednesday. If so, we'll sail with the evening tide."

The picnic food was consumed. The men leaned back against tree trunks or dropped into semireclining positions on the carpet of fallen leaves and talked through the lazy smoke of their long cigars. The forest was vibrant with birdsong and fragrant with the scent of rose apples and allspice growing in the pools of sunlight. Occasionally a flash of brilliant plumage marked the flight of a parrot.

Elizabeth stared contentedly up into the trees and listened to the talk droning among them. The captain and Mr. Richardson were telling about things that were happening in America, and though much of it escaped her understanding, she realized that much was going on in the world that she, on her narrow little island, had never dreamed of. How could anyone be so bold as to openly defy the king of England?

She glanced up as Tip-toe came running. "Mis' Lizbeth, Ah thinks we bettah go," he panted.

"Is this a model of your servant training, that they now dictate to their masters?" Hugh Purdie sneered.

She kept her voice low, and only he was aware of the anger underlying her words. "Mr. Purdie, you know that Tip is a good and faithful slave. If he has so far presumed, I know he must have a very good reason."

"Ah is, Mis' Lizbeth. Ah sho' is." His message came rushing out. "It's a meetin' of no-count niggahs ovah dat hill yonder. The people at LaRoque's tole me they was plannin' a risin', and Ah seed 'em a minute ago. Ah's powerful skeered we might git mixed up wid 'em effen we doan go."

"Why didn't you say so before, you black fool?" Purdie shouted, getting to his feet cumbersomely. All bullies are cowards basically, and he was no exception. He gave Tip a kick toward the waiting carriage and followed as fast as he could, not even waiting to assist his wife. John Richardson did that. He lifted her in his arms and set her gently down on the cushions.

"Have no fear, Mistress Purdie," he whispered as the horses moved off.

The vehicle rounded a curve facing a small natural amphitheater on the hillside below the road. Elizabeth caught her breath sharply.

"Look! There they are!"

Hundreds of blacks stood around a tall yellow Negro who was gesticulating and haranguing from a flat-topped boulder. They could not hear his words, but the voice was strong and persuasive.

Instinctively, at sight of anything unusual, old Togo stared and slowed the horses, but Tip-toe seized the whip and sent them into a wild gallop. At that instant the assembled slaves caught sight of the carriage. Intoxicated by the words of their leader, they surged up the hill, brandishing sticks and the long, curved knives used in cutting cane.

The majority were emaciated creatures—some minus one or both ears, the loss of which they had suffered as a punishment for attempting to run away. The tattered shirts of those who had shirts disclosed old welted scars, and the skinny wrists and ankles bore the thick gray marks of heavy chains. Their yells were wild and savage—many of them not even a generation removed from the African jungles.

They reached the road and began running after the careening coach. Hugh Purdie's face was as white as his stock.

"You should have stayed at home where you belong," he shouted at Elizabeth over the rumble of the flying wheels, and added, "You damned Americans should, too!"

Beyond a contemptuous glance at him, the other two men, riding backward on the opposite seat, held to the sides of the swaying carriage and stared at the oncoming horde as if they were merely interested.

Was nothing frightening to these Americans, Elizabeth wondered. She glanced back and, with relief, saw the slaves, seeing they were outdistanced, come to a ragged stop. Tip-toe looked back at her, the whites of his eyes showing.

"Is you all right, Miz' Lizbeth?"

"Yes. Go on!" She could hardly understand what she had seen. The slaves who had been around her all her life had seemed mild and gentle creatures—indeed, Mamba's kind old arms had been her refuge ever since she was born and she knew Tip would give his life for her. It had never occurred to her that the dark people could be like this until the other evening at dinner, and then she had not fully realized what Tim had meant.

The carriage now slowed somewhat and Hugh Purdie managed to speak, loosening his stock with a shaking finger.

"Go straight into town, Togo, to Government House. I will report this incident to the governor." He seemed to think that this settled everything.

But everything was far from settled. Rumors spread and grew. The handful of gentry composed of planters and shippers was hastily attempting to organize a militia to supplement the vastly inferior force maintained by the government. But this was next to impossible, for they disagreed among themselves as to concerted action, and many could not be persuaded that the trouble could be serious at all.

Hugh Purdie, at least in the presence of his wife, struck bloated attitudes of bravery, minimizing all reports and giving the impression that between himself and the governor the annoyance would soon be effectively settled. But there was not an hour that passed that the entrance bell did not announce some bearer of news that was fearful—of arson and killings and rape. Then on Tuesday morning his overseer, Carter, came in with a report that half the field hands had run away during the night.

"I can't understand it!" he kept saying over and over as he sank into a chair, the bubble of his assurance suddenly pricked. "I have never been a cruel owner."

And indeed, compared to some others, he had not.

Elizabeth dutifully suggested that he take a cup of coffee. She was touched with pity for his gray face and collapsed bravado.

"Now drink your coffee, Mr. Purdie, and don't fret so. We will manage somehow. We really don't need forty house slaves. They can be put in the fields."

"To do the work of four hundred? Don't be a fool!"

Then word came that the LaRoque plantation had been plundered and burned, that M. LaRoque was killed and the ladies in the house had suffered a fate so horrible that the messenger could not tell of it. He looked from Elizabeth to Mr. Purdie without speaking again, then turned, mounted, and rode off at a gallop under the waving coco palms.

An idea began to take shape in Elizabeth's mind as she realized the full import of the man's news. When Mr. Purdie had gone about his business, she slipped out to the stable, ordered her horse saddled, and made her way through the canebrake to the beach road, cutting through the thickets to avoid the highway.

The old cart in the cove at the foot of the cliff had given her the thought. She would leave the horse tied beside it, out of sight, and walk back up the steep, narrow path that came out at the back of the house. She knew that Mr. Purdie would never face the possibility of having to make an escape. In his smug and pompous mind he would refuse to admit that the god who watched over gentlemen would not step in and protect him even at this late date. Maybe he was right, but she would sleep more soundly tonight knowing that the deity's intangible protection was augmented by her own contribution of one little horse.

Toward evening a small cloud came up and scattered a few big drops of rain that kicked up the dust in little snuff-colored puffs. Not even a cooling wind accompanied it, and the sun sank red into a strangely calm, flat sea. The weather was most unseasonable. August had always been the month most feared for hurricanes and deluging rains—rains that poured in solid sheets and winds that tore and beat at the island like giant claws. But so far there had been only a few light showers, and the heat intensified as if the elements in holding off so long were saving energy for complete destruction.

Elizabeth was exhausted with the heat and the fearful anxiety. In the humid darkness she lay awake for a long time. She thought of her sister, who was half the world away—away in a strange world but a very gay one. She had become a popular lady of the French court, and scarcely a month passed that did not bring her letters and books, newly printed, each of which she described as "the rage" in Paris. Elizabeth hardly saw how they could be the rage of anything since they consisted almost entirely of long treatises on the subject of politics and a strange new doctrine of government wherein every man was to be equal, free, and rich. A man named Voltaire wrote that all property should be divided and all men educated to take part in governing. How stupid! Imagine slaves and overseers and dock workers having property—much less knowing the law! Mr. Purdie had denounced it all as trash, and she was much inclined to agree with him. How could anyone believe that such creatures as these rioting slaves should help to govern?

With this thought returned the present, stark and terrible. Suppose they came and burned Land's End! It was incredible that such a thing could happen, but it *had* happened at the LaRoque plantation. Evil forces were at large—it was like the tales the old Negroes told of the great earthquake a century before, when old Port Royal had slid into the sea, when houses had crumbled into dust and death and destruction lay everywhere. She thought of the Americans safe aboard their ship, and the knowledge of their presence in the harbor gave her a feeling that something still might happen.

When she went into the dining room next morning Mr. Purdie was already there and having his breakfast, the corner of a large napkin tucked into his shirtfront. His agitation had not harmed his appetite, but her entrance into the room dulled its edge. She seemed to be the embodiment of all he stood to lose by this trouble: a great fortune and a beautiful young wife. And he meant to keep them both, by God, in spite of all this silly confusion. He had not realized either how restive and out of hand she had become until she had openly defied him, and her obvious interest in these Americans infuriated him. Perhaps he was not giving her enough time—it was easy to forget, once one of the creatures belonged to you, what a lot of attention women required. After this trouble was over he'd give her a child. That was really what she needed to settle her down into a wife as proper as she was beautiful. His piercing eyes narrowed as they swept over her face.

He arranged some papers into a stack beside his plate and tried to be casual as he tilted a pinch of snuff from a small silver box onto the knuckle of his closed fist and applied it first to one nostril then the other. "This is Mr. Richardson's sailing day," he said, glancing at her to see how the mention of his name affected her.

"Yes," she murmured, "I had forgotten he was sailing with the tide." But she had not forgotten. If only something would happen to keep that ship in port!

He dabbed his face with the napkin. "There's not a breath of air stirring. The weather is making up to something," he said, observing her shrewdly from under the heavy brows. "I trust it holds off until he's at sea."

"I hope so." She met his eyes candidly, then bit the end of her tongue, partly in anger at perceiving the trend of his thoughts and partly in dread of the possibility of the *Celestine's* being caught in one of Jamaica's violent storms.

He pushed back his chair and went outside, where Carter had assembled the remaining slaves for instructions. Elizabeth followed to take a look at the sky. Overhead it was blue as lapis, but down toward the horizon it had turned thick and mud-colored. There was no doubt what that meant. But her attention was brought back to the more immediate crisis by Mr. Purdie's words giving orders for the defense of the house, telling the Negroes and overseers that at the first sign of trouble they were to come into the patio and barricade the doors. Then he asked with heavy sarcasm that carried a threat, if any more of them thought they'd like to run away.

Elizabeth looked at the cringing bodies and terrified eyes

and smiled at them reassuringly from behind Mr. Purdie's back. They were as bewildered as anybody else at the behavior of their kind, and she felt a tender sympathy for them. Afraid to join the rioters for fear of failure and subsequent punishment, they were almost as afraid to remain with their master and be punished for the sins of the others.

Pickaninnies clung to their mothers' skirts and stared like little owls, not looking very different from their elders. Fear hung over everyone, Elizabeth thought, like a cloud of dust.

Then from the back of the crowd she saw a big black Congolese Negro with a ring in one ear slink off under the banana trees and make his way toward the road. A woman near him half-turned to follow, sat down suddenly in the dirt, and began to scream, "He gone! He gone!" The overseer gave her a sharp kick and she subsided into a low moaning wail.

Mr. Purdie was so angry that he said not another word. With half his slaves gone, he knew the danger of trying to stop the Congolese Negro. One crack of a gun just now could turn the remaining ones into allies of their rioting brothers. He watched the dark form vanish in the thick undergrowth beyond the avenue, then turned on his heel and reentered the house, pushing Elizabeth ahead of him.

She felt the air pressing downward like a great weight, with the ominous stillness of a vacuum. Not a leaf stirred as they made their way through to the terrace on the side of the house overlooking the bay. Now, low in the south, heavy blue-black clouds were piling up and boiling toward the island. The sea was still flat and gray, for the sun seemed suddenly to have withdrawn into some far reach of the sky and drained the light out of the world. Presently flocks of sea gulls began flying inland. Elizabeth watched their frantic flight as they fled their own danger, and although Mr. Purdie was still too furious to speak a word of comfort or reassurance to her, her spirits lifted.

With the last of the birds came the first gust of the wind. It lifted leaves and dust and anything moveable and sent them whirling in wild circumfusion. It whipped the fronds of the palm trees and tore the shiny green leaves of the bananas to shreds. A queer yellow light spread over everything. Chickens and pigs ran squawking and squealing for shelter. Dogs slunk away out of sight.

She lifted her chin exultantly. There was something in the force and power of the oncoming storm that awakened an excitement in her blood. This was a new world, glorious and free. There was nothing everyday about it! She was glad, glad that something was happening—something big. Bigger even than Mr. Purdie or the governor or the rioting slaves. Everything was topsy-turvy. Not even the impending danger to herself or to the *Celestine* and the Americans reined her thoughts as they went charging down the wind, sailing the booming clouds, skyrocketing on the spears of lightning.

There was a sudden sound of calls and heavy, frantic pounding, and Carter was at the entrance with the faithful slaves behind him, shouting that a mob was in sight at the foot of the avenue.

The slave children were herded into the big sewing room at the top of the house. Groups of men were stationed at the windows with whatever weapons could be found, and the women huddled wild-eyed in the patio. There was barely room for all, but they managed to push the heaviest pieces of furniture against the doors and so make more space.

Elizabeth ran upstairs and sent Mamba up to settle the children. Then she went to her own bedroom overlooking the road and sat down on a low stool to watch through a crack in the shutter. When she could decide what was going to happen, she would tell Mr. Purdie about the horse she had hidden and they could make their escape.

The violence of the storm was increasing. Branches scraped and banged against the wall outside in bold relief against a mountain of sound. Rain pelted the windows. The darkness in the closed room was stifling. Tip-toe squatted silently behind her.

As the mob approached the house, pushing, straining, almost bent double in their efforts to walk in the face of the wind, she saw that many of them carried muskets. Cold fear gripped her. She had not thought them possessed of firearms. The only ones in the house were Mr. Purdie's pretty pair of dueling pistols. She half-rose to go and tell him of this new aspect of the situation when he entered the room, and she saw that he had them in his hand. His face was ghastly white, and somehow the sight of it stiffened her own spine.

"If I can only get a word to these blacks I should be able to stop them. If not . . ." How like him to think he could stop this black tide with a puny word! "Don't leave this room," he continued. "Tip will be here to guard you."

"I am not afraid," she said, moving away from him, "but I'm not going to stay here in this dark room and die like a rat in a clothes press!"

"But you are safe here!"

"Do you think I would be safe if that rabble gets into the house?"

He blanched. "Where do you think you could go in all this?"

"Oh, Mr. Purdie, listen to me. I have tied my horse down at the foot of the cliff. We can get there somehow and get away."

"What! And leave everything I own in the hands of these crazy Negroes? No! And, besides, you could not possibly get down to the beach. The road is cut off, and the storm would tear you to pieces."

As he spoke, the first wave of the wild and angry mob broke against the house in a maelstrom of sound and fury that could be heard above the roaring, screaming wind. Axes crashed against the shutters and outside doors, splintering the heavy wood. Those who could not get to the openings beat against the walls as if they would tear its very stones apart. The rain poured in solid sheets, blown horizontally in from the sea, so that they gained some protection in the lee of the house.

Elizabeth's eyes grew black with rage. "I'm going to Tim and Eulalie. You can't stop me!"

"You shall not leave this room." He turned and went out, and she heard him say something to Tip-toe. When the big slave came back into the room, he was wearing one of the pistols thrust through his belt. From outside the door came the sound of the heavy key turning in the lock. He was locking them in!

Savagely she turned to Tip-toe. "Can you open this door?"

"Now, Mis' Lizbeth—"

"Take a chair, take anything, but open it! I don't care if you tear it down, but get it open!" She went to the clothes press and snatched down a dark bonnet and cloak, and her eye fell on the new hat with the pink rose. A moment's regret assailed her. If the house fell into the hands of this mob, as seemed likely, all her beautiful things would be strewn to the ends of the island. But no matter . . .

Under Tip's blows the door finally flew wide.

"Now go and call Mamba—hurry!"

She heard the sharp report of a musket shot, followed by the anguished cry of the slaves inside. Footsteps clattered up the stairs and Carter burst into the room.

"It's Mr. Purdie!" he shouted. "They hacked through the

shutters and one climbed on the sill and shot—took him full in the face! We can't hope to hold them off much longer unarmed."

Elizabeth stared at him as if she had not heard. In the very center of wild sound there was the absence of sound; then, as she realized that Carter was stunned into immobility, her eyebrow lifted and her eyes snapped. "Mr. Carter, why are you not back at your post? Do you want them to come in and take us all?"

Carter came to his senses. "Go if you can, Mistress Purdie, for God's sake. We will try to hold them as long as we can." He stumbled through the doorway and Elizabeth turned to Tip-toe.

"Go bring me your master's keys."

Tip hesitated only a moment. The look on her face was more ominous than the sounds of battle, but Mamba pleaded with her not to wait.

"Hush, Mamba." She stamped her foot, but the little sound was drowned in the bedlam. "I've just remembered something."

Tip-toe came back with the keys. She selected one and went into the adjoining room to the big oaken chest where Mr. Purdie kept his valuables and his store of gold. The inside had been a mystery to her, fascinating at first, then disregarded as it became plain that she was not intended to know its contents. Mr. Purdie had always withdrawn from it such jewels as he cared to have her wear, then carefully replaced them under lock when she took them off.

Now the velvet-lined tray displayed such gems as she had not dreamed he possessed, pieces she had never seen before. But there was no time to stand wonderingly before them. She scooped them into a soft leather bag and lifted the tray aside to disclose the sacks of gold beneath. How that ragged mob would love to get their hands on such treasure! But they should not have it. She clutched the bag of jewels against her breast and went back to the bedroom where Mamba was stuffing what garments she could lay hands on into a bolster cover.

"Gawd's sakes, Mis' Lizbeth, les git outta here!" Tip-toe shouted, the heavy bags of gold in his hands.

Already the running feet of rioters were swarming up on the roof and the gallery at the other end of the house. Mamba straightened up and looked at him, her hands on her hips. "You ain't gonna walk out fronta all dem niggahs wid dem sacks in yo' han's. Gimme dat gole an' tuhn yo' back." She tore a strip of cloth from a sheet and tied the bags to each end, then lifting her multitudinous petticoats, knotted it firmly about her waist.

"We ain't goin' front of 'em nohow," Tip said, his face obediently turned to the wall as if they had all day, "we got to slip out on de ocean side ob de house an' go down de cliff. Dey ain't on dat side yit on account de wind an' de wet. Hit's ouah only chance. We got to hurry!"

When they reached the courtyard, they could hear the heavy, rhythmical pounding of a battering ram against the front door. The rioters would be inside in another few minutes.

Tip-toe heaved and pushed and finally wrenched the door open into the face of the wind. It tore at their clothes, sucked the breath from their nostrils with a steady, unceasing power. The rain was like a thousand silver needles against the skin.

They bent their heads, worked their way toward the retaining wall at the edge of the cliff, and scaled it—Mamba managing to get over with surprising agility, considering her own weight and the gold beneath her skirts.

As they started down the cliff, the big Congolese Negro who had left the day before stole around the end of the house. Knowing the premises, he had thought to come upon an unguarded door and make easy entrance for his comrades from within. But he had caught sight of the little party and gave a savage yell which the wind tore from his lips as soon as he uttered it, so that Elizabeth neither heard nor saw him until he was leaning over the balustrade close above her, his long curving cane knife upraised to swing. Then she heard the crack of the pistol Tip wore, and saw the Congolese Negro stumble back and fall.

The sharp report brought the first realization of her own personal danger. Everything had happened so fast since the beginning of the storm that it all seemed part of some wild dream.

The descent was perilous, but the wind for once became a powerful ally, pinning them against the face of the cliff while they clutched at trailing lianas and found each lower foothold in the rocks. Her hands were scratched and bleeding, and long red friction burns smarted on her arms and knees. Once she glanced down over her shoulder, but the sight of the sea boiling over the rocks below turned her dizzy. She shut her eyes and clung desperately for a moment to the trunk of a stunted, wind-twisted tree until her heart stopped its violent pounding and she could grope blindly for another step.

After what seemed an age, their feet touched the spongy sand. They found the horse in the shelter of the shallow cave where she had left him. The straw covering the bottom of the cart was dry.

Tip hurried them into the rickety vehicle and covered them with an old oilskin.

The wheels, merely two solid rounds cut from the end of a great log, crunched, bumped, and staggered along the road as he lashed the terrified animal. Out beyond the reefs the waves rose mountain-high. The bay was whipped to froth, and in many places the water was over the road.

Elizabeth felt that every jolt would tear through the top of her head. It was stifling under the oilskin, and rank with the African smell of Mamba's great fear. She lifted a little corner and peered out. Back toward Land's End there was nothing to see, but even while she gazed, smoke and flames shot skyward from the house. There was no one in sight—only the landscape gone mad with storm and fire. She pulled the covering hastily back over her head and crouched down again in horror, her whole body shaking with sobs.

Tip-toe's one aim, according to her orders, had been to get to Tim and Eulalie's house, but as they neared the town, he saw great columns of smoke rising and on closer view found all the streets choked with rioting slaves who were setting fire to everything in their path. He turned into a side street, grinning at them and waving his whip in salutation, hoping they would think the precious cargo of the cart was only loot pillaged from some plantation. The trick was successful, but he soon saw that the only entrance to the town would have to be made from the waterfront. When he reached there it was plain there would be no safety anywhere in the city. From every street he could see far up the hill the roiling, battling throngs. Fires were breaking out in every quarter.

"Lawd Gawd!" muttered Tip-toe.

Elizabeth stuck her head out. "What did you say, Tip? Where are we?"

"Ah say we cain't git nowhere in town. We's at de wharf."

"Oh!" She hesitated a moment, trying to orient herself, then an idea came. "Look quick, Tip, and see if you find Mr. Richardson's ship— Oh, there! I see it." She pointed. "Perhaps we can go aboard until this trouble is over. He can't sail now for the storm."

Tip-toe forced the horse up the barrow ramp onto the boardwalk and drove to where the *Celestine* plunged and tugged at her anchor. There was no one on the wharf, but as the cart came alongside the ship, he saw a sailor come on deck.

"Hey," Tip shouted. "Please, suh, call Mist' Richason—quick."

The sailor braced himself against the rise and fall of the vessel by holding fast to a stanchion.

"We's runnin' from de riots. Ah's got Mistress Purdie heah, bringin' huh to safety."

The sailor disappeared and in a moment returned at a run behind John Richardson and Captain Phinney. At the far end of the quay, heavy gray smoke began to coil around the buildings and drift low in the rain.

John shouted orders, and others came hurriedly to lower the gangplank. Captain Phinney rushed from the fo'castle. John leaped dangerously to the wharf, waited until there was some level between the ship and the dock, and carried Elizabeth aboard.

Mamba started up the plank, reaching back to steady herself and Tip-toe.

"You goin' to let these niggers on, Capt'?" a sailor yelled.

"Of course," Captain Phinney shouted. "She's got to have her servants." He well knew what would be the fate of these faithful ones if the mobs found how they had been cheated. He caught sight of the fires down the wharf and realized that the warehouses were being looted. Next would probably be the ships. He began to bark orders, and the vessel came alive. They would have to sail now, regardless of weather, or be burned at anchor. He had all an old seaman's respect for a blow like this, and the utmost contempt for a situation that made it imperative that he sail into the teeth of it against every principle of navigation. He had never encountered so perfect an example of the devil and the deep blue sea, but the choice had to be made at once, and a watery grave was better than a fiery one.

Down the way other masters were making the same decision, with vessels drawing out into the churning water as best they could, with no room to spare, bumping, grinding against each other, bending with the violent, unpredictable wind.

Elizabeth felt the toss of the ship where she sat in the captain's cabin. On a thin edge of panic she got up and went to look out the porthole. She could not just leave like this—just leave without anyone's knowing what had become of her. Why, she had never been farther away from Jamaica in her life than the little islands of the bay! She went back and sat down, a hundred confused thoughts shuttling through her head. Her teeth began to chatter. Mr. Purdie was dead. She was a widow. A widow! How strange. She felt no overwhelming grief, surprisingly, and crossing herself was only an absentminded gesture. By all the rules she should be draped in black, but there had been no time for such things even if she had thought of them, and so she was still clad in a damp, crushed morning dress. She shut her eyes and tried to feel shame that her heart was not in mourning either, though she knew that at the first opportunity Mamba would insist on all the trappings of conventional grief. Her eyes flew open at the thought. Then she shut them again and tried to call up a picture of Mr. Purdie, thinking that would bring a little dutiful sorrow, but all that came into focus were the heavy gray brows and, in her own body, the well-remembered spastic contraction of fear at the pit of her stomach whenever he started to make love to her. No, it was no good trying to think of Mr. Purdie.

She regarded the scuffed toes of what had been a dainty pair of slippers, and began to center her thoughts on the immediate future, thankful that she had Mamba and Tip-toe. John entered the cabin followed by a boy with a pot of tea.

He sat down wearily. "We're past the reefs, ma'am, safe if the blow becomes no worse. Your servants have told me of Mr. Purdie's violent and untimely death. I want to offer my sympathy."

Quickly and modestly she cast down her eyes. Condolences were a surprise. She had not thought of them. "Thank you, sir. I hope we won't be too great an inconvenience to you," she answered demurely. "We were trying to get to my friends' house, but it was impossible."

"No inconvenience at all," he said heartily. "I am glad you came to us—the town must be in shambles by now. But you must have no fear, for wherever this ship goes, as long as you are aboard her you are on British soil."

She could not help wondering, from what she had just escaped and from what she had been hearing of the world lately, if this could be the guarantee of safety it was intended to be. She sipped her tea and gave him a wan smile. Her spirits rose shamefully at the light of absorbed admiration that glowed in his eyes.

"What is your destination, Mr. Richardson?"

"Nassau first. We will complete a cargo there—several hundredweight of coffee, twenty or thirty puncheons of rum and sugar, if we can get it—then on to Connecticut."

"Perhaps there will be someone sailing back to Jamaica from Nassau with whom I can take passage."

"Oh, yes—yes, of course, that is possible. But I don't believe Jamaica will be safe for a long time."

"I don't know," she murmured, her eyes darkening with concern, "I don't know what to do."

"Well, we shall see," he said kindly, with a gesture toward patting her hand which he shyly arrested in midair. "In the meantime you must stay with us. Let us take care of you."

CHAPTER 3

Despite the meager wardrobe Mamba had been able to scramble together in their frenzied escape from Land's End, she kept Elizabeth bandbox fresh. She washed her clothing in the big wooden tub formerly used for the captain's bath. The fichu of fine white lawn she spread wet upon the looking glass to dry, and pleated the ruffles minutely between her gnarled old fingers next morning. Tip-toe did the best cobbling job on the ruined slippers that he could do with the inadequate tools from the ship's chest.

They were moving into the strange blue harbor of Nassau when Mamba came into the cabin where Elizabeth waited impatiently for her renovated garments.

"Oh, do hurry, Mamba," she said gaily, jumping out of the bunk, her tousled dark curls flying about her shoulders. "Mr. John and I are going ashore."

"Ah doesn't know what to make of you," she answered querulously, "yo' Ma woulda been prostrated by what you been thoo, an' you ain't even teched!"

"Well," she retorted, "I'm sorry all these bad things had to happen. I'm sorry for Mr. Purdie. I'm sorry as I can be, but I don't see how it would help any to moan around and look sad. Why, it's been three weeks! I can't spend my life grieving."

Mamba rolled her eyes upward with an exasperated sigh. "You hasn't got the mindfulness of a gnat. Ah is sho' gonna have mah han's full."

Elizabeth threw her arms around her. "Oh, Mamba, this is the first time in my life—"

"Yas'm, Ah knows. But Ole Miss look down she sho' ain't gwine 'prove of me lettin' you run wild. She liable to tell de Lawd what a wicked ole black woman Ah is."

"Then I'll tell Him you are an old black cherub!"

"Ah ain't heard you spendin' much time talkin' to 'Im lately," she answered tartly.

Elizabeth went out, slowing her feet to a sedate and dignified walk. John Richardson had admired her in the role of a modest housewife, and now as a widow. He must not learn too soon that she was enjoying these heady new experiences and looking forward to a life of her own. If she had kept one man interested all this time in the close quarters of a ship when she was hardly ever out of his sight, what might she do in America?

For she was going to America! The captain had scorned any idea of her trying to return to Jamaica at present. John had added the weight of his argument in trying to persuade her to make her home with his family in Connecticut—at least until conditions in Jamaica were more settled. In the meantime he had hinted that he hoped to endow her residence there with more permanence.

Ashore, they found the busy port full of excitement. A prize ship had just been brought in by a British schooner. They saw that she flew the Pine Tree flag of New England. The captive crew was being marched toward town with their hands tied behind them, their faces stony.

"I am a loyalist," John said as they watched the men filing along in front of the red-coated officers, "but the owner of that rebel vessel is likely a friend of mine. I know every shipper on the New England coast. It's sad to think that matters have come to the point where no ship is safe on the seas. Piracy in these waters was bad enough, now every sail will be a menace."

"Surely the *Celestine* is in no danger of capture," she suggested, hoping to be reassured, "since she flies the British flag."

"Yes, but don't forget that the rebels won't take these captures lying down. Both sides can play at such gaming." His face was heavy and stern, and she quickly changed the subject. This going ashore was a lark after the weeks at sea and she wanted no serious, depressing conversation.

At the inn, their dinner was served in the high-walled garden. Crimson blossoms spilled over the white stone. The tables were shaded by pepper trees and flaming poincianas. Her eyes were round with excitement at dining in public for the first time in her life.

Presently Captain Phinney joined them. "That prize was the *Macon* out of Savannah," he informed them as he slid into a chair.

"What was she carrying?"

"Powder and arms to Philadelphia. Looks like all hopes for a peaceful settlement are gone, John. Yes, and all hopes for shipping, too, unless we arm our vessels."

John sighed and shifted uncomfortably in his chair, any weighty problem habitually overcoming his enjoyment.

"It's running too close to the wind of piracy to suit me, and Father won't allow it!"

The captain regarded him with reproof. "The old man won't have much to say about this, son. I think it's time you stopped considering his word the law and gospel."

John flushed but said nothing.

Elizabeth interposed, "This is very confusing to me. You are British subjects and yet the British make prizes of your ships."

"Yes," the captain said. "It is a very confusing time. No one knows just where he stands or what he can do about it."

"Well, I know where I stand. The *Celestine* shall never fly any flag but the Union Jack," John said, and stared hard at the captain.

"Don't be too sure of that. I'm with your sentiments, but that don't alter the fact that if we hope to keep her under British colors we've got to take steps to insure it. We are unarmed because your father couldn't be persuaded of the wisdom of mounting a few guns. So, we've got to maneuver back to Connecticut without sighting a sail. A damned-near-impossible job—excuse me, ma'am. I think we ought to run into Portsmouth and—" He broke off abruptly and leaned forward, staring at the inn door. John turned to see what had affected him so and half-rose.

A young man stood framed in the doorway, handsomely attired in a flowing cloth cape faced back in red and a three-cornered beaver hat. Lace fell from below his square, deeply cleft chin. There was a look of power in the broad shoulders and slightly arrogant bearing as his eyes took in the garden at a glance. He tossed his hat to a porter and flashed him a brilliant smile as wide-cuffed gauntlets followed in rapid succession.

"James!"

A few long strides brought him to their table, and amid the greetings and handshakes, Elizabeth was conscious of a strange flutter in her heart. So this was the daring, gallant brother whom "half the belles of Boston" had hung on!

He bent low and touched her hand with his lips, but his eyes held hers the while. They were merry eyes—brown, with flecks of gold in their depths.

"Your servant, indeed, madam," he said, and his voice was deep and rich, with a peculiar warming quality like fine red wine. The sound of it flowed along the veins and imparted to the whole body a pleasant glow. Elizabeth had never seen anyone whose mere presence created such an electrifying air. The quiet and solemn dinner at once became a party! Thoughtfully, she rubbed the back of her hand where his lips had touched.

"Well, you do get about," John said when he had sat down, and in his tone was a suggestion of reproof. "How do you happen to be in Nassau?"

"I might turn the question back to you," he answered mischievously, "but no, I'll tell you first—I forgot that my recent travels are probably unknown to you."

"On the contrary, I had news of you in Jamaica. Pray tell me, though, that I was misinformed as to your taking a ship without Father's leave or knowledge."

"Now that I cannot do and be truthful, my dear brother, and a lie shall never pass my lips!" His dancing eyes sought Elizabeth's and he winked.

The captain saw the look, and he thought, Ain't that James to the life! Talkin' truth and flirtin' with a pretty woman in the same breath. He sure knows how to trim his sails!

It was a brief glance, but Elizabeth had had a taste of a new, delicious fruit.

He turned back to his brother. "Things have moved rapidly since you left. I hope Father's third of the money from my cargo may change his mind as to my ability as a businessman—though I doubt it." His white teeth flashed in a grin as he went on. "I sent it up to him by Captain Edmonds in the *Half Moon*."

John scowled, then changed what he had intended to say. "Then the ship is repaired? And if you sent it back home, how did you get here?"

"The repairs didn't take as long as we first expected, so as soon as she was ready I sent her home with a cargo of rice and tobacco. I came to Nassau in my own vessel—clearance out of Wilmington, North Carolina, sir! If you'd care to come aboard—"

"Just a moment," John stopped him firmly, "suppose you begin at the beginning. You sound as if you'd no intention of returning to Connecticut."

Elizabeth caught her breath awaiting his answer.

"I fear we are boring the lady." He smiled. "Later I'll be pleased to tell you all. It's a fair thrilling story—I'd like to hear it again myself!"

Through the laughter and talk that followed, Elizabeth observed the two brothers from between her lashes. It was plain that there was a change in John since James had joined them. He seemed defensive, as if he had drawn into a shell. But James was charmingly, gaily oblivious to anything save his own enjoyment. He looked as if he knew what he wanted from the world and meant to have it, but certainly to have a good time while he was about it. It was but a little time until she found herself rising to meet his spirits, laughing and talking with an ease and abandon she had not known since childhood.

John's disposition did not improve at this trend of things. Too often he had seen this sudden awakening of interest in his brother, followed inevitably by the lady's falling hopelessly in love and breaking her heart over him. That this should happen to Elizabeth was unbearable, but there was another and stronger reason: he wanted her for himself. He had never before wanted any woman, and his desire was the fiercer for being new. He had always regarded James' amorous escapades with scorn, knowing that he took none of them seriously. Indeed, he doubted if his brother were capable of feeling very deeply about anything.

The breach between them had started when they were children. John was obedient and steady and could be depended upon to return from an errand with whatever he had been sent for and not with an empty sack and a sticky mouth. Ezekiel Richardson could frown like a thundercloud and John toed the mark, but though James toed it when the birch rod hung over his backside, he did so with eyes flashing defiance.

As they grew up, John became more and more like their father: dignified, meticulous in attention to duty and business, in becoming a solid, solemn citizen. James, on the other hand, never allowed the more serious aspects of life to infringe upon his enjoyment of it. John sat in the family pew honestly interested in the seriousness of life and the fear of God. James sat and exchanged provocative glances with certain demure bonnets within his line of vision. It was only when this trouble with England had been dragged off the streets and into the pulpit that he became attentive to what the eminent divine had to say.

Secretly, John admired his brother because he knew that all the sterling qualities of character were there, but his admiration was colored uncomfortably by the knowledge that he himself could never hope to see his own virtues clothed with such charm. When he might have expressed approval, he met only the mocking smile and the mischievous twinkle of the gold-flecked eyes—a look James had long employed to silence the pious lectures, and whatever pleasant words he might have spoken shriveled within him. There remained only the difference of political opinion to make the rift complete.

Now, as they sat over coffee in the sweet-scented dusk of the garden, John refused to allow the subject to change. He took a perverse pleasure in hearing of James' adventures, which he knew he himself would never dare, but of which he would, by long habit, disapprove.

"Where did you acquire the vessel?" he asked, his voice suspecting a shady transaction.

"In Wilmington. And that's not all. I bought a plantation, too!"

"A plantation?"

"Indeed. You know, a sizable piece of land with a house, furniture, stock, slaves, carriages—the whole kit!"

John frowned. "I don't see what you wanted to buy so far from civilization for. Father has land to spare in New England."

"My dear brother, North Carolina is far from being the wilderness you imagine. 'Tis said that not even in Virginia can you find such thoroughbreds—neither among horses nor women! And such hospitality, such charming people. Why the planters live like kings!"

"I thought you had lost your taste for kings."

"Not so long as they create opportunities for a man to line his pockets!"

"And do you propose to give up your place in our firm?"

"Yes. I have already sent Father my resignation."

"It will be a blow to him," John complained.

"I think not a great one. He never approved of me much," James answered lightly. "There is too much for me in the South. Already I have a thriving plantation three times the size of our stony acres at home, a hundred slaves, and the *Quadrille*, in which I am shipping, among other cargoes, my own crops. Another ship, a schooner, I hope to have off the ways next year."

"*Quadrille?*"

"Yes, my brigantine." He was laughing again, and Elizabeth watched the ways his eyes crinkled up at the corners. "I call her that because she is light on her keel!"

"Oh," she cried, "can we see her?"

"Certainly. You shall be the first lady on board—and bring us luck."

"No," John said hastily, "we are sailing early. We can't take the time tonight." He did not know how soon he'd be aboard the *Quadrille*, an unwilling passenger.

But James turned to him quickly, "Oh, you must come. I want to deliver to you your share of my last cargo on the *Half Moon*—a sizable quantity of gold, most of it in good Spanish milled dollars."

"If you are talking about that cargo of gunpowder, I won't touch a penny of it!"

"In God's name, man, why not?" Captain Phinney wanted to know.

"Because I can't, with honor, take money derived from the sale of ammunition to be used against his Majesty."

The captain rubbed his nose and started to speak when he was interrupted by the arrival of a swarthy Levantine carrying a pack of jewelry, uncut stones, and various trinkets which he spread on the end of the table. Hastily he drew from a Morocco case a small pink shell. Thin, delicate, its fragile convolutions deepening in color to the apex where the lapidary's only touch was a piece of gold filigree through which ran a slender chain. He held it up to the light, then took the liberty of laying it against Elizabeth's fair skin. She gave a little cry of pleasure, and he hastened to press his advantage.

"See how the warmth of the lady's flesh gives life to it? Only a pound nine for such an exquisite piece!"

James laughed at the fellow's methods and drew the money from his pocket. "Oh, yes, 'twould be a pity to think of it lying on that cold velvet. Fasten it for the lady."

John followed the man with his eyes as he moved toward other tables with his pack. What he had feared was happening right before him and he was powerless. He knew that though he would give Elizabeth his life, he could never make her a present of a pretty bauble in so debonair a manner as his brother.

As they rose to go, James asked, "What's your destination?"

"Home."

"And Mistress Purdie?"

"I have persuaded her to take refuge with us in Connecticut for as long as she likes."

"So! That's the quartering of the wind is it? Brother, you amaze me!"

When Elizabeth came on deck next morning, the last loads of fresh provisions were being stowed on board for the voyage. Half-naked, brown-skinned boys filed up the gangplank bearing baskets of fruit, live chickens and pigeons, and cheeses wrapped in plantain leaves. Little Josephus, the cabin boy, addressed her, knuckling his forelock, "The captain's compliments, miss, and Captain Phinney says will ye be pleased to join him and the gent'men in the saloon for coffee?"

"Thank you, Josephus." She smiled into his freckled face.

"Mr. James come a while ago," the child volunteered. "He's gonna sail along with us."

This was exciting news certainly. Last night when they went aboard the *Quadrille* after all, there had been arguments on every point the two brothers could find to disagree upon. Twice it had been incumbent on her to pour the oil of a changed subject on the turbulent conversational waters. They had argued both sides of the trouble with England until they were almost ready for a war of their own, then jumped to the question of arming merchant vessels, and for a while it had been a verbal dogfight. Now, something had been decided while she slept. Something that meant perhaps this brief encounter with James was not to be the end.

She hurried her steps, arriving at the saloon to find John sunk morosely in a chair, his chin in his hand. James was standing over a big map spread out on the table. He turned as she entered and assisted her over the threshold before either John or the captain could rise. John motioned her to a seat beside him and began to tell her of their changed plans.

"Captain Phinney thinks we should be safer to accept James' offer to convoy us at least as far as the Carolina coast, then make a coastwise trip from there," he said. "This dancing ship of his is armed to the top o' the masts!"

"You really think so, too, but you are too stubborn to admit it," James retorted. "It is suicide to sail the Atlantic now without guns."

"Very well, but we'll not mount them until we can legally do so."

"Suit yourself"—James shrugged and half-sat on the edge of the table—"but you'll wake up some morning in a coral bed or in the hold of a strange vessel, your ship and your liberty both gone."

"Some are willing to purchase liberty at the price of honor."

James grinned. "That depends on your point of view."

"Well," John answered, rising, "I want you to understand that I am willing to sail with you not from fear of attack, but because I can give Father an account of your activities. The British flag has never yet skulked about the seas!"

Elizabeth smiled, more than half-understanding that John's submission to the plan, no matter what he said, was due to a curiosity to see his brother's plantation. But because her own spirits were so high over the arrangement, she clasped his hand comfortingly. Then she looked up at James out of the corner of her eyes.

"I think that I, too, should enjoy seeing your new home—and Carolina."

The little geste was experimental, and she was flustered by his leaning toward her, a quick response leaping into his eyes.

"I shall try to see to it that you aren't disappointed!" He slid his leg from the table and stood. "Don't you think, John, since you are unarmed, I'd better take your passengers with me?"

"On, no," Elizabeth answered for him quickly. "I'm sure we'll be quite safe." Far safer, she thought, than with you too near. The spark of interest she seemed to have conjured up in him, she suddenly discovered, could ignite the long-dry emotional tinder within herself and consume her prospects for a new and fascinating life of her own. That would never do for one so avidly anticipating arrival on shores that offered so much. America! La! She would enjoy herself in that land. The very word had a ring of freedom!

James stood on the bridge of the *Quadrille* in the bright, hot sun, his legs braced against the roll of the ship, and scanned the horizon through the spyglass. He had been caught in a calm this morning for an hour, and for the first time since they had cleared from Nassau he had lost sight of the *Celestine*. But the harpoon log which had been heaved out at intervals all afternoon now showed good speed. He ought to pick up her sail at any moment.

A strong breeze flapped the fine linen of his shirt against his back and through the full sleeves along his arms. It was good to be plowing through the swells again with the wind in his face after the stillness of the morning. He grinned a little at the thought of what Captain Phinney would be saying: "A fool for luck, that James!" Well, the weather had been perfect, and not a stranger had crossed their course. John was the one who should never have gone to sea, he thought idly, he simply had no feel for it, and the sea knew its own. Too bad his father never understood that. He had tried to force his material into the wrong molds, and as a result it had cost him not only in money, but finally a son.

There was no rancor in his thinking. He was merely reviewing the facts. His father would never consider him anything but a frivolous youngster, and so there was nothing to do but strike out for himself. There could not have been a more propitious time. The political rifts in families had sent more than one young man to seek his own fortune. Still, he knew deep inside him, there was a bond of affection there that would make him look after their interests whenever he could, whether it was appreciated or not.

Mr. Kendall, his mate, came up and offered to watch. He handed over the glass, glad to get the squint out of his eye, and went over to lean against one of the well-hooded six-pounders. But his rest was short-lived. Almost immediately Kendall shouted, "There she is, sir! But there's another sail coming up on her port side!"

James snatched the glass. Of course the strange ship might be only a merchantman passing within hailing distance. They were still so far away that the sails of both vessels were like little handkerchiefs against the sky. As the *Quadrille* dipped into the troughs, he lost sight of them, but as she rode the crest of each swell, he could see that the two ships were drawing nearer and nearer together. He noted that he was gaining on them now, and presently it was plain that *their* speed had slackened considerably.

A frown of annoyance crossed his sun-browned forehead. Name of God! Why hadn't Phinney tried to outrun the stranger? But even as the question crossed his mind, a puff of smoke like a cotton boll was tossed into the air.

"They've fired on her, sir!"

"So I see," he replied grimly.

The *Quadrille* had never been drawn into combat. There was not a stain of burned powder on her shining guns, and a swift surge of excitement rose in him at the thought of releasing their formidable power. Yet there was apprehension, too. A skirmish at sea was always of doubtful outcome, regardless of men and equipment. His lower lip thrust forward and the gold glints in his eyes turned to gilded steel. The *Quadrille* represented quite a slice of his worldly goods, and he did not intend to lose her. Yet he must see that the *Celestine* reached the Carolina shore in safety. He'd never hear the last of it if anything happened to her after his insistence that she sail this course with his protection.

The plan had seemed simple in Nassau, but even while suggesting it, the actual running into difficulty had been but a vague possibility in his mind. Perhaps he had suggested it out of bravado. Perhaps he had hoped to show John that the younger son who lacked experience had at least the foresight to arm his vessel according to the necessity of the times. Be that as it may, there was only one thing to do. It had been his own idea, foolish as it was to put his ship in danger of loss, and he must see it through. The devil of a spot to be in.

He lowered the glass abruptly. "Mr. Kendall, man the guns!"

"Aye, sir." The mate bawled out orders and men came running to their battle stations as others broke out ammunition. Muzzle covers were hastily snatched off, and skysails, which had been luffed earlier, were now run out. The *Quadrille* leaped forward like a stallion under the whip.

Then a thought struck James like a physical blow. The stranger had to be a rebel, since the *Celestine* was flying the British flag. He would not only look ridiculous, charging up to do battle with one of his fellow patriots, but if the news ever got back to Wilmington, his carcass would jolly well decorate a gibbet. How well he knew these fierce-eyed revolutionists whom he had joined more out of opportunism than anything else. Oh, he had learned all their arguments, and he knew all the catchwords they had used to stir up the people—it had been great sport to sit in the taverns with his friends and vie with each other with their oratory—and they fell from his lips as glibly as if his convictions were as deep as Sam Adams'!

What he did not realize was that they were as deep. The catchwords of liberty, freedom, equality, had struck root in the subsoil of his consciousness so far beneath the surface of his thinking that he himself did not know they were there. Like thousands of other young men, most of his thinking was done from the top of his head and from the lighter side. The leaders held out to them a complete change from the old ways, and a share in the ownership of America; there was everything to gain, and it appealed to the youth of the country as the new would always appeal to youth—especially when it appeared to touch their honor and involved the chimerical glories of war.

Now through the glass he could see the name *Diana* in gold letters on the stranger's bow, and the serpent emblem of the rebellious colonies streaming above it. The sight of the bunting exactly like the one whipping above his own deck brought the accustomed thrill. It represented his own freedom, and something deeper that he had not taken time to consider. But who was the captain of the *Diana*, and how could he be expected to treat captives? His brother was aboard the helpless *Celestine*, and a woman passenger—a devilish pretty one at that. The grimly humorous thought crossed his mind that there was something in the old saw about traveling alone and faster.

The memory of Elizabeth's face caught at him as any beautiful woman had always snagged his attention, and he chuckled as he thought of John's being in love. It was written all over him. Well, when he did find one to his liking, he had showed good taste. But he could not help wondering if, in his silent adoration of the seemingly demure young lady, John had sensed the fires smoldering not far beneath the surface of her tranquil gaze. He himself had, certainly, and he began to wish his brother had not discovered her first. She was too tasty a dish to be served to a New England farm! She should be in the center of his own gay circle in the South. But he was not the one to tell her what she was missing. From Captain Phinney's description of the old man she was married to, he had an idea that she was ready for a frolic. But it was high time John lay to and found his moorings, and if he wanted the girl, he would do all he could to help him win her. She was no more than any other pretty woman as far as he was concerned. There were plenty of these to be had, God knew, without tying yourself to one.

Through the glass he suddenly saw the *Diana* come about in position to use grappling hooks. He cursed himself for a fool for getting into the crazy predicament, then seized on the first solution that entered his head. "Mr. Kendall," he shouted without taking his eye from the glass, "do we still have that Union Jack?"

"Yes, sir, I think so."

"Bring it up, then strike our flag. And pray that no one sees you making the change!"

Mr. Kendall gaped at him for a moment, then turned to obey, since he could offer no alternative, and it was obvious that they could not attack a ship flying their own colors in defense of one under another flag.

But when he returned with the British banner over his arm, James' voice cracked at him like a pistol shot.

"Throw the thing into the sea, and run up the signal for a parley."

This was more to Mr. Kendall's liking, and he was relieved that for some reason his captain had not intended so dishonorable a move in the first place.

As he watched the king's colors float away astern of them, he handed the spyglass over. "Here, Mr. Kendall, give me the details." Then he stepped to the open hatch and shouted, "Holy, bring my uniform!"

"Oh, they've grappled the *Celestine*, sir, and are boarding her!"

"I saw that," James said, standing on one leg as he stripped off the brown breeches and took a pair of buff-colored ones from the hand of the tall, grinning slave. "What else is happening? Can you see?"

Kendall smiled. "Captain Phinney seems to be putting up a terrible fight, sir, unarmed though he is!"

When Elizabeth awoke, it was dark, but by the light of a small Betty lamp she could see that she was in a strange cabin. A very beautiful cabin with white painted paneling and a carved ceiling. Against one wall stood a washstand with a brass rail around the top, and on it a china bowl, pitcher, and soap dish. Opposite was a low dresser on which a wig stand rested and a man's silver-backed toilet set.

The bunk was soft and luxurious, and for a moment she lay drowsily observing the room. Then the realization that the ship was under way brought her wide awake and sitting bolt upright. She tried to think back, but the last she could remember was standing on the *Celestine*'s deck beside the captain while he tended the wounded sailors. She lay back on the pillow then and hid her face as the horror of the fight returned. But there was no shutting out the remembered sound of the cannon, the crash of the *Celestine*'s mainmast as the *Diana*'s forward gun sent it toppling; the heavy clank of the grappling irons, the rattle of small arms firing; or the sight of men being bludgeoned into the sea with every sort of weapon, heads split wide, the blood-covered deck. Then she had seen with relief the arrival of the *Quadrille* and heard the sudden, deafening quiet that followed. But Captain Phinney was in a shouting fury, and John was frozen with silent anger when they saw James in his splendid, gold-braided uniform push off in his gig toward the *Diana* instead of pounding her to pieces with his cannon. She had gone to the littered deck to be of such help as she could, held the captain's ditty box and the basin of water while he bent on his short knees and performed quick and clumsy surgery, cursing the Sons of Liberty in general and James in particular.

At first the horror before her had closed out every other thought; then, when she realized what the captain was saying, she was furious with herself that she could be so taken with a man who could perpetrate such an outrage.

"They're over there on the *Diana* now, laughing over how neat we sailed into their trap," she remembered the captain saying savagely. "I ought to have known better than to trust the young bastard!"

"Oh," she had said, "you don't suppose— Oh, he couldn't do such a thing."

"I don't suppose. I know!" he exploded, and rubbed his nose red on the top of his rough sleeve.

She wondered if John believed the same thing, and looked over to where he was splinting a sailor's broken arm. His mouth was hard and his eyes black with anger.

For a long time there was no word from where James sat in parley aboard the *Diana*. She went on shifting the medicine chest to more convenient positions as the nauseous task proceeded, trying not to hear the groans and the anguished curses following the cauterizing iron, trying not to remember the magnetic pull of James Richardson's gold-brown eyes. Then her ears were full of the screams of a sailor who was losing a leg. Her damp clothing clamped itself stickily against her body, and a terror started swirling round and round in her head. The last thing she knew was the deck rising higher and higher beneath her feet, and the sea and sky whirling into one nebulous mass of darkness—the voices of the men coming to her as if from a long way. . . .

What had happened since then? This ship was not the

Celestine. For all she knew it could be the *Diana* and she a prisoner aboard it. It might be the *Quadrille*, but if it were true, as the captain said, that James had deliberately led them into a trap, she'd as well be on one as the other! These rebels must be frightful people. Those who had clambered over the *Celestine*'s rail had looked like pirates. Where was everybody? Where were Mamba and Tip-toe? She swung her feet over the side of the bunk to the floor, her eyes dark with anxiety. Someone had unfastened her bodice. With shaking fingers she hastily buttoned it and moved cautiously toward the door.

The passageway was dark. Bracing herself against the toss of the ship, she walked out into the blackness and straight into the tall figure of a man.

She smothered a scream and gasped.

"So you are awake at last," came the rich, familiar voice.

Her legs gave way with a maddening mixture of panic and relief, and she would have fallen, but James caught her up and carried her back into the lighted cabin and dumped her rather unceremoniously on the bunk.

"Don't you know a lady shouldn't go charging around in the dark after such a swooning fit?"

"I'll charge wherever I like, James Richardson, and I should think you'd be the last person to tell anybody what they ought to do—getting us all into such trouble!"

Her eyes were blue-black, and her hair lay in a tumbled mass on the pillow. He sat down beside her on the bunk. "Et tu, my dear little Brutus?" He lifted her hand and pressed his lips where the faint shadows veined the underside of her wrist. Might as well enjoy whatever the gods offered in this nightmarish interlude, he thought. His generous intention to encourage his brother's suit with the widow Purdie had been swept away in the flood of bitter and unreasoning accusations John had heaped upon him.

Elizabeth snatched her hand away, her eyebrow lifted. "I should think you'd be ashamed to deliberately hand over your brother's ship to one of your confederates," she said icily, "no matter how badly it was needed."

He dropped her hand, his nostrils dilating. "Who told you that?"

But she refused to answer, and for a moment their anger held, matched spark for spark. Then he laughed lightly and rose. "Shall I try to convince you that you are wrong, or would it be worth my effort?"

"I don't want to be convinced," she said furiously, then

wondered fleetingly if she had told a lie. "But if it is not too much effort I would like to know where I am, and then you can please get out of my cabin!"

"How ungracious you are, madam. With one disgruntled passenger aboard I had hoped that you and I at least might enjoy pleasant company."

There was a gentle knock, the door opened, and John stood on the threshold, his face lined with fatigue and bitterness. "At your customary recreation, I see," he said sharply.

"Hardly," observed James dryly, remembering the new and titillating experience of being invited *out* of a lady's bedroom. "I was about to give Mistress Purdie some information, but since you seem to be so much better informed on what has transpired, I suggest you relieve me. I am sure she will be much more interested in hearing from you all about my base motives." He went to the dresser and gathered up his toilet things. His eyes were laughing as, turning at the door, he made a deep bow. "I trust, madam, that you will enjoy the conforts of *my* cabin."

When the door had swung shut, John said, "I apologize for his behavior. Are you feeling quite well, my dear?"

"Yes. What happened, John?" If she could start him talking, it would give her a chance to settle the seething emotions inside her.

He dropped wearily into a chair bolted to the wall beside the bed. He had changed his ripped shirt and put on a coat of dark-burgundy velvet that in the glow of the lamp deepened the color in his face. "We ought not to have allowed you to help with the men. When you fainted I was taking a stitch in a sailor's head and couldn't stop, but when the captain got to you, James was coming aboard from the *Diana*. Williams, the *Diana*'s captain, came with him bellowing that the ship was his and all the men except myself were his prisoners. James, I suppose to cover his embarrassment, lifted you and carried you down to his gig and onto the *Quadrille*, and left that loud-mouthed fool to give orders on my ship! I followed as soon as I could get my personal belongings together."

"Captain Phinney a prisoner! How horrid for him."

"Yes, and James said he argued for half an hour with Williams getting *me* off. If you hadn't been along, I'd have chosen to go on, a prisoner, and fight my way out when I could."

"But John, doesn't that prove James didn't intend all this?"

"Are you defending him?"

"Yes—oh, I don't know. It could have been just an unfortunate coincidence." She got up restlessly and went over to the little square port where the breeze was stirring the curtain, and stood looking out at the water rippling under a half-full moon. "Perhaps you don't understand—"

"You are mistaken, Elizabeth. It is not hard to understand these men who call themselves patriots. But though I saw all the beginnings of this trouble, I had not realized that matters had reached the stage where a man would betray his own brother!" He dropped his head in his hands and sighed. Immediately her heart went out to him.

"Well, he could not have fired on the *Diana*, could he? Since they were under the same flag?"

"Of course he could," he said. "Blood should be thicker than a piece of bunting."

"But if they had fired at each other, we might all be at the bottom of the sea by now."

"I tell you it was a rendezvous. A well-worked-out plan."

"John, I think you are being stubborn and unreasonable. You have no proof, yet you have made up your mind to believe him guilty and you won't hear any idea that it might have been accidental."

"The loss of our ship and cargo is proof enough, and I should think the loss of your slave would convince you!"

"*Who?*"

"Tip-toe. He was included with the men as a captive. I tried to save him for you, but Williams' greedy eyes had already spotted him for an excellent servant."

"Well, why didn't James tell him he was mine and not part of the crew?" she demanded furiously.

"You forget that my gallant brother had already picked you up and departed for this ship, leaving Williams to give us the result of their decisions. Would you call that the behavior of an innocent man?"

"Oh, I don't know. I'm all mixed up!" she wailed, pushing her hair back impatiently from her face and dropping down on the pillows again.

"Well, he's a scoundrel. There's no doubt about it now. He's always been irresponsible, but I've never known him to be vicious before." He got up, clasping his hands behind his back. His shadow undulated large on the wall as he passed and repassed in front of the swinging lamp.

Elizabeth looked at his streaked and smeared boots and reflected on his words. "What will you do now, John?"

"I'll go immediately to Governor Martin when we land in Wilmington and offer my services in bringing these rebels to justice, no matter what James promised his compatriots. 'Tis sure he had to agree to be responsible for me. If it gets him into trouble, so much the better. Maybe he'll come to his senses. My greatest regret is that it will not be possible for a little while to take you to Connecticut." He crossed the little space between them and took her hand. "I've dreamed of having you with me in my own country."

She looked up and smiled, purposely misunderstanding him. "Don't worry about me when you have so many worries of your own. Mamba will take care of me. She always has. And, John, please send her to me now. I'm very tired."

"Of course. Thoughtless of me to keep you talking so long. Good night—darling."

Presently Mamba came in bearing a dainty tray. There was a note beside the plate written in flowing script. Elizabeth read:

> This ship business was one of Lady Luck's little whims. I couldn't have managed better to get you aboard the *Quadrille* if I had tried! You are very beautiful with your head on a pillow—

There was no signature. Only a large *J* below, and she knew it did not stand for John.

She snatched a cup from the tray and threw it at the door, narrowly missing Mamba's head.

CHAPTER 4

The days swept by rapidly as the *Quadrille* sailed north. The moon filled and flooded the night seas with quicksilver, and presently there was a sharpness, a tang in the air. The lungs drew it in thirstily as if there were a limit to the supply, and by their own alchemy transmuted it into a golden elixir that energized the body and set it tingling with briskness and vivacity. It was autumn in America, and the bracing air was carried out to meet the ships on the wings of a north wind.

Elizabeth, accustomed to the languor of tropical Jamaica, had never felt so intensely alive. Her heels tapped up and down the deck and color whipped high in her cheeks. But the change in climate could not claim all the credit for her exhilaration. After the first days of strained politeness following the *Celestine* affair, she gradually warmed, then responded to the blithe, compelling gallantry of James Richardson. She knew she was far too interested in him and she fought a constant battle with herself to keep him from finding it out.

Mamba, with shrewd observation, had already startled her by saying, "Now don't you go gittin' buttahflies in yo' stummick to marry Mr. James, 'case he ain't doin' nuthin' but playin'."

"Who wants to marry him?" she had demanded, shying instantly away from a thought so menacing to her new freedom.

At first James had tried to explain what had happened and his position in the matter of the lost ship; then seeing it was useless, he had attempted to jolly John into better humor. But when that failed, he ignored him and turned his full attention to Elizabeth.

It was wonderful—breathtaking! Though in her heart there was a very real affection and admiration for John, she had been repressed too long not to enjoy riding the wave of gaiety and excitement that James created. She tried to draw John into the warm fun, but it was impossible. He believed, and nothing would change his mind, that his brother had played him false. He saw with impotent fury what was happening to his chances with Elizabeth, but he seemed powerless to behave so that he did not defeat his own purpose.

They had finished dinner on the last night out of Wilmington, but were still lingering at the table when James was called to see to some trouble with the binnacle light. Land had been sighted and it was wise to show no gleam across the water. When he had left the saloon, John still sat without speaking, turning the stem of his wineglass in his fingers.

Elizabeth regarded his doleful expression and finally burst out, "Why can't you get over your displeasure, John? What's done is done and there's no use holding your anger forever. You're not even civil to him!"

He pushed back his chair and rose. "You are not the first woman to be taken in by him. I hope you do not regret it. Good night."

She was sorry her words had not changed his humor, but he had been so angry at James that even she had been included in his churlishness. Now she was glad he had stalked off to bed and left her alone.

When he had gone, she ran up onto the deck. The moon was waning now, but it still rode high enough to make the night bright as day, and her heart made a little skip that there was a possibility of being alone for a while with James. She was not quite certain what to expect from such a meeting, for it had not happened before. Somehow John was always present, and too, she had to admit that James himself, for all his attentions and pretty speeches, had not gone out of his way to manage it.

She moved over to where she could see the men in the wheelhouse: Mr. Kendall at the helm, and James' tall body silhouetted against the pale sky. Still water lay in a shining sheet in the distance—the Cape Fear River. Soon the voyage would be ending, and she realized with a start that she had never really expected it to end. The *Quadrille* had become, as ships have a way of becoming to passengers, their little world, sufficient, complete. She felt a pang of jealousy that the land would make a difference. If only they could go on sailing! Once ashore, she would see little of James. He would be busy with his plantation and his voyages. And once ashore, she knew there was danger for them both in John's plan to go to Governor Martin offering his service against the rebellious colonies and arranging some sort of revenge for the loss of his ship. The future was very uncertain. Yet John still clung to the idea of taking her to Connecticut. That he hoped to manage this after telling her of the difficulties of traveling even so far as Virginia, seemed inconsistent.

She had thought little about her ultimate destination during the voyage, but now she decided that neither place suited her fancy. She knew none of her mother's people in Virginia; New England was cold and far away; but James was the embodiment of all he had told her of glamorous North Carolina, and in her mind there was no part of it against which he failed to move with his easy grace and teasing smile. This was North Carolina. This was what she wanted. And the cheering thought came that no one could tell her what to do. She was amply supplied with gold. She could live where she pleased!

As if her thoughts had called him, he came down the deck toward her. He pulled her hand through his arm and they strolled back toward the path of moonlight that lay beyond the stern.

The *Quadrille* had glided into the broad, flat river, but instead of keeping her to the middle of the stream, the helmsman was holding her as close as he dared to the west bank. Against the cypress forest that grew almost to the water's edge she would not be so plainly exposed to the view of the three dim, gray warships lying at anchor over to the east. They had come round the cape in safety and it was not likely that the lazy British would give chase at this hour of night even if they had been seen. However, it was well, James said, to proceed with caution. He had no intention of allowing the treasure of gunpowder in his hold to fall into enemy hands. The British would *take* it, but Cornelius Harnett would pay him handsomely for the precious stuff.

"Well, how do you like your first view of North Carolina?" he asked.

Accustomed to the mountainous terrain of Jamaica, she said, "It looks a little flat."

"It's flat down here. You are looking at some of the world's finest rice land. But wait till you see the rolling hills to the north." Then he grew thoughtful. "Not many hours ago this water passed my plantation."

Elizabeth caught something in his voice that expressed far

more earnestly than anything he might have said, his love of his land. It was one of the few times she had seen him serious, and she wondered if John or his father had ever known him like this. Then his look changed and she felt herself come back into focus.

"Wilmington should be very gay now despite the war clouds, with court in session, and besides that, everyone will be entertaining the militia."

For the first time she was not lifted by the thought of gaiety. "James, we've got to do something about John. I'm afraid he won't enjoy the festivities much—he is still so mad over losing his ship."

Once she had spoken, she saw her mistake. His pleasant mood might have been preserved, but it seemed that always one or the other made some remark that set them quarreling.

"John can't enjoy anything," he replied. " 'Pon my word, I don't see how he can be so dull."

"He is not dull," she retorted, "and you ought not to bait him so. He is brave and good and—and dependable, and—"

"And what does it get him?"

"Surely there are some things that even you can't arrange to take away from him!"

"*Touché!*" He laughed. "I was wondering about that!" His eyes swept down over her, and he caught her wrists, pulling her roughly to him. His arm went around her, crushing her against him, and he turned her face up to the moonlight. "God, you're beautiful," he said. Then his lips came down on her mouth—his hand cupped her breast, and a flame shot through her. The stars reeled in the pale sky.

Suddenly he released her. "You are far too provocative, miss. You'd better go get your beauty sleep—we dock at sunrise."

The spangled mantle of happiness that had covered the kiss was rent by his casualness. She was furious at her own heedless surrender. Her cheeks burned as she walked swiftly away.

At the companionway, a furtive glance backward showed him still standing there gazing out over the land of North Carolina. He seemed already to have forgotten her existence.

A cold, offshore wind was blowing as the *Quadrille* neared the wharf at the foot of Dock Street. The little town of Wilmington huddled at the edge of the river, wrapped in a cloak of rain. The sight was chill and gloomy, relieved only slightly by the sight of longshoremen in heavy boots and oilskins hurrying across the wharf at the vessel's approach. Could this be the colorful, exciting city about which she had heard so much?

The place was idle enough. Though there was no lack of craft about, most of them had a look of being deserted, their hatch coverings lashed and their sails clewed up. Small boats and dories were drawn up nose-first against the pier where they pushed and nuzzled like a litter of pigs at a sow's belly.

Elizabeth lifted her skirts as they picked their way around the puddles of water standing in the walkway between the wharf and the long raw wooden building that looked as if it had been thrown up in a hurry because business was so pressing it could not wait for seasoned lumber. Over the doorway swung a sign bearing a white painted schooner on a cobalt sea, proclaiming: MATTHEW ROWAN, SHIPBUILDER. The sound of hammers ringing rhythmically inside made a lonely accompaniment to the rain.

They found a carriage at the end of the dock, and once in the city proper, the aspect was more cheerful. Buildings were neatly ordered, the courthouse even imposing. James bowed to friends and acquaintances who happened to be hurrying through the rain or standing in doorways. Elizabeth glanced at him shyly. By neither word nor look had he made any allusion to the moonswept moment of the night before. His debonair gallantry was no more personal than ever, and she found herself miserably at a loss to understand him. John sat in his corner with his arms folded and said nothing. She turned her head and gazed unhappily through the streaked window of the coach. On the trees, autumn leaves that might have been bright in the sun blurred into dull blobs of color. A few late asters bowed their heads in the passing gardens. Broad Street was a sea of mud.

Finally, at James' direction, they drew to a halt before a red-brick house and the driver blew his horn. A servant came running to open the gates, the whip flourished and the wheels swirled up to the steps in a shower of gravel. An old Negro in dark-blue livery came to the top of the curving, iron-grilled stair and stood, bowing his kinky white head, but his butler's dignity could not prevent a grin of welcome when he saw James.

From the coach house grooms came hurrying. From the quarters a little Negro went hurtling across the back yard shouting, "Op'n de do'. Op'n de do'! Mist' James back!"

"Hello, Cicero! Is Mrs. Bell at home?"

"Naw, suh, she have gone to Vuginia, but she say we was to take keer of you right on same as if she was heah."

Elizabeth was disappointed. The plan had been for her to stay with Mrs. Bell, in whose house James kept rooms for such times as he was in Wilmington. Now she would probably have to take cramped quarters in some tavern.

But apparently James had another idea, for they were following Cicero into the wide hall.

"I 'specks you all would like some tea," he suggested as he led them into the drawing room, where a fire burned comfortingly in the grate.

"More than anything I can think of, and a spot of brandy, too. But when did Mrs. Bell leave, and when is she coming back?"

"She say she ain't comin' back till all dis here confusion settle down. She say she ain't gwine to stay here an' be insulted by bein' called no lobsterback."

James laughed. "Well, get us tea, and tell Trolcie I have brought Mistress Purdie to occupy my rooms for a time, so get them ready for her. Her maid is around at the back, see that she's taken care of."

"She can't stay here," John said firmly, as Cicero's coattails disappeared through the door.

"Heaven's name, why not? It's the finest house in Wilmington, and good houses with rooms to let are not easy to find."

"I will not have her here and subjected to gossip. No one here knows Elizabeth, and she may, from being in the same house, acquire the reputation of the lady who has just quitted it."

James laughed. "Cicero is crazy. Mrs. Bell will as likely be called a 'lobsterback' in Virginia as she is here. Besides, she has been talking about going back ever since Judge Bell died."

"And only your charming presence prevented it, I suppose," John said caustically.

"Yes, as a matter of fact. She disliked being alone, and she did me a very good turn—my place is too far to go back and forth." He was nettled at John's tone, but was in too high spirits over being back to take too much offense.

"I daresay. And how do you suppose it will affect Elizabeth when Mrs. Bell's friends learn that you have brought in a younger and no doubt more beautiful 'lobsterback' to take her place?"

"Just what do you mean?" quick anger demanded menacingly. John was being not only insulting but ridiculous.

"I mean that I will stay here with her myself before I'll have her presence misunderstood."

"Ah-h," James drew out the syllable with his slow, mocking smile. If he could only remember to hold his temper, he could always get the better of his brother.

John's face took on a mauve tint as he saw his own words interpreted against him. James' taunting look made him feel absurd, and indeed, he had to admit that, not knowing anything whatever of the Lady Bell, he *had* put up some foolish arguments.

They had both forgotten Elizabeth, standing by the fireplace, her palms spread out to the blaze. She stamped her foot and demanded their surprised attention. Her eyebrow lifted.

"Hush, both of you!" She turned about so suddenly that her skirts swished out and fanned the fire. "I am the one to choose, it seems to me."

John started toward her, then abruptly took his seat as Cicero came in with the tea tray and set it on a low table.

Elizabeth moved with dignity to the chair the servant held for her, and busied herself with the cups.

Cicero watched her pour and was delighted that the pretty, foreign-looking young lady knew how to handle a teapot. As he handed James his brandy, he bowed. "Excuse, Mist' James, but ain't you gent'men kin?"

"Right, Cicero, he is my brother." He cocked an eyebrow at John, who glared as if he would disclaim all relationship.

"Well, suh, I didn' know you had a brother. Trolcie say she havin' pigeon pie fo' dinnah ef you all keers to be in."

"Yes, do come," Elizabeth said sweetly, "I've decided to stay, and I'll be glad to have you."

James cast a triumphant glance at his brother and made Elizabeth a bow. "Thank you, ma'am. I'll be delighted."

"And may we count on you, John?"

"I suppose so," he replied ungraciously. He'd be damned if he'd give James the evening with her. "I don't suppose you'll give up this ridiculous idea of staying here?"

"Oh, no, I'll be quite comfortable, thank you." She smiled guilelessly. They both might as well understand from the first that she had no intention of having her life ordered for her.

James rose and put down his glass. "I must get back and see to my cargo." He gave her hand a little squeeze. "A pleasant day to you till six o'clock, when we'll see you again. Come, John, we'll see to a room for you at the tavern."

The old Negro held their triple-caped surtouts and deftly flipped their queues from beneath the collars. When he had put James into his, his hand brushed at an imaginary speck of dust—the gesture being as near a caress as he could allow himself.

When the dinner hour came, James arrived alone. John, he said, was nowhere to be found. Elizabeth felt no great regret at the news, but into her mind came his words when she had asked him what he intended to do. Suppose he *had* gone to offer his services to the governor! Well, he could take care of himself. Nothing should keep her from enjoying the very delightful novelty of entertaining a young man at dinner.

Over the pigeon pie she told him she had discovered through Trolcie that Mrs. Bell and her mother had been childhood friends.

"You didn't tell me Mrs. Bell was old," she said.

"You didn't ask me. But I probably wouldn't have told you anyway. No one ever thinks of her as old. I wish she were here. You'd like her."

"Well, I feel quite at home in her house already."

"By the way, I forgot to tell you, her carriage and driver are at your disposal if you want to go anywhere."

"I want to go shopping."

"No doubt. I seem to remember that your luggage was light."

"Light indeed! I have no clothes at all. Where do the ladies of Wilmington have their dresses made? But I don't suppose you would know about things like that."

"Ah, you underestimate me. I know all about it!" He leaned forward in deep conspiracy. "There is a Miss Sally Lamb on Market Street who turns out the most elegant folderols imaginable, and I've an idea you would be a model right to her taste. More than homely herself, she delights in clothing beauty."

He pulled out her chair, and as they went into the library for coffee, they saw that Mamba had taken up her position as chaperone in a straight-backed chair beside the hall door from which she had a commanding view of the room. Her head was tilted back and her eyes were closed, but Elizabeth knew she was not asleep. Better to disregard her than to be embarrassed by the reply she would certainly make if she were rebuked.

James whispered, "Let me see if I'm still good at outwitting the guard!" He pulled her up against the wall on the other side of which Mamba rested, and kissed her lightly. "What a delectable mouth you have, madam," he said, and proceeded to enjoy it further.

Her breath caught, but she turned her head aside and pushed him away. She had never known that kissing could be . . . like James made it. And she was on the verge of being sure that this thrill, this enchantment was love. But, after all, he was too masterful at taking liberties, and not a word of love had he spoken.

After last night on the deck of the *Quadrille*, he was somewhat surprised at the rebuff, but he was not one to be too easily discouraged by a feminine trick of resistance. The wall formed a splendid ally, but as he pressed her tighter against it, they heard Cicero coming along the hall with the coffee. Quick as a flash he whirled her around to face her inanimate adversary and a portrait hanging upon it.

"Yes, as you say," he said, gallantly inclining his chestnut head, "I sometimes think Mr. Sully's skin tones are a bit ruddy, but on the whole his work is very good."

She had been annoyed, but at the same time she could not keep the amusement at his wit out of her voice. "But you *do* think his work will live?"

"Oh, undoubtedly." They went on talking nonsense until Cicero left the room.

"Undoubtedly," he repeated, moving the little spoon slowly around in his cup and looking at her quizzically.

She rose with a flush in her cheeks and took a chair on the other side of the table, a safer distance away, realizing that she had had entirely too little experience to enable her to cope with James Richardson.

"May I take your cup?" This was dull ground, but solid.

"Yes, and by the way, may I take you to a party? I saw Thomas Brown in town. Their plantation is near mine. He and Sarah are having a barbecue and ball on Thursday next, and I told him I would bring you."

"A party! How nice!"

"Bring along a riding habit. There'll likely be a hunt before dinner."

"Do you suppose I'll have time to get one made?"

"Oh, yes. Miss Sally can whip one up in no time." His expression changed abruptly. He strode to the window, hands jammed into his pockets. "I can't imagine where John is. I thought sure he'd turn up before this."

"Did he leave you no message at the tavern?"

"No—" he turned to face her—"and none to you either, I suppose?"

"No." Though she had an idea, a very good idea, where he might have gone, she hesitated to mention it. But it *was* strange that he had sent *her* no word. Her vanity recognized the fact that he had had two very good reasons for intending to be present at dinner.

James turned again from the window, returning to the fireplace, where he stood frowning and running his hand down the back of his head in a way he had when he was puzzled or disturbed.

"I wonder . . ." she mused.

"What?"

"What is it, James? Do you fear for his safety?" She rose with impatient uneasiness and went to stand beside him.

"Not exactly, but in these times . . ."

"Do you suppose he could have gone to call upon the governor?" she asked hesitantly.

"What makes you ask that?"

"Well, last night he—he mentioned that he intended to."

"Oh, he did, did he? What a fool!"

"Why?"

"My God, child, don't you know the country is practically at war? If he were seen returning from the cruiser, he'd be swinging from a tree limb before morning."

"Oh, what can we do?"

"There's nothing you can do, and nothing for me but to go back to the tavern and wait." He reached for the bellpull and ordered his horse. "Why didn't you tell me this before?"

"I had no reason to," she answered haughtily. "And, besides, I had no idea a gentleman might not wait upon his governor if he chose."

"Be careful you don't make that remark to anyone else, or any others like it. You'll get yourself into trouble."

"I had been led to believe, sir, that in America one had the privilege to speak as he liked—or what *is* this freedom I heard you so heatedly defending to your brother?"

James was exasperated, but suddenly the gold in his eyes sparkled. "Look, suppose you just don't bother your pretty little hea—"

"Don't you dare say 'your pretty little head' to me!"

"All right, but keep your pretty little lips closed for the purpose of women's lips." He bent and, before she could elude him, dropped a kiss upon them.

Her stormy eyes leveled at him. "Don't do that again!"

CHAPTER 5

Not even to the threat of war moving southward could the hospitality of the Cape Fear planters quite succumb. Although much of the lavishness of their entertainments had been curtailed in obedience to the Continental Congress, their conviviality was too deeply rooted to be abandoned by forebodings of a condition that might not, after all, materialize.

In the main they were citizens whose forefathers had settled the wilderness of land along the river, hewn their homes from the great forests and the foundation of their fortunes from the rich soil. From the log cabins of the pioneer their homes grew into plantation mansions and their grandsons into fine gentlemen whose easily begotten leisure was used for the pursuit of pleasure and the arts and graces of culture. Even Governor Martin, the now-hated representative of the king, who had doubled the taxes to pay for his own love of luxury, having had occasion to reply to an address of welcome on his arrival in the colony, had described the district as "the region of politeness and hospitality."

But while with surprised approval the governor had noted that the leading men of his province bore the stamp of English gentlemen, he at first failed to observe the inherent purposes which also characterized them. In their veins ran the intrepid blood of pioneers, tainted with the spirit of independence, sullied with a buoyant disregard for the divine right of kings. They were quick to defend their rights as free men, quick to defend the heritage of their pleasant way of life, and the first to make willingly self-imposed sacrifices to maintain it.

They told themselves that a gentleman could become quite as mellow upon scuppernong or elderberry wine and peach brandy as on imported Madeira and rum, and the ladies were fully as alluring in homespun gowns as in Birmingham brocade.

On this occasion Thomas Brown had decided to have his friends around him for what might be the last time. Daily it became more evident that there would be no stopping the momentum of the coming struggle, but not yet were the lines so finely drawn that he could not entertain men in his home who had been friends from youth, regardless of their political convictions. Yet he knew that not much longer would this be so. And what better time than on the occasion of William Hooper's return from the meetings in Philadelphia? Perhaps some of the lukewarm ones might be persuaded even at this late date.

At his plantation, Oakland, the avenue leading up to the house was choked with horses and carriages, hacks, and gigs. At the edge of the yard the first-arrived conveyances stood with shafts down and their power unhitched and tethered in the rich green stand of winter rye sown for the purpose. The bare branches of great oaks met overhead and dropped an intricate weft of shadow on the backs of the horses, as the carriage passed up the avenue bringing the Richardson brothers, Elizabeth, and Mamba, like a somber afterthought, on the backseat.

John had returned from his mysterious absence. No questions had been asked, but both James and Elizabeth had insisted that he accompany them to this gathering.

A buzz of conversation and laughter greeted them on the gallery, and rugged, jovial Thomas Brown welcomed them into the long drawing room. His wife, Sarah, whom he completely dominated (he thought), overshadowed, and adored, waved Elizabeth up the broad stair to the ladies' room.

When she came down, she had made a perfunctory acquaintance with a dozen females who had already acquired knowledge of when she came, why, and where she was living. Amazed at the extent of their information, she nevertheless made her polite addresses with the graciousness of a naturally friendly soul—and also in accordance with Mamba's shrewd suggestions.

The night before, while she was trying on the ball gown just issued from Miss Sally's nimble fingers, the old woman had firmly delivered a host of precepts designed to set her on the path to social success.

"You has got to be 'traction wid all of 'em. Don't you dassent to let Mist' James think you is more interested in him dan de res'. Once he find out, he gone! Ah knows dat kine. Don't you let him take no libuties wid you neither. Yo' granma DeRossett wouldn't let none of 'em tech her, and dey crowd 'round her lak frawgs 'round a pool in summah.

"An' anuddah thing," she continued sternly, "You doan know womens. Day ain't likely to take kindly to a stranger what's nice lookin' an' got close and dey ain't."

"Oh, Mamba, they've got clothes. Miss Sally told me—"

"Yessum, but dey ain't new. Ah knows. Trolcie done tole me 'bout dese foolishments ovah heah: how de ladies ain't buyin' nuthin' cept'n homespun, lak dey was in sackclawf an' ashes, to save money fo' de waw. Hit ain't smaht neither. But howsomever, you be special nice to de ladies. But eben wid all de niceness you kin show Ah's 'fraid you is got a hahd row to hoe."

Now she began to perceive the old woman's wisdom. It was amazing how Mamba always knew about things, she thought, as she descended the stair. She had sensed the resentment and antagonism which lay thinly veiled behind the polite amenities fluttering about in that room up there, but she did not know all the reasons for it.

The ladies of Wilmington had heard all about the new wardrobe, which, in passing the way of many lips, was wildly exaggerated. They had learned of the fabulous jewels; the hard money with which she was well-supplied; and now one look at her confirmed the rumor of her youth and beauty. On top of it all, she had been escorted to this party by James Richardson, the most eligible bachelor in the county, who had, but charmingly, shown them that he was choosy about his women. Old Grandma Love opined darkly that none of these things went hand in hand with virtue, and powdered curls nodded in quick and comfortable agreement.

James was waiting for her at the foot of the stairs. Together they circulated through the thronged rooms, and Elizabeth forgot the strained atmosphere in the ladies' room, for almost immediately they stopped to meet Adam Boyd and his lovely blind wife, Mary. It was plain to see why they were so beloved. From them both emanated an aura of love and kindness, and a keen relish for living.

"What sweet hands you have, child," Mary said, "there's character in them. Welcome to North Carolina!"

"You have Agatha Bell's house, I believe," Adam was saying, "that's fine. You are just around the corner from us."

"Oh, yes. Do come around whenever you get lonely," Mary invited. "And Abigail will be delighted to have someone her own age so near."

"Abigail? Your daughter?"

"Our niece," Adam explained.

"She still here?" James asked. "I thought she had gone home to New York."

Adam chuckled. "No, she fancies herself quite indispensable to the young blades of the militia. And I daresay she is: I can't go in my own front door without stumbling over a baker's dozen of them. She'll be along in a minute." He rocked back on his heels, his hands clasped behind him, his smooth pink face beaming proudly. He was a fine figure of a man, which was surprising to those who knew he spent most of his time bent over his desk writing editorials for his newspaper, the *Cape Fear Mercury*.

John came up with Pitsy and Peter Slingsby. Elizabeth suspected they were on the loyalist side since John had formed an instant friendship with them.

"You're a good-looking wench," Pitsy said with her loud, infectious laugh. She had red hair and a forthright manner, and was too busy for malicious gossip. She scurried around to add to the group others she wanted to talk to. She declared Elizabeth must meet Cornelius Harnett, president of the North Carolina Assembly, and William Hooper on leave from the Congress at Philadelphia that had voted John Hancock to its presidency. "Now let's sit down. I vow I'm tired milling around."

As they found chairs, a peal of high-pitched laughter came in from the hall, and a moment later Abigail Bretherton sailed into the room, a young officer in a blue coat with a fall of lace at his throat in her beruffled wake. She made her entrance like a general, calmly assuming that the field was hers. She dropped an abbreviated curtsy to her aunt and the older ladies, then turned her full attention to the men.

Abigail's golden hair made a halo about her face, but her greenish eyes were set a bit too close together and her nose was sharply tilted.

"There you are, James Richardson, you handsome thing, you!" She smiled, and her lips were turned to a sculptor's dream.

Her glance swept down over Elizabeth, and for a moment a gleam of malice halted her volubility. Then she took a seat beside her, as if she thought it wise to reconnoiter as soon as possible and evaluate the enemy's strength.

Elizabeth was aware of the maneuver, but she spoke pleasantly.

"So you are the Mrs. Purdie?" Abigail asked.

"Yes. And I've been eager to meet you. Mr. Boyd told me of your visit."

"It's more like a residence! I came down from my home in New York to recuperate from an illness, and I've been having such a good time I've put off going back. *Now* nobody will *hear* of my leaving—they just won't *let* me go." Her fondly accusing glance swung 'round over the men.

"We can't have a light like yours going out of Wilmington, Miss Abigail," said the infatuated Lieutenant Randolph who had accompanied her, "isn't that right, gentlemen?"

The men said what was expected of them.

"Certainly," James said emphatically, "the Committee of Safety really ought to forbid all exportation of beautiful women, else they'll become as scarce as gunpowder."

William Hooper slapped him on the shoulder, "By the Holy Grail, sir, I shall vote for your excellent example of *importation—of both!*"

Lieutenant Randolph drawled, "Now, Miss Abigail, you know you wouldn't want to miss the militia parade. All you ladies must be there," he added gallantly, though he should have known that not a soul in the county would miss it.

The center of interest was about to be elsewhere, and Abigail immediately drew it back to herself. "Oh, Aunt Mary, Colonel Moore has asked me to ride beside him in the parade!"

Elizabeth caught Pitsy Slingsby's glance; she loathed Abigail and didn't care who knew it. That estimable lady's right eye closed in a slow wink. The attention to Abigail had gone far enough and Pitsy knew what to do about it.

"Cornelius," she asked Harnett, "how is the recruiting coming along?"

"Very well, indeed," he replied, his long sallow face drawing into a smile. "Matt Rowan says he's even having to give them lumber from the shipyard to put into barracks. Four hundred Continentals are to be stationed here as a precaution against Martin's designs to raise the Indians and the Negroes."

Somebody cursed Governor Martin, and the new subject was launched.

HARMONY HALL

Elizabeth was disappointed. James had led her to believe that Cape Fear was a place of pleasure and frivolity, and here she had arrived at her first party to find the men interested in nothing but politics and war. But she listened halfheartedly to the discussions of the proceedings at the Provincial Assembly and noted the pride with which they related what had been accomplished. From a legally elected body meeting under the existing British crown, they had, upon the governor's cowardly relinquishing his authority in flight from the angry people, formed a new revolutionary one along the lines drawn by the Continental Congress, ostensibly under the jurisdiction of the crown's representative, but, in reality, beholden to no one save the people. She realized with a shock that what all this meant was that they had simply seized the reins of government and were now administering it to suit themselves. It was no wonder that there were those who disapproved: it was treason against the king!

Peter Slingsby's face was open with disgust, and from his spoken opinions and questions she learned that he, like John Richardson and several others, was doing his best to remain moderate in a situation that before long would allow no moderation.

Mr. Harnett, head of the Committee of Safety, was saying, "So you see, at last, the powers of American government are where they should be—in America!"

"And what powers, sir," Slingsby wanted to know, "have you gentlemen of the assembly given to his Excellency the governor?"

"The power, sir," William Hooper flashed, "to remain aboard his floating palace and try to regain his province!"

John's face went red, and without thinking he exploded, "Palace, indeed! Why, in his enforced exile aboard that ship the man is almost destitute!"

Harnett rounded on him, his eyes narrowed. "Has it been your pleasure to visit him, sir?"

Elizabeth held her breath as John answered, "I have heard reports," he said.

James got up and moved to a seat between Elizabeth and Abigail. "You young ladies should now be entirely conversant with the affairs of the country. You will, perhaps, never hear more learned discourses concerning it than you have this morning," he said in his bantering way, and everybody breathed easier.

But Elizabeth, out of a sudden perversity and an attempt

to help John out of a spot, answered, "I understand a great deal more than I did, but it seems to me the governor is the one with a cause to fight—being run out of his house, and people taking his authority in their own hands when he was appointed by the king. Why, it's—it's anarchy! Gentlemen as learned as those in this—this Congress you speak of ought to be able to settle their quarrels without the use of such measures."

There was a moment of stunned silence. Her cheeks blazed with the realization of how badly she had blundered. John sent her a look of pride, but he was uneasy, too, that she had so courageously shown her loyalty in this hotbed of patriots. Cornelius Harnett's thin lips went white with anger, his hands making nervous movements, as if he would use them to throttle such speech. Hooper only stared hard because courtesy to a lady forbade the angry retort that rose in his throat.

Only in Adam Boyd's eye was something of appreciation for a woman who used her head, even if what she thought was all wrong. Here was a girl capable of forming her own opinion and speaking her mind in a forthright manner. He decided she was worth converting to the cause.

Abigail was annoyed. A new and beautiful young widow was danger enough to a reigning belle without the added menace of brains. She could see by the expression on James' face that he liked her fearlessness too, and James Richardson was one she had not succeeded in attaching to her train. She tilted her head back and regarded Elizabeth with half-closed eyes in a way she had of having given her words deep consideration.

"There might be those, Mistress Purdie, who would fail to understand your position. You are so lately come from Jamaica, where you must have been a loyal subject of the king, 'tis certain it would be impossible for you to understand any of the problems of the colonies. I think you had better not express yourself so frankly."

Elizabeth looked at her with a cool, blue stare, her eyebrow lifted. "Perhaps I am more qualified to speak than you think, miss. You probably don't know that your problems, as you call them, were quite well known to us in Jamaica. Indeed, they are responsible for my being without a home at this moment. So, you see, even if I were accustomed to having someone tell me when and how to speak, I should still express myself on this issue because I feel my viewpoint is somewhat broader than yours."

James was enjoying this parry of feminine thrusts, and Elizabeth's quick and fearless counter at Abigail contributed to his growing conviction that she was more a woman of the world than she pretended. She had certainly justified her attitude far more ably than anything he could have thought up in her defense—no woman could be too much blamed for resenting a situation that had deprived her of her home.

Before Abigail could move her furious tongue, the master of hounds appeared in the hall to announce the start of the hunt.

Before any of the other ladies came up to change to their ball gowns, Mamba was waiting with the sapphire satin over her arm, and a look on her face, Elizabeth told her, as if she were hopping up and down inside.

"Ah is. Ah knowed you was mah chile! Jes' yo' granmaw DeRossett all ovah agin. Puttin' that Bretherton woman in huh place!" From the depths of her bosom came the rumble of her mirth as she folded the riding habit aside. Elizabeth was surprised not only that Mamba already knew of the incident, but that she condoned it. All along she had expected the one obstruction to her freedom would be her old nurse. Was this strange America affecting her, too?

"How did you know about that?"

"Ah gits things," she answered mysteriously, "but the smahtest thing was you fallin' off that hawse, and havin' all them gent'mens ridin' back to see is you hurt."

"Why, Mamba, you don't think I intended to fall, do you?"

For answer the old woman only rolled her eyes and started on the long row of hooks up the back of the gown.

"Well, I didn't! It could have killed me."

"All right, honey, but you don't have to pertend wid me. This the third generation I bin keepin' secrets. Anyhow it was smart. After you showed yo' spo'tin' blood by goin' on an' jumpin' dat fence the gempmuns will likely forgit yo' speakin' outta turn this mawnin'."

Elizabeth gasped. So that had been talked about, too. Somebody had repeated everything; the slaves had picked it up, and here it was!

"Now, baby, you take mah advice, and leave the politics to de mens. Hit ain't women's business. Now you is ready. Go down theah an' show them folks who is de belle of de ball!"

Tallow dips had replaced the fine wax tapers of other years

in the drawing room, which had been cleared for dancing, but the light of one was as soft as the other and as effectively disguised the fact that most of the ladies' gowns were the finery of better times, that the richly embroidered brocade fashioning the gentlemen's clothing showed signs of wear. But hair was still powdered splendidly, the sparse pates of the older men were still secret beneath the wigmaker's art.

When Elizabeth came down the stairs, she saw that the ladies, lined up in their chairs along the wall, had folded the winnowing wings of their own talk that they might overhear what was being said by the men congregated in the middle of the floor. It seemed that everybody had forgotten this was to be a ball, she thought. How she had looked forward to the evening when there would be music and dancing, and now—politics again! Leave it to the men, indeed! There was no separating them from it.

Lucy Moore, a kitten-soft, appealing girl from down river, beckoned her to a seat at her side, squeezing her hoops over to make room, and it was almost the only friendly gesture from the whole roomful of women. (Mary Boyd, of course, could not see her.) She was conscious of the unspoken antagonism that greeted her entrance, and she felt a warm rush of gratitude toward the pretty little orphaned cousin of Robert Howe who made her home with him and his sister in Brunswick.

"They're talking about independence," Lucy whispered.

"Do you want it so much?"

"Oh, yes. We're no more than slaves under the king."

Elizabeth doubted but pondered this, feeling the trouble-breeding crosscurrents through the room. Her eyes sought out James, smiling, elegant, handsome, his cuff laces falling more richly than anyone else's from his bent arm, and his silken hose shining in the candlelight, then John, frowningly disapproving of all that was being said, though he was making a valiant effort not to show it. That he had seen the governor she was sure now, and the fact that his manner toward James had become more amiable had not in the least allayed the uneasiness about what was to happen between the two. What did they want out of this turmoil? John wanted herself and his quiet New England farm. He wanted to go on under the protection of the king with his trading and his shipping, and his patriarchal father in the background. But James must uproot tradition and carve out his own destiny. She sensed the danger between the two extremes—danger for them both in these times. As for herself, she could not be sure. Though she had told Mamba she did not intend soon again to give any man the right to command her days and nights, she knew her old nurse was right when she had replied that the goal of every woman was a home and a husband.

But her marriage to Mr. Purdie had been too appallingly unhappy for her to enter that state again without a sure knowledge of love surrounding it. And of love she knew nothing. Whether it was the quickening pulse she felt with James or the feeling of strength and security in John's presence she did not know. She wished the men would stop talking and the dancing begin. But in spite of herself she began listening to them.

Someone asked, "When *will* Congress declare for independence?"

"We must be patient a little longer," William Hooper said, "and there must be more patience before these thirteen colonies are united in a common-enough view to take a strong and definite stand. 'Tis not easy as it must seem to you here at home. Imagine the difficulty of getting all the representatives to one mind, the confusion of a multitude of committees, the innumerable speeches! But I will give you this for encouragement: the idea of independence, which was anathema to most when Congress first assembled, is gaining every day. It has been like a snowball rolling down a hill."

Thomas Brown slapped him on the back. "I'll warrant you've been giving it a push or two yourself."

"I've not held it back!" He grinned.

"Who's holding it up, Hooper?"

"Oh, Georgia hesitates, South Carolina wavers, and God only knows what Maryland will do. Three or four of the other middle colonies are not quite ready, but I think, even so, it will not be long."

They went on and on: Boston was still in the hands of Lord Howe; New York was overrun with Tories, and a powerful British fleet was on its way to the harbor. Congress was urging General Washington to make haste, but, far from the scene, they did not understand that he could not secure harbors without ships, that he could fire no guns without powder, and that added to all his vexations was the crowning one of having the personnel of the army continuously changing by the termination of short-term enlistments and the constant influx of raw recruits.

The prospects, all in all, were discouraging, but still the

snowball gathered weight and rolled on with an ever-increasing force, and the faith of Americans in America strengthened as it rolled.

Hope of getting aid from France was discussed, but Adam Boyd doubted the possibility. Even though it seemed logical that France would help if only as an excuse to make war on her bitterest enemy, England, it was not likely that such an autocrat as King Louis and his Catholic ministers would lend their support to the establishment of religious freedom anywhere, lest his own colonies get ideas.

It dawned on Elizabeth that there were more sides to this conflict between England and her Atlantic seaboard colonies than the purely commercial one which had so affected Jamaica. She remembered that her grandmother DeRossett, a French Huguenot, had come with her family to Virginia to escape religious persecution. The thought conjured a vision of people streaming impossibly across the water to reach the freedom of American shores, but it faded quickly when Thomas Brown, suddenly remembering his duties as host, signaled the musicians to begin.

The gentlemen rushed to request her favors. Mamba was right: they seemed not to hold her blunder of the morning against her at all. Only from the women was there coldness. Out of the tail of her eye she caught glimpses of hands lifted to guard whispers as she danced by. She tossed her head. Let them talk. Let them think whatever they liked. She was having the first good time she had ever had, and nothing was going to spoil it.

She tried out some of Mamba's suggestions for coquetry, found them satisfactory, and invented a few of her own. She had entered a new set with John, and now with her hand in his big one, warm and strong, she felt a wonderful happiness in her knowledge of his love for her. James had not yet asked her to dance, and she shifted her eyes around to where he was gracefully and absorbedly performing the minuet with Sarah Brown. No doubt a great part of his charm lay in his unfailing courtesy to the older ladies. He invariably danced with them first, leaving the younger girls to stew with anxiety lest he had forgotten them. Sometimes he had been known to do so too, dividing the entire evening between the smoking room and what appeared to be a fascinating conversation with a woman old enough to be his mother.

But when the set was over he came to her.

"Well, I see milady has set all the gentlemen on their respective ears," he said as they moved across the polished floor.

"Yes, isn't it fun?"

"Why, you shameless baggage!"

"Why am I?"

"You're the first I've known to admit being deliberately enticing."

She glanced up at him out of the corners of her eyes. "Aren't they all—really?"

He threw his head back and laughed. "I suspect you're right!"

During the *embrassement* she allowed her warm slimness to melt toward him, withdrew with arch dignity for the *pas de bourrée*, the blue satin shimmering out over its paniers as she went around him, their hands held high, then sank into a softly rustling curtsy, her tiny lace fan fluttering up to cover all her face except her invitation-filled eyes.

As the music stopped he looked at her speculatively. She was drawing him on, certainly, but how far he had not determined. He murmured something about a breath of air and led her out onto the gallery. Frequent visits to the punch table had not lessened his intention to get her off by herself and enjoy more, at least, of her delectable brand of kissing.

The garden was pale with starlight, and in the deep shade of a magnolia that grew at the end of the veranda he slipped his arms around her and quickly sought her lips. But she struggled to get away as the music started up again.

His voice came warm and rough against her mouth. "No—no. Don't you like this?"

"Yes," she murmured, her better judgment confused into giving up to her body. Her arms slipped up and tightened around his neck. Oh, this was love! What did Mamba know of being young and in love, of starlight and shadows? Her head was reeling and her heart pounded as his lips left hers and traveled down to her bare white shoulder, his hand pressing low in her back.

An instinctive warning shot through her. She struggled up through the warm red mist that seemed to be suffocating her, and began to beat against his chest with small, rapid fists. "Stop—"

He lifted his head, though he still held her tightly against him, and his low laughter was light. "Let's go to my plantation, it's not far," he whispered.

"Oh, could we leave the party? I do want to see it."

"Of course. We'd never be missed."

"I'd like to see it, but we'll have to hurry right back. I have all the next dances—"

He looked at her quizzically. "I'm not taking you to hurry right back. This party will go on till dawn."

"And I want to be here for it! I won't go unless you promise to bring me—"

He let her go suddenly and leaned against the banister rail as if he had no further interest. "You are exquisitely clever, my dear, but you can drop your pretty pose of innocence with me."

"What—what do you mean?" she demanded, stung into stillness.

"I mean that John and all the rest you seem to have hoodwinked very neatly. Surely they are enough scalps for your very tiny belt!"

Pose of innocence! She longed to cry out denials and explanations, but no words came through the choking anger and the hurt. She drew back the hand clutching the fan and brought it smartly across his face, then turned and, lifting her skirts, flew down the steps into the garden.

As she reached the path she heard John's voice from the gallery, "You scoundrel! You unforgivable—"

There were more words, but she sped down the path, her eyes blinded with tears, and at a sudden turn she came upon the tense little figure of Lucy Moore, standing white and strained in front of her.

"Oh—oh, it's you, Mrs. Purdie! Please come over here."

Elizabeth forced her tears back. "Lucy, what is it?"

The girl half-turned and spoke to someone back of the shrubbery. "It's all right, Gordon. This is Gordon Denny, my—my fiancé. He has come with the most frightful news. He told me to meet him here in the garden tonight, that he wanted to tell me something, but I didn't dream it would be—I don't know what to do."

Denny wore the plaid of his Highland clan, with the long, basket-handled claymore hanging at his side. In his face was an expression of almost feminine sweetness, yet the mouth was firm and his legs, where they showed between tartan and hose, were heavily muscled. In his voice was the burr of all the thistles of Scotland.

"Mistress Pur-r-die," he said, "the loyalists are massing at Cross Creeks with the intention of marching doon the river. I came tae warn Lucy, for I want her to bide in a place of safety. They will overrun her uncle's plantation, for they expect to meet Clinton's forces at Brunswick."

"If I go in there and tell our people, and they've *got* to know," Lucy said, "they would know where I got the news and come and find Gordon. They'd never believe that he doesn't care who governs the colonies just so—"

"Just so I can have my fields and this bairn here, it makes na' difference tae me!"

The girl looked at him with adoration, and Elizabeth was touched that Lucy felt she could trust her with such a secret when she had only known her since morning.

"Oh, Mrs. Purdie, can't *you* tell somebody?"

"Perhaps we can think of something, Lucy"—she glanced around—"but it would be wise for Gordon to leave at once if you don't want him found here—someone may come."

"But where will ye go, Lucy? I *must* ken where ye are!"

"She can stay with me at Mrs. Bell's house," Elizabeth offered impulsively, "if her uncle has no objection."

"Oh, can I? Uncle Bob's gone, and Cud'n Belinda won't care."

"That's well then. It's kindly I take it, mum." He kissed Lucy and she came out of his arms in tears. With a quick salute he vanished into the thicket at the end of the garden.

Elizabeth put her arms around Lucy's shaking shoulders. "Don't cry, honey. You must think of what you're going to do with this information Gordon's brought you."

"I know, but it seems so awful for us to be on different sides. Gordon doesn't care, but his family does and mine did, and I care terribly. It was the British that killed my father—dragging him off to England to try him for something he didn't do."

"Well, don't cry anymore. Here, take my 'kerchief. Let's sit down here on the bench and give Gordon a chance to get away. There must be *someone* you can talk to."

"No, don't you see? *Any* of them would know who told *me*."

Elizabeth was thinking fast. Though her quick sympathy was hotly on the side of anyone in distress, should she be the bearer of tidings which she neither understood nor felt strongly enough about to put herself perhaps in a questionable position on account of them? She had made a bad mistake this morning. Could she afford another one? How vital was it that the patriots, who seemed to compose most of this party, should know? She could go to John, but he was not the one to receive this information, surely. Perhaps if she told *anyone* John might be in danger, but if she did not, James would be. Her anger, temporarily forgotten in Lucy's affairs, flared anew. Let them take him prisoner and hang him! She would not lift a finger to save him!

"Mr. Boyd," she said suddenly, "I can talk to Mr. Boyd. Now, listen, Lucy. You go around the house and up the back stairs. Then come down the front, as if you had only been up to comb your hair or something. And pray do, because it's badly mussed. I'll go back in the front door and manage to get Mr. Boyd where I can talk to him alone."

Elizabeth was not sure why she felt so trustful of Adam Boyd, yet, when she found him a little later, the feeling of confidence was stronger than ever. She took his arm and acquainted him with the fact that she had something of the utmost importance to tell him.

"Let me get you some punch," he said with a smile, as if he were accustomed to confidences of the young. He went to the table, poured out two cups, then led her to the library across the hall.

When he had closed the door, she said, "You must promise not to ask where I got this information, for I shall certainly not tell you. I do not myself know the importance, or whether it is important at all. I am merely obeying a request, so please don't tell anyone it came from me. It seems I've already said too much today!" She grinned.

"It shall be as you say, my dear." There had been a twinkle in his eyes, but now he became quite serious. "Let me give you a little advice before I hear your news. Don't express yourself so openly on the political situation. I should hate to have you get into difficulty, and besides, I think you might feel differently if you understood our cause entirely."

"All right. But here is what I was asked to say: the loyalists are massing at Cross Creeks with the intention of marching down the river to meet Clinton's forces at Brunswick."

Adam choked on his drink and coughed before he could speak.

"Where— Oh, I promised not to ask," he sputtered, "but are you sure?"

"I have every reason to believe so, sir."

"Well, my thanks to you. Now—"

"Please wait for a little, so that the news will not be connected with our talking together."

"Yes, of course. You have done us a great service."

She remembered her speech of the morning with some embarrassment. It must seem inconsistent to Mr. Boyd now that she was assisting the patriots by bringing them secret information.

Some time later, amid the sound of music and dancing feet, she was conscious of a muffled uproar of excitement issuing from the library. The door opened, and Cornelius Harnett, Adam, William Hooper, James, and several others came out. Like a breeze before a squall the result of their meeting swept through the rooms. The music stopped. Men and women gathered in excited groups around them. How soon would the Scotch march? No one knew exactly, but not likely for a day or two. Was the big British fleet already on its way to the Cape Fear? Did this mean the southern invasion that had been threatened so long?

Cornelius Harnett took the floor. He was tall, thin, dyspeptic, and his clothes had the appearance of having been hung up for the night rather than put on for the day, but in his piercing eyes burned the spirit that made him so intense a patriot. He was able to fire the people's enthusiasm like no one else, and his never-ending zeal in stimulating the half-satisfied wealthier groups in favor of American patriotism made him one of the most-valued men in the province.

"There is nothing in this situation to cause too much alarm," he said. "Recently I was instructed by the Committee of Safety to try to learn the truth of rumors that the royalist Scotch were recruiting to the north of us, so you see we have for some time been aware of the possibility. We have now received word that such is actually the case and that the British fleet is expected to make a junction with them at the mouth of the river. But"—and here his eagle eyes began to snap and his voice to be laden with the heavy, famous sarcasm—"are we to be dismayed by the devil-spawned enemies of freedom? No! When they come down the river and the admiral comes up it, we shall be ready and waiting for them. We are prepared!"

In the midst of the cheering that followed, Elizabeth's relief was of a different origin than that of the rest. How neatly Adam Boyd, true to his word, had kept her out of it! Lucy squeezed her hand. John stood silently behind her, but James was smiling and clapping and saying "Bravo" with the rest.

On the long drive back to Wilmington that night, John

looked down happily on the head that had sought his shoulder when Elizabeth could no longer keep her eyes open. Dear little naive, artless child! How young and unprotected and helpless she was! And the little streak of stubbornness she had shown in insisting on taking Mrs. Bell's house only made her more endearing. He could overcome that in time.

But Elizabeth's eyes were only narrowed to slits between her lashes. She would get even with James Richardson for treating her in so insulting a manner. She would never let him know. She would make him fall in love with her; then, when he was begging for her hand, she would just calmly marry John. In her mind she made it a wonderful scene, but even as the picture grew, his tantalizing, half-mocking smile told her there was scant chance of bringing it off.

CHAPTER 6

Despite the gathering clouds of war, the ladies of Wilmington kept an eye on their social life, and the brass knocker on the front door of Mrs. Bell's house was kept busy.

Continued fear of the British landing at Brunswick had kept Lucy Elizabeth's guest. Here she was welcome to meet without opposition her Scotch loyalist sweetheart whenever he found it expedient to come to town. It was a pleasant arrangement, and it kept Elizabeth from being lonely.

The women came to call on the doubtful Mrs. Purdie, with the excuse to themselves that they were also coming to see Lucy, whose patriotism was well-known. Some came out of pure curiosity, and some for fear of not having established relations in case Elizabeth "took on" and became the social leader her predecessor in the house had been.

Mrs. Pitts, treasurer of the Ladies' Assistance Society of the Episcopal Church, placed her well-upholstered buttocks in the straightest chair in the room, planted her feet squarely on the floor, folded her hands piously, and extended an invitation to Elizabeth (whom everyone knew to be possessed of a well-filled purse) to become one of their members.

But Elizabeth, remembering long, dull afternoons when a like organization had met in her mother's sitting room, thought fast for a polite way to refuse.

"How nice of you, Mrs. Pitts, but I don't belong to your church," she said sweetly.

"In what faith *were* you christened?" Mrs. Pitts' eyebrows rose. If you weren't Church of England, regardless of politics, you simply weren't anybody!

"The Catholic."

Mrs. Pitts looked as if she had found, just in time, a fly on the cream pitcher, and as she stalked down the steps, even her rigid back gave no indication of the relief she felt at the narrowness of her escape.

Grandma Love and her daughter-in-law, Emmy, a pale, washed-out rag of a young woman, paid their call next day. Grandma was a virile, hawk-eyed old lady who used a cane more as a weapon for emphasis and a threat than for its manifest purpose. She immediately began asking questions, the answers to which she already knew.

"They said at Sarah's you had arrived only a few days before—last of October 'twas."

"Yes, Mrs. Love."

"Your husband was killed in the Jamaica riots?"

Lucy tried to break in with a new subject, but Grandma picked up her own again as she would have retrieved a dropped stitch. "That would be about the last of August?"

Elizabeth did not answer this time, and again Lucy attempted to stop what she feared was coming. "Elizabeth, don't you think I might call Cicero for some tea?"

"Just a moment, Lucy," she answered, an eyebrow lifting and calmly fixing Grandma with eyes in which there was a cool, blue intensity. "When I have found out what seems to be the purpose of Mrs. Love's call, I'll decide whether or not I want to entertain her at tea."

Lucy patted her hair nervously, but looked at Elizabeth with exultant pride. This horrible old woman had wanted taking down a notch or two for years, only nobody else had ever dared do it.

Emmy giggled fearfully, then sobered at her mother-in-law's angry glance. Grandma herself was shocked. Her ivory teeth clicked.

"Well, miss, the wicked fleeth when no man pursues," she misquoted and misused, for the "wicked" was not fleeing, though she was certainly being pursued. "From your own mouth I have learned that what they said at Sarah's was true: not three months a widow, a widow by violent death, and already gallivanting around the country with *men!* Come, Emmy!"

By the end of the week, Elizabeth's reputation was on the griddle in earnest, even though there was a grudging admiration for the way she had handled old Mrs. Love, who had been so furious she had made the mistake of telling on herself what had happened.

But it remained for Abigail to plant the little seed which, in this fertile soil, would grow into such a dangerous plant.

She threw back her head and half-closed her eyes. "There's something about her I don't trust."

"There's something about her none of us trust." Rebecca Higgins laughed. "But I don't worry. My Tom is too satisfied—"

"That's not what I meant," Abigail snapped.

"What *do* you mean?" They crowded closer, the better to hear something new on the fascinating Mrs. Purdie.

"Well, figure it out yourselves. How do we know she actually had to leave Jamaica? She's got plenty of hard money. Where did it come from? She *says* her husband left it to her, but how do we *know?* It *could* be coming from the British government. You've got to admit she's clever."

"That's a lot for you to admit, Abigail. She must have got under your skin plenty!"

Abigail flushed. "Well, if you don't care to hear what I have to say . . ."

"Oh, yes, we do! Be still, Rebecca!"

But if Elizabeth knew what was going on among the gossips, she paid no attention. There was too much to occupy her thoughts and time. There were John and James and her emotional tangle with them both, and she knew that despite his more amiable behavior John was still strong in his intention to "bring these rebels to justice." She knew what he was doing was dangerous. He was in constant and secret touch with Governor Martin, he and Peter Slingsby and some others. The loss of the *Celestine* still rankled, and there was a fear that what he and the governor might be plotting to avenge it would prove dangerous to James, whose presence spiced every occasion for her. Though she was constantly surrounded by his rivals, which fact seemed to worry him not at all, he always left her with a feeling that he'd as lief be elsewhere if the company were as good. It was most aggravating.

She and Lucy took long walks together and rode the saddle horses Mrs. Bell had left in the stables. The sight of the two pretty girls in their flowing habits and plumed bonnets riding about the countryside and through the town became one delightful to the gentlemen and frowned upon by most of the women, who huddled indoors with their knitting and their gossip.

It was on one of these excursions that they found the little boat in the rushes at the mouth of a creek that emptied into the river on the edge of town. Obviously it had been left to rot in the winter weather. Laughing like mischievous children, they bailed it out and made fast the muddy sail, using a strip torn from a petticoat ruffle in lieu of a rope. After that there was nothing to be thought of but trying it out.

The river was wide at this point, and there was no one near. Lucy sat in the stern while Elizabeth pushed off and expertly set her course down the broad expanse of the Cape Fear.

"La! It's good to have my hand on a tiller again."

"However did you learn to do it?" Lucy asked.

"What? Sail? I don't know. I've done it all my life."

"It's wonderful, but—but don't let's tell a soul about it."

"Why?"

"Oh, it wouldn't be considered proper for us to go sailing about alone."

"How silly," Elizabeth said as she ducked skillfully under the little boom. But when they returned to their small, snug harbor, she had agreed to keep it their own pleasant secret.

At teatime, Adam Boyd stopped in on his way home from his newspaper office. He came, he said, to bring Lucy a dispatch which had come from her uncle, Colonel Howe, who was leading the Continental forces in the battle for the possession of Norfolk, but he remained to take the excellent opportunity of trying to make a patriot out of Elizabeth. He was one who believed the best of people he liked, and he was sure that a woman of intelligence could be won over to the cause if only she could be made to understand the principles involved.

Heavens, she thought, laughing to herself, politely bored, he sounds like one of his own editorials.

But more of his well-phrased ideas stuck in her mind than she realized, and she found herself meeting his arguments.

"But, Mr. Boyd, you don't mean that *all* the people have a divine right?"

"And why not, my dear? Are we not all God's children?"

That gave her pause. But it seemed strange that all those stevedores, the dockhands, the slaves, the bondsmen, should have as much to do with government and God as did the aristocratic group of which she was by birth a member, and she said so.

"Ah, yes, it must seem very strange to you. But see here, Elizabeth, brought up as you were, you could never have known the type of man that makes up the great majority of Americans. In Jamaica the social line is more precisely drawn: planters and slaves. Here there are thousands of small farmers, tradesmen, smiths, carpenters, and common workmen all of whom are fired with a belief in their rights as human beings—to enjoy the fruits of their labor without exploitation and to have a voice in the assemblies that govern them."

"Perhaps I shall understand sometime," she said, her interest lagging again. God's whiskers, she thought, borrowing an expression from the very proletariat she had been reared to ignore. I didn't come to America to associate with workmen!

Suddenly she said, "There is something I want to ask you, Mr. Boyd. You spoke of religious freedom. Why was Mrs. Pitts so horrified when I told her I was born a Catholic?"

"That old war-horse!" He smiled, then looked grave. "Are you a devout Catholic, Elizabeth?"

"No," she answered, dimpling. "Father and I let Mother and Constance do our share of the churchgoing."

He made no comment on this. He seemed deep in thought. "Well," he said at length, "unfortunately, Catholicism is regarded in our country as almost synonymous with slavery. Perhaps you have not heard of the Quebec Act, which was another of the decrees of Parliament designed to infuriate America."

"What's the Quebec Act?"

"Well, it's a long story, but briefly, it was an act by the king giving the French in Canada the right to exercise their Catholic religion."

"But you said this country was *founded* on the principle of religious freedom among other things."

"My dear," he said with no little amusement, "you should have been a barrister! It *is* founded on such principle, but not for the freedom of the churches to make slaves of the people. And the Church of England has not stood still herself while the secular government was encroaching on our rights. She has become almost as tyrannical as popery."

"Why, Mr. Boyd! James told me you had studied in the ministry—the Church of England ministry—until you were just ready to—"

"Yes, but we have not been allowed to ordain our own men. They must go back to the Bishop of London for that ceremony," he replied, with a near approach to bitterness, "and I could not afford the trip. So I started the *Cape Fear Mercury*, which has been a fair substitute for a pulpit. But someday soon we'll have our own bishop, and then there will be many changes, Elizabeth. Some are immoderate and go too far and too fast toward trying to force what they believe, but there is a middle ground, and the rights we fight for and win will give every man the privilege to stand forth in freedom and dignity."

"And the slaves, Mr. Boyd?"

Adam laughed. "Elizabeth, you do beat all! I think I'll have you nominated for a seat on the committee! The slave question has been pondered under many a learned wig. The Tory gentlemen have asked us over and over how we reconcile our cries of liberty and equality with the possession of slaves. And I admit, on the face of it, there is an inconsistency. Yet we who own them know that as yet they are but children mentally and must grow up before they can assume their place as men. You and I may not live to see it, but mark my word, the day will come when even they shall come into their own, and with education and the right to vote, assume their obligations as citizens."

It was Elizabeth's turn to laugh. Imagine such ideas!

The knocker sounded. Adam rose, pulling a large watch from an embroidered fob. "Time completely forgotten in such good company." He smiled. "Mary will be waiting dinner on me. Oh, good evening, Mr. Richardson. I'll be getting along. Good night to you both."

"John, you are freezing! Come over to the fire." She looked at him searchingly. His lips were blue and his body shivering. "What is the matter? Where have you been?"

Before answering he went to the window and peered out into the gathering dusk. "I think I was followed."

Cicero came in to light the candles, and so her alarmed questions must wait.

"Cicero, bring Mr. Richardson a glass of brandy. Now tell me, John."

"I have been out to the cruiser, and as I landed from a small boat, I heard voices and the sound of a horse stamping. As I started to move on, I heard footsteps behind me. Perhaps it was imagination. The nature of the interview with the governor was not pleasant, so it might be that I was imagining someone following me, but I do believe it." He accepted the drink from Cicero and sank into a chair.

"John, why did you go? You know how dangerous it is."

"In the service of the king one does not consider danger, Elizabeth." With the double comfort of the fire and the brandy, a warmth began to steal through him and he relaxed.

"Oh, drat the king! I'm sick to death of politics tonight. You'll get yourself killed, sir, if you don't be careful."

"Am I to hope"—he smiled—"that such an occurrence would grieve you?"

"Well," she replied with a mischievous glance, "you saved my life once. I am certainly interested in preserving yours. I might need saving again sometime!"

He leaned toward her. "Tonight it is James I'm trying to save."

She kept her gaze steady, though she was irritated at the pang of fear that went through her.

"The governor and I have made a plan whereby we hope to dissuade him from his present course."

"And how will you do that?"

"By making him discredit himself with his own party." John would not perhaps have been so open with this information had he not believed that James' behavior on the night of the Browns' party had killed any romantic interest Elizabeth might have had in him. Now he dared to believe the way open for himself.

"Oh, John, is that safe?"

"As safe as anything these days." He shrugged.

"You are wrong to tamper with another person's life! How do you know *you* are absolutely right—or your party either?"

"Right, Elizabeth? Right? Can you think of anything more wrong than being one of those who are trying to overthrow government? You yourself said it was anarchy!"

"Oh, John, maybe you don't understand! Mr. Boyd said—"

"Mr. Boyd! What right has he to implant his radical ideas in your head? Really, Elizabeth, I don't consider him a wholesome influence for you."

She was sorry for him, for he was sincere in his beliefs and it was plain that he was honestly worried over James, but at his words she felt the old net closing around her. She would not have her thoughts ordered for her by anyone!

"I think Mr. Boyd is a lovely gentleman," she said firmly, her eyebrow lifting, "but what you think of him is beside the point. James is your brother, and you are plotting to destroy him!"

He threw out his big, kind hands in appeal. "I am planning to *save* him!"

But an icy fear clutched her. What if this scheme placed James in the light of a traitor? John didn't realize what he was doing, and the governor wouldn't care. Swiftly she decided to write James a note of warning the very minute John had gone.

CHAPTER 7

The smell of frying bacon drifted up from the tavern kitchen and filled the room with an enticing odor. A shaft of sunlight, bright and cold, shot through an open shutter and pried persistently at the thick brown lashes clamped together tightly in an effort to keep it out.

James stirred in the great featherbed, turned and stretched, buried half his face in the pillow, and let the sun have its way with the other. One eye opened slowly and shut quickly. But he was suddenly wide awake. There was something in the air that reminded him of frosty mornings in New England, when, long before he could possibly collect himself from sleep, his father's voice was bellowing up the stairs. He remembered the soul-shattering contact with icy water at the pump outside the back door, then those interminable morning prayers which seemed a sort of mental purgative for his father and purgatory for his own freezing knees. He could scarcely have endured it had it not been for the comfort of breakfast which followed in the great, steamy kitchen. Yet the thought of home and his father was good—in memory. He'd stop by to see the old man on the next voyage that took him in that direction.

The odor of bacon came again insistently. He kicked back the covers and thrust his long legs into his breeches, went across the room, and gave the bell cord a tug.

The clean freshness of the air carried an exciting scent of the sea, of rope and tar and salt. Over the roofs of the few low buildings between the tavern and the river, he could see a long barge gliding through the yellow water, and the flash of wet oars lifted to the sun in slow rhythm. The sound of a ship's bell floated up to him; from the backyard of the inn came the sudden, haughty, challenging crow of a cock. He grinned as the thought came that a good hearty crow must be a very satisfying sensation: proclaiming to the world that you were a man, answerable to none, and that all your women were well in hand.

The sights and the sounds were pleasing, for nearby the acres of his own plantation spread over the undulating fields and pine-covered hills. Indeed, he was now a man of parts. By Jove, he could never have got anywhere if he had remained under the autocratic thumb of his father. The idea occurred to him that perhaps there was an analogy between his career and that of the colonies—they had both outgrown parental dominance.

There was a timid knock on the door.

"Come in," he called cheerfully, turning from the window. It would be the tavern wench with his hot water.

The door swung wide enough to admit a view of thick ankles clad in white woolen stockings below a skirt of linsey. The rest of the figure was hidden by a large can. Only a pair of chapped, red hands showed as they clutched the handles.

The girl leaned backward balancing the weight she carried, moved into the room, and kicked the door shut behind her.

James laughed. "If you'll come out from behind that pot, I'll say good morning to you." Susan had served him at the tavern when he first came to Wilmington, and he had a cheerful fondness for the girl and her comfortable contribution of scalding water. She had been indentured to Lal Dorsey since childhood, and James knew that if the truth were known she had long since paid for her freedom. She worked from dawn until the tavern was deserted at midnight, after which, it was understood by Lal's more-favored patrons, she was available for an even more comforting service than the bearing of hot water.

He reached for his shirt and put it on as Susan went across to the washstand and emptied the contents of the can into the pitcher. Her stocky back, bisected by a loose, mouse-colored braid, was toward him, and he saw her shoulders heave with a soundless sob. He crossed the room and laid a hand gently on her arm.

"What's the trouble, Susan?"

She turned and faced him with tears streaming down her cheeks. He was shocked at the sight of her.

"Oh, sor, I didn't want you should see me like this—you as is the only real gintman I know. Mr. Dorsey has never beat me much, but last night—" Her face grew red and a line of sweat appeared on her upper lip as she drew from her bosom a letter which had been badly crumpled then smoothed. "Last night this come for you, sor. A black man brought it and I knew it must be turrible important because 'e called me off private and said to see it got into no hands but yours. Mr. Dorsey was a-comin' through the kitchen and 'e seen me take it, but I run till I could 'ide it on my pusson, sor, and then when 'e caught me 'e hit me down the head with 'is cane. 'E'd of found it shore if Mr. Tucker hadn't of started hollering for me, so I 'ad time to run away and 'ide it some place else afore I 'ad to go up to 'im. And then—"

"Lower your voice, Susan; somebody will hear you."

"And then, Mr. Tucker was awful drunk, and I was afeared of 'im. Oh, I don't mind some of 'em—some of the ones as smells nice and all—but when 'e grabbed me like—I was so scared then I run back to Mr. Dorsey thinkin' I could beg 'im not to make me go back, and then, Mr. Rich'son, 'e was so double mad at me 'e tied me up and beat me turrible!"

Before James could stop her she had slipped the blouse from her shoulder. "Look!"

He pulled her clothes back into place. "Susan," he said sternly, "you are legally bound to Lal Dorsey, and there is nothing I can do. It was good of you to bring me the letter."

He glanced at it—a woman's handwriting, unfamiliar—and thrust it into his pocket. All this excitement and this poor girl taking a beating because some fool woman considered one of her silly notes important!

"Here," he said in a kindlier tone, "take this and buy yourself a pretty."

Susan rubbed her nose down the length of her forearm, then lifted her apron to dry her face. She took the coin offered, but still lingered hesitantly before him.

"I thank ye kindly, sor." Her rough red hands twisted together. "I 'opes ye'll not take it amiss if I asks ye somethin'. Would ye speak to Mr. Dorsey for me? Ast 'im to let me come to you nighttimes? It wouldn't cost ye so much as ye've already gave me, and if I told 'im ye didn't want me to go to nobody else I wouldn't 'av to—"

"Susan, I couldn't do that," he said kindly, "I don't want a girl." His eye fell on the thick ankles and the heavy hips—God's teeth!

"But, sor, I'll—"

He would have to be stern to get rid of her. "The answer is no. I'll be glad to give you money from time to time toward your freedom, but I prefer to sleep alone."

HARMONY HALL

She turned then and fled through the door like a frightened rabbit.

"God's teeth," he said again, and going over to the salt box hanging beside the washstand, he vigorously scrubbed his own.

He was half through with his breakfast when Cornelius came through the doorway. He heard Lal Dorsey say, "There he is over there, sirrah." Lal was putting it on for Mr. Harnett, bowing and scraping, his moon face beaming and his fat hands rubbing together under his apron. It was seldom that this distinguished gentleman visited the tavern. He had a comfortable home and a bad stomach, which seemed to him sufficient reasons for not doing so. He brushed past Lal with something between a grunt and a snort, and came straight to the table.

Cornelius lifted a finger without bothering to turn his disordered bag wig. "Here you, girl, bring me a cup of hot water and milk. Can't stand this stinkin' stuff you call coffee."

James rose. "What brings you out so early sir?"

"Important business." Mr. Harnett leaned forward and fixed him with a steady, yet friendly eye.

Susan set the cup of cambric tea before him. "Now, girl, take yourself out of earshot and see that we are not disturbed." He paused for her obedience and continued, "The Committee of Safety had a meeting last night. 'Twas decided to ask you to join us. I trust, sir, that you realize what a grave and signal honor is bestowed on you, and that you will honor us by accepting."

"Why, sir, I'm profoundly touched by your confidence. I—er—" Indeed, this *was* coming on—being taken into the holy of holies of the most representative citizens in the county. True, his liberties would be somewhat circumscribed—there could be no dashing off to foreign parts for the sheer love of the voyage; he would have to be seriously attentive to the business of the committee.

"Well, what do you say, sir?"

"Why, of course I'll be delighted to take my place among you."

"Good. Meeting will be held tonight, after the militia parade, in the small assembly room at the courthouse. You will take the oath. Nine of the clock, sharp. That's settled. Now another matter. Keep your eye on your brother. Hate to mention it and that sort of thing, but a man answering his description was followed last night from a small-boat landing. Got away before our man could be sure of his identity.

There's been some important information leaking out lately. We can't put our fingers on it, and we're watching everybody of whose attitude we're not certain. Hate to have him get into any trouble."

"No, sir. Thank you. I'll see to it. But John was here for dinner last night and brought Mrs. Purdie with him, so I've an idea it must have been someone else. I came in rather late myself and haven't looked in on him this morning."

Harnett picked up his effects from a chair, came around, and laid a hand on James' shoulder. "As a member of the committee, it will be your duty to keep a sharp lookout for any and all subversive activities. Your servant, sir. Tonight at nine."

James left his buttered spoon bread unfinished, leaned back in the chair, and studied the toes of his well-varnished boots. His lips formed a tuneless whistle. What was John up to, if anything? He had given him little thought lately and had not seen him often either. To be sure, he had seemed a little jumpy and nervous last night, but he thought that was only because he had Elizabeth with him. He would have to find out just what went on, but, gad, he disliked keeping watch on his own brother. The tables had certainly turned. It had always been John's self-appointed task to police *his* activities. Well, he thought grimly, it looked as if he must return the courtesy.

Passing through the taproom on his way back upstairs, he glanced at the two men who had been sitting there since he came down to breakfast. They were a swarthy pair in sea boots and pea jackets. One of them eyed him keenly as he passed. The fellow's black eyes were bright and beady, and a crop of whiskers grew like a strange black forest up to the shores of his moist, red lips.

Upstairs, James passed through his bedroom and rapped gently on John's door. He rapped again, and still no answer. He opened the door and glanced at the bed. It had not been slept in. With a slight frown he was about to withdraw when he turned to find the stranger from below stairs inside the room and regarding him with a disparaging smile that made him feel as if he had been caught snooping.

"Well, what do you want?" he said, flushing angrily.

For answer the man kicked the door shut behind him while a heavy pistol appeared from beneath his coat. "I dislike this method of invitation as much as you do, undoubtedly, sir," he answered pleasantly, running his hand adroitly over James' clothing to make sure he was unarmed. "And now, if you will be so good as to step out into the hall, quietly, a friend will join us."

"May I ask what the idea is, my good man?" His voice was scornfully patronizing.

"Oh, I'm sorry. I forgot to mention that you need have no fear. Just be certain that you give us no trouble. Now, go out the door and we will take the carriage waiting in front of the tavern. Make no move to attract attention, or you will undoubtedly regret it."

The second man joined them and the carriage headed toward the river road. James sat stiffly between them.

"If this is a jest, I should not plan anything for tomorrow if I were you."

"I think, sir, you will not find it a jest." The man was sadistically enjoying mystifying his prisoner.

They traveled a mile or two, then turned off into a lane. At the end of it they got out and entered an old cabin that stood in a small clearing, and James saw that the one bare room showed signs of recent occupation. There was no fire in the grate, but the ashes still sent out a feeble warmth. There were only a rickety table and two old chairs.

"Please sit down, Mr. Richardson. There is someone who wishes to speak to you. I'll go and fetch him. I volunteered to bring you to where he could talk in the utmost privacy, and thereby earn my fee." He laughed and went out, closing the door.

Furious at the man's manner, James was also intrigued by the mystery. He made a circuit of the room, then moved a chair over into the band of sunlight slanting through the paneless window. It was getting on for noon and the militia parade was slated for two o'clock, but he supposed there was nothing to do but wait. There seemed to be no reason to try to escape. He jammed his hands in his pockets and encountered the letter Susan had given him.

"I must see you," it read, "as immediately as possible." The brief note was signed, "Elizabeth."

Well! He laughed to himself, a new approach, to be sure! And he wondered amusedly if it had been she who had had him abducted. She was a clever little piece, but if this was the game he'd teach her a few things right here in this cabin! He had no intention of becoming involved in the impeditive tangle of a serious affair. Failing a little caution, a man might awake some morning to find himself committed to matrimony. Time enough for that when he had accomplished, unfettered, all the things he meant to do. Time then to cast about for a generous dowry and a suitable, settled young lady; sow the seed of his posterity, and sit back for the rest of his life enjoying his plantation. He crammed the letter back in his pocket.

These pleasant thoughts were interrupted by the entrance of a man wearing a voluminous cape which he threw off to disclose the uniform of a British officer, who held out his hand.

"Mr. Richardson? Captain Glick, of his Majesty's ship *Viper*."

"Servant, sir," James returned coldly, and kept his hand in his pocket.

If he noted the insult, Glick's mission was too important to allow him to take offense. "Sorry to inconvenience you by bringing you out here, but as you know, the sight of a British uniform doesn't evoke the kindest regards around Wilmington at the moment."

James clamped his mouth in a hard, unyielding line.

"We have the intelligence," Glick went on quickly, "that your ship, *Quadrille*, is to sail the day after tomorrow to Nassau for a cargo of gunpowder for the Committee of Safety."

James concealed his angry surprise at the extent of the man's information. "So?"

"Ah, I see you are noncommittal. You are also wise. It does not pay to answer too many questions these days, does it?"

"Suppose you state your business," James said with an edge of contempt.

"I have come to make you an offer—one which I think a rising young businessman would be foolish to refuse. To wit, sir: when your vessel returns with this cargo, we will meet you at some given point offshore and pay you double for it whatever you have been offered by Mr. Harnett and his gentlemen." He spoke the last word in deep sarcasm. "It seems that it is worth more to the governor to pay you than to watch you. You are an ingenious navigator, Mr. Richardson."

James was thinking rapidly. There was something decidedly fishy about all this. The proposition was insulting—still—double the price of the cargo, by heavens, it would make him a very rich man. And here he was about to become a member of the Committee of Safety! He almost laughed.

"I'll have to think it over," he said. Either way, the situation was fraught with too much danger for a snap judgment.

Who had instigated this tempting offer? And who had gleaned so much information on his business?

"Very well, sir. Tomorrow morning someone will be in the taproom to receive your answer. The gentlemen who brought you here will see you safely back to town and give you details of how your answer may be given." He clicked his heels and went out quickly.

James picked up his tricorn and greatcoat and walked slowly out into the sun. The officer had vanished, but the carriage and his two escorts stood waiting for him.

On the highway, the man with the red lips said, "I hope you hold no offense, sir. You see now why it was so necessary to guard you. Our necks would have been in the stocks by now if you had tried an escape in town, and if I mistake not, a valuable offer would have been lost to you."

"No offense," James said shortly.

"Well, if you will read your history, sir, you will find that there have always been those wise enough to pick up a little cash wherever they could in times like these." And he displayed, clinking the coins together, a neat stack of British gold. "A man can't be blamed too much for preferring this to that paper stuff the Congress is printing."

As he got down at the tavern, the man said, "I shall see you here tomorrow, sir. Signal an affirmative answer by shifting your hat from one arm to the other."

So this man would receive his answer. By gad, it was a well-worked-out plan!

He went into the taproom and selected a long clay pipe from the rack over the fireplace. He broke off an inch of the stem. This thing wanted thinking out. Gold lay heavier in the pocket, but indeed, it made a more durable lining.

Groping through his small change, he drew out one of the large George III pennies and dropped it through the slot in the top of the brass tobacco box. On receipt of the coin, the lid flew up, and on its face was engraved the one word "HONOR."

Slowly he took a paper spill from a container on the mantel, stooped to ignite it at the grate, then turned and regarded the tobacco box again. As he knew, the word had been put there as a polite reminder to those gentlemen who might be inclined to take more than the pipeful they had paid for. In the light from the burning spill it glowed as if written in fire. The room was so still he could hear the heavy, sudden pounding of his heart. Up to now he had taken it for granted that, despite all the talk to the contrary, peace would be restored and business go on as usual. It had not occurred to him that he would ever have to make such a decision. But never in his life had his honor been sullied. His friends here had accepted him, a stranger, at face value, had put their faith in him, and he had given his word to Mr. Harnett.

He replaced the pipe, closed the box with a decisive snap, and took the stairs in rapid strides toward his room and the donning of full regimentals for the parade.

Neither Adam nor Mary Boyd had ever seemed to recognize the enmity which had lain between Abigail and Elizabeth since the moment of their first meeting, and it was because of their warm, graciously extended friendship that Elizabeth made every effort to conceal the way she felt about the girl. It was the least she could do, she thought, to express her gratitude for the many little acts of kindness she had received from their hands. It was not long before she had fallen into the local habit which Lucy had of addressing them as "aunt and uncle," though they were no more kin to Lucy than they were to her. It was merely a southern custom, a mark of affectionate respect.

The morning of the militia parade, Mary's little black slave came to the back door with an invitation to the girls to ride to the parade grounds in the Boyd carriage. Lucy came flying up the stairs with it and waited while Elizabeth wrote their enthusiastic acceptance.

"Abigail's going to ride in with Colonel Moore, so we won't be bothered with *her!*"

Elizabeth grinned. "Good. Here, this is ready, and tell that little spot of ink to go straight home with it. Last time Aunt Mary sent her with a note she loitered half the morning in the quarters."

When Lucy had left, she sat on before the desk, the tip of the quill caught between her teeth. The small French clock on the mantel pointed to half-past ten. Not a word had she heard from James, and by the minute her anxiety was increasing. She had tried to word the note to him so carefully—the wastebasket was half full of the torn attempts—so that by no suggestion could John be involved. Perhaps she should not have written at all, but even last night she had succeeded in convincing herself that her real motive lay in trying to prevent John from causing trouble he would regret for the rest of his life. Suppose James misunderstood the message. He was so—so arrogant. She threw the quill down with a spattering of ink. Half a woman's life was spent in some sort of concern over a man!

The Boyds' carriage rolled along under the leafless trees at what seemed to Elizabeth, sitting forward in eagerness, a turtle's pace. She anxiously watched for James in the milling crowds moving toward the parade ground, but the only familiar figure was a big slave with a tray of sweetmeats on his head who reminded her sadly of Tip-toe.

When they reached the area, Adam called her attention to the companies forming over beyond a low hill. The wind brought snatches of clipped orders and the muffled attempts of the drummer boys to hold off beating their drums. That was where James would be if he were here at all. She must get back there somehow.

"Uncle Adam," she said, turning to him quickly, "don't you think this is a good time for me to meet some of these 'common' men you told me about? There must be a lot of them in the army, and they're likely to be more convincing on a day when their enthusiasm is so high, don't you think so?"

"I do, indeed," he said, entirely unaware of her guile. "Mary, you and Lucy go on and take your seats and we'll join you presently. I want to introduce Elizabeth to some of our democratical ideas."

"A very fine thing, Adam. Keep your eyes open, child."

"Oh, I will!"

Arrived on the other side of the hill, Elizabeth saw that it was a regular campground of the militia. Men lounged in front of their tents or stood in little groups talking and joking, some busy practicing formations and manuals.

Her eyes ran rapidly from group to group, so that she was scarcely paying any attention as Adam stopped to speak to a sergeant who had come forward eagerly at the sight of him. He was a big, burly fellow with a shock of tawny, uncombed hair and wide-apart hazel eyes.

"Elizabeth, let me present Sergeant Anson."

Reluctantly, but because they seemed to expect it, she laid her small, dainty hand in his big grimy one.

"Pleased to meet yer, miss." And he turned his attention back to Adam. "You are just the man I wanted to see, Mr. Boyd."

"Good, Zed, what's on your mind?"

Elizabeth slanted her eyes around again toward the drilling men, anxiously now. James should be here, unless—oh, unless . . . All kinds of horrible possibilities occurred to her. Then she saw him, sitting his great bay mare as if he owned the world, his resplendent uniform bright in the sun, his head thrown back in laughter. Her relief caught her breath and kindled a sudden hot anger against itself. Why should she have bothered with warning him at all? He was perfectly capable of taking care of himself. Her note he had completely disregarded. Quickly she turned back to face the sergeant so that James would not catch her looking at him, and then it was that she saw the man on the ground.

"He's all right, miss. I jes' laid him out, but he'll come 'round in a little while."

"What's the trouble, Zed? Isn't that George Holmes?"

"Yessir, that's him all right. And that's what I wanted to see you about."

Elizabeth saw that Holmes was clad in a fine new uniform.

"He come 'round with his boots and ordered me to shine 'em. Jes' because while I was indentured to his pa I took orders from him I reckon he thought I still would. But the old man give me my freedom to go to the army, and as I understand it, it's freedom I'm a-fightin' fur." His face was suddenly hard. "I don't aim to take orders from no man no more as long as I live, 'cept maybe the general."

Elizabeth had never heard such talk, but as the sergeant continued, she thought what he said sounded reasonable enough.

Anson jerked his head back toward the unconscious Mr. Holmes and shifted his quid into the other cheek.

"He never done a lick o' work in his life, Mr. Boyd, and he wouldn't of got a commission if his pa hadn't boughten it fur him. Popinjay!" He spit out of the corner of his mouth.

"You had no cause to obey him, true, Zed, but you didn't have to knock him out."

"Well, sir, he come 'round so abusin'like, and when I refused to shine his boots, he begun to hop up and down and say who was I to be puttin' on airs, that my ma was even now a-workin' on his pa's ropewalk. It was the first I knowed, sir, that Ma'd went and sold herself into service. I been doin' everything I could to help her, but I guess things got pretty bad with that passel o' brats she's got. I seen red when he said it, Mr. Boyd, and my fist jes' went out hastylike. The first thing I'm a-gonna do when this here war's over and I get into the legislature is to vote some other way o' treatin' paupers."

Elizabeth, who had been listening with increasing sympathy to the man's words, was brought up sharply by this last statement. The man was preposterous. Who ever heard of a freed bond servant going to the legislature!

"And how will you get into the legislature, Sergeant Anson?" she asked with an amused little smile.

"By savin' my pay, ma'am, and buyin' me a little piece o' land." He seemed for the first time conscious of her presence and her interest. His wide eyes looked into hers with no embarrassment, no suggestion of a knowledge of inferiority. "Can you imagine, ma'am, how it feels to be a man grown, sold into bondage, with no right and no way to help your own family? And all you've got at the end of a day's work is a bit of bacon and a bed in the hayloft? No'm, it ain't right. With a piece of land freeheld I can vote—maybe congress'll give me a little tract if I sojer good."

There was a quickening all about them. An officer dashed by on his sweating mount shouting directions. When he saw Elizabeth and Adam, he pulled up short.

"Clear the field, please, we're ready to begin. Sergeant, order your men to fall in. Here, what's this?" He dismounted and stooped to examine Holmes. "Who is responsible for this?"

"I am, sir," answered Anson promptly, and began to explain when the officer cut him short.

"You'll get some time in the guardhouse for this. Fighting on the campground!" He was the typical tidewater aristocrat, elegantly accoutered, haughty, proud. "You scum don't know what this war's about. I wonder why we put up with you."

Elizabeth started to speak—a furious defense of Anson—but Adam laid his hand on her arm. "I'll do what I can for you, Zed."

"Well," he said as they started around toward the grandstand, "I could have asked no better exposition of what I have told you."

"What right did the captain have not to let Zed Anson explain?"

"Oh, he's another one of our mercantile patriots. Holmes' father owns more land and more ships than any man in Newberne, so of course the captain is on his side. If it had been the other way 'round he wouldn't have said a word. That kind cares plenty for his own interests, but not a tinker's dam for the common man. They are only patriots on account of their financial interests. I am glad his type doesn't understand that in this fight for freedom there is another class for whom it means a different thing, for we need the support of their prestige and they would not give it if they knew how surely complete control will pass from their hands."

In the grandstand they took their seats. Mr. Harnett sat next to them, leaning forward, his wig and clothing askew as usual, resting his arms on the railing as if by the very force of his will he might cover the field before him with well-equipped, smartly drilled soldiers instead of the raggedly disciplined, poorly accoutered lines that would presently appear. John had come in and, finding Lucy and Mary, had chosen the seat by the one Elizabeth was to occupy.

James was safe, so far, and her concern over Zed Anson's problem slipped from her lightly as her spirits rose to the holiday level of the celebration. She was here for a good time, and John's frowning disapproval of Adam's taking her behind the lines was not going to worry her in the least.

The sound of fifes and drums announced the appearance of Colonel Moore heading the first regiment on his big white stallion. Beside him, in a garnet-red habit, rode Abigail, sitting her horse like a queen, the plume on her small hat dancing in the gentle wind. A prolonged cheer arose as they passed the reviewing stand. Many of the men who followed had drilled with the regulars and had a finished, military bearing. Their dark-blue, brass-buttoned coats were faced back in buff; the crossbelts and gaiters were white with pipe clay; their white-breeched legs made lines as straight and even as the keys on a harpsichord. The principal officers were well-mounted and, in addition to the regular uniforms, were further distinguished by red sashes and gold-fringed epaulets.

James led his company behind his colonel, Thomas Brown, and the soldiers passed on and on in review. Drums beat and rolled, fifes shrilled, flags snapped in the wind, the people cheered. But after the first well-dressed, well-drilled companies, the ranks became ill-assorted and poorly clothed. Those who could not afford uniforms wore what they happened to have, which lack dampened their ardor not at all. Men from the northern counties, from the mountainous terrain at the headwaters of Cape Fear, had joined up in their leggings of deerskin, fringed buckskin shirts, and homespun. They bore a miscellany of firearms: fowling pieces, muskets, muzzle-loaders, blunderbusses. They were the "long knives" from the north; they were big and husky and rough and untrained, but to the wide turned-up brims of their hats and their coonskin caps was pinned the red cockade. Doggedly, with the silent, catlike tread of Indians, they moved across the hard-packed field—out of step, out of rhythm.

Elizabeth, accustomed only to gentlemen soldiers, made the mistake of laughing, and no other thought than amusement was in her mind as she said, "Why, the British could whip an army like that with their hands tied!"

Heads turned, shocked, in her direction. Lucy nudged her gently with her elbow. Cornelius Harnett fixed her with a grim eye.

"They can hit a snake's eye at a hundred paces, miss," he said.

John, immediately defensive at his tone, said, "I am sure, sir, Mistress Purdie has a right to speak if she chooses. They *are* a queer-looking lot of soldiers, though the sight of them is not so new to you as it is to her."

Mr. Harnett allowed his sharp eye to run up and down John's spare frame. "They are men, sir, willing to do their duty for their country!"

"Are you implying—"

"Oh, do sit down, John. It doesn't matter. I was wrong. I'm sorry, Mr. Harnett."

John sat glowering. Lucy looked over and saw the cat-and-cream expression that flickered across Abigail's face.

After the parade, everybody went home to change for the ball which was to be held in the assembly room at the courthouse in honor of the visiting officers of the militia. In the vacant lot across the street hoi polloi would have their barrels of beer and dancing on the common.

Elizabeth could scarcely wait to get back to the festivities, but Lucy decided to stay home.

"It's no fun for me to go to a dance when Gordon can't be there," she said. "You go on and have a good time."

"I hate to leave you here alone."

"I won't be alone. Mamba and the others are here. I'd rather stay. Please."

So Elizabeth went on without her, picking up the Boyds in her carriage. But on arrival she found John awaiting her at the door, a heavy look on his face of mingled sorrow and fury. He drew her hand through his arm and finally succeeded in making way for her and the yards of rustling silk fashioning her skirts through the press of people to a corner of comparative privacy.

Before she had time to voice the sudden questioning anxiety that flashed to her mind, he spoke. "A letter came by packet this evening for James. When I saw that it was from my father I opened it, as James was nowhere about." He drew a long breath. "This is the end of our world, Elizabeth."

"What's happened, John?"

"He has been run out of his home, everything he owned confiscated, and has fled for his life to Nova Scotia!"

"Oh, how terrible. But why? Who?"

"These damned swine who call themselves patriots. They have done their country more harm than good, I tell you. One of the finest men who ever lived! Our dignified and beautiful home the rendezvous of thieves and riffraff!"

"Where is James?"

"I have no idea. But have no thought of him—he wouldn't feel any concern." John would have been doubly sure he spoke the truth had he known that at that moment his brother was taking the oath of allegiance to the Committee of Safety.

"I think you are wrong. And, anyway, the letter was to him, he has a right to know its contents. Come, let's find him, and you'll feel better for talking with him. It may change everything."

"No, go along and enjoy yourself. Here comes a gentleman to ask your favor. I'll find James later, but it will make no difference."

She saw that the young lieutenant approaching was George Holmes, whom she had last seen stretched out by the hasty hand of Zed Anson. But there was nothing to do but dance with him. Perhaps John preferred to be alone. She kept a sharp watch on the door, but James did not come.

Then she became conscious of the man lounging against a window across the room. He was staring at her with his bright black eyes. His cherry-colored lips were smiling. That Abigail was standing beside him and disapproving of the direction his interest had taken, she also noted.

At the end of the set, obviously because he had asked it, Abigail brought him up to be presented. "Mrs. Purdie, David Fanning."

Fanning gave her his full attention and asked for a succession of dances. In a capricious desire to annoy Abigail, she gave them to him.

He was an excellent dancer, and his conversation was smooth and flattering. The knowledge of Abigail's fury only made her enjoy herself the more, and she became aware of the admiring eyes following the couple who seemed to be having such a gay time.

"Ah, Mistress Purdie," he whispered, holding her more closely than was necessary, "you are very beautiful. The powder in your hair is like stardust."

"Oh, it is, sir?" she said, laughing. "I always have a star or two ground up for my toilette!"

"Perhaps I was greedy to try to monopolize you," he said, squeezing her hand, "but I am one of those who believes in increasing opportunities for taking. Given one chance, make three out of it!"

She did not hear the rest of what he was saying, for she had caught sight of James in the doorway. He made straight for the punch table. Quickly she looked around to where, only a moment before, John had been standing with Peter Slingsby, but they were gone.

"Mr. Fanning, I am like to faint with thirst." If only she could get near to James she might reiterate the necessity of talking to him, though a precious lot of response she had gotten from her note.

James gave her only a brief glance, then his eyes fastened intently on David Fanning.

Fanning raised his glass. "Liberty and justice," he said with rather a mocking tone, "and God save the king!"

James hesitated only a moment, then tossed off his drink. If the Continental Congress had opened its session with a solemn prayer for his Majesty, it could not hurt a member of the Committee of Safety to drink a toast to the old fellow.

He continued to stare at Fanning until the other dropped his eyes. "I believe we have met before," he said curtly.

"It is possible, Mr. Richardson." And with that he set his glass down, gave Elizabeth his arm, and turned to join the promenade around the room.

Fanning returned her to her seat beside Mary Boyd, and suddenly she was sick of him. She had missed another chance to speak to James, and it appeared that he had weightier matters on his mind than asking her to dance. She would go home. Perhaps he would wonder why and—

Pleading fatigue, she said good night to Aunt Mary, and went across to get her wraps.

On the other side of the paper-thin wall of the cloakroom she could hear two men talking in tense, low voices. "I tell you, Mr. Harnett, someone got this information to the cruiser that was plenty smart."

"Was the powder totally destroyed?"

"Yes, sir, there isn't a pound of it left—even the magazine is wrecked beyond any repairing."

"I can't understand. No one knew of its whereabouts except the committee."

"But, sir, there are some here lately who are mighty close to the members."

"Whom do you suspect, Hayes?"

"I dislike to say exactly, Mr. Harnett, but I do think there's a man about that ought to have been watched more carefully."

Elizabeth's heart began to pound. She could not have moved if she had tried.

Hayes was speaking again. "All the way to town I pondered on it, sir, and the man that best fits the shoe is John Richardson."

"You do not surprise me, but it would have been impossible for him to have gotten this information from his brother. He was taken into the committee only tonight, as you know, about the time this occurred."

"He may have had other ways of finding out. We know nothing of him, sir, and his movements have been strange. Today a letter came from his father, who is a well-known Tory, saying that he had been forced to flee to Nova Scotia and expressing a most bitter invective against the cause. I think he ought to be taken into custody—"

Elizabeth waited to hear no more. She sped down the stairs and to the carriage where Ephraim slept at the reins. The street was bright with the glow of bonfires on the common, and noisy with the people's celebration. She climbed into the carriage and shook the old slave awake.

Only a single candle burned upstairs in her bedroom, but in passing through the hall she was attracted by a low call from the drawing room. It was Lucy's voice, and the ring in it told her more quickly of Gordon Denny's presence than his own immediate word of greeting. This of all nights for Gordon to come! Adding the anxiety for his safety to everything else she had on her mind!

"Lucy! Everybody in town will talk about you—sitting like this in the dark—" In her desperation she spoke sharply.

"No'm they ain't," came Mamba's voice from out the dark. "Ah bin settin' rat here all evenin'."

"Oh, Elizabeth, what's the matter?"

"Somebody destroyed the powder magazine belonging to the Committee of Safety tonight, and they are looking for the man who told them where it was. John is suspected, and, Gordon, if they found you here, after you declared yourself at Cross Creeks—"

"I'd hang, ma'am, that I would."

"Oh, Gordon, don't say it! You must go."

"And have him caught in the streets? No, he must stay here until we know—"

A low knock sounded on the front door, and they froze in silence. It came again insistently.

"It may be John," Elizabeth whispered. "Be very quiet, I'll see."

"Oh, don't answer it. It might be—"

"I must. You and Gordon get to the attic as fast as you can."

"Elizabeth!" It was John, and in a moment he had slipped into the hall. He was breathless. His stock was loosened and crumpled, and his queue ribbon hung down untied. "Get your cloak. We must make our escape now or never," he panted.

"Oh, John, you are in great danger!"

"Danger! My God, I know it. They're after me in full cry, and if I mistake not, they'll be in this street and this house before many minutes looking for us both."

Elizabeth felt the blood ebbing from her head. "For me? Why?"

"There's no time for questions. In their present mood over the loss of the powder there will be no mercy for anyone who's not been licking their boots. Your remark of this afternoon—men have been shot for less! Come now, quickly. We can take Mrs. Bell's horses and send them back later." He tried to draw her toward him. "We can yet have our chance for happiness despite a crazy world."

But this last remark gave her back her nerve. Surely no one would hold a half-jesting remark against her. She had done nothing, she would not run away, and besides, his calm assumption of the story's ending was not to her liking. Better be free and suspected than safely in bondage again!

"John, I am not going with you." She whirled about. "Come, I'll hide you till this blows over. You didn't fire the magazine, did you?"

"No! Before God, I didn't even know they had one. But why stand there asking foolish questions? And speak no more of not going. I wouldn't dream of leaving you here to face this mob."

"Listen!" From the end of the street came the sound of shouting, and a flickering glow of torches turned the night outside to a murky rose.

"Oh, John, hurry! To the attic!" But Gordon was in the attic, and if searchers found them both in her house . . . What a fool she had been to keep the boy here when he had had so much more time to get away. "Wait," she cried softly, her foot already on the stair. "Would you go to the cruiser?"

"How, in God's name?"

"I have a way." She snatched up her cloak and, pulling him after her, went swiftly to the back of the house. The light from the torches did not reach into the darkness along the sally port leading to the quarters. An outside stairway ran to the loft over the stable, and from there it was an easy step to the coach-house roof.

"You are mad, Elizabeth."

But she ran along the slanting shingles, steadying herself by gripping the ornamental iron railing extending only halfway to her knee, and at the roof's end dropped with a soft thud into the alley. Here they stopped to listen, then she led a devious way to a thick grove of trees. She looked back, but they could see nothing but a glow in the sky.

"Come on, we can make it now." If they searched the house, how would she explain this absence? Perhaps she had better go on with John after all. So hard was she thinking on this problem that at first she paid no attention to John's surprised questions when she left the small path and made her way in through the dry, rustling reeds to the little boat she and Lucy had stowed away so carefully.

"What are you doing, Elizabeth?"

"Oh, do hurry, John. Get in!"

"You mean to sail to the cruiser in this little shell?"

"We've not much choice, have we?"

"Ah, then," he said with relief, "you mean to go with me after all!"

She did not answer, but busied herself with setting her course toward the faint, far light of the cruiser, which cast only a feeble gleam across the water. Then, all at once, she began to doubt the wisdom of her impulsively made decision. With John gone, her feeling of security would be gone with him. She had not realized until the thought came that she might never see him again, how much it meant simply to have him near. Like solid ground beneath her feet—like a wall at her back. But once aboard the cruiser neither the British nor the Americans would allow her to come back to Wilmington, and she would have to live on weevily biscuits and salt fish—a virtual prisoner as Governor Martin was. Without any of her pretty new clothes, without Mamba. Oh, Mamba could not be left alone, and there was Gordon in the attic, and James—

"John," she demanded suddenly, "what did you have planned against James? Was tonight a part of it?"

"Good Lord, no! You didn't think I wanted him killed, did you? No, I thought it might prove effective to try to change his mind through his most vulnerable spot: his pocketbook. We offered him double the price of his next cargo of gunpowder, but that fool Fanning we hired to bring James to meet our man doubled back and sold the information to the Committee of Safety that it was probably I who had instigated the temptation of one of their patriots. That, followed within the hour by the destruction of the powder magazine, was what set them after me. Such perfidy! How he managed it without putting himself under suspicion is more than I can understand. But he's a smooth eel."

That John seemed entirely unaware that his own action in thus attempting bribery against his own brother was perfidious in the extreme, whatever his motive, she let pass without comment, for another thought had taken possession of her mind. "Did James accept the offer?" So intent was she on his answer that she failed to see the spit of land jutting out perilously close to the boat. With a desperate pull on the tiller she managed to avoid it, but the little sail dipped far over and an icy spray drenched them both.

"Lord, that was narrow," John exclaimed. "What? Oh, I don't know. He was to give his answer tomorrow morning, but there's so much treachery there's no telling what may happen."

Somehow she could not picture James as one who would accept a bribe, and knowing he had just become a member of the committee she felt he could not possibly be such a turncoat. Only tonight at the ball, Aunt Mary had told her that he had been selected to join, and if he *could* be tempted so far, it would mean his death, she knew.

Abruptly, the gray sides of the cruiser loomed above them. The night was so black it was difficult to maneuver the small craft alongside.

"No, don't tie the painter. It will be easier to make connection with the boat loose. If it's tied she may swing 'round," she said.

John called and men came running across the deck above. Standing, he made himself known, then turned back to Elizabeth. "Well, we made it! Up you go, now."

"After you, John."

"How like a woman! Even at a time like this to be bothered about whether a gentleman sees her legs! But have it your—"

He never finished his sentence, for halfway up the ladder he realized the little boat beneath him had vanished.

Elizabeth heard the calls, and she saw the flare of torches lighting up the river around the cruiser, but she had too much the start. Thank God for the good wind and for the fact that the condition of the sail was by age and mud so dark a brown it would be invisible to those who might try to follow her in a small boat.

The creek was not hard to locate on account of the trees at its mouth. She tied the boat up and began to make her way back toward her house. But now, alone, every rustle of the brush and weeds along the path was frightening, in every shadow lurked danger.

Reaching the alley, she started to run. Her skirts caught and she jerked and tore them loose. She stopped to listen and realized that the street was quiet and there were no more torches. That someone might be lying in wait slowed her pace to a more cautious tread, but she was shaking and chattering with terror.

How formidably high was the garden wall! And the gate would be locked. There was nothing to do but to try to climb back up to the carriage-house roof again. But as she reached the gate, it opened silently, and James stepped out, glancing quickly up and down the alley. Her relief was almost overwhelming, but he must not find her here.

Instantly, she crouched back into the shadows, but she was too late. He reached out and caught her wrist, pulling her roughly after him as he made for the small toolshed at the end of the quarters. He shut the door behind him, took care to do it silently, but did not relax his grip.

"You are hurting my arm," she said icily.

"You little fool," he answered savagely, "prowling about alone with half the county searching for you! Where have you been? Where did you hide him? Answer me!"

"Who?" she asked. If he had been in the house, she thought, he just might have learned of Gordon's presence.

"You know very well who. That treacherous scoundrel, my brother. His dastardly attempt to ruin me, to get me hanged! I'll replace his black heart with the lump of lead it so resembles!"

"Then I think it will not do you any good to know his whereabouts."

"Nor him, I assure you, but I will know, and now, unless you prefer to have it choked out of you!"

"Very well, then," she said coolly, "I am but just come from sailing him out to the cruiser!"

"Gentle God! You—"

"Yes, and if it please you, I am wet and cold and would like to get to the fire."

He convinced himself that she spoke the truth by feeling her gown. "I can't see what you look like in this darkness, but it couldn't be much. Come, there is no time to lose." He dragged her toward the house, across the garden. "Change your dress and join me in the library. We'll have to make it appear that we've been out for a drive and have just returned. The searchers may be back any minute. Why I should bother with you, God alone knows."

She flew upstairs where Mamba was already laying out dry garments. To her surprise the old woman was in high glee.

"Ah ain't had sich goin's on 'round me since de Injun waws, and yo' grandmaw thowed bilin' soap on de chief!"

Suddenly it was very good to laugh. "How on earth did you know I needed dry clothes?"

"Ah heered Mist' James thoo de back window. How you git so wet?"

"I'll tell you later. Where did you hide Gordon?"

"He's in de prayer closet back o' dis here wardrobe. Trolcie tole me 'bout it when we fust come, but Ah forgit it till de Lawd brung it back to my mind rat when we need it most."

"Did someone search the house? James said they might be back."

"Yas'm, dey even went thoo de attic, but dey ain't find nothin'. Dey lookin' for Mist' Jawn. Dey axe me is he here. Miss Lucy she run jump in de baid and kivver up. Hit sho' was a sight to see dem big mens a-tippin' 'round to see is dey anybody in dah wid her."

"Mr. James doesn't know Gordon is here!"

"No'm, Ah ain't told nobody."

"Well, don't. There may be another search. You just sit over there with your knitting as if you were waiting up for me."

"Which Ah is."

She had no sooner taken a chair by the library fire opposite James than there was a loud knocking and the scraping of boots outside. James got up.

"Do as little talking as you can and take your cues from me. Remember, we've been out for a drive."

She was bursting with questions, but she no longer trembled with fear. The little interview with Mamba had eased the tension, and she was feeling a little thrill that James was going to all this trouble for her. She heard the men in the hall addressing him with respect, for he was still in full regimentals, but after a few minutes they entered the library.

"Mrs. Purdie, these men are searching for a man and they want to look through the house."

"They are free to do so, I'm sure," she said with a mildly haughty air, but she was thankful to note that these were enlisted men who had not attended the ball, and so would not notice that her gown had been changed. "But why?"

"We are looking for Mr. Richardson, ma'am. Mr. John Richardson. But first I'd like to ask where *you* were when our men were here earlier?"

"Why, we have just returned from a drive."

The spokesman turned to James. "You his brother, sir?"

"I am, and greatly as I regret our differences of opinion, I could scarcely be expected to go on a manhunt for him. So, to keep out of the way, when I learned what was up, Mrs. Purdie and I went for a ride. Naturally, I was not in a very happy frame of mind."

The men shuffled their feet, suddenly ill-at-ease, sympathetic for their superior officer forced into such an unpleasant situation.

"I understand, sir. And you swear that this ride had nothing to do with his escape?"

"I do. As a member of the Committee of Safety, I should not likely be one to aid the enemy, even though he happened to be a relative."

Elizabeth slipped off her soaking shoes and pushed them back under her skirts. She had completely forgotten to change them.

"And you have no idea where he might be hiding?"

"Not the faintest."

"And you, madam?"

"I? How could *I* possibly know?"

"Because he was often seen in your company, and Mr. Harnett seems to believe you may know where he is. He feared the others had not been as thorough in their search as they might."

"Well, my maid tells me they covered the house," she answered sharply, her heart beginning to pound again at the thought of a more meticulous search. If they found Gordon, they would all be in for trouble.

He was looking squarely at her, piercingly, as if he could see the dark secrets behind her eyes. "I hope you are telling the truth, for your own sake, ma'am. My apologies to you, sir, but we have our duty."

"Well, go ahead and get it over with," James answered with a well-simulated yawn, "it's getting late."

A man was left stationed in the hall, so the conversation must be a masterpiece of casualness. If the situation had not been fraught with such dire possibilities they would both have been convulsed with laughter.

At length the search was ended, and by a miracle Gordon's presence remained secret. When the men had gone, Elizabeth's eyes flashed at James.

"Now tell me," she asked, "where were *you* when the men were here before?"

But he was in a black humor, in no mood for answering questions. Yet he made no move toward leaving.

"I was explaining myself to the Committee of Safety!"

"Yourself! Well, it's your own fault if you're in trouble. I tried to warn you, but you disregarded my note in a very highhanded manner."

He stood in front of the fire, perfectly groomed and poised, unruffled in appearance by the wild evening. She had never seen him so handsome.

"You tried to warn me of what?"

"That there was a plot being formed against you, but I couldn't put all that in a note. All I could do was to tell you I must see you, but you paid no attention!"

"Oh," he said, and smiled suddenly, then became serious again. "I see. Then the gentlemen of the committee were not so far wrong."

"In what?"

"Your note was found by someone in my room, and may it please you, madam, it was that which drew their attention to your own uneasy head."

"But who? Why?"

"Elizabeth, these men are not fools. They think you knew something that had to do with the loss of the powder and with John's escape. Coming on the heels of your remark at the parade this afternoon— They will watch you like a mouse from now on. Yes, and the cats are watching too, never fear."

"Who told *them* what I said?"

"I'd think you'd know who told them after the flagrant

manner in which you relieved Miss Abigail of her most cherished beau."

"Oh, of all the—"

"I'm in no mood to listen to a plan of campaign for a women's war, madam, and I think that tomorrow you will regret that you made such a spectacle of yourself with that charming gentleman."

"What do you mean? I will not stay here and be—" She rose, and the green watered silk of her skirts made an indignant rustle. But she had forgotten to step back into her shoes, and suddenly James was laughing at her. Abashed that the hauteur she had intended was lost, she lashed out, "You can't talk to me like that!"

"Oh, yes, I can and will." He gripped her shoulders. "You have been warned before, now I'm *telling* you: I'm slipping out to sea tomorrow, so you will have to take care of yourself."

"I can certainly—"

"Apparently you can't. I have saved you from a pretty bad scrape tonight; at least let us hope so. I don't want to have to marry you to keep the Committee of Safety off your neck," he finished sarcastically.

She could only stare at him in surprised fury, while he, with an amused smile, looked down at her stockinged feet. "Go put some shoes on before you catch your death of cold."

She heard the heavy front door close behind him.

CHAPTER 8

Next morning the weather, which had held good for so long during January, became a thing to be reckoned with. Snow whirled out of blue-gray skies on a wind that carried a knife. Fences disappeared, and shrubbery began to look like old women in white wool huddled against the houses.

At first it was fascinating to Elizabeth, who had never seen snow, but as the day wore on with no other activity than alternately hugging the fire and watching the unbroken expanse of white, she began to be bored.

Lucy looked out the window and reported that Uncle Adam was coming in the gate. He had brought them a copy of the *Mercury*.

"It should have been out this morning," he said, "but I held up the press to get this story in."

Elizabeth suppressed a gasp as she read that David Fanning was under arrest. So *that* was what James had meant about regretting Fanning's attentions to her! The charge against him, the article stated, was that of "representing his Excellency Governor Martin and attempting to bribe a member of the Committee of Safety. And but for the cleverness of Mr. James Richardson in seeming to consider the offer, thereby drawing Fanning into a trap, he should even now be at large to continue his treacherous business wherever he might by so doing, indulge his appetite for British gold."

Elizabeth did not ask why there was no mention made of the fact that he had also indulged his appetite for colonial paper by accepting a fee from the committee in payment for information concerning John's part in the scheme. She was feeling a strange relief that James had not accepted the offer, but she said nothing because even Uncle Adam must not suspect her own knowledge of the affair. What would he say if he knew that she herself had helped John escape, and that a man who was certainly a Tory by background, if nothing more, had been hidden all night in her house?

Suddenly, to her horror, she realized that Lucy was laughingly relating the latter fact, embellishing the story with the ruses she and Mamba had used to effect Gordon's early-morning departure on the old mule Judge Bell had used to plow his garden.

"We blacked his face with a cork, Uncle Adam, and dressed him up like a darky in a lot of old clothes, and—"

"Wait a moment, Lucy. You mean to tell me that you girls took a chance like that at this of all times?"

"*I* did," Lucy bubbled on. "Now, Uncle Adam, you know Gordon is not a Tory. Why, it was he who brought the report of the Scotch massing at Cross Creeks!"

"That is beside the point, Lucy. I don't doubt that you are speaking the truth: you have every reason not to give aid to the loyalists, but please consider how it would look to others. And, Elizabeth, you can't afford this sort of thing. I had all I could do last night to convince some of the gentlemen that you were merely a harmless child without enough knowledge of what went on to be responsible for any assistance to the enemy."

"Thank you, Uncle Adam," she said, stung a little by the characterization.

He refused their invitation to stay for tea and shrugged back into his coat. "I must go to Newberne tomorrow for a few weeks."

"Oh, Uncle Adam, the weather!"

"The weather can't be helped, my dears. There is much to be done if it is true that Cornwallis and Clinton are on their way here." At the door he drew on his knitted mittens. "You girls be cautious, now. Confine your walks to the city streets and, Elizabeth, do be careful of every word you speak."

In the copy of the *Mercury* there was a report of the condition of the American army lying before Boston at the year's end. There was nothing encouraging in it, since, with scarcely a blanket to a man, little military equipment, and a questionable food supply, the forces had braved the violence of the winter storm with no action against the comfortable, well-equipped enemy except the strengthening of fortifications and minor skirmishes. Though General Washington wrote to Congress a formidable list of his absolute necessities and drew a dark picture indeed of his situation, there could not be read into it by even the most sanguine English officer any infirmity of purpose or flagging enthusiasm for the cause.

As she read, Elizabeth realized that she had begun to some extent to share the hopes of the colonies. She was entirely individual, yet despite herself she had become involved in the tangle, and her sense of fairness and logic caused changes in her thinking. She had been pulled this way and that. While John was there, he had kept the Tory attitude ever before her—many of his ideas were her own; she had been born with them and accepted them without question. But there was Adam Boyd, and James, and, yes, even Sergeant Anson, who had given her a new set of values. And so it was that while one half of her hoped for the achievement of colonial aims, the other half clung to the old established order under the king.

It was difficult to know, she thought, and still more so when one day toward the end of March, her budding interest in the cause of the patriots was almost crushed.

She and Lucy had been staying close at home, not only in obedience to Adam's warning, but on account of the continued cold and unpleasant weather. Now spring was in the air, although snow still lay in patches here and there.

Curled in a chair by the library window, Elizabeth thought of the green palm trees waving against a blue Jamaican sky, the arms of crimson vines reaching over garden walls white hot in the sun. But the brief clutch of homesickness left her with the realization that she would not go back if she could—not even if Land's End were still standing in all its splendor. Came then that exasperating tug inside her at the thought that she was missing James. She had been furious at him the night of John's escape, yet now that he was away she passionately wished him back. Ridiculous! John was the one who loved and needed her, and he was like a rock for her own refuge. She had not realized how much she would miss *him*. Maybe it was real love she felt for John, after all. Maybe like any greedy child, she had too much eye for the glitter rather than the gold.

She turned from the window as Cicero came into the room. Lucy sat morosely staring out at the street.

"Dey ain't no mo' sugah," he said. "I done bin to town an' we cain't buy none."

"What do you mean you can't buy any? Why not?"

"Hit's all went to de army. We is gwine have to use molasses when we kin git dat."

"Well, of all things!"

"Yas'm, an' dey is some news, too. Dis here Mist' Fannin' done 'scaped." He waited for their exclamations, enjoying being the bearer of information, and continued, "An' it's hunnerds of dem Scotch people from up at Cross Creeks country comin' thoo on their way to Floh-da."

"The *who?*" Lucy cried, shaken out of her lethargy.

"De Scotch. You 'members, Miss Lucy, Mist' Hahnett say a long time ago dey was goin' to confistocate dere propity effn dey didn't sign up wid de 'sociation. An' sho' nuf, dey is leavin' in droves. Ah seen 'em mahchin' long wid de wimmins an' chillens, an wagons full o' stuff. Hit sho' was pitiful." And tactlessly but sorrowfully he added, "Ah ain't much surprised ef Mist' Gordon wid 'em. Ah seen his ma. Howsomever, he may not be, 'cause dey say most of de mens was stayin' back to fight."

To Lucy's frantic questions, Cicero could add no more— nothing except his own lamentations at the increasing scarcity of food.

"Oh, come on, Lucy, let's ride!" Elizabeth felt she could not stay indoors another minute, and Lucy was more than willing, despite Uncle Adam's warning.

Instead of the river road, they took one that paralleled the North East branch, passing Hilton, Mr. Harnett's plantation, then Jones' sawmill whirring noisily farther down the road. After this one sound of industry, the countryside was still and quiet. They galloped over the muddy ground until they reached the edge of the big swamp, and pulled up.

"Shall we go on?" Lucy asked, looking into the narrow aisle where the trees grew right up to the ends of logs laid closely side by side on the spongy ground forming a wooden road through the swamp. "I've always wanted to see what this place looked like."

"Yes, let's go. There isn't a soul in sight, and we can turn back any time we want to."

The horses picked their way carefully along the uncertain footing, and the forest closed in about them and shut out the sun. Cypress trees spread their enormous knees in the black water, tangling their tops overhead.

"Oh, I do so wonder where Gordon is. You don't suppose he would have gone with his people and left me, do you?"

"Of course not, Lucy. He's doubtless one of the men who stayed to fight and defend their properties. You love him terribly, don't you?"

Lucy lifted soft brown eyes, shining with the gentle glow of a woman who loves and knows she is loved in return. "Oh, so much that I want—I want to live inside his body with him!" A deep blush crept up her cheeks. "He's all I have. I never knew my mother, and since my father— Well, he's just everything. Elizabeth, have you ever been in love like that?"

Elizabeth looked at her with eyes that were very wide and very blue. "No," she said slowly, "heavens, no!"

The blush stayed on Lucy's face. "I thought maybe—well, I thought you might—I knew your husband was old, but I hoped you might feel like that about James." She finished in a rush, hopelessly bogged down in embarrassed fear of having been tactless, and Elizabeth waited so long to answer she glanced shyly down, miserable that she might have offended her.

But at length her voice came, low and untouched by anger. "I don't know, Lucy. I honestly don't know. I like to be near him, yet we quarrel—and sometimes I think, for all his charm, he's not worth half of John."

"Oh, he *is!*" Lucy surprisingly flared in his defense. "You don't know the good he's done. Why when the governor had my father taken to England for trial for something he didn't do, James worked day and night to get him released—he and Uncle Adam. And then, when nothing did any good, he tried to persuade the governor to let him go with him, all the way to England, to tell the judges the straight of it. Of course, they wouldn't let him go, but he tried all the same. And that's not all, he saved Mr. Nielsen's groom from a tar-and-feathering—it wasn't the poor man's fault he was indentured to a Tory, and James wouldn't let them touch him. And look what he did about not letting the British get by with this affair of David Fanning!"

Elizabeth took refuge in laughter, "Oh, Lucy, he—"

"Yes, but you could make him! Every girl in town wants him, but I want him to have someone good, that's really—"

The road turned abruptly across an island of solid ground, and the brush grew thickly matted up to its edges. Suddenly, from one side there came the sound of twigs snapping and of something stealthily pushing its way through the undergrowth. The horses shied violently, pointing their ears toward the noise. Lucy broke off in her speech and looked around in terror. Elizabeth pulled up her reins and tried to turn.

Then a face was peering through the branches, almost unrecognizable with caked mud. A voice said wonderingly, "Lucy?" as if the mind were playing tricks, and Gordon ran up into the road.

"Hurry! They're after me!"

"Oh, Gordon, darlin', who?"

"Soldiers. There's been a fight at Moore's Creek and

they're scouring the country for what's left of our forces." He glanced down the road and stopped, listening. "I hear them," he cried, and started back toward the brush.

"Wait," Elizabeth said, dismounting and throwing her reins to Lucy. "Stay here, Lucy, and if they question you, say—say that your cousins have gone into the woods for a moment." The merest smile was in her eyes as she pushed Gordon ahead of her into the thicket.

Once screened from the road, she began removing the thick outer skirt beneath which she wore a dark woolen dress, and one of the petticoats from the "skin layer."

"Here, put these on." She wound her kerchief over his head and tied it under his chin. With the addition of the voluminous cape Mamba had insisted on, he could pass nicely for an unmodish but warmly dressed woman. She washed the mud from his face with swamp water and pulled the scarf high so that only his eyes were in view.

"Mrs. Purdie, I don't know if Lucy will like what I've done, but we were cruel put oot o' my father's house, and I canna help but fight."

"Don't try to talk now, Gordon. Hurry." What difference did it make whether he was fighting or on which side as long as they loved each other as they did?

From the road they could hear shouting and loud voices. Then a surly voice, vaguely familiar, said, "How now, little lady, what are ye doin' here?"

"I'm waiting, sir, for my cousins," Lucy answered.

"Well, now, ain't that interestin'?" said another, "and where might they be—wadin' in that black cold water?"

"Your question is embarrassing, sir, but—"

"Well, ma'am," asked a third in a more gentle tone, "have you seen a fellow anywhere around here looked like he was trying to hide?"

"No-o, I can't remember seeing anyone at all on the road."

"Why hev ye got two horses, if ye got mor'n one cousin in the bushes?" the second one asked, suspiciously.

"Two of us ride one." Then she added more loudly, "You see, one of them is getting old and she fears to ride alone."

"Well, we'll wait and see 'em anyhow," persisted the burly one.

Elizabeth whispered to Gordon, "You hear that? You're old and you're deaf, too. Come on. Keep your hands under the cape."

Before they reached the road she called out, "Who're you talking to, Lucy?"

"Some soldiers looking for a man."

"Oh, I wager that noise we heard back there in the log road was somebody. I told you so at the time!" She turned a brilliant smile on the soldiers and pointed in the opposite direction. "Nearly frightened us to death. La! I wish we'd had some gentlemen along to protect us then!"

She saw that they all wore cockades, and one the uniform of the Continentals. To her surprise she found that the familiar voice belonged to Sergeant Anson. She allowed her eyes to grow wide when she saw that he recognized her as well, and whispered fearfully, "Oh, was he a Tory, do you think?"

"Sure he was, the damned swine. I'd like to get my hands around his th'oat."

Elizabeth shuddered, remembering the last man she had seen laid low by Anson's hand.

The man in the uniform turned toward Gordon in order to scrutinize this silent one more closely. "What's your name, lady?"

Elizabeth directed the full battery of her blue eyes at him. "She's deaf as a post, Captain."

Pleased at the advanced rank, but still not liking to leave a word unturned, he wanted to know if she was dumb as well. Elizabeth leaned toward him slightly and giggled. "Sometimes I think so, sir!"

He started to laugh, but recovered his dignity as Anson said, "Let's go, men, we're a-wastin' time. I'd advise you ladies to get home as fast as you can. There's been a battle at Moore's Creek bridge, and pretty soon the roads will be full."

"A battle?"

"Yeah," proclaimed the uniformed one, feeling like a captain, "we licked the daylights out o' them lily-livered Scotch from Cross Creeks."

Elizabeth felt the muscle of Gordon's arm twitch beneath her hand, and was relieved at Anson's order.

"Well, let's get goin'. You say you heard something in the swamp back thisaway?"

"Yes, about half a mile up the road—it was right by a big magnolia tree."

Thinking their hoax successful, with the men already starting to move off, Gordon went quickly over to Lucy's side. She kicked her foot free of the stirrup so he could mount, but as he raised his leg to the iron, the long skirt fell back disclosing his shoes and tartan hose. To Anson, who had glanced back, it was a red flag.

"Wait," he bellowed to the men. He leaped from his horse

and seized Gordon's leg, pulling him down. Lucy's riding crop struck him a murderous lash across the face. He loosened his hold and Gordon stumbled into the brush.

"Hold these women here," he yelled.

Two of the men slid from their mounts and grabbed the girls' bridles, while another plunged after the sergeant. Lucy was screaming hysterically. The man holding her horse looked up and laughed contemptuously. "He ain't got a chance, not with them skirts. The ones he's used to is shorter."

Elizabeth could hear the men thrashing about in the thicket. She ought to be able to think of something, but the only idea that entered her numbed brain was to dig her heel into the horse and ride over the man at its head. But this, she knew, would be unwise, for he was the only one with any gentlemanly manners at all. With him out of the way, there was no telling what might happen to them. Though she had once been ready to defend Sergeant Anson, she had no illusions about how he would feel toward an enemy. If only John were not away, or Uncle Adam, or even James! She must think of something! But all she could do was stare at the spot where Gordon had disappeared, clutching the long, hindering garments she had put on him.

They heard the sergeant's victorious roar, and presently the two men returned, half-carrying, half-dragging their prisoner. Lucy's cries diminished to moans, and as Gordon looked up at her, he seemed to realize for the first time *her* danger. He tried to shake off his captors, but the sergeant gave him a heavy blow with his fist. His head jerked back and he stumbled to his knees.

"Oh, don't," Lucy cried.

"So, you don't like to hev your pore old cousin played about with!"

"There's no reason for you to be cruel and insulting," Elizabeth said in a deadly voice. "Sergeant Anson, do you allow your men to speak so to their betters?"

Anson gave her a straight look. "One assistin' the enemy ain't better."

"'Their betters,'" mimicked the other, making a lunge toward her. "Why, you little bitch, I'll teach you to trick us and then try to be high and mighty!"

But Gordon caught him a glancing blow with his fist. He spun around, wild with rage, as the fellow holding Lucy's horse reached out with the butt of his pistol and brought it down on Gordon's head.

"That settles that," said Anson. "Tho' him over yo' horse, Steve; George, you and Luke tek charge o' these women. I'm sick o' the sight of 'em."

The soft-spoken one said, "Sergeant, I think this one's fainted."

"Put her up with the other'n then, and let's get movin'. It's gettin' late."

The man lifted Lucy's limp body and laid it gently across the saddle in front of Elizabeth. "Can you carry her, miss?"

"Oh, yes!"

She rode along silently between the men with their jingling harness and their loud, coarse talk. Her arm was numb with Lucy's weight, and she was uncomfortably conscious of displeasure at herself. Why should she have been embarrassed by the look of surprised disappointment from a crude sergeant? "One assistin' the enemy ain't better," he had said. She was furious because there was no denying the fact that what he said was true.

A dull red sun lay against the western horizon, turning the snow patches faintly pink, and across the sticky road in front of the horses, a frightened deer leaped like a shadow, without sound.

In Wilmington, the little cavalcade stopped for inquiries amid the gaping wonder of those on the streets at the sight of the two women in custody and the man who looked to be dead draped over the back of a horse. When the sergeant had the information he sought, he turned their direction toward the courthouse, and there, leaving Lucy, who was still in a faint, in the arms of the gently spoken soldier, he escorted Elizabeth up the steps without explanation. She was tired and hungry and angry, and only when the door had opened into a small chamber and she saw that she was face to face with the Committee of Safety, did she realize how deadly might be the consequences of the afternoon. If, as Adam had said, they suspected her before, this would finish her. If he were only here now! The faces of these men, most of whom she knew, looked strange in the candlelight. They were here for attending to serious business, and there was no laughter in their eyes and no pretty speeches on their lips.

The sergeant told his story, and as it unfolded, though every word was truth, Elizabeth knew there was not a man among them who would not believe that she had gone out for the express purpose of helping the loyalists in some way. No one offered her a seat. She stood with head held high. Not a word would she speak unbidden.

At length the sergeant was dismissed with approbation, and for an hour they questioned her without obtaining any more damning evidence of her hostility than attempting to save her friend's sweetheart. Lucy's patriotism was unquestioned. She was the ward of Colonel Robert Howe, and though she was wrong to oppose him in her choice of a lover, she was certainly, at heart, a patriot.

It was Cornelius Harnett whose piercing eye she had dreaded, who finally stopped the tiresome questioning, offered her a chair, and asked the members to withdraw into the next room for deliberation.

The clerk was left to guard her. Impressed with her beauty, he attempted a conversation, but she was too frightened and too angry to answer him civilly, and he gave it up, resuming his quill-scratching over endless sheets of reports.

When the committee reassembled, Mr. Harnett took the floor. He drew from beneath the papers before him a closely written document and handed it to Elizabeth for her signature.

"We shall have to ask you to sign the association paper, Mrs. Purdie. After that, so long as your conduct is unquestionable, you may remain in North Carolina."

Elizabeth took up the article and scanned it. Upon oath she must declare that she believed it "unlawful for the English Parliament to impose taxes and to regulate the internal policies of the American colonies," and so forth. (Remain in North Carolina? What did they expect to do with her?)

"How do you expect me to swear to all this when I don't know whether it's lawful or not—I don't know anything about all this!"

The men permitted themselves a smile at her astuteness. Most women had signed without even reading it.

"That is not the part we are so interested in in your case. If you will read further you will see that you are enjoined to 'support, maintain, and defend all and every the acts, resolutions, and regulations of the Continental and Provincial Congresses to the utmost of your power and ability.' If you sign this, you have sworn not to aid the enemy or to use your influence against the cause of America."

"If you can tell me how I can sign one without the other, I will do so." Why must they be so stupid? She had not been assisting the enemy—only helping her friends. But with John safely away and Gordon already in custody, she supposed she would have no further occasion to do so.

"Madam, I hope you are not rewarding the leniency of this committee toward you by making sport of it."

"I assure you, sir, that nothing is further from my intention, but I dislike much to take oath to something I fail to understand."

Several of the men chuckled, but Archibald McLain, of the fiery temper, addressed the chair. "I told you, Harnett, she was clever. You will either sign this, madam, or go to jail!"

"That remark will be stricken from the record, Mr. Clerk. Mrs. Purdie," Cornelius continued, ignoring McLain, "since you are not a man, to be concerned with a point of honor, the first part of this article need give you no uneasiness."

"Yet my name appears before the world attesting that I hold a belief I do not, in truth, hold. My honor, Mr. Harnett, is quite as valued to me as yours is to you. Indeed, 'tis a new theory that virtue makes discrimination between the sexes!"

Cornelius looked at her, but allowed none of the rising admiration he felt to show in his face.

McLain leaped to his feet. "You see, Harnett, the woman is a British agent. She has been well-trained to confound us!"

Elizabeth turned toward him, her eyebrow lifting high. "May I ask you, sir, would it necessarily be true that you were an enemy of freedom because you refused to sign a paper before you had read it?"

She had used, without knowing, a proper phrase to gain sympathy. An uncontrolled murmur of assent went around the table.

"But you have read it," McLain said, flushing.

"But I do not understand such things, which is the same."

Mr. Harnett called the clerk. "Please make a special copy of the oath to the association and leave space for a signature. Only the second part, please. Now, understand, Mrs. Purdie, that we are making quite a concession in your favor, and because of it you will continue to be watched. We must also ask that you deliver up to us the store of gold which you brought into the country."

Elizabeth gasped, but Harnett continued, "You must see that we cannot allow someone of whose convictions we are not sure to be in possession of funds which might enable that person to work against us. Oh, we will give you enough to live on, but if you are sincerely desirous of becoming a citizen, you will not object to sharing our sacrifices."

The men who had been disapproving of Harnett's manner

of handling of the case now began to feel a wholehearted appreciation of their leader's cleverness. Why had they questioned his actions? He had never yet failed to bring them out on top, despite the wiliest adversary.

Elizabeth was suddenly more furious than she had ever been. Her precious supply of gold! The gold that could buy such lovely clothes and keep her in the style she had always known. If only Uncle Adam or James were here—someone to protect her from this greedy committee. She faced Mr. Harnett with blazing eyes. "The one thing, sir, that I *had* understood of American political doctrine was the inviolable right of property! I think if you continue thus to fail in practice what you profess to believe, you shall have done your cause more harm than good. This is not a very thorough way of converting recruits!"

The clerk laid the paper he had finished before her, and seeing that the committee had no intention of remanding the edict, she scrawled her name, threw the quill across the floor, and swept out of the room.

CHAPTER 9

When the *Quadrille* docked, those at the wharf who knew James Richardson thought he had got himself a new slave, for as he came down the gangplank he was followed by a huge, fine-looking young Negro in bright-colored pantaloons and a yellow turban. He had a peculiar gait, against which the long-tailed parrot perched on his shoulder seemed to have difficulty in maintaining its balance.

Matthew Rowan stood in the doorway of his ship chandlery. "Glad to see you back, James. Did they throw in the parrot with the nigger?"

"Sure, got a bargain. What's the news, Matt?"

"Good God, man! Forgot for a minute you had just got in, and me standing here watching you come ashore. We've really got news, and just today, too."

"Well?" One had to be short with Matt. If not, he'd ramble over every possible field of conversation before he said anything.

"Well, I believe you was gone when we got word there was danger from up at Cross Creeks, wasn't you?"

"There's always been danger from that hotbed of loyalists, Matt."

"So there has. But this was more definite like." He turned slowly and spat tobacco juice over his shoulder. "The Scotch and the regulators from all over that country was organized down to a flea's ear, and the word come through that they was marching down the Cape Fear." A sudden thought struck him and his already bulging eyes seemed to protrude even further. "How in tarnation did you get in, anyhow? There's a whole British fleet laying out there!"

James shrugged. "Ways and means. But you're wrong about there being a whole fleet. They're shy one ship."

"How do you mean?" Matt's mouth hung open.

"I mean we sank one."

"The hell you did! How?"

"Oh, we fired a couple of guns at her and down she went. Let's have the news, Matt. I've got to be getting on."

"Well, it was like this: right after you left, the governor got anxious for some reason and sailed off down to Charleston, but he come right back. I guess he was scared he'd miss the big fleet, which ain't come yet, thank God. He didn't want McDonald to start before Clinton come, but you know how them Scotch is. When they're ready to move, hell or high water ain't goin' to stop 'em. Well, they heard General McDonald was headed for Wilmington. Colonel Lillington and Colonel Ashe and Colonel Moore started out of here, and Colonel Caswell was comin' over from Newberne to meet 'em. Now they didn't make connections right at first it seems, but—"

"For God's sake, Matt, come to the point."

"James, we licked all glory be to God and halleluja out of them Tories!"

"Where?"

"That little bridge over the Widow Moore's creek, you know where 'tis."

"Did you take prisoners?"

"Did we take prisoners!" One would have thought that Matt had not only been there himself, but had brought off the battle single-handed. "Hah! And that ain't all we took. You never heard the like: guns, rifles, powder, and all their wagons and horses. But what do you suppose was the best we got: A chest of fifteen thousand pounds sterling!"

"When did all this happen?"

"Just today! News just come in."

As he hurried toward the tavern, James reflected on Matt's amazing story. A real scrap. Too bad he had been on this voyage when the thing came off. Such plunder! Even in Nassau it had not been easy to obtain guns, or powder either for that matter. It had taken him a month or better to make the trip, secure the supplies, and get back with them, and here the committee had all this stuff dumped in its lap right here at home. He quickened his steps until the big slave had trouble keeping up with him.

"I'll take you to Mrs. Purdie when I've eaten and dressed," he said, as he sent the boy around to the quarters at the tavern.

In the taproom Lal Dorsey raised his voice above the din,

"Misteh Rich'son has returned from his voyage! Here's a flip coming up for you, sir!"

James took the one empty chair at a table where several of the members of the committee, having just returned from a meeting, were celebrating the victory.

"Well, old man," Parker Quince said, "your prisoner got away." They had covered the subject of the battle and turned to a new one.

"Who's that?" James asked, sipping his drink and making a grimace. After the rum in the Indies this stuff was of poor quality.

"Fanning! There's been no sight of him since, but yesterday we had a report from up-country of a band of Tories with a man at its head answering his description; he has terrorized three counties. They have looted plantations and destroyed everything they could belonging to the Whigs."

"Where did you have him lodged? I never did know."

"Locked in the storeroom at the rear of the *Mercury* office," said McLain. "It was the strongest place we could think of, outside of the jail, which would have been unwise under the circumstances."

Ben Jepson, who was assistant editor to Adam Boyd, wrinkled his forehead. "There's only one small window, barred on the outside, but the bars weren't touched. When I sent in our 'prentice with the man's food that morning, the door was locked just as it had been the night before by my own hand, but the prisoner was gone."

"Could the boy have let him slip by him?"

"No way he could have. I always lock the door at night and take the keys to Mrs. Boyd, because the boy sleeps at their house, and he usually opens up in the mornings. But that day I happened to be there just as he was arriving. I went to my desk, and the boy went in to carry Fanning his breakfast, found the door locked and the room empty. There's no way out other than past my chair."

"Well, it does seem to me," James said with a jocular pretense at being aggrieved, "if I can catch a scoundrel you fellows could hold him."

Susan came in with a platter of meat and a mound of fresh-baked bread. The men began to ply James with questions about his cargo.

"It was difficult to get the powder, but it was finally managed," he reported. "I was able to get quite a store of quinine."

"Good! And the boots?"

"Only a hundred and fifty pair."

"How much will they cost us?"

"I'm donating the boots."

"But why? Nobody can afford a thing like that these days!"

"Well, I can't afford to stay awake at night thinking of what Adam told me happened to the soldiers' feet in Boston this winter. They aren't too costly. I can possibly pick up a few pairs every trip."

They knew what boots were selling for, even in Nassau, but they saw that any word of praise would be embarrassing. Parker Quince said quickly, "By the way, we almost forgot to tell you: the beauteous Mrs. Purdie signed the association this evening."

"She what?"

The tempestuous Archibald McLain flushed scarlet as his companions, each seeking to tell the story, began to twit him about the lady's getting the upper hand of him in an argument. Harnett, too! She had had the last word at him as well.

Amid the good-natured raillery, it was some time before James had the whole story, and he was conscious of amused satisfaction at Elizabeth's behavior, and annoyance that he felt it. He had known all along that she was far brighter than they knew, and furious as he had been with her for effecting John's escape, he nevertheless began to look forward to another tilt with her himself. Though he was returning Tip-toe to her, he knew that before the evening was over something would be sure to set off that tinderbox temper, and he would feel the sweet fire that always rose in him at sight of her beautiful anger. Ah, that was the *raison d'être* of woman! Certainly not the confuting of learned gentlemen.

He pushed back his chair and rose, explaining that he was on his way to return her manservant he had lost for her and had had the luck to pick up again in Nassau. "And perhaps," he added, laughing, "by so doing I'll reinstate the committee in her good graces."

As he bade them good night, Parker Quince said suddenly, reaching into his pocket, "Here, I almost forgot to give you this. Hooper sent it down from Philadelphia and asked me to deliver it to you."

James broke the seal. "My letters of marque for the *Quadrille!*"

The men crowded around and eagerly read the document over his shoulder. This was getting the job done! A tangible order from the Congress, giving official permission to capture British ships, assuming the authority and responsibility in the government of a unified nation. It was the first one they had seen and it seemed to prove to them all that their labors were at last bearing fruit.

During their descriptions of the Moore's Creek battle, James had about decided to make Kendall master of the *Quadrille* and turn over the subequent voyages to him, but with the letters of marque in his hand, he changed his mind. There was much of interest going on on land, to be sure, but land skirmishes paled in contrast to a good fight at sea. He would not be able to dispatch so much business for the committee, but his usefulness to the country as a privateer would be greater by far.

Arrived at the Bell house, James saw that he would have to exert more effort than merely the presentation of a pleasant surprise to lift Elizabeth out of a despairing mood.

She met him at the door, mixed emotions in her eyes. Sorrow was there, a smoldering anger, and defiance in the set of her chin.

"Oh, why couldn't you have come sooner?" she burst out.

"Why, my very little dear, had I known a lady was in distress I—"

"Oh, do be serious. Such frightful things have happened!"

"What," he asked, smiling, "beside the loss of a little money?"

"You didn't know that Gordon is in jail, and Doctor Tucker says he'll be dead before morning! And Lucy is so badly off he says she may never be in her right mind again—"

"Where is Lucy?"

"They took her back to Brunswick to her uncle. Oh, it was all my fault," she wailed, "because I suggested the ride."

He felt a sudden tenderness for her, standing small and wretched before him. He gathered her into his arms and turned her face up until she looked into his eyes. "Well, now, cheer up. Nothing's as bad as it seems. Gordon may recover after all, and Lucy will be all right once he's well again."

"Oh, you couldn't be so optimistic if you had had all these terrible things happen to you, and on top of that had everything you owned taken away from you," she cried, trying to pull away.

But he held her fast, and at the concern in his voice she was quiet. "How do you think I felt," he said soberly, "when I learned that my father had fled the country, or when I found out that my own brother was conspiring against me? Believe me, my dear, everyone has his troubles these days, and you are not alone. For Lucy and Gordon I feel very sad because I have watched their little romance from its beginning. But you, you can't say I didn't warn you that the Committee of Safety was not to be trifled with."

She jerked free then. "Yes, that was very kind of you! But you didn't tell me they were a band of robbers!"

"Ay, my lady, you could be tarred and feathered for a speech like that. Shall I volunteer for the privilege of being your executioner? I could use the plumage from a parrot I know—"

"I don't find your jesting, sir, funny at all."

"Very well, then, we'll be serious. I think their decision was quite logical. How could they leave funds of such size in the hands of one whom they suspected?"

"If they consider loyalty to one's friends being an enemy, then I am one! I'm glad I sailed John to the cruiser. I would do it all over again, despite that silly thing I signed!" She was in a fine rage. All the pent-up anxiety and fear and fury that could not be expressed to anyone else came rushing from her lips. "And here is something else you don't know: the night John escaped, Gordon Denny was hidden right in this house from those two searching parties!"

He had stood amusedly watching her tirade, which had risen according to his anticipation, but now at the realization that he himself had been hoodwinked, it was not nearly so amusing. He reached out and gripped her shoulders.

"Do you tell me that while I was here protecting you against one piece of folly you were perpetrating another beneath my nose? God almighty, what do you think would have happened if Gordon had been found and we both had been caught after my lies to save you? I, a member of the Committee of Safety!"

The capricious dimple suddenly appeared at the corner of her mouth, but there was no laughter in the still-smoldering eyes. "Suppose you tell me, sir; you seem to have all the answers!"

As quickly, his own expression changed and a sudden mesmerism locked their glances. Her slightly parted red lips were an overwhelming invitation, but there was always fascination in an expected kiss withheld.

"I have a surprise for you," he said, and according to a prearranged signal, there came the sound of footsteps clumping down the hall.

She turned, bewildered and still angry. There in the doorway stood Tip-toe, and from behind him came the excited whispers of Mamba and Trolcie and Cicero watching to see her surprise. The parrot still teetered on Tip's shoulder uttering unintelligible protestations at all the confusion.

Tip's wide mouth split into a gleaming grin, and forgetful of the bird, he fell on his knees at Elizabeth's feet.

"Oh, Tip-toe, is it really you?" Gently she loosened the black fingers grasping her skirts. "Stand up and let me look at you! Why, you look as if you had had very good treatment."

Anger forgotten now, she cast a grateful, joyous smile at James, then turned back to her slave. Mamba, she had inherited, but Tip-toe was her own, bought with her own pocket money. She had created him out of a cringing creature under the lash into a proud and loyal servant. "How ever did you get away? Tell me!"

"Well'm, hits a long story, but Ah slip off de wawf when de *Diana* was unloadin' in Nassau, an' Ah runs till I cain't run no mo'. I'ssa yaller gal what took'n me in an' hid me till de ship sail, an' she got me some clo'se an' a job. An' 'en Mist' James he come 'long an' heah Ah is."

Mamba's face was beaming. It was evident that her opinion of James, whom she had heretofore considered a scamp and a menace to her child's happiness, had undergone a change. "Mist' James, you sho' is a good man down unnerneath all yo' foolishments."

"Why, Mamba, I don't know when I've had finer or less-expected compliment." He laughed, then leaned toward her with mock fierceness and whispered, "I always bribe my women with presents before I make off with them!"

Elizabeth gave him a sidelong glance. "One could hardly consider the return of stolen property a bribe, sir, nor yet a present."

"Ah, this is but the beginning, madam. Tip-toe, fetch those boxes."

He knelt and slit the cords, scattering pieces of finery about in display before her delighted eyes. Even if the committee had not relieved her of her gold, there were not such things to be had now in all the colonies. She finished fastening the little silver buckles on a pair of blue Morocco slippers and stood twisting one foot this way and that.

"Do they fit?"

"Almost! I can put a bit of wadding in the toes." She laughed.

At length the servants were dismissed, and they sat alone before the library fire. Close on the sofa, he showed her the letters of marque for the *Quadrille* and told her of his now-discarded plan to hand over the ship to Kendall. It was a complete change from his usual attitude of teasing, frivolous gaiety—the first time she had sensed a deeper side of him since the night, nearing Wilmington, he had told her of his plantation, and she was swept along in the rush of his enthusiasm so that for a little while, in the joy of their companionship, she forgot the troubles besetting her. She also forgot that this decision would take him to sea again for no telling how long and into the ever-present danger of battles on the ocean. She shuddered, suddenly remembering the one she had seen.

Although almost three hours had gone by, it seemed but a moment when he rose to go. Her eyes were glowing and her heart had set up that rapid beating again as he drew her to her feet. He kissed her long and hard, then lifted her gently and laid her on the couch, a strange look in his eyes.

"Good night," he whispered, and was gone. She heard the hoofbeats of his horse echoing down the street.

CHAPTER 10

Elizabeth sat before the secretary in her bedroom in half-stays and petticoats, curls tied high on her head and her bare arms showing round and white in the morning sunlight. The sheet of paper before her bore three columns of figures, each composed of the same numerals and each with a different total written below it. Impatiently, she threw the lead down, then picked it up again with an exasperated sigh and began again.

Mamba paused in her tidying about the room. "Effen you clean off that desk Ah 'specks you have mo' luck. Hit look lak a rat nes'."

"Now you've thrown me off again! Do be quiet till I'm through." She started down the column once more, her fingers tapping out the numbers softly in the process of addition, and this time got an answer to match the last one. "There, I suppose that's right. Mamba, one pound, one shilling, and a sixpence is all we've got until the committee softens its heart enough to give us more. What'll we do?"

"Honey, I sho' doan know." She stood looking down on the meaningless figures, hating to admit that for once in her life she was stumped. "Is you sho' them markin's mean what they says?"

"Of course they mean what they say."

Mamba frowned. Miserable Elizabeth might have been married to Mr. Purdie, but at least she had never had to concern herself with such a low-class thing as money. The security of her white folks she had taken for granted. That the men in the family did some mysterious things that turned crops and cargoes into the wherewithal for living she was vaguely aware. That was their business. But since the loss of Elizabeth's fortune, her whole dimly perceived idea of economy had become a hazardous, floating thing without the accustomed keel of plenty.

She fixed Elizabeth with a speculative stare, as if doubtful of the reception of the suggestion she was about to make. "Mis' Lizbuth, a man is a necessary sumpin'."

"Don't change the subject. We've got to think of what to do."

"No'm, Ah ain't changin' the subjeck. Ah'm jes' sayin' Ah doesn't see why in all dis time and wid all deshere nice young mens buzzin' 'round, you ain't found yo'self another husban'." She fired the shot, then took herself off to other regions of the house before the repercussion could break upon her wooly head.

But Elizabeth pretended not to hear. She ran a hand over her forehead and stared at the disorderly pile of papers, her eyes narrowed and her lips in a pout.

Mamba had an idea all right. But a year is a long time to hold out, then give up just when success might be near. A long time to deny the importunings of half the male population of the county because the one man you loved had been all this time a prisoner in France.

It would be just my luck, she said to herself, to marry one of these calf-eyed boys, and about that time James would come back and there I'd be!

Out of a pigeonhole she pulled two letters: one James had written her from Charleston in South Carolina, and the other more recently sent from France. He had happened to be in port when the great British fleet finally arrived at the Cape Fear, but when Admiral Sir Peter Parker had sailed away, having decided to invade South Carolina instead, James had gone with the army in a hurried march to the defense of Charleston. Certainly the letter was no billet-doux, and yet it was marvelous how like James himself it was: gay and flippant, taking not even the battle in successful defense of the city seriously. John, he wrote, of whom he had had a distant glimpse, was elegantly accoutered in the red coat and gold braid of his Majesty's officers, an aide to Lord Cornwallis, and the account of his haughty, Tory attitude was so droll she laughed again as she reread the lines. There was a disappointing lack of reference to herself, and he merely closed with the laconic supposition that he would be seeing her soon. Army life was not his dish; give him a helm and a sail, or a quiet plantation when the visited ports ceased to yield a crop of pretty girls! There was not even the fashionable, "Believe

me to be, madam, your most obed't and hon'ble serv't—"
Only the sweeping signature swung halfway down the page.

In the few days after its receipt, she had gone over and over it, seeking to find something to hold against the bleak days of change. Most of the army had gone south; Uncle Adam had left to join General Washington as chaplain; and every day marked the lack of some article or supply she had always considered a necessity.

There had been bloody skirmishes throughout the vicinity in the early spring, and the town had been hard-pressed to care for the refugees in addition to the wounded who were brought into the makeshift hospital. The ladies worked from dawn to dusk with dressings and bandages and cooking. There must not be an idle hand, and Elizabeth was swept into the feverish activity along with the rest. The younger women had to take their turns nursing, too, and Elizabeth, who had reported for duty in high spirits over the romantic idea of nursing the soldiers, returned to Mamba in the evening, worn out, nauseated, and angry.

But Mamba wisely kept her at it by saying, "Ah knows you want to be dere in sich case as Mist' James come in entertainin' a bullet."

But after his detention in France, this had ceased to be a charming possibility.

The days were growing warmer, too, and the men cursed at the flies buzzing incessantly around them, and demanded so much attention it made her hot and irritable. She gave them as tender care as she could, but it was difficult to keep down the rebellion at the necessity of being so engaged.

But in July the Declaration of Independence had been signed, and since then the work had not been so hard. The men were so happy they ceased to complain; they stopped cursing their luck and the insect world, and yearning to go back to their occupations. Now all they thought about was getting well enough to rejoin the ranks to uphold this wonderful new declaration.

She remembered the evening the news had come. In the hot dust of the street, men were slapping each other on the back and shouting, and at five o'clock Adam Boyd himself had come to the hospital with the ink still wet on the *Mercury*. Elizabeth was perched up on a table surrounded by a group of men in varying stages of convalescence, and they were all singing at the top of their voices. Even the fellow at the end of the ward asked to be propped up so he could join in.

The scene would have been shocking to Dr. Tucker, who

had followed Adam into the room, had he not been instantly aware that this medicine was doing his charges more good than all the pills and ointments in his bag.

For in his elation over the great tidings, each man became a man again and no longer a patient. What did shattered bodies matter in the face of such glory as a country—their own country, made up from Maine to Georgia of men, plain men, like themselves, rising up and daring to be free? They had fought for this wonder and this glory and they would fight again. Something had happened deep down inside them that created the need for singing, and involuntarily, because the old tune had always been their musical expression of patriotism, they began with "God Save the King." But now the words were new. At first, almost shyly, then more boldly as improvisations took on a competitive spirit, they composed new lines cut to the old measures, wove them with the bright threads of liberty, embroidered them with sentiments of freedom, and the walls rang with their gladness.

Then Adam's voice had come quietly through the sudden hush that followed his entrance. "Gentlemen, I give you the Declaration of Independence of the United States of America!" He paused and cleared his throat, almost as if he found it hard to speak. " 'When in the course of human events it becomes necessary—' "

Elizabeth had felt the greatness of the moment, but her treatment at the hands of the committee still rankled, and she wondered, in the days following, why she should be working and giving up everything she had for a country that was not even her own. But she dared not stop. There would be talk if she did, and she was still being watched.

It was October by the time James returned from Charleston to go to sea again. He was forsaking the short runs to the Indies for the bigger game offered in the Atlantic, he had said, and by Christmas his reputation as a privateer was widespread. Hardly a packet or ship came in that did not bring news of some spectacular exploit of his against British shipping. She was filled with pride, but there was the awful fear for his safety, as well as the safety of John, who was somewhere in the British army.

It was a dreary time. Even in the comparative unimportance of the household there was little to lift the spirits. Tiptoe's parrot died of the cold. Cicero reported that there was no more coffee; the drought had dried up most of the corn; and all the meat went to feed the soldiers.

Aunt Mary sent for her one day to show her something,

and when she arrived, she found spread out in the sitting room a large colored pattern for a flag General Washington was urging all the colonies to fly. There were alternate red and white stripes, and a blue field carrying a circlet of thirteen stars.

It was the first time Elizabeth had ever heard a complaint against her blindness from Mary.ABY streamed from the sightless eyes as she said, "If only I might see my country's flag!"

"Oh, Aunt Mary, darling, I'll make one for you!"

"You are a dear child, but I have already commissioned Miss Sally to fashion one. She does need the work." Quickly she dried her eyes and attempted to smile away her weakness. "Why not make yours for James for the *Quadrille?*"

Abigail, who was sitting with a book, but hearing everything, said, "It certainly is a better-looking one than that snake thing he's flying now."

Elizabeth was nettled at her speech, but she made her flag for James and folded it away against his return. It was pleasant to anticipate the day when she would shake out its folds and have him admire her handiwork.

But then had come the shattering news of his detention in France, and suddenly nothing had seemed of much importance. She continued to work at the hospital and the public kitchens, but the salt had gone out of living. There was one hope: that France would soon sign the treaty with the United States, in which case all American prisoners would be released.

Eagerly scanning the *Mercury*, which was now edited by Ben Jepson, Elizabeth had watched for developments. Mr. Benjamin Franklin had arrived safely in France as ambassador from the United States, despite his age and a long, perilous crossing. The jovial old man had created a furor in the French court. The country that had produced a Voltaire, a Rousseau, a Diderot, took him to its heart—a symbol of their own new thinking, an incarnation of a spirit that made America dare to step forth and do what other nations only dreamed and wrote and talked of doing. So reported Mr. Jepson, and Elizabeth took heart.

In April she had a caller. He was Captain John Paul Jones, and had put into the Cape Fear for supplies. When Cicero had brought word that he was awaiting her in the drawing room, she had flown into such a state of excitement that Mamba had difficulty in pinning up her hair. His was already a big name on the sea, and she half-suspected his call might have something to do with James.

He advanced to meet her, surprised her with a hearty handshake, while she surprised him with a sweeping curtsy.

"Captain Jones! To whom do I owe debt of gratitude for your knowledge of my existence?"

The pleasure of such a fashionable speech was still new to the hero of the *Bon Homme Richard* with his humble background, and the lady did have the face of an angel. The captain smiled his delight. "You do me too much honor, madam, but if gratitude be in order, 'tis due to a young man, homesick, impatient, and technically a prisoner of France."

"James Richardson," she breathed, "but tell me, who—why—I had understood the French were most generous toward our—toward the Americans who took their prizes into her ports."

"That, Mistress Purdie, is a story of some involvement."

"But what has he done? Why, the *Reprisal*, the vessel in which Mr. Franklin himself reached France, took two British brigantines into Quiberon Bay! Oh, do forgive me—please be seated."

"That is true, ma'am," he said, perching on the edge of a chair, "the French government has given us great encouragement, but France treads lightly for two reasons—I might say three. First, England is her most ancient enemy and she will take advantage of any opportunity for revenge; second, if England wins this war, which God forbid, France stands to lose her own West Indian colonies and the American trade as well; and third, it amuses the French to see how much they can put over on the British."

Good heavens, Elizabeth thought, can't men ever tell anything without going off into politics? He tells me he has seen James and immediately starts talking about things that don't matter!

"They soothe the British ambassador," he went on, "with one hand while they beckon American ships into port with the other!"

"But tell me, did you see Mr. Richardson? Is he well, or languishing in some foul dungeon?"

"There are those, ma'am, who consider the court of King Louis foul, but not by a biggin of rum could it be called a dungeon!" He slapped his thighs uproariously.

"But you said—"

"He is a prisoner in name only. Just now, ma'am, we Americans are a fad in France, and you may be sure that the ladies of the brilliant court at Versailles would not allow a gentleman of Mr. Richardson's, er—parts—to languish!"

It did not occur to him that she might have preferred to picture James in the Bastille.

As the captain took his leave, he put into her hand a letter—a single sheet, folded and sealed. There was a little thrill that in the midst of his gala sojourn in Paris he had taken the trouble to write. At least he had not forgotten her. But later, when she broke the seal, she found that the missive could have been written to any one of a hundred people:

My dear Elizabeth:

I wonder if you would be so good as to get word to my overseer, Bill Lipman, and acquaint him with my anomalous, though delightful situation? And kindly tell him that he is to discharge the selling of the crops as best he can.

This will be handed you by my good friend Captain Jones, who will doubtless enlarge upon my circumstances sufficiently that any who might be interested may know that I am in no immediate danger of the hangman's noose! This court is gay beyond one's wildest dreams of gaiety, giving almost the impression (to a backwoods provincial like myself!) that the wheel turns too fast and may, one day, fly off into chaos.

From what I can learn in various circles, our agents here are well on the way toward effecting a military alliance with this nation, in which case I should soon be free to return to the *United States*—wonderful two words!

This time he ended with a complimentary close, and its formality was somehow less welcome than its omission had been before. But the captain *had* said he was homesick!

She sat for a moment longer, staring at the two letters in her hand, then stuffed them back into their place as the little French clock on the mantel daintily and musically struck the hour. Daydreaming over the past months would not solve her problems. Perhaps she should have found another husband, as Mamba had suggested. Well, she could marry George Holmes, the son of what Uncle Adam called a mercantile patriot, and be the richest lady in Newberne, but there was no compensation in the thought. She would not go into marriage merely for security. If only James would hurry back so she could be sure just where she stood with him!

The long-hoped-for treaty with France had been history for some time now—he should be home any day. If only he would ask her to marry him, it would settle everything. A swift memory came of being in his arms and was as swiftly followed by the delicious thrill the reality had evoked. But was this love? At least she thought so. All that remained was for him to convince her, but whether or not he would choose to do so was doubtful.

She shut her eyes and tried to visualize his greeting: would it be with a formal bow or with one of those blinding, breathtaking kisses that left her weak and pale?

But when at last he did come, she was seized in a great bear hug that she felt would break a rib. She wriggled down finally until the toes of her slippers touched the floor and pushed backward, laughing up at him with ripe lips and shining eyes.

"James! Is it really you?"

"I wasn't sure"—he laughed, squeezing her up to him again—"until I knew I remembered correctly how nice it was to have an American woman in my arms!"

"You are terrible as ever! Come and sit down. I've a thousand questions. Anyway, from what Captain Jones told me, you have not suffered from want of feminine companionship!"

"Ah, that rogue! I'll shoot a hole in his hull for that. Never let your women on one continent know what you are doing with those on the other!"

"Oh, but I must hear about Versailles—'tis said to be fabulous."

He laughed and launched into a detailed and comical description of the events, the people, the fashions current at the French court. She was fascinated with the pictures he drew of the ladies' enormous headdresses, festooned with ropes of pearls, with flowers and plumes and ribbons; the voluminous hooped and panniered skirts, wilder in width and elegance than anything ever designed in America. He described the jewels that adorned Queen Marie Antoinette, and as well in only slightly less degree, the persons of every other woman at court whether matron or mistress or both. One of the duchesses walked her little dog in the gardens on a golden leash studded with rubies and diamonds, the gift, he told her, of some handsomely satisfied lover. Coaches were gilt, satin lined; halls were hung with priceless tapestries; exquisite bibelots adorned bonbon-box boudoirs.

She was unconscious that the picture he painted was that of a decadent society which had reached a degree of pleasured frenzy that foretold its ruin in tragedy; that it was the thin crust over which skated frivolity and greed, delight and lust, perilously near the seething anger of the masses whose viciously exploited travail was forced to uphold it. James did not enlighten her, partly because he found it so enjoyable to see her eyes widen.

"Did you chance to meet my sister? She is Constance Le Clerq, and a great favorite of the queen."

"Not that I know of. Sorry I didn't know to look for her. If she has half her sister's beauty I could scarcely have resisted—"

"Nonsense, she is happily married."

"Then she's a rare one and doesn't go to court. There's no such thing as a happy marriage at Versailles." He laughed. "The only requisite for a gentleman looking over the field to see who'd likely make the most charming bedfellow is but to have his pockets well-lined and be certain of the whereabouts of a secret door!"

"James, you are the very limit." She smiled, then sobered sedately. She was torn between appearing naive in his eyes and, as well, lacking in propriety. She looked at him, suddenly really shy. How splendid he was in these new clothes of French cut and fabric! He was unchanged, and yet there was that about him now that bespoke the cosmopolitan. It was easy to picture him at home in the sophistication of a king's court.

But his next remark delighted her. He would not be going to sea again for an unforeseeable time, for with the acceleration of the war in the South he was more urgently needed on land. The *Quadrille* he had turned over to Captain Jones under Kendall, and manned it with French volunteers and such American seamen as could be found idle.

Then he asked, "Apropos of nothing, how are you getting along with the Committee of Safety?"

"Very well," she said, wrinkling up her nose at him. "I decided it wasn't worthwhile to do anything but play safe, but I'm a little weary of the role."

"I can imagine," he said dryly. "You know, you are quite a paradox. It worried me like an itch while I was away."

"Is that supposed to be complimentary? Is that why you

didn't bring one of those ravishing French creatures back with you?"

"Entirely complimentary. But as to your second query, I thought I might just do better here without the bother of a transplantation." He was looking at her with his head on one side, the gold lights in his eyes dancing. "I can't quite decide whether you are a lady or a baggage at heart!"

"And what difference, sir, when you are certain?" She laughed.

He encircled her waist quickly with one arm while with the other he reached up and grasped the curls at the back of her head in a gentle imitation of a violent gesture. "Just this: I've a wonderful idea! Come live at the plantation with me. You would have few difficulties out there, and think of the fun we could have!"

Her heart began to beat with suffocating suddenness, but she had learned from past experience to give her replies the light touch. Her lashes swept up as she glanced at him. "Is this a proposal, sir?"

He pretended to look startled. "Not of matrimony, my sweet. Surely *you* know how tedious the bonds of wedlock can be." He bent and his lips brushed hers.

The old flame flashed through her, but was quenched in a wave of anger. She slipped from his grasp with a forced laugh. "I think, James, that your little French interlude has given you delusions. This is America, remember? And, besides, I've had better offers."

"Of marriage, perhaps?"

"But of course!"

"Then, milady, you have more courage than I."

"Oh, I have the courage to take what I want—if I can get it!"

When he had gone, she dropped her pose of light humor and burst into tears. He had seemed so glad to see her, she had dared to hope— And seeing him again was all she needed to convince herself that she loved him deeply, even though he had treated her like a tavern wench with his insulting proposal. For all his attentions to her, he had never mentioned love, and he had never spoken of marriage except once. Except once! She sat up suddenly, her lashes still starred with tears. Once he had said, "I don't want to have to marry you to keep the Committee of Safety off your neck!" Those were his very words!

It was certain, she thought, that he was not in love with

anyone else, and she more than half-suspected that he really loved her. He just didn't want to give up his freedom. His freedom. Well, she would see. Treating her as he had today, he deserved to lose the battle for it.

She dried her eyes and ran up the stairs. Mamba followed her into the room, her arms full of freshly ironed linens, and a broad smile on her face. "Mist' Boyd done come home."

"Uncle Adam? When? How do you know?"

"He jis' got here. Dey hawse groom come wid de news, but say he sho' is sick. Po' Mist' Boyd. Ah sho' glad he here." Adam was favored of Mamba. She knew, despite his being a member of this outrageous committee, he was solid protection.

"What's the matter with him?"

"De boy say hit was 'sposure an' asthma."

"No wonder. Valley Forge was enough to kill anybody, let alone the rest of the winter."

Mamba paused in her task of laying away the clothes and gave her a shrewd look. "You ain't soundin' as glad he home as Ah thought you would."

"Well," she answered carefully. "I've decided I don't want to do any more of this silly war work. I'm tired of it, and it's too bad he didn't come home when I was doing so much of it. He won't like it."

Mamba regarded her darkly. "What is he mattah wid you?"

"Nothing! I'm just tired of it, that's all."

"Ah ain't rat certain what you is up to, Mis' Lizbuth, but Ah doesn't lak de smell of it somehow."

"Why, Mamba, I vow you're too vulgar for anything."

"Mabbe Ah is, but when you gits that look on you Ah knows you is up to sumpin'. Ah ain't knowed you all yo' life fo' nuthin'. How come you don't like Mist' Boyd comin' home rat now? He sho' bin yo' bes' friend."

There were extremely few secrets it was possible to hide from Mamba's bright old eyes, and Elizabeth's relief was great when just then Cicero rang the supper bell.

He held her chair with the same ceremony as when the table had groaned with luxuries. "Tell Trolcie to come here," she said as he served the usual rice and beans.

Trolcie appeared in the doorway, no farther. If this were to be another complaint about the food she preferred to be at a distance. But Elizabeth only smiled and said, "Trolcie, I've got to have some new dresses."

"Aw, Miz Lizbuth, I'se 'fraid you is gonna look onstylish.

All de other ladies be roun' in homespun, an' you gonna 'pear bang up in satin."

"I am if you can find some."

"Well'm, I'll see what Ah kin do. Ah sho' does lak to see you lookin' purty."

On Mrs. Bell's departure for Virginia, she had given the slave her discarded dresses, but Trolcie had left them untouched in the attic. Once before, when Elizabeth had bewailed the lack of a decent garment, she had extracted one, ripped it up, pressed it, and offered it to her with a gleaming smile. It had only remained for Miss Sally to refashion it into a fetching little frock decorated with roses out of her scrap bag, and Trolcie had been delighted to exchange the useless treasure for a small box of snuff.

Elizabeth was almost too excited with her plan to have much appetite. She would stop all the war work; she would appear everywhere in a new frock. There was not much doubt of being able to draw suspicious attention to herself. The women would be in a buzz when she failed to appear at the hospital, let alone what they would say when they saw her in what they thought were glamorous new clothes. And with all the information of army movements leaking out of Wilmington these days, Mr. Harnett hardly trusted even the other members of the committee. What would he say of a lady who had no money yet managed luxuries?

There were several drawbacks, of course. It would be easy to fool everybody else, but not Mamba. Uncle Adam's return just now was most unfortunate, too. He would ask awkward questions, and then finally intercede for her as sure as the world, and James wouldn't have to. But that was a chance she would have to take.

There was to be a ball next week to raise more money for the army. George Holmes had asked to escort her, and she would attend, dressed in a costume designed after James' astonishing description of the French mode. How surprised he would be! It would be fun to see everybody's surprise, and if she were tasked about it, no one could prove that the dress was new.

Next day, Abigail gave a tea party at which she offered a pledge she had composed to the assembled girls for their signatures, stating that they would not receive attentions of men who refused to join the militia. There was a great deal of excited chatter and gabbling over the importance of seeing their names in a column of the *Mercury,* for Abigail, being the editor's niece, was in a position to hand out this bait, and she knew her own name would head the list. It was a wonderful idea for regaining ground with the officers who had strayed from her side with Elizabeth's arrival in Wilmington.

Elizabeth waited for the hubbub to subside, dropped the bombshell of her refusal to put her name to the paper, saying she had signed all the patriotic papers she intended to, and swept out of the house.

There was a moment of stupefied silence; then, before she got to the gate, her satisfied ears caught the explosion of their shock and wild speculations.

Miss Sally was called in again, somewhat dubious now that people were talking so about Elizabeth, and set to work on every scrap of lace and ribbon in the house for a wardrobe designed to rock the town. Elizabeth drew a fantastic sketch before her horrified but fascinated eyes of how the ball gown was to be made.

She could hardly wait for Thursday evening and the ball. The days seemed to creep by, but a chance encounter with Cornelius Harnett one morning revealed the fact that her plan was being furthered faster than she thought. She was walking down Broad Street in one of the new-old frocks when he stopped her with a curt greeting.

"Why, good morning, Mr. Harnett." She smiled as sweetly as if there were no rancor in her heart against him.

It was plain to see he had something on his mind. "The committee is still watching you, Mrs. Purdie," he said without preamble, "and we don't like what we see."

"Indeed? And what have you seen?" She had him there—all they had was women's gossip.

He looked at her sharply. "You have ceased all patriotic works. Why?"

"I stopped because there's not been enough work lately for the women they have. Mr. Harnett, I don't believe you are very well-informed on your ladies' committees. Most of them, I assure you, find it more entertaining to run around doing war work than to stay at home and do their own."

He covered what may have been an amused smile at the probable truth in this by a hand and a slight cough. "Can you explain your rides in the country? We are beginning to think it strange that every time something happens there is a report that you were seen in the vicinity only shortly before."

"I don't understand you, sir. I ride because I like to."

"I think you do understand. A wagon train of ammunition was attacked by a party of Tories on the river road two days ago, and Miss Abigail happened to speak of having seen you out that way during the morning."

In spite of her, her temper flared. "I was not on the river road two days ago. In fact, I have not been riding all week. So Miss Abigail has told you a lie!"

He didn't intend to get himself embroiled in women's fights, and he was vexed that he had thoughtlessly mentioned Abigail's name.

Elizabeth continued quickly, "Now that you have mentioned her name, what, pray, was she doing on the river road?"

This he disregarded and indicated the silk of her gown. "These clothes, madam, where do they come from?"

"They are some of Mrs. Bell's dresses that she gave her cook, made over," she answered with a level stare, and knew he did not believe a word of it. Furious as she was, she began to enjoy confusing him.

He saw that he was getting nowhere, which nettled him. "Well, madam, I ask you to remember what I told you before. Don't pretend you were not warned. I bid you good day."

She walked on, boiling inside that Abigail had lied about her, and wondering why. Come to think about it, Abigail was more to be suspected than herself—or could be. Suddenly it occurred to her that Abigail was the only one who could have taken the keys from Adam's office and opened the door that allowed Fanning's escape. Certainly, she had access to them.

At the same time she was pleased to have confounded Mr. Harnett, and that she was innocent of everything he had suspected her of. She had done nothing against his precious colony, but unless her little scheme worked, it made little difference whether they sent her away or not.

As she passed the tavern, James was coming out. He invited her in for a cup of makeshift tea, and she was glad of an opportunity of finding out if he intended staying over for the ball, but she spoke coolly, as if his presence were of no particular concern.

"Don't tell me the longbeards are permitting such frivolity."

"They are this, because they need to raise money for the army," she said. "It's to be a very patriotic affair. The older ladies will have a spinning bee to make cloth for shirts in one room, while the younger ones will dance with the soldiers."

"Well, I shall certainly be there, if only to see you at the wheel!"

"You are a horrid creature! Quite the most unchivalrous man I ever knew." Though she had the pleasure of refusing him as an escort, when they parted she was at once more doubtful of her success and more determined to bring him to heel.

The day of the ball, Wilmington was full of dreadful excitement and foreboding. News had come that Savannah had fallen to the British, and rumors spread like prairie fire of their intentions to make good at last their previously abandoned threat to invade North Carolina. Patriotic zeal was whipped high.

Indicative of the feeling was the fact that, as in other evenings, the doors were not opened to the elite alone. This time they were flung wide to all. There were no barrels of beer on the common, and no dancing in the streets. Democracy jammed the hall, and its walls bulged with the crowd. The women showed their devotion to the cause by wearing gowns homespun, home-dyed. There would be no rich brocades which had ever issued from English looms no matter how old and worn they were. Hands were lifted a little higher, curtsies were a little deeper, as if the dancers must compensate with exaggerated elegance of manner for the diminished grandeur of their apparel. They would fling their sacrifices gaily into England's face—and win the war!

It was into such a scene that Elizabeth, in all the splendor of the French costume, made her dramatically late appearance.

The music lost tempo and dwindled away as the musicians, then the dancers caught sight of the slight figure poised in the doorway, smiling over the assemblage. They stared for an instant at the spreading skirts touching the door jambs on either side, the yards of delicate pink and the festoons of lace ruffles. Full stays had drawn the tiny waist into a pointed bodice as slender as a young sapling, the firm breasts curving from the low décolletage. Her jewels flashed, and crowning all was a towering headdress, topped with plumes, looped with pearls.

For a moment there was no sound except the whirring of spinning wheels in the room beyond. Then this, too, stopped and there was a sudden indrawn breath as from a single throat, exhaled into a babel of indignation.

She was sharply aware of the reaction, but she was not

prepared for the too serious temper of the crowd. There was nothing to do but try to carry it off. George stood, uncertainly, his face going red and white with perspiring uneasiness.

The musicians started up again guiltily in a nervous, rapid rhythm, and because people were too stunned to do otherwise, they returned to their interrupted patterns.

"Well, George, aren't you going to dance with me?"

He ran a shaking finger around his stock and stammered, "Yes—yes, I guess so."

At first sight of her this evening he had been so captivated by her beauty and so enamored of her that he had not even thought of her costume.

As they entered the set she saw James leaning against the wall, watching her with a lazy, crooked smile. But she was disappointed because disapproval was there as well.

With one accord, the other couples indignantly withdrew from the set, but she pretended not to notice.

When the music stopped, she sank into a pink and billowing curtsy, every scornful eye in the room fixed upon her. And in the split second of the tableau, a recruit in buckskin sent a well-aimed stream of tobacco juice arching across the room to flow from bodice to hem of the shining gown.

She looked down, horrified and furious, and when she looked up again, George Holmes had taken to his heels. Instantly there was pandemonium. The crowd surged forward with snatching hands and clamorous voices, and she found herself the center of a pushing, hysterical melee, defenseless and alone. Then she felt her headdress topple, and raking fingers that tore at her bodice. Panic-stricken, she tried to fight her way through the mass of straining, lunging bodies, but it had now become a free-for-all into which everybody had entered as viciously as a pack of wild animals. Desperately she looked for a friendly face and straight into the eyes of Grandma Love, whose vengeful, clutching hands were tearing at her skirts. It crossed her mind, in the brief instant, that the so-called aristocrats had as much of the mob spirit as the multitude.

Cornelius Harnett leaped to the platform and demanded silence, but his voice carried no more into the babel than a whisper. She felt an elbow sharp in her ribs, then a blow from behind sent her to her knees. I'll be trampled to death, she thought with a staggering attempt to rise out of the tangle of dangling lace and satin.

Then came a strong grip on her arm and she realized that

miraculously she was being propelled out of the vortex and through the door. She wanted to stop a moment to catch her breath, but James hurried her down to the street and into the first carriage he found, which he ordered driven home at top speed.

Not a word was said until Cicero had closed the door upon them. Then he remarked coldly, "Well, I hope you're satisfied."

"Oh, James, how could I know—"

"You've been warned often enough. I don't believe there's an ounce of brains in your pretty little head!"

Before she could retort, the doorbell rang and Harnett and Adam came into the room.

Harnett said, "Mistress Purdie, you are under arrest. I can no longer control public opinion." Then he turned to James, "I'm not sure you will care to attend the meeting of the committee that's now awaiting this woman's presence."

"I shall certainly be there," he answered evenly. "I could hardly allow a lady to be killed by that mob, could I?"

Adam was looking at Elizabeth with sorrowful eyes. She noted his pallor, the shaking of his hands, and hated the anxiety she was causing him.

"My dear," he said softly, "I believe you will tell me the truth. It will be better for you if you do. Did you have anything to do with the burning of Jones' mill and the skirmish there that resulted in the death of twenty of our soldiers?"

"I didn't know anything about it," she answered fearfully.

James looked his surprise.

"News just came in," Adam told him, "and there are many who believe Elizabeth was late to the ball because she took the time to betray our encampment."

"Oh, Uncle Adam, that is the most preposterous thing I ever heard!" She saw the disbelief in Mr. Harnett's eyes, and it seemed suddenly incredible that she could have been so foolish as to appear in this costume on this of all nights. She could not tell them why with James standing there, and they would not believe her if she did. She turned to Mr. Harnett with such dignity as she could muster in her bedraggled state. "Will you permit me to change my dress?"

"Pray do, madam," was his caustic reply, with a flicking glance at the low-cut bodice, "I desire that the gentlemen of the committee keep their minds solely on the business of the evening."

The night wind of early spring came softly into the little

room in the courthouse where Elizabeth and Mamba were seated. It flickered the candles and cooled somewhat the flushed cheeks of the girl sitting straight in her chair, the white collar of her prim gray dress caught high at the throat with a modest brooch, hands gripped tightly in her lap.

Mamba's lower lip was distended to twice its normal size as she stared at the window, but she did not speak. Her torrent of words unleashed on the three men had finally been stopped by the threat of not being allowed to come with them. She glanced at her mistress and drew a breath.

"I'll send you home if you say a word," Elizabeth hissed. She was straining to hear the discussions going on in the next room. Some of the voices clearly penetrated the wall, others could not be understood at all. But she heard enough to be amazed at the way her most guileless act had been misconstrued. Everything she had said or done, and a great deal she had not, since arriving in Wilmington was brought up and used against her, and presently even the chairman's mallet was powerless to stop the flow of angry talk.

She heard snatches of speech, interrupted, drowned out, confused, but it all added up to show that with this latest tragedy of Jones' mill so near town, coupled with the realization that the war was sweeping perilously near home, the honorable gentlemen had become uneasy to the point of striking out ruthlessly at anyone against whom suspicion had been cast.

"If they'd all only stop talking at once I could hear," she said to herself.

"All circumstantial. Not a word of it proves her guilty of—" That was Uncle Adam. Her heart warmed toward him.

Then Cornelius Harnett's voice rasped, "Gentlemen, we are accomplishing nothing in this manner. If you will be so good, I will ask for a vote. Is it the opinion of the committee that this woman is guilty as charged?"

If there were any "noes," they were drowned in a flood of "ayes." The gavel came down again. "And what is your advice as to the disposition of her?"

"Jail! Until we can prove—"

"The stocks!"

"The pillory!"

"One moment, please," Harnett shouted, finally silencing them. "I agree that some steps must be taken, but I'll not agree to punishment of that sort for one who *could* be innocent. Now, there is a West Indian packet due to leave Newberne in a fortnight which will touch Jamaica—"

Elizabeth gasped, and her eyes went wide. In the horror of the evening she had forgotten that she herself had planned this. What a fool she had been! But she was lucky that, in their present mood, they had not thought of hanging.

A chair scraped back then, someone rose, and even Mr. Harnett's voice dropped to silence. "Mr. Chairman, gentlemen." It was James' voice, and his tone was overlaid with a faint, almost disparaging amusement. Elizabeth crossed the room swiftly and laid her ear against the door, her heart racing. "I think," she heard him continue in a maddeningly slow drawl, "that you have allowed the ladies to warp your judgment."

This was so largely the truth that an indignant murmur went around their table. "So far as I can see, you have offered not one actual proof of Mistress Purdie's guilt. Indeed, you sound much like a flock of gossiping hens! As for her costume of this evening, I think I can explain that to your satisfaction. On my return from France I brought her a description of the mode at the French court with which any woman would be fascinated—particularly a beautiful one. And on one of my trips to the Indies I brought back some fabrics and furbelows to her as a present. I can see nothing indicative of espionage in her wearing them if she chooses. Her choice of an evening to do so, I will admit, was unfortunate, but—"

McLain pushed to his feet. "You confess to spending your money on fripperies when the country is so badly in need of it?"

"Are you questioning my patriotism?" James' words cut across at him like blown sleet.

"Here, here!" Adam shouted with the first anger Elizabeth had ever heard in his voice. "No one can question James Richardson! There is no man here who has given more unsparingly of himself or his means. His reputation both on land and sea is too well-known to permit a question!"

McLain sat down unwillingly. It was true. There was no way they could get at James, but they refused to revoke their decision.

"Mr. Harnett," James declared surprisingly, "I will vouch for Mrs. Purdie. Make myself personally responsible for her actions."

There was an immediate uproar of "noes."

"Has this committee no confidence in its own members? If not, my resignation—"

"The committee has every confidence in you, James," Cornelius said hastily, "but, after all, you are but a human young man. It's possible that you yourself may be duped."

Elizabeth heard a palm go down on the table with a crash that silenced the murmur of approval at the chairman's speech, and the anger in James' voice was the crack of a pistol shot.

"Then, by God, I'll marry her! As my wife she will be beyond even your questioning. I'll see to it. I bid you good night, gentlemen!"

She had reached for the moon, and now that it was in her hand she found the silver platter too big to hold. Trembling, she slipped quickly back into her chair and folded her hands to wait until he came through the door.

CHAPTER 11

They were married next afternoon by Adam Boyd. It was the first exercise of his office since his American ordination, and his face beamed because this was one of the things he had always looked forward to among ministerial duties, and because he still felt that his beloved cause was going to gain a fine recruit even if it was by marriage. The compunction he had felt last night when James had made his startling proposal, he had dismissed on the conviction that these two young people were well-suited, which, after all, was perhaps as good a basis for wedlock as any.

Mamba stood scowling with the rest of the servants smiling fatuously behind her in the doorway of the chintz-hung library during the ceremony. By his championship of Elizabeth in the face of the committee, James had reinstated himself again within the exclusive confines of her affection, but she was darkly disapproving at the vague uncertainty that all the shenanigans of the past week were a part of a brazen plan of Elizabeth's to get him. A blind man could see she was in love with him, but Mamba was disconcerted over the absence of an orthodox courtship.

"Gentle Jedus, what is you done wid yo' pride?" she had demanded the night before.

"Why, Mamba, you are the very one—"

"Yas'm, Ah knows. Ah did say you oughter git a husband, but Mist' James ain't marryin' you fo' de right reasons."

"Well, you always said a girl had to make a man want to marry her. What difference does it make how she does it?"

"Hit's diffrunt," she persisted, "you ought to uv made him want you fo' yo'self."

"Oh, he does," she answered gaily, "he just doesn't know it

yet. And by the way, Mr. James says you and Tip-toe are to follow us day after tomorrow with the rest of my things."

"You means Ah ain't goin' wid you tomorrow?"

"No, he doesn't have time for you to pack. He's going to be busy with the planting and can't wait."

It had been a long time since Mamba had felt the iron arrangements of a man's hand and she resented it. "You cain't go off widout me to take keer of you," she said with bitter disappointment but no conviction, for she knew too well the price of security was the unequivocal acceptance of the master's will.

At last the cylindrical hide trunk was being slid into the springs of the coach, the bandboxes piled on the seat beside the driver by the grinning Tip-toe, and they were off.

It was late spring. There was sun, and the skies were a high, windswept blue. Trees draped themselves in pale-green lace, and peaches and wild plum had burst into sudden bloom, standing like dainty nosegays about the countryside. Cherokee roses embroidered zigzag rail fences; the forests along the river, swollen with early rains, revealed long drifts of dogwood. There was the mingled scent of daphne and fern and last year's rotting leaves.

James was conscious of an exhilaration which seemed to have completely overcome the concern he had felt when, on awakening this morning, he had realized he was caught in a noose his own temper had fashioned. In a moment of anger at the Committee of Safety for a seeming lack of confidence in himself, he had forsaken his pleasant, solitary, free existence, but though fate had overtaken him rather more quickly than he would have fancied, she had at least been kind enough to hand him an utterly charming woman—one for whom he had felt a certain ardor since the first moment he saw her.

Looking back, he realized that Elizabeth had been on his mind a good deal, whether in pleasure or exasperation. Whatever this marriage was to be, it would not be dull. When this occurred to him, his naturally bouyant spirits rose, and he had been amused to make of it as well-trimmed a wedding as possible in the limited time. He had bought a ring and a most elegant bouquet of wax flowers.

As the coach swung into the rutted river road, he glanced down at his wife, slipped his arm around her, and pulled her close to him. "I trust, Mrs. Richardson, that you will be able to keep out of trouble in the country."

"When you get that look in your eyes, sir," she replied archly, "I begin to think I might be into more than I'm out of!"

They broke into peals of laughter out of all proportion to the wit. She wished he would be serious and tell her he loved her and how beautiful she was, but instead, he kept up a bantering, gay conversation that partook not at all of the talk of lovers. So far, he had treated the whole affair with his usual levity, but he had looked at her seriously when he said, "I do," and she *was* married to him—nothing could change that. It was some happiness just to be alone with him, riding toward a home they would share.

At the ferry across the Cape Fear, they got out and walked to the edge of the water. The blare of the coach horn reverberated through the green glow of the forest and echoed back and forth across the river, but there was no answering shout from the other side. It was getting on toward sundown and James frowned with irritation at the delay. He called to the man to sound the horn again, and strained his eyes to try to detect some sign of life where the big log craft lay in a shaft of golden mist slanting down through the pines. Shadows flickered among the yellow globules of light reflected from the water on the underside of the ferry's up-curved end, but nothing else moved.

He cupped his hands and sent his voice in a ringing call. Then, when there was no answer, he ordered the driver to swim over and get it. The man went upstream and disappeared into a thicket, and presently they heard a splash and watched the regular sure strokes of the glistening black arms. Then slowly he pushed the ferry ahead of him.

When he rejoined them, his high cheekbones still shone with drops of water and a puzzled frown was on his face. "Ain't nobody there at all, Mist' Rich'son. Been a fyah, though. Sump'n still smokin' on tuther side."

The four reluctant horses were hurried onto the ferry, and the logs began to creak and groan against the current. Halfway across they saw a thin spiral of smoke lifting from behind the trees.

"What is it?" Elizabeth asked, anxious at the halffrightened look on James' face.

"I don't know. It might be Podge, the ferryman's house, or

... the plantation lies only a short way beyond in that direction."

"Oh!"

The craft pushed up on the muddy approach with a jolt. The horses struggled up the bank, and a few more yards brought them to a clearing a safe distance from the river, at the edge of which had stood a little house. It was now a smoking ruin. There was no stock in sight, though a small haystack stood nearby. Against what had been the chimney lay the carcass of a cow, the choice portions of her meat cut away, and a little aside, the body of an unborn calf. The charred remains and some bits of crockery were all that was left of the ferryman's household.

Elizabeth got down and ran over to where James was already searching among the still-glowing coals, his face a mask of fury.

"Vandalism!" he said. "God only knows what they have done with the old man."

"Who do you think—?"

But James did not hear her. He had caught sight of something almost hidden behind the small haystack, something that moved. He hauled it out. It was Podge, trussed up like a chicken for the spit.

Together they loosened the rope that wrapped him and took the gag out of his mouth.

"Podge, old fellow, are you all right?"

"A-course I ain't all right! I'll skin 'em alive I will—I'll—"

"Who? What happened?"

"Come and sit down and tell us," Elizabeth said gently.

"No, ma'am, it ain't no time to set. I'll have their hides. I'll—"

James gave the old man's arm a shake. "Here, stop all that raving and tell me who burned your house."

Podge looked up at him with a rheumy eye and suddenly ceased his gyrations. "Tories, they was, by God! They come up on tother side the river and called for the ferry and—"

"I knew you'd get yourself into trouble. I warned you, Podge."

"Well, how in tarnation was I to know? I conversationed with 'em like I allus does with you and tother gentlemen, and when we got over to this side—"

Podge was violently against the British, but James doubted if he really understood the long political speeches with which he regaled his passengers.

"Who were they? Do you know?"

"I'd know 'em if I'd see 'em. Leader had a funny red mouth. He had a little *mus*tache and eyes black as shoe buttons."

"Think I've seen him," James said grimly.

"Yes, sir. They was havin' a rollickin' time, damn ther hides. One o' the men tied me up and throwed me over in the haystack, then this here leader he come over and said did I have any gold hid around, and if I told anybody 'bout 'em bein' here they'd burn *me* up next time. Then one of 'em said he was hongry, so they up and kilt my cow. And her with a calf in her, too. They fried ther meat over the fire from my own house and set and et it right afore my eyes." He started waving his rope-toughened hands again. "I'll skin 'em alive, I will!"

"Well, come on over and I'll give you a bed, and tomorrow you can have a carpenter and some lumber. Then you take my advice and don't talk so much."

The old man fixed him with his one good eye. "Ain't nobuddy yet told Podge to hold his tongue," he stated indignantly, " 's why me and the old lady parted company back in sixty-two!"

There was a strained silence in the carriage as it rounded the curve and drew in through the brick pillars at the foot of the avenue leading to James' plantation home. Dusk was settling quietly over the fields despite the nearby violence, and beyond the trees they saw the chimneys of the house rearing black against the evening sky.

"Thank God they left my place alone," James said. He was furious at the almost certain knowledge that it was Fanning who had burned Podge's house. "I knew he was a scoundrel! He will likely go into Wilmington now and blame this thing on a party of Whig soldiers!"

Elizabeth said nothing, for she had an uncomfortable feeling that the less she had to say about Fanning the better. Though she knew all the things that had been said about him she could not believe that he could be so cruel. She had thought all along that he was harmless enough—merely making money out of what everybody else seemed to be losing on.

They reached the carriage block and James swung her down from the step. His lightheartedness returned with their arrival.

"What an experience for a wedding journey! Sorry I could not have provided better entertainment. But that's your friend Fanning!"

"He's not my friend," she protested, knowing he was thinking of the night of the first militia ball. "Do you think he'd really go to Wilmington now?"

"Oh, he's brazen enough to do anything as long as there's money in it. I heard recently that he'd signed the association and now they're perfectly willing to trust him. Sometimes I think there're a few fine fools on the Committee of Safety!"

"I'm the first to agree with you on that!" She laughed.

Sound of the approaching vehicle had brought a few of the outside slaves to peer around the corner of the house. Old Tobe appeared in the doorway holding a candle above his head.

"Tobe, this is your new mistress."

"Yassuh," Tobe said calmly, then stared. "Well, fo' Gawd! Welcome, ma'am. Welcome. Ah well 'members when Marse Pahkah brung his old lady home!"

"Well, get along now, and tell Mariah to get Mistress Richardson's room in order, and have Beezie get us some supper." James laughed and shied his tricorn onto the hall table.

Elizabeth took off her bonnet before the mirror and smoothed her hair with fingers that were suddenly shaking, a slow, beating agitation beginning inside her. James was playing the gracious host, ordering her room made ready as if he had no thought of occupying it with her. Did he intend to offer her merely the protection of his name and his house with no idea of consummating their marriage? But, from his behavior on other occasions, she could not believe it likely. Crosscurrents of disappointment and anticipation threaded painfully through her mind.

They went into the drawing room, and she watched him pour glasses of wine from a bottle out of a cabinet by the sofa.

"To the bride!" he said gaily, and it was impossible to tell what went on behind his smile.

She laughed and raised her glass. "And to you, sir, the groom. And thank you for the small effects you so kindly provided for making our wedding conventional."

"Is it not to be a conventional marriage?" His eyes were boldly probing.

Before she could delicately pursue this opening there came

the interruption of Bill Lipman, the overseer. He came in with his sandy, sun-streaked hair, and his limp in one leg, bringing a sheaf of papers. Tobe announced that supper was ready, and all during the hastily prepared meal the men discussed affairs of the plantation.

The taste of home-cured meat was heavenly, and the eggs were fresh and well-cooked. She ate hungrily, glad that James was too immersed in his business to see how much she consumed. A full stomach eased the tension within her. I was just hungry and tired, she thought, and tomorrow, when Mamba comes, everything will be all right.

Bill finally took himself off, and they were left alone. Tobe appeared in the pantry door, but James waved him away. "That will be all tonight, Tobe." He glanced at Elizabeth, then got up and poured two glasses of brandy. "Here," he said, laughing, "drink this. You are the perfect picture of the terrified bride!"

"Oh, do I look as bad as that?" As long as it pleased him to be flippant, she would be so, too.

"No, you look very beautiful," he said gently. He took her in his arms, twining his fingers in her hair. Then, on a sudden thought, he released her and pulled her after him out onto the gallery. "I forgot something—to carry you over the threshold for luck!"

"Is that another American custom necessary to a proper wedding like a ring and flowers?"

"Yes." Outside, in the darkness he gathered her high in his arms and ceremoniously walked back through the doorway. There was a subtle change in him now. A tenseness and a strange look wiped the laughter from his eyes. Without putting her down, he turned and blew out the candles Tobe had left on the hall table, then his mouth closed her lips before she could speak.

She felt the urgent tread of his boots on the stair and the heavy hammering of his heart close against her body. Her arms tightened about his neck, and bright rockets of light flashed behind her closed lids and broke into showers of stars as his kisses covered her face and moved downward to the pulsing hollow of her throat. Her bodice had suddenly grown too tight. As if he knew, his fingers found and loosened the lacings.

A candle burned on the dressing table beyond the open door of her room. He slid her to her feet, then stooped and kissed her again. "Don't be too long," he said, and gave her a little push into the room.

She closed the door and stood against it for a moment, her breath catching in little gasps, her head thrown back exultantly. "He loves me," she cried softly, "I know he does!"

James went to his own room and poured himself another light brandy. His hands were not quite steady, and he was amused as the question passed through his mind as to whether this superlative emotion he was feeling could be love. Ridiculous! He certainly had no intention of allowing his heart to become too much involved. That way lay all the danger to a man's freedom. No, he had been about to mistake desire for love, possibly because he had had to marry Elizabeth to have her. Quite possibly she expected no avowal from him. She had been in a tight spot and had accepted him without hesitation. Well, it was a fair bargain, and from the eager promises of her kisses, it was evident that she was as well-pleased with it as he.

Her little trunk had been unpacked and the nightdress folded across the foot of the bed. As if the sight of these familiar things had released her from a spell, Elizabeth ran to the mirror, laughing at her shining eyes, and with trembling fingers began to struggle with the hooks and buttons of her clothes. That brandy has made me awkward, she thought happily. But she knew it was not the brandy.

The nightgown finally slipped over her head, she returned to the mirror and began to take the pins from her hair. As it fell in dark coils about her shoulders, James followed his light knock into the room.

He took the brush from her hand and drew her to her feet. A vibrant current flowed between them that was sweetly dizzying. She turned her face up to him. In the glow from the candle his eyes had never been so full of golden glints.

Her heart was bursting with love for him, but she was afraid to speak lest the fragile moment be shattered. Tensely, she searched his face and saw there a fleeting glimpse of what she wanted—then it was gone behind his smile. With a gallant gesture he raised her fingertips to his lips.

"You put me to unnecessary trouble for this moment, my dear, yet I begin to think it worth it."

She moved backward in his arms with sudden bitter hurt

and disappointment, which he misunderstood. "Surely you're not drawing out on your end of the bargain," he said.

Again she searched his eyes, but there was nothing there but the old teasing look. She might have known! Her own love had tried to force into his behavior on the stair a quality that was not there. She quickly lowered her lashes that he might not see what lay behind her own eyes. Then the DeRossett pride pointed up with her own sense of fairness shot through her wretchedness. After all, he had been honest. He had told her he wanted her—had even told her he did not want to marry her. There was nobody to blame but herself. She had tricked him into it. Now there was nothing to do but play the game by his rules.

With a sidewise lift of her head, the heavy curls fell back from her face, and she forced a smile. Her voice was very low. "I think you have mistaken a natural reticence for reluctance."

"Ah, there's my lady!" His laugh was soft and exciting even at this moment as the rich tones of his voice. His eyes measured the distance to the bed. The candle was snuffed, and she felt herself swept up in his arms, felt the softness of the bed beneath her, and his mouth hungrily hard upon her own.

She tried not to feel the touch of his hands, the burning kisses, or to hear the broken, murmured words, but the mad darkness was reeling with a roaring in her ears like distant thunder drawing nearer and nearer, and his lips and his hands were forcing her uncontrollably, relentlessly to strange and wonderful sensations. And the swirling vortex became a crucible, burning away all fear and disappointment and pain, leaving only the molten thrills that ran like wildfire through her veins.

When she awakened, it was noon, and the April sunlight coming through the white curtains was warm where it made a yellow wedge across the wide, high bed. For a drowsy moment she stared at the strange wall. Almost she had put out her hand to ring for Mamba when she remembered. A quick glance found the other pillow crumpled but empty and the covers thrown back only enough to allow a quiet exit.

She stared up at the ceiling, wondering with some dismay if she could possibly play her part in this game to which she had assigned herself so sternly last night. There was a light knock on the door and she jerked upright, hugging her knees up to her breasts under the covers.

Without awaiting permission, James came striding into the room. He was in riding breeches with a rough jacket thrown carelessly over one shoulder. "I thought you were going to sleep all day. It's awful to be married for life to a lazy woman."

She made herself smile. "I almost did. What time is it?"

"Almost noon." He sat down on the side of the bed and ran his fingers through the long curls spreading over the pillow, then pushed her down and bent to her lips. "You know, you are a very satisfactory bride, madam. I have decided to keep you."

"I do hope so," she answered with mock concern. This was not hard to say—maybe it would not be so difficult after all. She certainly did hope it. And it was not hard to return his light caress. The only thing that required an effort was to veil the love she felt welling into her eyes.

There was a shuffling step on the stair, and without moving, he called, "Come in. It's quite all right," he added, grinning as she made an uneasy movement. "Beezie knows we are married. She is bringing you some coffee."

Beezie set the silver tray on the table beside the bed. She was very black and small, her skinny hands like bird claws. She wore a bright head rag, and her smile was nearly toothless.

"Here is your new mistress, Beezie. But I warn you, one grain of salt out of the soup and she's likely to beat you!"

"Aw, Mist' James, I ain't never been beat in mah life."

"Don't put on airs. Everything's got its first time to happen."

"I'm wondering if you have any salt to *put* in the soup, Beezie." Elizabeth smiled. "We had none in Wilmington except what we could make from seawater."

"Hyah, hyah," she screeched. "Dat's a proper mistus, Mist' James! An' we *is* low on salt! We ain't got moan a teacup lef'."

"Well, you'll have to figure out a substitute. I'm not going to town for a week or two," James said.

"Naw, suh, I doan 'magine you is." Her implication was so plain as she went out grinning that James burst into laughter, and though Elizabeth colored to the roots of her hair, she made herself join in.

He got up and gave his attention to pouring the two cups

of coffee. "We won't have any more of this pleasant drink when the present supply is gone. I brought this in from the last trip to Nassau."

Luxury at her fingertips, she thought, then snatched away by the ever-present annoyance of the war. But somehow it did not seem to matter as much as it had.

"Shall you miss the sea dreadfully?" she asked, casting about for something to say.

"Possibly, but there are other things. I'm glad to give the planation some attention for a change, and unless I miss my guess, we will all be too busy before long to worry about what we're missing." He jammed his hands into his pockets and walked to the window, then came back and sat down again on the bed. He was so casual, she thought, they might have been married for years. "I want to ask you something," he said finally, looking straight into her eyes, "and I want the truth. Were you guilty of any of the things the committee accused you of? Had you been meeting Fanning secretly?"

This was so unexpected and so ridiculous that she gasped.

"Certainly not!"

Quite suddenly he laughed and gathered her up, bending her head back into the crook of his arm. "You can get madder quicker than anybody I ever saw." He kissed her hard, and her pulses began to hammer as she pushed against his chest. But he only lifted her out of bed and put her on her feet. "Put some clothes on. I want to show you over my—*our* domain."

"Well, go out so I can," she said stormily, clutching at his dressing gown that lay carelessly thrown over a chair.

Like most of the planters' houses along the river, this one had been built for gracious hospitality. It sprawled over its rise of ground as comfortably as a dowager with her stays off. Ivy draped its brick bosom, and billowing lawns spread about its feet.

There was a wide hall that ran straight through, opening out on both the east and west sides to identical white pillared galleries. The west one was the destination of the magnolia-bordered avenue that led into the property from the river road, but the one on the east overlooked three semicircular terraced slopes that swept down to the river itself and the boat landing. There were lagoons on the bottom level, lying on either side of the broad walk shaded by magnificent elms and oaks.

South of the house were the camellia gardens, broken into formal paths edged with moss-covered bricks, and beyond was the woods garden. To the north stood the slave quarters and the workhouses.

Under Sims Parker's ownership, the plantation had been solely in use for his pleasure—the planning and planting of gardens, with perhaps a handful of tobacco and the small crops the slaves could handle with no attention from him. Hence, it was by far the handsomest place on the Cape Fear. But it had remained for James Richardson to see the unlimited possibilities of the great pine forests that stood to the north, the size to which the tobacco fields might be extended, and the indigo that would thrive in the virgin soil beyond.

When the virile New Englander took possession, the overseer and the slaves knew their long, lazy days were over, and accepted without much reluctance the harder work for the satisfaction of now being part of an efficient, productive organization. It was not long before they took pride in the humming sawmill that grew up in the heart of the forest, the great rafts of lumber that floated down the Cape Fear, and they sang as they rolled the endless barrels of tar and turpentine down to the landing.

Elizabeth had recovered her good humor. When she came downstairs in riding habit this morning, James gave her a little mare named Dolly for a wedding present, and she was extraordinarily pleased that he had thought of it. If only I could forget how much I love him, she thought, and just act like I did before! But I'm different now. Our wedding night seemed not to have changed him at all, but I—

"You are not listening to me, madam, and I am endeavoring to explain to you how tar is made."

"What do they use it for beside to mix with feathers?" she asked pertly.

"Numerous purposes"—he laughed—"but this is headed for the government shipyards to go into vessels for the navy."

"You are *selling* it to the government?"

"Of course. You didn't think I was giving it away, did you? I have to get a price and a good one to pay the higher taxes they are going to be levying on us one of these days."

They started cross-field over the soft, plowed loam toward the sawmill. A hen quail led her brood of precocious miniatures out of a deep furrow a little distance ahead and scurried into the safety of a blackberry thicket at the field's edge.

The remains of a blackened chimney reared incongruously out of the vines.

"Used to be a prosperous farm there. It belonged to the Widow Crane and she was as expert at running it as a man. But the governor, that was in Tryon's time, kept getting more and more careless about the tax-gatherers he appointed, and finally he put in a real villain. The old lady tried to keep up with his demands, but the more she paid him, the more he took out of her, until she had nothing more to give. Then he got his band of cutthroats and they came down with a lot of legal talk and paper, and when they left, they took her livestock, what little money she had, and her daughter. She tried to protect herself, so they shot her and burned the evidence with the house. That was one of the first things to stir up the people against the way they were being treated by the English. Nobody knew but what he'd be next."

"That's horrible! Where are they now—those tax-gatherers?"

"Oh, they lost their jobs, as far as the people were concerned, when Governor Martin lost his, but there are bands of Tories that carry the old records around now and try to collect in the outlying districts."

Elizabeth shuddered, wondering if that was the system Fanning used.

The sawmill made a welcome change of conversation, and she watched with interest the long yellow planks issuing from the chutes into the hands of slaves who stood waiting to stack them into crisscross piles.

"Thomas Brown's place is not far from here through the forest," James said as they remounted.

"Of course! I remember, we came through this wood on the hunt from Oakland that day. It seems a time ago, doesn't it?"

They started back along the sandy road that was known as the horse-pond road. It branched off the main highway, the river road, and ran through the plantation, striking the avenue leading to the house at right angles. A small section of it, some distance from the house, was built above the swampy ground formed by springs bubbling out of the earth. The dairy was here, and so constructed as to make use of the icy water to cool the great crocks of butter and milk and cheese.

James tried the door. "Tobe keeps it locked on account of the travelers that frequently make use of the detour through this part of the property to water their horses and take advantage of the shade of the apple trees—and generally the fruit, too!"

"Show me your spinning rooms and the loom house. I want to see my part of the job."

"There's been precious little use of those," he said, turning off toward the slave quarters. "The women have grown lazy, but there's no need for you to fool with all that stuff. I'll buy you some dresses when I sail again."

"The very idea! How little a man knows about a plantation, after all! You've got to clothe your slaves; you must have linens for the house, and, oh, a hundred other things. You've probably made little use of household equipment up to now."

"All right, all right! If you start being a scold, I'll find me a ducking stool. But come on, if you must make all the gestures of a housewife."

"Don't you expect me to be one?"

He didn't answer, and they dismounted at a low whitewashed building in the shade of a spreading elm. Sodden bits of cotton and wool lay about the door, and inside they found the wheels and swifts covered with dust and cobwebs. There was only one small island of cleanliness in the whole room that showed signs of recent use. Elizabeth gathered up the skirts of her riding habit and went across the littered floor to inspect a wheel. "Why, this measuring hammer is even *broken!*"

"You surprise me, my dear," James drawled from where he leaned against the side of the doorway watching her in amusement. "I thought the ladies of Jamaica toiled not and neither did they spin. How did you know about such things?"

"You forget I've had to supervise all this before," she said, and it crossed her mind that it would be good to have again the familiar role of looking after the business of many hands. *I'll keep busy and I won't have time to think.* She dropped her eyes, veiling a sudden despair. *Here I am,* she thought, *back in the same old pattern. But before, I was doing everything for a man I didn't love, and now I want to do it for one who doesn't love me!*

"Then perhaps I have married well after all!" He laughed and swung her back onto her horse.

In the orchard young boys were slathering whitewash down the trunks of blossoming fruit trees, cautiously eyeing the thousands of bees buzzing above them. And in the vegetable garden an old Negro strightened from inching along on the seat of his canvas breeches plucking weeds.

"Good morning, Jonas. I see you're hard at work."

"Yas, suh. I'se got to he'p Gawd 'long wid dis here gyarden. He ain't never gwine git hit to grow by Hisse'f."

The smokehouse hung chockful of meats. Slabs of bacon and great russet hams hung from the rafters; the blocks and shelves held a tempting array of beef and pork. Indeed, the place was like a small village, happily ahum, productive, sufficient unto itself. Elizabeth's heart lifted. This is my home, she realized suddenly, with a queer little surge of pride. Surely with everything else so perfect . . .

They turned back toward the house. In the middle of the graveled drive they found Mamba and Tip-toe, with the help of the house slaves, unloading the wagon in which they had arrived.

CHAPTER 12

It was not long before the household was transformed from a bachelor establishment into a plantation home. Smoke rose from the chimneys long before the sun was up and gave the signal for the pleasant, muted bustling of a well-run house. Elizabeth reorganized the servants to make for efficiency where there had been shiftlessness. Under Tip-toe's hand the wine cellar came into orderly disposition, and the silver plate in the scarlet-and-white dining room began to gleam. Neglected floors and furniture to shine, windows to glisten; flowers appeared in sunny, fragrant rooms. Mamba could have achieved all this single-handed, but Elizabeth insisted on supervising every minute detail. She was all over the house, skirts aswing, high-piled curls bobbing, orders issuing crisp and certain from her lips.

"They've been allowed to be lazy so long they don't know how to do anything," she said one morning to James in answer to his sleepy questions as to why she felt she must be up and about so early. She had taken to rising before he was awake because, though the nights were wonderful, they were only intervals of time swung between restless days that had to be filled with any sort of occupation to keep her from thinking.

But today he caught her at it and pulled her back on the pillow. "What difference does it make if they're a little slow? Besides," he added, burying his face in the soft curve of her neck, "you know it's nicer here."

She stiffened involuntarily, then relaxed, as quickly established habit threw up the guard she had worn for the past week. It was not too difficult to be gay and flippant when they rode together or met at dinner after a busy day, but with the tender sweetness of his lovemaking her surrender was too complete to allow light and airy words.

"I didn't bring you here just to be a housekeeper," he said.

It was on the tip of her tongue to ask a question out of her heartbreak to which she already knew the answer, and which he would certainly interpret as an invitation. And then a queer thing happened to the flimsy mental structure she had built on her wedding night. It came with a sudden bright and exciting clarity that she had been allowing her love for him to submerge those very characteristics that had attracted him; that this was the sort of thing she must say to be perfect in her self-assigned role. The rules were his, but the game could be hers if she played a little more from her head instead of her heart. She would be exactly what he wanted her to be, but with trimmings he had not expected; she would vex and delight him, flatter and annoy, tease and indulge—and, oh, but such a lady to the world!

She looked at him out of slanting eyes with the most wanton air. "And what *did* you bring me here for?"

He grinned. "I'd think you'd know by now, or have I not—"

"Yes, but man cannot live by bed alone! He must have his house well-ordered, his meals on time, and I must be about my work." She laughed, slipping out of his arms and pulling the covers over the foot of the bed so that the morning wind struck at him with chilling discomfort. "I vow, it's terrible to be married for life to a lazy man! Get up and get busy, or do you want your wife to starve?"

He swore savagely between clenched teeth and made a hilarious lunge for her, but she vanished into the clothes press and shut the door.

As they sat down to breakfast, she noted with pride that the table was well-ordered and beautiful, according to her careful instructions. The sun poured in through the scarlet damask draperies and turned the white-painted paneling to a faint and lovely rose; it caressed the yellow daffodils in their milk-glass bowl and struck glittering shafts from the silver coffeepot. Tip-toe, with his finest air, mincing in an endeavor to walk softly, served the plates at the sideboard from platters of fried ham and stewed, dried apples, spoon bread, and eggs.

"We are going to set tobacco plants today. Want to come watch?"

"Oh, yes," she answered, "after I see to a few things up here. You know your old Lulu in the weaving room is really a genius. But she isn't very anxious to get back into the habit of work. She's getting so old I'd let her off if she'd tell some of the younger girls how she makes up her dyes. But she won't. She only shakes her head and says, 'Nobody know how to do hit but me.' And that's all we can get out of her. I could choke her!"

James laughed at her mimicry and started to speak, but broke off at the sound of a horse stopping at the block, and rose hastily.

Elizabeth smiled and went on with her breakfast. That he was pleased with her domestic arrangements it was plain to see. It was gratifying, because she recognized in his satisfaction one of the more prosaic strands with which she could bind him.

Then he was calling her to come to the library.

"Why, Mr. Kendall," she cried, putting out both her hands, "how nice to see you again!"

"He just came in at Wilmington, Elizabeth. The *Quadrille's* in port!"

"Oh, how fine!"

"Have you breakfasted?" James asked delightedly.

"Yes, thank you. At the tavern, early."

"Then you must be ready for coffee again," Elizabeth said, ringing for Tip-toe and turning all her charm on Mr. Kendall.

"Indeed, yes. After that ride," he said, rubbing at the seat of his pants. "I'm not much of a land traveler!"

"Tell us the news, Kendall," James demanded eagerly.

"Well, what I came for was to bring you Captain Jones' compliments and tell you that he offers you the *Quadrille* back for shipping your own crops. I ran across him in Wilmington. Said he thought you had done enough to deserve your ship back if you needed it, which I thought was damned generous of him in view of his shortage of vessels."

James did not answer at once. He went over to the mantel and stood with a propped elbow and a hand running slowly down the back of his head. Elizabeth watched him and understood uneasily something of what he was thinking.

Tip-toe came in with the coffee tray.

"Darling, do come and have your coffee. How do you like yours, Mr. Kendall? Cream, sugar?"

"Aye, both, please. But say! Something goes on here I hadn't known about," he said, looking from one to the other. "When did all this happen?"

Elizabeth allowed her eyes to drop demurely, then looked up at James. "Just three weeks ago, wasn't it, angel?"

James gave her a quizzical look that said what-the-hell-is-all-this, and answered politely that it was exactly three weeks.

"Well, I'm the son of a hurricane! I was so intent on my business I didn't tumble at first. Just seemed sorter natural to see you two together."

"Now, I think that's very sweet of you, Mr. Kendall. Tell us, how did you do at sea?"

"Oh, we added a few notches to our guns. Took a brigantine, and a sloop off Hatteras last week," he said with satisfaction, then turned to James. "I don't want to seem to lead your decision, but the *Quadrille* is worth two of any other ships to the government as a privateer. She's so maneuverable and speedy, a victim don't have a chance. But I guess you need her pretty bad yourself, and we do need to keep our exports up."

Elizabeth stole a quick glance at James. She could see that a conflict of no little intensity was going on inside him, and she knew it was composed of several things. But if he kept the *Quadrille* for his own use, there would be the constant threat of his going to sea again hanging over her head, and she had enough on her mind without that. There was nothing to keep him from using the vessel for his own use and privateering at the same time. She knew there was the struggle within him to decide to keep the money-making ship for himself or to make the patriotic gesture of giving it back to the use of the country, the desire to take charge of it again as a privateer himself, but something was holding him back. She had a fluttering hope that it might be because of her, but the almost certain knowledge that it was the new projects with the planting that could not do without him.

Mr. Kendall stirred his coffee reflectively, his sea-tanned face bent over his cup, waiting for James to speak. But Elizabeth could not wait. He might decide wrong!

"Oh, Mr. Kendall, James would not think of keeping the *Quadrille* when the country needs it so badly. It was fine of Captain Jones to offer it, but, no, we couldn't allow him to sacrifice so valuable a weapon to our personal needs, could we, my pet?"

James sent her a shocked and venomous glance, but she crossed over and slipped her arm through his, looking up at him with demure admiration.

"No, of course not, love," he said through his teeth, and

tried to keep the fury out of his voice. She had him tied and delivered, and there was no way out of it without losing face before Kendall.

"I never saw a man," she chattered on, beaming at him, "so afraid of doing something that might appear the grand gesture. He's so modest! No, you just go on sinking the British, Mr. Kendall, and we shall hear with pride of your exploits. Oh, wait, I have something for you."

James was, to say the very least, nonplussed. He watched her graceful exit from the room and heard her footsteps up the stair. What could she possibly have for Kendall? What had he married, anyway? Fortunately, Kendall was delightedly pumping his hand and congratulating him on marrying himself such a proud and loving wife, so he didn't have to answer except with a forced and uncomfortable smile.

Elizabeth came in again with a bundle in her arms which she unrolled and spread out over the sofa. It was the flag she had made from the pattern William Hooper had sent Aunt Mary. There was a low whistle of pleased surprise from Kendall.

"I really made this for James while he was in France, but since he won't be going to sea I want the *Quadrille* to have it anyway. I want to feel I have some small part in her fight against the enemy," she said, one hand lightly poised on her breast and her eyes dreamily on the distance.

The captain was completely taken in, but James made a choked sound, somewhere between a laugh and a cough.

Kendall said, bending gallantly over her hand, "I am profoundly touched, ma'am. The *Quadrille* and I will fly your colors with pride. I have been wanting the new flag. Mr. Richardson, I am more than ever impressed with your good fortune! Allow me to wish you both long years of such happiness as you have at this moment." He picked up his hat.

"Keep in touch with me, Kendall," James managed on an outgoing, exasperated breath, which his erstwhile first mate interpreted as the fullness of emotion.

"Indeed I will, sir. Put a horseshoe over the door for us."

Whe he had gone, James turned to face his wife. He was in such a state she knew he hardly knew where to begin, so she decided to beat him to the draw.

"There! Didn't that go well? No one in the world would dream that we were anything but the most happily married couple!"

"Well," he shouted finally, "of all the— I'll have you

know, madam, that I am capable of making my own decisions."

"Oh, I know," she answered equably, "but see how pleased he was over your situation. He thinks I am a perfect hostess, a devoted wife, and a great patriot. What better impression could anyone ask? I think I did you handsomely!"

"Yes, you made a charming impression. Mr. Kendall was quite overcome," he said scornfully. "And you did me out of a ship—" He broke off and ran his hand down the back of his head in an exasperated gesture. "All your little pretties: 'darling this' and 'my pet' that! Bah!"

"But, James"—she made her eyes widely innocent—"we've only been married three weeks. I'm supposed to be acting like a bride!"

"A bride," he sneered. "You certainly dripped honey equally on us both."

"Why, James, could I possible construe that as jealousy?"

"Jealousy!" He was goaded now beyond speech other than a final "bah" and flung out of the house.

His bad humor was short-lived, partly because he was too busy to remember his anger and partly because he was secretly glad that the matter of the *Quadrille* was settled and he did not feel pulled away from the plantation. Everything was going well with the plantation, his house was perfect, his food excellent, and his wife damned intriguing. This last item gave him some moments of reflection. Somewhere along the line since his marriage, something had changed so subtly he could not put his finger on it. Something that seemed vaguely to threaten his position as master of the situation. In the back of his mind he had had the comforting bulwark for his masculine freedom that whenever he chose he could always go to sea again, or to the army, or anywhere to escape the toils of a too-loving female. But Elizabeth, he discovered with no little discomfort, was very much an individual. She was not running true to form, and it upset him. Gad! He was beginning to go in circles like a mule in a sugar mill. But, by God, there was plenty to enjoy without worrying over what made people tick, himself included. And enjoy it he would. Let tomorrow take care of itself.

However, he found the determination simpler than the doing. It was easy to dismiss everything from his mind when he was astride a horse and busy with the thousand details of the plantation, but Elizabeth was too compelling a presence to disregard. The whole house echoed to her clicking heels, her bubbling laughter, her sharp commands. She was as capricious as a butterfly. Sometimes sweetly submissive, seeming to hang on his every word, and then, before he knew it, she had changed into the most utterly annoying minx, tempestuous, turning everything upside down, putting him on the defensive, and at the same time managing to be tantalizingly desirable.

The morning after Kendall's visit, he had occasion to return to the house, where he found her seated before his big desk, with the plantation books spread out in front of her. She looked up as he came in, with a vacant stare, and when he spoke, held up her hand for silence.

"What are you doing?" he asked, nettled at her preoccupation.

She threw the lead down with sudden anger. "I am merely trying to see if I could keep your books for you. I was adding and you've mixed me up!"

"Who asked you to meddle with that? My God, haven't you found enough to occupy you?"

"Well, I was only trying to please you," she said icily. "You mentioned your dislike of having to keep track of things and I thought I would relieve you, that's all." She rose and stood facing him, her eyes dark and the brow lifted.

He felt the usual flare of desire her anger always stirred in him, the fiercer for being mixed with the knowledge that she had put him in the wrong again. He seized her shoulders and pulled her up to him, intending a light reply that it didn't make any difference. But instead of resisting as she had never failed to do when she was angry, she melted suddenly in his arms and began to sob against his breast.

This was so strange a denouement that he was shocked into an abject apology. Only once before had he seen her in tears, and because she was not a crying woman, which he loathed, it moved him to unusual tenderness.

For the remainder of the time he was in the house, she was as sweet and solicitous as a little wren, but when he returned from the sawmill in the late afternoon, he saw that the account books had been put away, and with the change of her gown for supper, she had donned a different mood. In a frock of blue silk over high stays, she was coolly indifferent and as smilingly serene as a royal princess.

Over the lighted candles, he watched her soft red lips lead the conversation into the broad channels of world affairs, and was surprised at the extent of her knowledge. This was a challenge, and he found himself giving tongue to many ideas, the skeletons of which had laid unclothed in his mind.

While they were at the table it began to rain, softly at first, then increasing to a steady, constant fall. There was no wind and no rushing downpour that would have beaten the young tobacco leaves into the ground. There was only the soft whisper of moisture soaking into the greedy, fertile soil.

James broke off in the middle of a sentence and went to the window. "Planting just finished today. Perfect! A rain like this at this time is worth a thousand pounds. We'll have a crop this year to boast of!"

Elizabeth looked at him thoughtfully. He was, she supposed, what Uncle Adam called a mercantile patriot, despite his fine phrases. For still his own affairs, the welfare of his own possessions, were of paramount importance. Yet, after all, everything stemmed from a personal impetus, and it did not greatly matter whether your convictions were based on a right to freedom or on your desire merely to be free to pursue your own selfish interests. But there was still the nagging idea that it did matter.

She changed the subject quickly. "What finally persuaded the king of France to align himself with American struggles? Oh, I know all that Captain Jones told me, but I remember somebody said he would be afraid to have anything to do with a fight for freedom. You were over there, and I'd like your opinion. You know," she added, smiling, "when you came back you gave me only the lighter side of the picture."

"Well, in this case, certainly, the threatened loss of his colonies. But his hatred of England played a part, too. However, I don't think it will matter much longer what he does. It's fine to have France on our side, and it's fortunate we needed her help now rather than later, because later she may have no help to give."

"What do you mean?"

"I mean that the people of France are as sick of their burden of government as we were of our own. They are being bled white for the money to keep their glittering courts in a splendor at which they are not even allowed to look. The same had begun to happen to us, but we had guts enough to kick about it. Those poor devils are forced to take bread from their children's mouths to buy diamonds for the king's mistresses, and men won't stand that forever. Anyway, I don't think the king had much to do with it. His ministers wrangled him into it and made him think it was all his idea."

"They treat royalty like children," she said scornfully.

"Sure they do, because they act like children, and no American at least is long going to be ruled by a man he considers mentally inferior. I am surprised at the men who still cling to the old feudal principles under the king. My father, for instance, and John. You'd think he'd be young enough to take up a new idea."

It was actually the first time she had thought of John since her marriage. "Where do you suppose he is, James? How I should love to see him!"

"He is wherever Cornwallis is, I imagine"—he scowled, still bitter at the thought of his brother—"and that, the last report, was headed for trying his hand again at South Carolina. I must go to Wilmington soon and find out what's going on. They may need my company again down there."

But he was spared the trip to Wilmington, for Sarah and Thomas Brown arrived shortly after dinner. The rain had stopped and a light wind had sprung up, tearing the clouds into thin wisps. They had walked out onto the gallery in the cool evening that was fresh with the mingled scent of earth and rain, and spring like a heady perfume in the darkness.

It was too much for Elizabeth's formal manner. "Oh, doesn't it smell delicious?" she cried.

"Wonderful," he answered gaily, thinking that his work had been well done and that nature had given him a hand at the propitious time. He felt the love of a man for his land, for the season of the year which shared the power and youth of his maleness, and a great hunger for life and labor and achievement. In the fullness of enthusiasm he turned, according to the nature of man, to his woman, swinging her into his arms as a need for expression of his elation. He kissed her, lightly at first, then hard, with passion, and she returned the caress out of her own compulsion to make the moment articulate.

They heard the carriage coming up the avenue beneath the massed blackness under the magnolias. They drew apart quickly and stood looking down the dark tunnel of leaves with a sudden, spent quiet. Swiftly it crossed his mind to warn her for God's sake not to put on an act for the visitors, whoever they might be, but if he did there was no telling what she might do, so he held his tongue.

"Good evening, good evening, folks!" Thomas Brown

called jovially, and Sarah's greeting was a pale echo. He was in a planter's good humor over the rain. "Well, we gave you a little while to get settled and then the weather almost kept us away. But we'd have come tonight anyway. I've a deal of news."

They moved up the broad steps and into the library.

"Get your tobacco in?" James asked.

"Finished yesterday, and a good thing. James, all hell's broke loose to the south. General Lincoln is facing Clinton at Charleston as you probably know, but it looks like this time there's too big a hole in the dike. Colonel Washington is in Wilmington now, and he sent word our company was to stand ready to march on notice. And there's something else nearer home. Did you know there was a posse out looking for this fellow Fanning?"

"No. But I'm not surprised." He went over and leaned against the mantel. "This thing in the south looks bad if they're calling out the home militia." His brows drew together. The actual possibility of a British victory seemed to have just struck him.

Elizabeth had been trying to give her polite attention to Sarah's compliments on the improvement of the house and to hear what the men were saying at the same time. Now they both frankly abandoned their conversation.

"I had hoped to see this crop through this summer, but I suppose there never would be a convenient time to go," Thomas was saying.

"They simply ought not to take men with families," said Sarah with despair in her voice.

"Why now, love, would you trust our land entirely to the efforts of our young lads?"

"Yes, I would," came the thin answer, "and think how awful it is for Elizabeth—a bride of only a few weeks!"

A mischievous impulse rose in Elizabeth. She did not actually believe James would have to go. Armored in her own preoccupation, since her marriage, she had almost forgotten the war, and it seemed a remote chance that James would really ever have to leave. She had been acting most unbridelike—making no protest at all.

She was so quiet that James glanced at her with vague apprehension, but he was prepared for anything save her reply to Sarah.

"Yes," she said, "but this is war. I shall be proud to lend

my husband to his country. I believe I can take care of things here."

"That's the spirit, Miss Elizabeth," Thomas boomed, and James was relieved that only he himself was aware of her histrionics.

"When do you think we'll move?" he asked quickly.

"Next week likely. Can you be ready?"

"I'll be ready any time." He grinned, feeling excitement rise at the thought.

It was easy for Elizabeth to see what he was thinking. She began to hold her breath, literally, willfully, though it was quite an effort. Constance had told her how to do it once when she stood in imminent danger of corporal punishment, and sure enough she had fainted dead away.

The Browns were preparing to leave and she had risen with them when the room began to swim before her eyes. Everything went black. She put out her hand for support in the suddenly terrifying whirling, to grasp something solid, and her lungs finally demanded and gulped a quantity of air. This gave her back enough consciousness to think, as her eyes closed and she sank to the floor, "This is perfect. Just enough—"

There was a gratifying amount of excitement, and she caught snatches of words—"tried to be brave," "poor little thing—" She kept her eyes closed as James lifted her to the sofa, but as he turned back and said, "Pull that bell cord, Thomas," she took a quick, one-eyed peep to see anxiety on his face. He was actually quite pale!

"Here, I have something," she heard Sarah say.

There was the flutter of a handkerchief against her cheek, and suddenly her whole body was galvanized by the strong whiff of something in a bottle she had not known was being thrust under her nose. Involuntarily, her eyes flew open and she jumped upright, with an angry stare, almost striking the heads bent above her.

"Well," piped Sarah, "I never saw smelling salts act so quickly! Are you all right now, dear?"

"Yes," she stammered, feeling a hot surge of blood in her face with the fear that they might have suspected her trick.

But Thomas was saying excitedly, "By God, Sarah, you fixed it! Now don't you be embarrassed, ma'am. I've seen grown men fall out when they got their marching orders. 'Tis no disgrace for a new bride to faint when her husband gets his."

Sarah still fluttered over her, stroking her hands, fanning her with her handkerchief.

"I—I'm all right now," she said with relief, but one look at James' face showed a wickedly knowing gleam dawning in his eyes.

He pressed her back on the couch as she started to rise, and with irony that was plain to her ears alone, he said, "Now you lie down, angel. I'll see our guests to the door and they will excuse you, I'm sure. You must not exert yourself." He bent and kissed the top of her head, then straightened and beamed fatuously, with a beautifully pretended delicacy, at Thomas. "I suppose this is to be expected. They generally do, don't they—that is, when they are—" His shrug was eloquent.

Sarah said, "Oh, a baby!" And Thomas roared, "Oh, Lord, of course they do! Congratulations, Mistress Elizabeth!"

When James came back from seeing them off, her eyes were blue-black with a fury by no means lessened by his hearty, triumphant laughter.

"That, madam, will teach you to play little tricks on me!" He could not stop laughing. "If you could have seen your face! Come on to bed, my lamb. I swear I've half a mind to make it *so!*"

CHAPTER
13

Next morning, the peace and quiet that had lain over the greening countryside was suddenly gone. No one could say at exactly what hour the faint rumblings and distant sounds had begun that made tense the very air itself. One day there was such a stillness and a lack of anxiety that it was hard to imagine a war going on beyond the rolling blue hills to the north and the flat rice fields to the south, but the next, the road paralleling the Cape Fear began to echo to the steps of marching men, the jangle of chains and harness, and the roll of heavy wagons.

At the plantation, it had begun with Adam Boyd's arrival on a sweating horse with orders for James to gather such members of his company as lived in the vicinity and proceed at once to Wilmington, where they would join the main army for the march to Charleston. Elizabeth caught her hands together to still their trembling as he dismounted and poured out his message, almost before they could give him a greeting.

"I didn't think it would come so soon," James said. "Thomas was here last night, thinking it might be another week."

"Yes, I know, but a dispatch came through in the night from Ben Lincoln, saying he couldn't hold out much longer without reinforcements, and the people of Charleston were pleading with him not to surrender the city, even though it would be sounder strategy to pull out and make a stand farther inland."

"Uncle Adam, you aren't going back into the army, are you?" Elizabeth pulled the back of her hand across her forehead. It came away damp, though the April morning after the rain was almost cold.

"No, they refused to allow it. Say I can't stand another campaign. Bah! I can still show 'em a thing or two! There's plenty to do for us they claim are too old to fight, by George!"

James slapped him on the back. "You're right, sir. It'll be a comfort to us all to know you're around looking after the home front. Are you riding to Oakland?"

"Yes. I'll get the message to Thomas and anyone else you can think of. You might as well be getting ready at the same time."

"Let me see. There's the Bonners, George Cramer, and Alec Simpson."

"I'll get 'em." Adam was like an old war-horse hearing again the sound of drums.

"You come in, Uncle Adam, and have some tea or something," Elizabeth said. "You have plenty of time."

James excused himself as they went into the house. "I must be about my preparations, Mr. Boyd. Tell Thomas I'll meet him at the ferry at three o' the clock this afternoon." He hurried out of the room, shouting for Holy as he went.

Elizabeth unleased a pack of questions on Adam.

"How do you expect me to know how long he'll be gone, child? Ask me how long the war will last. I could answer that as easily."

She dropped her eyes. She had been living in a fool's paradise that, if not completely delightful, had been all-absorbing. Now it was about to be invaded. She had not realized that James would really have to go away, not even last night when Thomas had so plainly told them so. Even then, she had gone on playing her little role, visualizing only what might happen in the pleasant days stretching into summer. But now it had come. She would be alone. Panic seized her at the thought of long days and nights of utter loneliness, without even the sure knowledge of his love to comfort her.

Over his teacup, Adam thoughtfully regarded her stricken face. "You're in love with him, aren't you?"

"Most awfully"—her chin started to quiver, but she steadied it, blinking her eyes rapidly—"but don't you tell him."

"Trust me not to meddle in a love affair," he said with his kind smile as he prepared to leave, "but isn't that a bit of an irregular request?"

"Yes, I guess it is, but—"

"You've cut out a large order for yourself, my dear, and I wish you all the luck in the world."

"Why, Uncle Adam, you talk like you—"

"I think I understand completely. I had my suspicions the night the committee had you on the griddle, but I didn't let on, did I? Though I never would have let them harm a hair of your head. I think, really," he went on softly, "James is in love with you, too, but he's like many another young man caught up in all this turmoil. They are feeling their oats, and what with the war and all they don't rightly know what they do want. Give 'em time and their heads, and they'll come 'round."

Impulsively, she threw her arms around him and the curls at the side of her cheek brushed his ear. "Now, now," he said, patting her back.

"By the way," he said, "almost forgot to tell you: I'm sending Mary and Abigail to Oakland to stay with Sarah until we know what is going to happen. Maybe that will help to keep you from being too lonesome."

"Oh. Oh, that will be nice." She couldn't hurt him by letting him see that Abigail's presence in the vicinity would be no pleasure to her.

When he had ridden away, she went up to the bedroom, where James was supervising the packing of his equipment. Holy, in a pair of his cast-off boots he had varnished to brown mirrors, was excitedly bustling about, his arms full of garments, and a face full of grins because he was being taken along.

James was standing by a window, bent over a long pistol, running a greasy rag through the barrel. He straightened as she came in and faced her with a serious glance. "I've got to talk to you before I go."

"I rather hoped you would!" She tried to give her words a lightness, but it didn't come off very well.

"Holy, take your packing into the other room. You've got everything out of here I'll need."

"Ain't you gwine take dem other black boots?"

"Yes," he answered shortly, "get 'em and get out of here."

"Aunt Mary and Abigail are coming to Oakland for the duration of the war," Elizabeth informed him.

"Good. They'll be company for you, or do you resent the fact that Abigail's gossip had a good deal to do with your being where you are?" He, too, was trying to lighten the moment and the sudden surprising feeling that he'd as soon not

HARMONY HALL 179

have had to go away just yet. He aimed the pistol out the window and squinted down the barrel. "You owe a lot to the jealous nature of women, my dear," he added, throwing her a teasing smile.

"And you, my love, would still have been a lonely old bachelor but for that charming attribute!" she retorted, taking up the gauntlet. "Can I help you do anything? Most wives do."

He finished cleaning the gun and slipped it into the holster. "No, thanks. Holy is quite capable, and I'm glad to see him work for a change. But there is one thing I want to tell you, and I don't know—"

"Oh, really, Mr. Richardson, this is so—"

"If you say 'sudden' I'll slap you!" He laughed. "Be serious for a minute."

She sat down and folded her hands piously.

"As I was saying, I don't know where to begin because I can't know what may come up. I never thought to leave my affairs in the hands of a woman."

"Well, you aren't. Bill's here. He handled things while you were at sea and in France, didn't he?"

"Yes, but poorly. He's not capable of doing more than overseeing. He has no business judgment. His only value is his honesty and the fact that he gets on well with the Negroes."

"Well, I don't see any help for it, or is this your delicate way of asking me to put on breeches and start plowing?"

He threw back his head and laughed. "Might do you no harm at that! But rather let us say it's my clumsy and indelicate way of suggesting that you give him a hand occasionally when it comes to making a real decision. 'Two heads,' you know, even if one is very beautiful and very flighty, and the other practically empty—" This was a touchy point. If he told her flatly to leave it all alone, she'd be likely to take over the whole management out of pure stubbornness; if he told her to run things God knew what she'd do, and something had to be said on the subject. Gad, how women cluttered up a man's world!

"Indeed, sir, I think you are too flattering. Being beautiful is nothing unusual—a common enough characteristic—but 'flighty'—ah, there's a compliment of fine subtlety, a fine and feminine adjective, a—"

"Oh, for God's sake," he said, laughing and pulling her

into his arms, "I never know but one way to stop your prattle!"

She was glad of her helplessness against his strength and his demanding lips. It had been so hard to be flippant with his leaving staring her in the face. Now, in his arms she could give up pretending, for she knew he believed her submission only the answer to a need as urgent as his own.

"Miss me while I'm gone?" he whispered.

"No!"

"Wench!"

She rode to the ferry with him on her little mare. The avenue had never seemed so short, nor had she remembered that the distance around the curve, past the giant oak that split the river road briefly into twin lanes was such a little way. A field spread paralleling the river, then the gentle slope down to the slow, yellow water—that was all. And he was gone. There had not been enough time. Unspoken words that could not pass the constriction in her throat now rose in a wild rush to her lips. She pressed the back of her hand to her mouth after his last waving salute and stood watching the little cavalcade disappear under the canopy of leaves beyond the river. A bluejay planed low over the water, swooped up onto the limb of a pine, and sat scolding and preening his feathers.

Podge brought the ferry back and came up shaking with laughter. "Didja see that nigger of Mist' Richardson's? Funniest thing I ever seen. Thinks he's a general, at least!"

The lump in her throat gave way a little as she remembered Holy on his mule, weighted down with paraphernalia, his feet proudly encased in the shining boots, and a fierce and warlike expression on his face. But still she did not trust herself to speak.

Podge scratched his sparse pate with fingers gnarled by years at the ferry rope. "You know, Mist' Richardson is a damn fine gentleman. I hope he don't get hisself kilt."

"Oh, Podge, don't say it! Don't even think it! He won't."

"I ain't so sure. Them redcoats'll do anything."

"You're coming along splendidly with your house, Podge," she said, to change the subject.

"Yes'm, I am, and if them bastards burn this un down, they'll answer to me!"

"What made you hate them so, even before they burned your house?"

The old man looked at her with the less opaque of his

eyes, as he lowered himself to a seat on a blackened stump. "They taken everything I had in the world, ma'am. My pa and me staked out a parcel o' land, cleared it, and built us a house. We worked day and night tryin' to feed our family, but we never could keep ahead of the quitrents. My little boy was a baby then, just about two and learnin' to walk. Well, he tooken sick, and the circuit preacher that was kind of a doctor, too, said he wasn't gettin' enough to eat. He got somebody to lend us a cow so's we could have milk for him—a lent cow, mind you, but when them yellow-livered skunks come 'round again they took her. 'Twarn't nothin' we could do. They said how was a king to keep a crown on his head if we didn't send him money. Well, little boy died." His voice trailed off into the past, and he rubbed a hand over his face. "I ain't never had no likin' for nothin' much since."

Elizabeth laid a hand on his shoulder. "I'm sorry," she said gently. "If you need anything from the house let me know."

Riding slowly home, she added the old man's story to the growing collection of individual and personal reasons for the conflict, and it occurred to her that there was not a great difference between the colonists under English rule and the Jamaican slaves. Both were human beings, as Uncle Adam said, though she had never given it much thought. In the slaves, with their undeveloped mentalities, the revolt had stemmed from physical causes—empty stomachs and tortures—but in these good people it came from causes proportionately higher as they were higher in the social scale. They had pinned their faith on this new country, upon their right to "life, liberty, and the pursuit of happiness." But the strong and powerful had exploited them viciously, had threatened that right—and now again was revolt.

Perhaps James had understood more of these things than she had thought. In any case, he had gone away to fight for them, and her heart slipped quickly down from consideration of abstractions to its own very real loneliness. Everything had happened so fast that time was telescoped into this heavy and poignant moment.

As she reached the house, the supper bell rang and night came down softly over the fields, darkening the river.

The days were not so bad. She made the rounds in the morning hours to see that everyone was at work: the laundry first, with its steamy air smelling of damp linens, the sadirons, and the big pot of boiling soap outside; in the loom house the women sang in rhythm to the whirring wheels and the measuring hammer tripped with a sharp knock every time eighty yards went around the reel; to the shack where the younger girls made candles. She liked to watch them dexterously pour the boiling wax into shiny molds, then hang them by their white wicks from cooling frames. Old Lulu was back, ruling with an iron hand, stirring her colored brews. In the dairy, crocks of yellow-topped milk stood in rows along the brick troughs, and churn dashers plunked in ragged, reluctant rhythm in the hands of little Negroes.

Everywhere there were details to engage her attention. One morning she went into the kitchen, where Beezie, like some scrawny seeress, muttered incantations before pots hung in the huge fireplace.

"Beezie, haven't you some cake or something I could take Podge?"

His new little house was finished, and Elizabeth had a basket packed with some odds and ends of pottery for his cupboard.

"Yas'm. Got some liddle meat pies, jest finished."

A detachment of cavalry passed her on the river road going toward the north; a column of infantry on a southward march, was up ahead, and on the far bank several wagons waited for the return trip. Podge would have all he could do this morning with no time to cook himself even a meager meal. The foot soldiers were already boarding the ferry as she pulled up in the shade at the side of the road, and the old man's head was bobbing as he regaled his passengers with his customary invectives against the British and the Tories—not taking James' advice at all.

Watching the wagon-loaded craft come back across, Elizabeth recognized Grandma Love, sitting atop her high-piled household goods, and Emmy, big with her sixth child, beside her. They, like many others who had places to go, were seeking the comparative safety of the country. The children were hanging over the railings, and their two spotted mongrels skipped back and forth, barking, under the restive feet of the horses, between the legs of standing passengers, frenzied at the novel transportation. And over all came Grandma's scolding voice.

"I'd as soon stay in Wilmington and take my chances with the redcoats! Leemie! *Git* down off'n that railin'!"

As they pulled up the slippery bank, Emmy lifted her hand in a half-embarrassed salute. Grandma's rigid back turned when she saw Elizabeth and she gave the girl a sharp slap. But Emmy waved again as soon as her mother-in-law's eyes were in the other direction.

Elizabeth smiled, lowered the basket to Podge's doorstep, calling to him that she had brought him some things, and rode off home at a canter. As she reached the house, another detachment of cavalry approached from the horse-pond road. Their sabers glittered in the sun, and as they drew up the leader dismounted. He took off his cap.

"Captain Smite, madam, your humble servant. We are sent by Colonel Reese to the plantations along the river for a handout." He smiled.

Her hand went to her throat. She had heard neither of Smite nor of Reese. Were they loyalists or colonials? The uniform told her nothing, for it was different from any she had seen. Just what did he mean, "a handout?" Were they eating at every plantation along the river?

"I suppose we could fix you some food," she said uncertainly.

"Oh, ma'am, you don't understand." He grinned, suddenly embarrassed, as if his past position in life had not accustomed him to begging. "Colonel Reese wants supplies."

"What—what kind of supplies?"

"Meat, meal, food of any kind. Forage for the animals. Our wagon train was attacked a few days ago, and the loyalists got the whole thing."

"Oh," she said with a relief which Captain Smite recognized at once. His pleasant, boyish face brightened. "You thought we were Tories?"

"I had no idea," she said with dignity.

"Well, ma'am, I've been accused of a lot of things, but that's not one of 'em!"

She smiled then, but doubts and uncertainties were rapidly going through her mind. Would they pay for this stuff? How much to let them have? James had not mentioned such an exigency. "How much do you want? How much do you pay, for instance, for meal?"

Smite looked at her queerly. "We've been having it given, ma'am, but the colonel says we are to pay if it's demanded. I'd say sixpence for five pounds of meal."

She felt the vague rebuke and her cheeks flushed. "I'll call my overseer and see what we can let you have." But to her annoyance, she found that Bill had as little idea of prices as she did. However, the deal was finally settled on a hundred pounds of meal, on a wagonload of hay, eight hams, six sides of bacon, half a beef, and a small cask of scuppernong wine, which all together added up to fifteen pounds, nine shillings.

Payment was offered in Continental paper, which Elizabeth was about to refuse, being sure that James would be furious at her taking anything but hard money, when Smite said, "The Lord knows, ma'am, I'd give you hard money if I had it, but"—he grinned ruefully—"if I had fifteen pounds in gold, I could buy you out!"

It was most upsetting to find that the paper money was so near worthless, and more so not to be sure what to do, but she had to accept what the man had to offer. So she stowed the money away in the attic and, because it was the first she had ever made, despite its apparent deflation, it looked like a splendid amount.

But on her tour of inspection the next morning, she decided that the production of the plantation would have to be increased if drains like this came very often. There were all the slaves to be fed, the household, and all their own livestock. She had a talk with Bill, and together they worked out a few ways whereby savings could be effected and more produced. Bill was little help, however. She had to think up everything herself. But two heads at least made things easier on the one accused of being "flighty."

It was not even by a gradual process that in Elizabeth, Bill Lipman recognized a shoulder of relief for his load of responsibility, and she began to learn what a planter did with his time. Household management was turned over to Mamba, as the broader field challenged her, and she accepted it as a refuge from the loneliness and heartache.

Early mornings found her in the saddle, as the tours of inspection widened to include the sawmill, the fields, the blacksmith shop, the loading landing; found a frown of concentration on her face and a determined set to shoulders bearing for the first time a load heavier than a silken gown. James had asked her to give Bill a hand, but Bill demanded an arm, once he found the hand so sure. No matter, she would show James that a woman could make money as well as a man.

But when at length a second officer from the commissariat arrived with a predetermined quota for woven cloth, she realized that it would be difficult if not impossible. She was not dealing now with a Captain Smite. This was a hard-bitten veteran who laid his demands before her and expected no argument.

"We got Mr. Richardson's plantation down for a hundred yards of cloth. Part linen, part cotton; don't make no difference. How can you let us have it—I mean, how soon and in what amounts?"

"Are you paying in paper or gold?"

The man fixed her with a frown. "We ain't payin'. This here's a contribution everybody is got to make."

"Why, I can't possibly afford to give you that much without payment!"

"You can't afford not to," he retorted. "I reckon there's many a soldier thought he couldn't afford to go to war either, but he's there all the same, a-fightin' for you and everybody else that stays home. The least you can do is to keep a shirt to his back."

This was true, she thought, but James expected the plantation to make money. How could it do so if she had to give away all the produce? "They paid for the food I furnished, why can't they pay for the cloth?"

"Because people have got to have food, but they don't have to have new clothes. Look, lady, I got business. When do we send for the stuff?"

There was the well-remembered look of ruthlessness in the man's eye, which told her that the patriots meant to have her cloth whether she gave it willingly or not.

"I have about ten yards of stout fustian on hand now that was intended for the slaves' clothing. I suppose you can have that."

"Good, I'll take it along now. When can you have the rest? Can you make the most of it linen? Better for bandages."

"I suppose so." The new bed sheets would have to wait. "It ought to be ready by the middle of July."

When she went in the house, she was not much in the humor for Mamba's scolding. "Miss Lizbeth, Ah sho' hopes you doan git a gleam in yo' eye. Doan nobody lak a hahd, schemin' woman."

"I can't help it. I've got to do these things, don't you see?"

"Ah doan see nuthin' but yo' han's is gettin' rough, an' you is out in de sun so much yo' skin gonna look lak a ole boot."

"Well, you don't want us to be without money again, do you?"

"No'm, but you ain't gittin' much, 'pears to me. An' you

ain't wore nuthin' but dem ridin' clo'es since Mist James lef'—you eben smells lak saddle leatheh an raw pine!"

Though she was stung by Mamba's observation that she wasn't making much money, she laughed. "Just wait till Mister James comes back, I'll turn into a lady again!"

Maybe I will get hard and ugly, she thought as she rode along the soft, sandy trail toward the sawmill, but I've got to show James I'm not just "flighty." Behind her the leaves of the tobacco already stood broad and shiny in the sun. The army certainly didn't have to have tobacco. Just wait till the first buyer for that commodity came along. She'd make him show hard money before she even talked to him. And that went for lumber, too!

As she crossed the road and entered the woods where the mill was busily whirring, she saw Abigail riding toward her. She came up at a trot with a friendly greeting, to which Elizabeth replied with some constraint. She had not seen Abigail since her marriage, nor had she had occasion to learn how the girl felt now about her turncoat lover. It was not a pleasant thought that her presence at Sarah's might draw Fanning uncomfortably close.

"We're going to be neighbors for a while," Abigail said in as friendly a manner, as if she had nothing but the kindliest feelings. "Heavens! Don't you find it dull in the country?"

"No, so far I've not had time."

"Come, ride up to the Bartletts' with me, Elizabeth. I haven't had a visit with you since the day you left my little tea party in such a huff. You were so naughty not to sign my pledge. But, of course, you weren't married to a patriot then."

Elizabeth choked back the retort that rose to her lips, but she looked at Abigail steadily until the other lowered her eyes. "I have an errand at the sawmill," she said evenly, turned her horse, and rode off down the path.

She abhorred the thought of the girl's being so near that she would have to see her frequently, for she knew how Abigail had lied about her and done everything she could to get her into trouble. She was a two-faced vixen—a dangerous woman—and knowing she was near was just another worrisome thing she would have to put up with.

CHAPTER
14

It was not many days before every quartermaster in lower North Carolina knew that supplies were to be had at the Richardson plantation, and every officer with orders to proceed up or down the Cape Fear was certain of a good meal and a half-hour respite from the rigors of the march in a cool and beautiful house.

As rumors spread of these patriotic deeds of Elizabeth, there were many who raised surprised, amused eyebrows. One of the men who had known of her situation in Wilmington made one day a chance remark to Podge concerning her apparent change of attitude.

"Well"—the man laughed as he pushed his horse onto the ferry—"Richardson really made a patriot out of her!"

Podge slackened his grip on the rope so that the craft slowed and regarded the man with one-eyed venom. "I'll ask ye to explain that remark, sir. I don't like the sound of it."

"Oh, no offense, old man. I merely meant that it took a good man to make a good woman out of her."

"Thought that's what ye meant," said Podge, and his nose and chin almost met over his firmly clamped lips as he began to pull the ferry back to shore.

"Here! What are you doing? I've got to get across this river."

"No, sirree. Nobuddy rides this boat that don't have a good word for Missus Richardson. And nobuddy had to make her good, either. She was borned like that."

"How the devil do you think I can get across? Come on, get this scow moving."

"It ain't nuthin' to me how you cross. You kin swim fr'all I care," and he started tying up the ropes, so that the passenger, fortunately a good-natured fellow and tremendously amused, had to make some fancy apologies in a hurry.

It was nearing sundown, and waiting on the farther side was a small company of horsemen. Podge had been so riled that he did not notice who they were until they had embarked and were well out into the steam. Too late he realized he was carrying Fanning and his band, who had burned his house. He answered their banter in monosyllables, and when they had ceased to torment him, he listened, much against his will but in favor of good advice, and the burden of their planning sent a horrible fear through him. They would sweep up the river, pillaging plantations for supplies they could turn into cash, and if the owners resisted, there was always the torch.

Podge slyly pretended not to hear or to recognize them, not even when they asked where he got his new house. One of them tossed him a penny for the trip and they clattered away up the road.

He delayed only long enough to spit on the penny and drop it in the water. He tied up the ferry and cut out though the woods that grew along the river to the Richardson plantation. He had not for years exerted his old legs to such speed, and when he rounded the house, he hardly had breath enough to speak.

Elizabeth was going over her accounts when she heard his running steps. "Why, Podge, what is it?"

"They're a-comin'. They're gonna take everything they can find!"

"Who?"

"Men that burned my house. I heard 'em a-talkin' it on the ferry."

Fanning! What on earth was she to do? There was only one gun in the house, and what good would it do against that band? They heard the pounding hooves coming up the avenue.

"Mamba! Tip-toe! Get in here, Podge. They'll kill you if they find you here. Hide him, Mamba." She drew back out of sight, peering out of the side of a window. Tip-toe had whipped out a long-bladed knife. "Put that away, Tip. They'd shoot you in a minute if they saw that knife."

They were almost in front of the house, but for some reason it appeared they were not going to stop. They rode through the horse-pond road with no diminishing of speed and presently could be heard turning back into the highway. Why they had passed her by with only this frightening show she could not imagine. She leaned weakly against the wall, trembling.

Podge was shaking with relief and amazement. "Said they was gonna hit ever' plantation on the river. I cain't understand—them snake-mothered bastards!" He spat in the direction they had taken, without regard for Mamba's shining floor.

Elizabeth said nothing. At their pace she could identify none of the band except Fanning. For some reason she had been unmolested with but this crazy gallop through her property, but the other places beyond might not fare so well. This thought sent her into action.

"Get Mr. Lipman's horse, Tip," she said, running toward the sally port where Dolly was tied, waiting to be unsaddled.

Mamba shouted after her, "Whah you goin'? You cain't go nowhere off by yo'se'f wid dem mens loose in de country!"

But she spurred Dolly into a run and took the little cow path that ambled along by the river bank, Tip-toe loping hard behind her. It was only two miles to George Love's place this way and four by the road. Twilight began to spread over the land, and a breeze from off the water rushed against her hot cheeks. If only she could hurry faster! Emmy's confinement so near, and all those other children—war was bad for the soldiers, but it was no play for those at home!

The supper lights were on in the Loves' house as they drew up, but there was something else happening outside. Figures moved stealthily from the smokehouse to dairy to loom house, and each was loaded down. Suddenly there was loud talk and confusion, and over all Grandma's screeching voice rising in frenzied vituperation.

"You cain't go up dah now, Mis' Lizbuth," Tip whispered fearfully.

"No, I'm too late, but maybe we can make it on to warn the Bartletts."

They pushed on another three miles. She left the Bartlett boy flying toward the house on his fat legs to give the alarm, and turned back down river. They had gone but a mile when they saw the dull, red glow that spread fanwise over the tops of the trees.

"They're burning the Loves' house, Tip!" Quite suddenly, tears were running down her face. It's nothing to cry about, she told herself, angrily brushing them away, but they kept flowing, out of excitement and weariness and dismay.

In the Loves' yard they could see the line of slaves passing buckets of water hand over hand from river to house. Tip tied the horses well out of range of the heat, and dashed up to lend a hand with a great, heavy bedstead being hauled outside. Emmy's children were standing about in their nightgowns sobbing; Grandma was racing around like an old charger, giving conflicting orders, screaming threats and vengeance, and otherwise spreading hysteria.

Emmy sat dry-eyed and stunned a little aside. But at the moment there was no time for comforting words. Elizabeth saw that a brick addition to the house was not yet touched by the fire, and quickly ordered the slaves to change the direction of their buckets to where it might do some good. At least there would be shelter if they could save this wing. But a door was open into the hall connecting the two sides of the house. If the flames began to lick through there would be no chance. She ran to the far end, into the door farthest from the fire, and made her way through the red murk and stifling smoke and banged the door shut. Instantly the pull of the draft stopped. If they could get enough water now at the juncture of the two wings . . .

Outside again, she saw the wooden part of the structure had crumbled inward, and after one great flare the flames began to die down. Her face was stinging with heat, eyes and nose smarting from smoke, and her hands were blistered from contact with the bucket handles she had snatched from the slaves in order to direct their puny force to better advantage.

Grandma looked up, saw her, started to speak, then shut her mouth. The screeching stopped, and presently, shoulder to shoulder, they heard the last hiss of the wet embers.

Weakly, Elizabeth dropped down beside Emmy on her pallet of quilts. She pushed her damp hair out of her eyes and managed a smile at the girl's torrent of grateful words.

"I'm sorry I couldn't get here in time."

A few feet in front of them Grandma stood and surveyed what was left of her house. "The low-down, sneakin', yellow-bellied sons o' bitches!" she croaked, and they suspected that for the first time in her long matriarchy the old lady was close to tears.

Elizabeth flung herself out of the saddle and into Mamba's arms.

"Praise Gawd you is back." Mamba pushed her off and

looked at her. "But I cain't see is you black or white. It's a gent'mun in de library waitin' to see you."

"Oh, Mamba, send him away. I can't see anybody tonight. I'm too tired. We've been trying to help save the Loves' house. Those men set it afire!"

"Well, dis here man's been waitin' a good little while. Say he a frien' o'yourn. Seeks lak a perlite young man. He ain't gonna hold yo' looks again' you when he know you been at a fyah."

She dragged herself into the house, and there, comfortably ensconced on the sofa, sat David Fanning.

"What are you doing here?" she demanded, her breath catching less in fear than in anger.

"Good evening, Mistress Richardson," he said, rising and coming toward her, "you've changed your name since I saw you last and, it seems, your manners too. You are not so gracious. I came to pay my respects to the bride. It's been too long since I've had the pleasure of your company, and when I heard that your husband was away, I hastened right out to call. He does not care for me, and you remember I always take advantage of my opportunities."

"Well, you have no opportunity here, unless, of course, you came to treat my house with the same charming courtesy you showed the Loves'."

"Oh, that," he tossed off lightly, "I try to hold the boys down, but they get excited and playful."

"Playful! Get out of here," she stormed between clenched teeth, "get out, and don't ever set foot on my property again." She was so furious she was entirely careless of his ability to take revenge.

"How beautiful you are," he said, moving closer. "Now, now, don't throw that quirt. It wouldn't hurt me in the least. I had hoped we might be friends. Don't you get a bit lonely with Mr. Richardson away? I remember a time when you encouraged my attentions."

"That was long ago, before I was married and before I learned what a scoundrel you are. Will you leave, or shall I have you thrown out?"

"You seem to have a flair for attracting scoundrels," he said, his black eyes very bright and his cherry-colored lips wet and smiling. "Come over and sit down. I know you are tired from fighting that fire we started." He grasped her arm, trying to pull her to him. "I'd like to start one you wouldn't care to fight."

"Don't you dare touch me! If you don't go—"

"Perhaps I can tell you something to make you more, shall we say, cordial?"

"Nothing you could say would interest me in the least, and now—"

"Not even if it were something pertaining to the scoundrel who so gallantly offered you the protection of his name?"

Did he really have news of James?

"I should not consider a marriage binding," he continued, "if one of the partners attached to himself a third party."

"You would not likely consider a marriage binding," she retorted contemptuously. "What are you talking about?"

"About the very common practice of the officers taking women on the marches with them. I assure you it's done by some of our finest gentlemen, and it's very convenient. They wash your clothes and warm your bed, but I think if I were the wife left at home, especially one so young and beautiful, I would not feel strictly bound to celibacy during his absence."

A slow beating pounded in her throat, and he saw that his shaft had struck.

"My husband took no woman with him."

"My little dear," he said, throwing tenderness into his voice, "how little you know. I was at the tavern when he arrived in Wilmington, and heard him bargaining with Lal Dorsey for his bond girl, Susan. And when the column marched, there she was with her bundles and a grin a yard wide on her face, matching steps with others of her kind."

"It's not true," she shouted, trying by the very force of her words to wipe out the fear that it might be.

Swiftly he pulled her into his arms, and before she could turn her head, the red lips had covered hers. "I'll come again when you've had time to think it over," he whispered, releasing her in his own good time. "Maybe you'll decide I'm not a bad substitute."

Spent and sick and furious, she flew up the stairs and scrubbed her mouth.

June came in with humid, dizzying waves of heat. With voluptuous abandon, with orgiastic extravagance, the rich earth poured forth abundantly everything from reaching vines to a multitude of mosquitoes. The tobacco flourished in the fields, and in the bottom lands along the river the corn stood shoulder-high. Elizabeth threw herself into the work with a passionate disregard for everything but the money to be wrenched from the men who came to claim the largess of her land, and the gift of whatever could be spared to the army. But more and more she found herself sacrificing her hard-won produce on the basis of the almost worthless Continental paper. She kept Podge supplied with food and shared the rapidly decreasing stock in her own smokehouse with the Loves. It could not be built up again until fall, she knew, when cold weather would allow the pigs to be turned into pork and the great sides of beef to hang in the hickory-scented darkness.

Wearily, she went over her accounts, trying to make the figures add up to a more imposing total. James would expect a full till when he returned. She wondered why she cared what he expected or why she continued to work and worry for a man who loved her not at all. She tried not to believe Fanning's story, but there had been something in his eyes that had told her it was true. No word had come from James, and there was no happiness or joy to uphold her through the long days of labor—labor that had begun to be not entirely for his benefit. She had to admit that. Into the more obvious reasons for keeping things going to the best of her ability, another had forced its way into her consciousness. In helping supply the army, she was fighting like any soldier to keep the British from her home. From the stories of Podge, the Widow Crane, and others like them, she knew what would happen if the king's men won the war. There would be no more clear-eyed young officers who came and asked politely for "handouts." There would be only with horrible regularity the ravening tax-gatherers who would make the greater part of one's labor count for nothing and, in the end, claim even the goose that was laying the golden eggs.

This was a burning fear; her love for James, a slow, consuming fire; and the only solace, sleep, which came with aching shoulders at the end of the long days. She had neither the time nor the inclination to attend the spinning and sewing bees of the other women along the river, and only occasionally did one or two of them come by to pass her news they might have gathered, or to sit companionably for an hour with a lapful of knitting.

Abigail drove Mary and Sarah over one evening after supper. Elizabeth had gone out onto the gallery to sink tiredly into a chair and watch the past-full moon slip up over the river and turn the terraces into grassy gold, when she heard the carriage in the drive. And suddenly she was glad of company, even though it entailed having to be civil to Abigail.

She led them through the house and to the back gallery. Frogs down in the lagoons made a monotonous accompaniment to the field slaves in the quarters near the swamp, half-crazy with the mosquitoes, singing to ease their troubles.

"I had a communication from Adam today," Mary said. "He sends you his regards."

"Oh, thank you. Where is he, Aunt Mary?"

"He's in Halifax, trying to frame a suitable constitution for the state, and the Democrats and the Conservatives are quarreling among themselves as to which way it ought to be."

Sarah waved her turkey-wing fan. "The Democrats seem to think everybody ought to have a place in the government whether they are landowners or not. It sounds very well to say that all men are born free and equal, but they're not and never will be."

"Well, unfortunately, your point is still open to argument, Sarah," Mary replied, and Elizabeth found herself wondering. A year ago she had thought the idea ridiculous. She listened in silence to the discussion, glad not to have to talk.

"But Adam's burden at the moment," Mary went on, "is, while granting them the right to vote, to hold in check the element of recklessness engendered in those people who suddenly find their hands full of a power they've never had before. He says that some of the judges they're trying to elect never even studied the law."

"Imagine *electing* a judge, anyway!"

"Yes, I agree with you there, Sarah. William Hooper wrote what he thought on the subject. He said, 'I admire no part of the Delaware plan more than the appointing of judges during good behavior. Limit their political existence, and make them dependent on the suffrages of the people, that instant we corrupt the channels of public justice.'"

"Well, it's all too bad," Sarah murmured, "I don't suppose any country ever started off with a cleaner slate politically than Ameri— I mean, the United States. I do hope our good men up there in Philadelphia will see that it's founded properly."

Abigail stirred from where she sat on the gallery floor leaning her back against a pillar. "All this talk of democracy is one thing, but Caesar proved long ago in Rome that a government loses strength and finally falls by making too many concessions to hoi polloi."

HARMONY HALL

Elizabeth felt Mary's sigh as she changed the subject. "Wasn't it terrible about the Loves' house being burned? I just wonder what sort of renegades that band was!"

A quick glance at Abigail gave no clue as to whether she knew, so Elizabeth said nothing. Aunt Mary had enough on her mind without knowing any more about David Fanning.

But Abigail said, "It seems strange to me, Elizabeth, that you were unmolested here when others farther away were not."

So she *did* know it was Fanning!

Before she could form a reply, there came a vigorous tug on the bell down at the river landing. They all rose, startled, as a man came up the walk in the moonlight. His left arm was missing, the sleeve of his shirt pinned up against his shoulder. As he drew nearer they could see that he was quite young, with a boyish face and a thatch of hair so curly it defied all attempts at clubbing it into a queue.

"Hello!" he called. "Is this the Richardson place?"

"Yes!"

"Well, ma'am, Colonel Richardson asked that I stop and say he is well." The young man had served many such commissions along his route and had learned to pour out his good news first.

"Oh. Oh, thank you," she said, her fingers twisting together. "How does the fighting go? We hear it's very fierce."

"General Lincoln has surrendered Charleston to the British, ma'am."

"Oh, no!" the ladies cried in a breath.

"Yes, he couldn't hold out with what he had. The North Carolinians got there in time, but Colonel Buford was intercepted on his march from Virginia by Colonel Banastre Tarleton and cut to pieces. I mean literally, too. He killed nearly every man of them, brutally, viciously, not to have to bother with prisoners." His voice became louder and more excited as he talked.

"Where is Colonel Richardson?" Elizabeth asked quietly.

"He led his company in a very fine escape, ma'am, for I was with him. I reckon they're somewhere on their way out of South Carolina, but the forces in the city were all taken prisoner. Charleston is a mad house. They're compelling all the citizens to take the oath of allegiance to the British crown, and many are doing it to save their lives and property. They can't do anything else hardly, but I've an idea most of them don't consider it binding. A few of them like

Marion and Sumpter and Pickens wouldn't take it and have fled to the woods and swamps to organize everybody they can get into guerrilla bands to strike back when they get a chance. It would break your heart to see women and children from the finest homes in Charleston camping around fires in the swamps. Clinton is leaving Cornwallis in charge of South Carolina, and you never saw such plundering and murdering. They are capturing the slaves as fast as they can and shipping them to sell back in the Indies."

He paused for breath, and Mary said, "That means they'll be on our own soil before long."

"I'm afraid it does, ma'am. Our armies are so worn out and disheartened and the British have got Georgia and now South Carolina, and everything in the East practically except West Point, that a lot of people doubt if it's worthwhile to go on fighting."

"Do they really feel that way?" Abigail asked with a certain quick intensity.

The boy looked at her curiously. "I've talked to some who do, but I can't say I liked 'em better for their opinions."

"Well," said Sarah in a pained tone, "I wish they would stop, sometimes I honestly do. Sometimes I think we ought to have accepted the peace proposals England offered us in '78—they granted nearly everything we asked for."

"They will not stop fighting," Mary said with quiet conviction, "until we have made sure and safe the independence we've declared."

"Have you had your supper?" Elizabeth asked, seeing the boy sway slightly.

"No, but that's all right, ma'am. I've my men in the boat down there."

"How many are there?"

"Five."

"Oh, you sounded as if you had a regiment." She smiled. "Ask them in."

The men ate with starved relish, talking all the while of the hardships of their flight from the south as though they were parts of some sport. They had all been wounded and were going home on furlough, where they had volunteered to raise such recruits as they could from among the population in their own districts. They had had their horses shot from under them, and had walked all the way to Wilmington, hiding in the swamps and forests from Tory parties, eating berries and roots, catching rides whenever they could with a wagon train or a farmer, and finally managing to borrow a boat for the last lap up the Cape Fear. But their enthusiasm still ran high, and to a man, they intended rejoining the forces as soon as they were again in fighting condition.

This is the kind of man I've been keeping shirts on, Elizabeth thought, with a feeling of pride because she had.

"We ought to be getting home, Aunt Mary," Abigail said, and Sarah heartily concurred. The tales of horror they had listened to had not made more attractive the thought of driving back through the forest in the dark.

When they were gone and the last clunking sound of the soldiers' oars had died into silence up the river, Elizabeth went back to the gallery and sat alone in the hot, still semi-darkness. She ought to go to bed. Tomorrow would be another busy day. Matt Rowan had sent word that he would come to buy lumber, and she must have a clear head to bargain a lot of hard money out of him. Besides, she would probably have to take a hand with the spinning herself to have ready the rest of the cloth she had promised the army.

But James had sent her word. He was well. Nothing more. For all its brevity, the message spun a thread from somewhere across the lonely miles to her heart. A meager evidence that his thoughts had turned toward her, however briefly, even though his body claimed the comfort of other arms than hers. It was enough to live on—for a while. But, oh, where was her pride?

A mockingbird in the climbing rose at the gallery's end awoke with a chirp, then poured a flood of silver song on the night. The cape jasmine forced their heady fragrance into her breathing, and as she looked out over the sleeping fields, she felt that here was pride—enough, perhaps. To keep in peace and fruitfulness these rolling lands, to know the joy of working hand in toiling hand with "Nature's God," was a transcendental thing that sustained and lifted the soul above the lesser tribulations of the heart. This, in truth, made all men equal: the Tidewater aristocrat, the backwoods farmer; this, the taproot of all humanity thrust deep into the earth, drawing forth the vital essence for the burgeoning of human life and personality. There *must* be freedom in this land!

Vaguely comforted, she went up to bed.

Clouds obscured the moon, and all night long a downpour rattled on the roof in gusts and flurries. But when morning came, the sun broke through and the birds in the ivy vines against the walls went wild with joy. Elizabeth dressed quickly, eager to match wits with the first customer she would feel no shame in besting if she could.

After breakfast, she went down to the landing and soon recognized Matt Rowan in a small boat, standing upriver.

"Well, well," he said effusively, stepping out onto the dock. "How is Mistress Richardson this fine morning?" He touched his rusty bag wig with a scarred forefinger in salute.

"Quite well, Mr. Rowan. I have your lumber rafted for you," she answered coolly, fixing his protruding eyes with a look so level that his wavered and slipped around to take in the raft lying at the mouth of the creek.

"Sure nice place James got here. Done a lot to improve it, he has. You oughter seen it before. Old Man Parker didn't do a thing but putter around in his gardens."

She made the same discovery that others had made: Matt would talk all day if allowed. He sat down on a pile of cloth bales and took snuff from a cracked tortoise-shell box.

"The lumber, Mr. Rowan, I will sell you for nine pence per foot."

"Oh, yes, the lumber. Pretty good this year, is it?"

"Pine trees don't change a great deal, Mr. Rowan."

Matt roared with laughter. "No, don't s'pose they do. Hope we can make a deal." He looked up at her, seeming to change the subject. "You know, James' new ship has been on the ways at the yard all this time." It was a statement that admitted of no argument, so she did not answer. "So busy in the spring, didn't get it finished. He still owes me a thousand pounds on it."

"I'm afraid that's Mr. Richardson's business, sir," she said sternly, so as not to let him know she was terrified lest he go away without buying.

"Well, now, I was thinkin' it might be sorter nice if you let me have the lumber for the balance due on the ship, and"— he glanced up with a quick movement of his shifting eyes— "when James comes back home he'd have his nice new vessel all paid for by his clever little wife."

Elizabeth knew of the schooner—had known of it since the night in Nassau when she first met James. But she also knew that James had purposely held up completion of it until times should be more settled. However, now that the *Quadrille* was gone to the navy (she herself had worked that!), wouldn't it be fine to present him with the surprise of a new one for shipping his own crops? She made some rapid computations:

HARMONY HALL

a thousand pounds due on the ways, and two thousand pounds worth of lumber here. The gleam Mamba feared came into her eyes.

"You mean *part* of the lumber, of course?"

"Well, you see, the ship's got a monetary value way above the raw lumber—way yonder."

"Mr. Rowan, I am very busy this morning, and I'm sure you are, too, and yet here you sit wasting both our time." She smiled at him sweetly, but with gentle reproof.

Matt squirmed on the bales. He began to be less enthusiastic over his idea of coming to buy while James was away.

"One thousand pounds *and* the finished schooner," she said firmly.

"Now, Mrs. Richar'son, I know your husband well, and I don't think—"

"Mr. Rowan, that is my price, and I'm making a great concession in taking the ship at all. Perhaps I shouldn't anyway, since I don't know his wishes in the matter."

"Oh, it's what he intended, ma'am." Matt was getting uneasy. He had to have the lumber, and he had put over the ship idea, even though not so cleverly as he had expected. Women were funny critters. She might change her mind on even this much of a bargain. He'd better take her up on it before she did. Though he had assured her to the contrary, he knew there had been some doubt of James' ever taking title to the schooner. There had been some talk of selling his equity to the government.

Matt had a thought, then, that was not much to his credit, but he had made his brags in the taproom that he could best any woman in a deal, and he dare not take back the story of this one up to present negotiation. Well, it would be a word-of-mouth sale—no papers—women didn't know about such things, and who was to say he hadn't got the whole raft for a thousand pounds? He could convince James he'd never heard anything about the ship's being mixed up with it.

"All right, Miz' Richar'son. I'm a soft touch for the ladies! One thousand pounds and the schooner. Sold!" He pulled out a wallet fat with Continental paper.

"You sent word to Bill that your payment would be in gold, else I would not even have talked with you. Was that a bait to make us hold the lumber against other buyers?"

"Why, there must of been a mistake."

"There was no mistake, Matt Rowan."

Reluctantly then, he pulled upon the drawstring mouth of

the leather bag beneath his coat, dumped out a pile of gold, and started to count it. Couldn't get by with the paper money, but he'd still get the lumber without a bill of sale.

But as he handed over the heavy coins, Elizabeth called to Bill. He came forward from the little shack that served as the loading office, bringing a sheaf of papers in his hand. When Matt looked up and saw him, his jaw dropped. By durn, she had him hog-tied! He slowly scrawled his name on the bottom sheet.

Jubilant at her success, Elizabeth went hurriedly back to Mamba, the bag of gold clutched against her breast. This would swell the account!

Mamba listened, grinning at the story of the bargaining, then sobered when she got to the part about the ship. "How you know Mist' James want you t'sell his lumber fo' dat boat?"

"Well, of course he wants it. He can't use the *Quadrille* and we've got to have a ship for the tobacco in the fall. And look, Mamba, I got gold for it!"

"Mens doan lak fo' de women to be *too* smaht, honey."

But she only tossed her head and skipped up to the attic, where the paper rewards of her previous salesmanship nestled in the metal box hidden back of a loose brick in the chimney. This will please him tremendously, she thought, out of her own high spirits.

She was interrupted by Mamba's excited calls. "What is it?" she cried, hurrying down the steps, the bedraggled train of her riding habit swirling out behind her.

"Come and see!" came the thrilling tones of James' voice up the stairwell.

CHAPTER
15

Now in the half-hour before supper, Elizabeth sat at her dressing table. About her the floorboards creaked beneath the weight of the excitedly attendant Mamba.

"Ah is thankful to see you in a decen' dress agin. Ah sho' is," she growled, anxiously keeping up a flow of talk designed to be diverting. Her sharp eyes had taken in at a glance the loving relief flooding Elizabeth's face at James' arrival this morning, then her quick withdrawal into a pose of indifferent gaiety. She had been hopeful that something would happen to dissolve the lump of uneasiness in her own heart that what she had feared from the first in this marriage was true. But the hope was pale now.

She brushed the black curls around her twisted fingers with a skill that denied rheumatic joints, then reached for the powder bowl. "Ah laks to see you lookin' purty, honey."

"I don't want any on my hair tonight. It's silly to waste flour now."

Mamba, with a look, supplicated the heavens for knowledge to understand this victory of economy over vanity, and handed Elizabeth her hoops. "You is gonna weah dese, Ah hopes. Dat dress ain't look lak nuthin' widout 'em."

"All right, give them here. I promised you I'd be a lady again." She buckled the contraption around her waist and put her arms into the sleeves of her gown. Downstairs, she could hear the monotone of conversation between James and Colonel Washington, whom he had brought home with him, over their glasses of rum. "If I can get through this evening, I can do anything," she said to herself, her mind running rapidly and fruitlessly over the day.

When the men had arrived this morning, she had wanted to rush wildly into James' arms, but remembered to slow her steps in time. After nearly three months of his absence, and the awful thoughts of that bound girl possibly being with him, it was not easy to push herself to reach again that stage of easy, careless bantering. Nor was it easy to drop the load of anxiety and responsibility she had carried. There was so much that must remain unsaid, and much that must be talked about. Now that the time was here, she felt dubious about the wisdom of her negotiations with Matt Rowan, and also that she had not stuck strictly to the letter of his orders to give Bill merely a hand.

Colonel Washington's presence had helped, of course, and in spite of everything, she had been relieved when they stayed at the house only long enough for light refreshment before remounting and riding off to various nearby points in search of gunpowder and recruits. It had given her time to put her thoughts in order, and Mamba time in which to do the same for her body.

The old woman had helped her into the little tin tub of hot water into which she had dropped the bruised leaves of rose geranium. Her skin emerged soft and rosy, and the relaxing bath took most of the aches out of her shoulders, so that when James came upstairs, having sent Colonel Washington to his own room, she had her courage back and was well on her way toward really feeling the lightheartedness she must assume.

Though he did not know the effort it cost her, she was sweetly yielding in his arms. She recognized at once, and with some gratification, that the force of his ardor was not diminished by the tavern wench. Perhaps this Susan person was more satisfactory at washing clothes, she thought contemptuously.

When at length he took himself off to his own room to shave and dress, she must come along and tell him all that she had been doing. The fields appeared to be in good shape, but then they always did under Bill's hand, he had said. Had any buyers come? Had she found it necessary to send to town for anything?

And so the stormy session had begun.

She perched on the edge of a chintz-covered hassock and began by answering his questions. Of her long hours of labor in taking over, out of necessity, the whole management of the plantation, she said nothing, and she knew she was safe from Bill's telling him. Preferring to have him believe she had done but little, playing at the business, she told him lightly and not in too much detail what had gone on during his absence.

Surprisingly, he had not seemed much perturbed at her taking paper money for the stuff she had furnished the army and only a little less pleased at her gift of the cloth. Emboldened, she began to tell him of the sale of the lumber.

"Mr. Rowan thought he had me when he said you owed him a thousand pounds for the schooner you've had on the ways all this time, and he wanted the whole raft of lumber for the balance!"

James whirled to face her, the razor suspended over the bowl. "You mean he had the gall to—"

"Oh, but I didn't let him get away with it! I made him give me a thousand pounds *and* the schooner!"

"But there was three thousand pounds worth of lumber— even more now that prices have risen. You mean you let him talk you into making a deal on that ship when God knows when it'll be usable?"

"Yes. I thought you would need it in the fall, now that you don't have the *Quadrille* anymore."

"Well, I'll be everlastingly— Don't you know Clinton is on his way to Wilmington, and unless we can raise a bigger and better army than we've got now, the British will take everything there for their own use?"

"How could I know all that?" Her anger was rising at his lack of appreciation, when she had thought her deal so clever, so designed to please him.

"You might have guessed it. I am surprised at Bill's letting you do it. You might at least have consulted me on a matter as big as that. A thousand pounds is not easily come by, and here I've got a useless ship instead. You tricked me out of a vessel I might have used, then hand me one I don't want. Good God! Women in business!" He threw down the razor and buried his indignant face in the towel.

"You're the most unreasonable person I ever saw," she flared back. "How could I consult you? I just had to do the best I could. Bill didn't know *what* to do. The trouble with you is that you want to win the war but you don't want it to cost you anything—that's the trouble with a lot of people!"

"That doesn't excuse you for giving Matt Rowan a raft of lumber for a schooner I haven't intended to finish since the war began. Matt knew that," he declared angrily, uncomfortably conscious that she had put him in an unfavorable light.

"No, I confess I did that because I thought it would please

you, but you liked almost as little the fact that I have contributed to the commissaries cloth and food instead of turning it into money. Don't you think I'd rather have kept the fine linen for the house, the cloth for our slaves, and the food for our own use?"

"When did you become such a patriot as to make such willing sacrifices for the cause?" he scoffed, turning the tables on her, making an acrimonious climb back from the momentary decline of his self-esteem.

When, indeed? She had no answer for that. She had merely done what seemed right and necessary at the time. Her heart was pounding with disappointment and fury topping the emotional turmoil she had been living in, and she could not trust herself to speak.

"Another thing," he continued, wanting to wound, "how does it happen that David Fanning so courteously left this house alone when he caused such havoc up above?"

"He did come here," she said, surprised at the firmness in her voice. "He and his men galloped through the horse-pond road with apparently no intention of stopping."

"Did they stop?"

"No."

He would have liked to shake more information out of her, but he only looked at her with elaborate disbelief.

"All right!" she cried. "If you don't believe me, ask Podge, ask Mamba and Tip-toe! And if you don't like the way things are going around here, stay and take care of them yourself!" And she had swept out of the room, slamming the door behind her.

Now, getting into her dress, she tried to still her shaking hands. To appear the loving wife, the charming hostess, would take all the force of will she could muster. Mamba fastened around her neck the little shell necklace James had given her in Nassau.

"A man is a unappreciative sumpin', Mis' Lizbuth," she grumbled, as if she had been attending the trend of her thought. "All dey wants wid a woman is somebody to brag to an' to sleep wid. Yo' granmaw DeRossett knew she wuzn't 'sposed to have no sense, but she jus' went on her smaht little way, doin' what she want, payin' no 'tention to yo' grandpaw, and purty soon he come a-cottonin' back, all smiles, thinkin' he wuz de big strong pusson put all de ideas in her haid."

She did not answer Mamba's attempted comfort. Curiously,

she was thinking of John. He would have been proud of her efforts even if they hadn't been directed exactly to his liking. No matter what she did, it would have been right with him. She wondered, if it were possible to go back, if she would choose the quiet peace of a love like his for the anguished but thrill-packed relationship with James.

"Miz' Lizbuth," Tip-toe called from the foot of the stairs, "suppah is served."

As they sat down to the table, her spirits rose. She was well-gowned again, the table was beautifully appointed, and there were two gentlemen to furnish conversation. Even if one was an irate husband, it was a far cry from the evenings when she had sat alone, not bothering to get out of her dusty riding habit, not even caring how her food was served. She glanced at James and felt her resourcefulness challenged at the sight of his easy grace as the good-humored host.

"I was most surprised to see you here so soon after we had word of you, James," she said pleasantly.

"When did that messenger arrive?" he asked, having forgotten all about commissioning the man to stop.

"Only last night, dear. You must have followed close on his heels."

"Something must have delayed him then. His group left me in the south two weeks ago."

"Colonel Washington, I am glad you were one of the few who escaped Banastre Tarleton."

"And I, madam, thank you. There has seldom been such a butcher in all the annals of warfare." His face looked like a moon face painted on—so different from General Washington's one could scarcely believe them cousins. But the colonel was quite a charming man, with a sense of humor and no shrewdness at all. Elizabeth decided she could put on a pretty good show without arousing his suspicions. She allowed her eyes to widen at James, "Oh, my darling, do keep out of his way. You can't think how it would grieve me if you became a victim of his sword!"

Colonel Washington looked at his host enviously, with twinkling eyes. "James, I think you are an extremely lucky devil!"

"Oh, he is! He always manages to take care of himself, and to come out on top of every situation even if—"

"That was not my meaning, Mrs. Richardson. I heard in Wilmington of your patriotic works out here, and now to find such devotion hand in hand with beauty and a heart afire with love—the man who has all this for his own is undoubtedly lucky."

"You honor me too much, sir," she murmured demurely, observing from between her lashes that the young man whose good fortune was being lauded looked ready to burst.

"In truth, I do not. Not upon another estate have we had so delectable a meal, nor found a house so tidy, the mistress so agreeable."

It had been a long time since men had had time or been in the humor to pass compliments. But the "delectable meal" almost made her laugh. There was only ham and bacon in the smokehouse, and to keep James from being aware of the frugality of their board she had sent Tip to the woods to find mushrooms and wild raspberries; Mamba knew all the wild herbs; Beezie had a way of making an honest vegetable out of a rutabaga; and she herself had sacrificed one of her setting hens to the pot of dumplings.

"I could only wish, Colonel Washington," she said, "that every woman had the incentive for trying to make her home the happy, comfortable place that I am blessed with! My dear husband is so appreciative of my efforts, 'tis a privilege to work for his approval."

James coughed into his napkin, recovered himself, and joined in the game of self-defense. "I beat her when she doesn't do to suit me." He winked at the delighted guest.

"Oh, he does no such thing, Colonel." She laughed, and treated James to a brief but evil glint of her eyes. " 'Tis only a tongue lashing, and that as gentle as a cat licking a newborn kitten!"

William Washington shook with laughter. "I think the war must be hardest on happy people like you. Some couples don't care about being separated, but you must miss this jollity in each other's company most cruelly."

For his benefit, Elizabeth threw an exaggeratedly wicked and teasing glance at her husband, which the colonel considered most captivating. "Yes," she said, dimpling, "once when I was a child, I had a loose tooth which I enjoyed pushing back and forth with my tongue. When my father pulled it with a string, I missed it no end."

Even Tip-toe could not resist a grin contracted from the laughter around the table.

"Well," said Washington, wiping his eyes, "I shall certainly hate to take you away tomorrow, James, but Gates needs recruits and we've got to help him get 'em. Haven't had such a pleasant time in months, and I shall never forget—what did you say the name of your place is?"

"Why, I never have—" James began, but Elizabeth stopped him.

"Oh, James, aren't you ashamed not to have told him? The name of our plantation, Colonel, is Harmony Hall. We named it that because it's filled with love and happiness. A cross word within its walls is a thing unknown!"

And the evening wore away in such merriment that when their guest had bade them good night and gone to his room, they were both in the humor to continue the badinage for the sheer fun of it.

To see him go this time was worse than it had been at first. For a day and a night she had had the joy of his presence, whether in good humor or bad, and she had been able to drop the load of work and worry for a pleasanter role. Now again the long, lonely days stretched ahead. He had made no more criticism of her transactions, but she knew his disapproval was still there even though, according to his nature, he already considered it water under the bridge. It had shaken her faith in her own ability—not a very comfortable frame of mind in which to approach the work that must be done. She wondered dully how long she would be able to spring back to play this game so lightly at a moment's notice if necessary, in the days to come.

After the fall of Charleston and the success of the British throughout South Carolina, the river road began to be more congested than ever. It was the main artery from the sea to the northern counties upon which Cornwallis had his eye, and the logical march for regiments going either north toward Hillsboro, where General Gates was trying desperately to collect enough troops to attack the string of British strongholds reaching all the way down from Camden, or toward the defense of Wilmington, which was rumored to be the first place the redcoats would strike North Carolina from the sea.

As the heat of summer advanced, Elizabeth saw that more and more travelers were inclined to take advantage of the horse-pond road for the comfort it afforded both men and animals, and her resources were strained to the limit trying to feed the hungry Continental soldiers who had been told they could get a meal at Harmoney Hall. The name had caught on, and many a soldier passed on the word that here was to be had a gracious welcome and a full stomach.

The only advantage in so constant a flux of traffic was the accessibility of news, and the officers she fed seemed to feel that the least they could pay for her hospitality was a report of what went on in the war. Clinton, they told her, had inaugurated a policy of the utmost severity in South Carolina and Georgia, and Lord Cornwallis was only too delighted to carry it out. The name of Banastre Tarleton was becoming as terrifying to the people as the name of the devil himself. The patroits were being worn out gradually, but, they feared, surely, for neither the Congress nor the population at large was doing enough to support the armies—there were too many people who wanted nothing more than to be sure of being on the winning side. The only bright spot was the French fleet that had just arrived at Newport with six thousand troops which General Lafayette had pried out of King Louis.

It was mostly very depressing. Then one day Adam Boyd arrived, bringing her the news that James had left for the south again to join forces with Sumpter and Marion to harrass the British and loyalist outposts until General Gates should be ready to move.

"Oh, how did you learn of him, Uncle Adam?"

"Gates told me. James and Colonel Washington did what recruiting they could for a while, but soon decided they were wasting time doing work that somebody else who couldn't fight could do as well."

"But why? Why does he have to put himself in the most dangerous places of all?"

"My dear, your husband is a patriot and a very brave man. He's not waiting for anything. And I must not either, as much as I enjoy your company."

Elizabeth could not help but think that Adam was a remarkable man in making people be what he wanted them to be. She had suspected that James' love of adventure had sent him south again, but here was Adam attributing his movements entirely to bravery and devotion. He forced his friends to the best that was in them by his own belief in their motives.

"How long will you be in Wilmington?" she asked.

"Only long enough to gather up a sizable quantity of paper I had on hand, for the army stores for making cartridges. There's almost none to be had anywhere and they've got to have it."

"What will the *Mercury* do without a supply?"

He pinched her cheek as he remounted. "We are living the

news these days, and there's little sense in printing it when we need ammunition worse than we do reading matter. Do you want to ride over to the Browns' with me?"

"I'd like to, Uncle Adam, but there's so much to be done. I've got to ride the tobacco and go to the mill, and a hundred other things."

As she rode along toward the sawmill, she pondered on Adam's willingness to sacrifice his newspaper, the thing he loved most in the world, for a cause that might be lost. If everyone were like him, she thought, the cause would not be lost!

The tobacco was velvety green in the sunny fields, and at the thought of the possible value of the crop, she fell to computing the amount of the more immediate lumber sales and saw the gold growing like a strange yellow fungus in the dark of the tin box. The more money she could make on crops the army didn't have to have, the more she could afford to give to the poor men who looked so hungry and so ragged and who let their own affairs go neglected to fight the enemy.

Crossing the road, she saw Abigail talking with a mounted soldier. One could hardly be upon the river road long before seeing her. She was always around, chatting and flirting with the men, her golden head a bright spot to the march-weary.

As Elizabeth drew near, the man touched his cap and rode away. Abigail turned her horse and came to meet her.

"Hello, Elizabeth. I've just had the most interesting news: General Washington has given the command at West Point to Benedict Arnold! I know him so well. Isn't it lovely?"

Elizabeth knew nothing of her friends and cared less, and General Washington's appointments were of no particular interest to her. "Very nice," she said in a tone of dismissal, then changed her mind. "Listen, Abigail, you knew it was Fanning who burned the Loves' house and others, too. Why are you keeping it from Aunt Mary? And why are you still seeing him if you're such a patriot?"

The girl's eyes narrowed. "David didn't do that, his men did. He's not responsible for what they do."

"Of course he's responsible! And I see you don't answer my question. But I warn you, you'd better keep him and his gang away from here."

"Why didn't they attack your place?" The glitter of jealousy was in her close-set eyes, and Elizabeth decided she might as well use what had happened.

"Because he came to my house alone, and with a very insulting proposal which he expected me to accept, for obvious reasons," she said calmly.

"Oh," Abigail said furiously, "you leave him alone!"

"That seems to be our mutual desire. But you are the only one who can see to it—unless, of course, you want Uncle Adam and Aunt Mary to know you are still seeing him."

A shrewd expression came over Abigail's face. "How do you think James would like knowing you had entertained David during his absence?"

"You wouldn't dare such a lie!"

Abigail's lip curled. "Some say there have been many lies about you, one more wouldn't matter. After all, you got a husband out of lies, even though he did prefer taking along a tavern wench when he went south!"

The wound of hearing it the first time was too raw, and to have salt from a vicious tongue rubbed into it was too much. A blaze of fury whipped the blood to her cheeks. The hand holding the riding crop drew back and the braided leather thongs slashed down across Abigail's face.

The girl stared blankly for a moment, her hand covering the quickly reddening welt. Then she turned and galloped off into the forest.

The August sun was beating down mercilessly as Elizabeth made her way back to the house. Her head ached and being on Dolly's back was like sitting over a teakettle. She dropped down on her bed exhausted.

It seemed only a matter of minutes before she was conscious of voices on the gallery. Forcing herself awake, she heard a man say, "Well, this *is* the place they call Harmony Hall, ain't it? Is the missus here?"

"State yo' business, man. Ah'll see ef she heah."

Elizabeth flew down the stairs. She saw that it was late— she had slept almost till sundown. "I'll see what he wants, Mamba."

"Oh! It's *you!*"

"Why, Sergeant Anson! What do you want?"

The sergeant looked at her suspiciously. "Are you Mis' Richardson?"

"Since April."

"Well, I'm a son of a gun! He must of give you a good goin' over to git you doin' all these here good works I been hearin' about."

"Suppose you confine your speech to what you came for!"

The sergeant had his orders, even if he was dubious now

about carrying them out. But there had been things before he didn't understand, and orders were orders. A court-martial, and he never would get his tract of land.

"General Gates sent us here"—he jerked a thumb over his shoulder indicating the three men squatting over in the grass—"to make a little headquarters sorter, for army stores. As we gather up stuff it'll be stored here till they need it."

"In the *house?*"

"No, we got a couple tents, but the general thought maybe you'd let us have some outbuilding you ain't usin' for the perishables."

"Where do you want to place your tents?"

"Best we put 'em right close to the house so's if we get attacked we'd have some pertection."

With sinking heart she could see unsightly stacks of accumulated hay, fodder, and goodness knew what else cluttering up the place and inviting raiders; the men forever underfoot and doubtless expecting to be fed. But there was nothing else to do, and there was the advantage of having armed men on the premises.

"All right," she agreed, "pitch your tents on this side of the house so you can watch the road. Did you expect to eat here?"

"Oh, no. We got cookin' tackle."

But after the first few days of seeing the meagerness and smelling the unmistakable quality of what went into the single pot, she could not resist sending out a few morsels to improve their miserable fare. Another responsibility, she sighed. She knew that Podge no longer even pretended to cook for himself, but waited more or less patiently for whatever she chose to send him. Well, the old man had little enough time off the ferry with the road so full these days and nights, and Anson and his men rode hard scouring the countryside for provisions. It was little enough to spare them a bit of food now and then.

She gave them the use of an old shack back of the loom house for storing the meats, blankets, pumpkins, the extra guns and powder, and she herself added the contribution of several cheeses. They took great pride in the accumulation of these things, and eventually delighted in reporting to her their progress in procuring them. Unquestionably, it took some wit, skill, and certainly diplomacy to extract from uneasy householders provisions that had been stored for their own use.

"One thing is certain," she told Mamba one evening after

an inspection of the place, "marauders will think twice before attacking such a well-guarded storehouse."

"Yas'm, dey sho' is big husky fellows. Ain't nary inch on 'em ain't ahmed, neither. Hit do make us safer, but Mis' Lizbuth, you quit axin' dem mens to have a cheer on de gallery an' you settin' talkin' to 'em. Tain't fittin'. Dey ain't quality folks."

"Oh, for heaven's sake, Mamba, what do I care about that? They're right amusing company. That big one called Buck tells the most fascinating tales of when he went to Kentucky with a man named Daniel Boone. And, besides, I've at last convinced Sergeant Anson I'm not such a dangerous person as he once thought."

"What you keer what dat trash thinks o' you?"

"I do care," she said firmly.

She undressed and went to bed, but sleep was miles away. Mentally, she checked off the work for the week. The tobacco had been topped and the suckers removed. Bill said it would be a beautiful crop. Already he was getting the charcoal ready in the drying kilns. There was a thrill of eagerness in thinking of the day when she would see it in bales, ready for buyers. She would get hard money, too. James could not fail to appreciate her efforts this time.

She heard a rider in the horse-pond road, and voices as the sergeant challenged the arrival. Presently footsteps were on the gallery and someone was knocking. Tip-toe was lifting the chain from the lock as she ran downstairs, buttoning her dressing gown. It was not late, but hurrying hoofbeats might mean news at any hour.

"Mrs. Richardson? Captain Hugger, at your service. I've come to ask if you have any sort of ointment to spare? We've discovered several cases of smallpox in our encampment up the river."

"Oh, how terrible! Yes, I think we have some. My maid makes it from herbs and it stops all kind of itching."

"Git back, Mis' Lizbuth," Tip ordered, his eyeballs showing white and big, "Ah'll git it an' han' it out to 'im."

The captain smiled. "She won't take it from me. But I do advise you to be extremely cautious, ma'am. If this thing spreads . . ."

Tip came back with a jar and handed it gingerly out the door.

"Thank you, boy. This is going to comfort some mighty sick men."

But in the ensuing weeks the dread disease struck everywhere, apparently without the necessity of contact. There was greater fear in the faces of people now than had been caused by the war, and the first of September brought reports that the army was full of it and men dying like flies. Elizabeth had as great a dread as others, but she took what precautions she could and went doggedly on with her work.

The ripened tobacco was at last in the kilns, hanging in heavy bunches to dry; the corn was ready for the mill, and every hand on the plantation had more work cut out for him than could be done in a day. Timber cutting had started, and all day long the ring of axes sounded from the pine forest. This was the time Elizabeth had looked forward to. She could hardly tear herself away from watching over the tobacco, and she rode rapidly from the kilns to the mill to the forest. She would have been exultant had it not been for the background of a war that was gradually being lost.

General Gates had confronted Lord Rawdon's forces at Camden, but had hesitated too long to give battle, hoping to have time for his men to recuperate from the ravages of smallpox and the weakening August heat. Lord Cornwallis had rushed up with reinforcements, and the Americans had suffered overwhelming defeat. The loyalists everywhere grew bold. Tales of atrocities, of carnage, of arson, swept up and down the river and stopped the heart with terror. Banastre Tarleton had struck with lightning speed and mysterious suddenness in eastern North Carolina, murdering men in front of their women and children, burning houses over the heads of helpless victims. No one knew at what moment or where he would strike again. His aim seemed to be only to destroy everything and wear down the patriots into giving up.

To Elizabeth's own fear and heartaches was added the anxiety for James' safety. Was he dying of smallpox in some filthy prison camp, or lying wounded and uncared for somewhere back of the British lines? Nobody knew for sure. Nobody knew anything for sure.

With the first hard freeze, she ordered the hog killing. The smokehouse had been empty since the middle of August. Meals had degenerated to corn pone, chicken every now and then, such vegetables as could be stored and preserved in a cool cellar, and whatever wild game Bill Lipman could locate enough powder and ball to kill. An occasional fish came from the river whenever anyone found time to catch it.

The Negroes came from the quarters with their little buckets to receive their share of the fresh meat, and watched with greedy eyes and watering mouths the extraction of the various visceral organs from the dangling pink bodies which were allotted to their consumption. Elizabeth turned away from the gory sight. She knew the Negroes had had too little to eat, but then so had everybody else. She had done the best she could, but evidently it was not good enough. The only consoling thought, the only thing she could pin her hopes on was the tobacco, she told herself as she made her way toward the barns, where the small bales were being stored against any possible drop of rain. An exultant pride rose in her as she watched the golden parcels hoisted to the backs of the ragged slaves. This will take care of us, she thought, and had a comfortable feeling of financial security as happy as it was brief.

Back at the house, she found Captain Hugger had arrived again. "I'm really a beggar this time"—he smiled, with a broken, pathetic forlornness—"but would you have any gold, Mrs. Richardson? If we could get hold of a little we could get quite a store of medicines. You can't imagine how we need them!"

"Oh," she said, about to deny the possession of a single farthing when the picture flashed in her mind of James, maybe sick and in need of help. What good was gold lying in the attic when it might be exchanged for the lives of soldiers? There would soon be more from the tobacco. "I can let you have a few pounds," she said.

"I don't know how to thank you, Mrs. Richardson, but then I won't try to. We're all in this together, and times are mighty discouraging. Cornwallis has taken Charlotte and—"

"Oh, not in our own state!"

"Yes, ma'am, our men are fighting like fury to dislodge him, and fortunately his force is not too big. By the way, have you heard the news from New York?"

"No."

"Biggest scandal in the whole war. They caught General Benedict Arnold in a plot to sell out West Point to the British. Can you imagine? He got away, too, but they got Major André. Caught him with all the papers in his boot."

She wondered what Abigail would think of her friend now. She had known of his appointment soon enough—strange. "Why, I thought General Arnold was one of the staunchest patriots in the country."

"Many people thought so, including Washington himself,

but others say he's always had loyalist tendencies. Looks like you don't know who to trust. I guess this is about the blackest time this country's had."

When he had gone, Elizabeth sat down at the desk and bent over the big ledger. On one page she entered the number of bales of tobacco in the barns, and on the other the number of pines felled to date. Laboriously, she estimated the cash yield, then sat back, relaxing with the thought that the simply awful busy season was over, and after all, she would show a nice profit. Buyers would come soon, and she would haggle over a half-penny to drive a hard bargain. No matter what James would say about it she would give half the money to some responsible person for the purchase of equipment for the army. The enemy could not be allowed to take North Carolina! What did money matter if you had no house and no land? What good was anything if your home was lost?

She closed her eyes and wondered how it would feel to have James back home—no longer to be tormented by the thought of this Susan creature. To begin living a normal life again, with a man doing the work and a woman making herself and her house beautiful and comforting to him. This was what men fought for, this privilege to live and labor in peace, and governments were supposed to be instituted to safeguard it. And hope sprang up again that James would some day come to understand that the basis of it all was love.

She heard Tip-toe passing through the hall toward the door. His ears had caught a sound hers had missed. Now the unmistakable vibrations of hooves thundering into the horse-pond road brought her out of her reverie and to the window, and her heart became a lump of ice.

There were some twenty men. Their leader rode a great white stallion, and above his short green jacket his helmet sported a long, white hair plume. Banastre Tarleton! Behind him his men swayed easily in the saddle, smartly accoutered, jocular, confident. She had had too many descriptions of him and his company of cavalry to have any doubt of his identity.

She heard Tip-toe come quietly back inside the hall and the door close. The cavalcade had passed beyond her line of vision now; they were halting at the avenue in front of the house. She could not move. Why, oh, why, did they have to come in the middle of the afternoon when Sergeant Anson and his men were away? In panic she began to pray for some miracle of help, for stories of Tarleton's utter ruthlessness left little doubt that only a miracle could save her.

Then she heard his contemptuous voice. "That's irony for you! Hear of a good meal to be had with one o' these bloody patriots, among other possible delights, go out of our way to come here, and find the place a pesthole!" And there followed a string of oaths that would have made even General Washington pale.

She could not imagine what he was talking about. "Pesthole," indeed! It seemed as if they did not intend to enter the house. But why? She was afraid to move from the spot where she stood, but something was happening and she had to know what it was. Slipping to her hands and knees so as not to be visible from the windows, she crawled out to where Tip-toe still stood by the door. His back was pressed against it, and his face was lighted by a tooth-revealing grin. With Tarleton's next words, however, the smile faded.

"Come on," they heard him say, "we won't get what we came for but we can have a little sport, then be off for cleaner premises."

Elizabeth got to her feet. She was furious.

"Cleaner premises! Where are they going, Tip? What are they talking about?"

"Ah don' know whah dey goin', but dey sho' ain't comin' in dis house."

"Why? How do you know?"

"'Cause dey thinks we got de smallpox, on account o' mah yaller dustin' rag Ah hung up on de gallery when Ah heard 'em comin'. Ah knowed none o' dem raiders wouldn't come neah no smallpox sign!"

Elizabeth ran for a quick look through the dining-room windows and the sight turned her sick. The entire company had deployed rapidly, skillfully, as if by a long-used plan, about the plantation buildings. Tarleton himself made the barns his goal, as if he knew that a well-directed blow here would most effectually cripple his victim.

"Oh, Tip," she cried, covering her eyes with helpless, trembling hands, "he's going to get my tobacco!"

Tip-toe was quite gray with fear. "No'm, look lak he gonna buhn it."

Her precious tobacco! The crop she had worked so long and so hard to make! The crop that was to have carried them through the winter, that was to have helped the army fight off such invaders as these forever! The winter feed in the lofts;

the newly filled smokehouse—Harmony Hall itself. "God, please don't let them burn my house. I'll do anything, but just please don't let 'em burn Harmony Hall."

Mamba lumbered down the stairs, saw the two huddled by the window, and peered out. "Oh, gentle Jesus, sweet Jesus! Mis Lizbuth, dey is burnin' usses tobacco!"

Elizabeth couldn't answer. The slaves at work had suddenly discovered the smoke and flames rising from the outbuildings and had begun running in wild confusion across the fields, into the quarters, out of the quarters. Some ran screaming toward the big house, clutching their children by the hand and were shot down, writhing where they fell; others made for the swamp; still others for the river.

She looked on in growing horror and impotent rage. The barns were now enveloped in flames, the workrooms, the weaving rooms, the stables. They could see men trying to get the horses out of the burning stalls, and hear the terrified screams of the animals they could not budge. The quarters caught the blaze and their dry pine planking burned like kindling.

The yellow rag flag waved menacingly from where Tip had hung it on the gallery, so they did not approach the house—not even at the length of a torch—and it seemed to make all the more frenzied their efforts to lay waste everything else. What livestock they could see was shot, and any slave who dared make a target of himself suffered a like fate. Their purpose was not to pillage for their own use, but merely to destroy, and the wind brought the smell of smoke, of burning tobacco and grain and cloth, and the nauseous odor of burning horseflesh.

The tobacco was gone. It would be consumed slowly, to be sure, but Elizabeth knew more than to hope there would be any salvage from it. If only they did not learn the whereabouts of the sawmill! If only Bill would stay there and not come over to see what was happening! If only he would have that much sense!

There would be no hard money now from the shining bales she had set such store by. They would be lucky now to scrape together a decent meal.

She was desolate, but even as the flames crackled and roared, she began to think of what might be counted on to have escaped the vandalism. The smokehouse was at the back, and too close to the house they believed infected with smallpox to tempt them; Dolly was tied in the sally port on the other side; and she remembered that one milk cow with her calf had been set to graze in the rich little meadow beyond the woods garden. With only these she would have to carry on.

Suddenly she realized that, as swiftly as they had come, Tarleton and his men were leaving. At a signal, they reformed and rode rapidly away to the north, and a deathly silence settled over the fields and the devastated, smoking buildings.

Followed by Mamba and Tip-toe, she moved out onto the gallery.

What had been a thriving, prosperous institution was now a shattered, blackened ruin. There was no comfort. The long, hard, hot months of watching, of anxious planning and anguished waiting had culminated in a nothingness too vast to comprehend.

Sergeant Anson and his men flung themselves off their horses and rushed up to the sorrowful little group. They had returned not five minutes after Tarleton's departure, and their faces showed a grave and awful fury.

At the sight of Elizabeth's dry, hurt eyes and the beaten droop of her shoulders, Anson put out a hairy, condolent paw and patted her gently on the back, repeating over and over, "We'll get 'em yet, Missus Richar'son. We'll get 'em yet!"

Bill Lipman heard the gunfire, saw the smoke, received from one of the fleeing slaves report of what was happening and, fortunately, decided that he'd better save his skin by staying where he was. To give him credit, he also figured that, unarmed as he was, there was nothing he could do against a band of soldiers, and there was no point in disclosing the whereabouts of the mill. Fire here would be disastrous. He gave orders instantly ceasing all sounds that might attract the marauders to the depths of the pine forest, thereby saving himself, the lumber, and the twenty-odd slaves working there.

"At least we have this much left," Elizabeth said the next morning as together they rode over the plantation inspecting the damage. "That makes your horse and mine, a cow and calf, a sawmill, and a handful of slaves." She looked up at him with a twisted, broken smile. "Not much to show Mr. Richardson when he comes home, is it?"

"Not much," Bill agreed, running a hand through his sun-streaked hair, "but I reckon we'll manage somehow. You've still got the house, thank God. How did you manage to save *it?*"

She told him how Tip-toe, realizing the company of horsemen was too big to mean anything but some kind of trouble whether friend or enemy, had hung the square of yellow cloth he used for dusting out on one of the pillars of the gallery as a smallpox warning, and Bill began to laugh. "Can you imagine the fierce and mighty Tarleton shying away from a little piece o' yellow petticut? Tip was goshamighty smart to of thought of it."

But Elizabeth had no laughter. In the face of her overwhelming loss she wondered if anything would ever seem funny to her again.

"You'll have to move to the house now, Bill. You can take the little room off the kitchen, and we'll have to use what lumber we've got cut to put up some kind of shelter for the rest of the slaves. Do you suppose the others will ever come back?"

"I doubt it. They've all got wind of the promises the British have made 'em, and I hear they've been flockin' by the hundreds to their armies."

"Oh, Bill, what are we to do? We can't run these big places without them!"

"I shore don't know, ma'am. It's lucky it's comin' winter. Mebbe by springtime we can make some kind of arrangements in time for the planting."

The tobacco was a total loss, still smoldering in the ruins of the barns, and the corn crop burned to a parched crisp in the bins. Only a few bushels that had already gone to the mill on the creek had escaped the fire. The house Negroes and some of the hands from the sawmill were set to work dressing the hogs and cattle that had been shot to add to the little meat in the smokehouse; Anson and his men buried the dead slaves during the night in their cedar-shaded cemetery down by the river.

Elizabeth shivered in her threadbare riding habit and at length rode back to the house. Some of the trees were already bare, but a few maples and sweet gums in protected places still flamed like red-haired women. The earth turned on, she thought, and attended to its seasons regardless of what happened to its people. There had been only one real freeze, but today the sky was overcast with lowering gray clouds that carried a threat of snow. She felt a sudden dread of winter: for the slaves in their ragged garments, for the soldiers in their broken shoes and flimsy blankets, for those in devastated homes who would face the cold without shelter, without warming food, for everybody—except the British, with their full bellies and warm backs.

When she reached the block she saw Sergeant Anson riding hard up the avenue toward her, waving a letter in his hand. He pulled up, bringing his horse to a gravel-scattering halt.

"Letter from Mr. Richar'son," he shouted, glad to give her some cheer.

"Oh, thank you." She ran a shaking finger under the seal and looked up, her eyes like blue stars. "Where did you get it?"

"Fellow handed it to me up the road. I been up to see what Tarleton done to the rest of the river folks, and we shore was lucky. You never seen the like. The Loves' house is plumb gone now, and they're livin' in what's left of a little feed house and cookin' on the ground. They took all the Bartletts' niggers or run 'em off and finished burnin' what Fannin' had left standing."

"How about Oakland, the Browns' place?"

"You mean where Missus Boyd and Miss Abigail is a-stayin'?"

"Yes."

"Never teched it, for some reason. Ain't you gonna read your letter? I'm powerful anxious to know is he all right."

If you'll stop talking, I will, she thought, then smiled. "Why, I didn't know you knew Mr. Richardson."

"Yes, ma'am." He grinned. "I've knowed him a long time. We marched from Wilmington to Charleston in his company."

She gave only a quick glance at the letter. "Well, he's all right, Sergeant."

"Good! I'll be goin' now so's you can read it all."

She went slowly up the steps, the letter gripped in her hand. She sank down on the sofa in front of the fire, wanting yet dreading to read what he had to say. The tobacco would not matter, nor any of the losses if only this turned out to be a real love letter. Nothing would be hard or discouraging again, neither the work nor the worry nor the fear, if only she might be so brightly armored at the heart. With shaking fingers she spread the letter on her knee.

My dear Elizabeth:

I am seizing this opportunity to write you, not knowing whether this will ever reach your hand. But I must pass on to you the first good news we have had for months. We are resting at the moment, after a battle which we hope will have the result of drawing Lord Cornwallis out of Charlotte. He had sent Ferguson westward almost to the Alleghanies to gather recruits and re-join him, but he reckoned without the temper of the mountain men. They came swarming out to join us as we pressed Ferguson further and further into the trap, and at last there was nothing he could do but give battle. Much to his cost, he was foolish enough to take up his position on top of King's Mountain. The location was well suited to our frontier fighters, as the slope was covered with big rocks and pine trees, affording ample protection for our charge, and having, as it did, a precipitous cliff on one side, rendered it impossible for him to retreat. When the white flag went up and a count was made, we had a loss of only eighty-eight to the enemy's four hundred. I had the pleasure of seeing a ball put through Ferguson, who heretofore has been in the habit of killing his prisoners. The men in these parts are fierce fighters, and had begun to hang loyalists in retaliation when Col. Campbell stopped them.

The sacrifice and courage I have seen demonstrated here among our people gives one the belief that as long as there is a drop of American blood flowing, the fight for freedom will go on. A few more battles like this one, and it might be won!

We hear that General Washington has appointed Gen. Nathaniel Greene to the command of the Southern Division. Let us hope that he will display more military strategy than his predecessor!

This leaves me in possession of all my arms and legs, and in a state of health that might be described as robust despite the food, which is consistently bad when not nonexistent, and the chill of these nights. I hope to come to Harmony Hall soon (I must say I like the name you bestowed on our dwelling, even if in a spirit of buffoonry!). My wardrobe is badly in need of repair and replenishing.

I am all eagerness to know what disposition you made of the tobacco crop.

Col. Washington, whom I saw recently for a day, asked that I remember him to you which I do here with pleasure.

Believe me to be—etc.—etc.

That was all—nothing personal, nothing endearingly intimate. He might have been writing to Bill Lipman, with the one exception of the allusion to "our dwelling." Her spirits, which had hoped for so much, drooped, and she sat for a while staring into the fire. Then, as she thought back over the letter, she realized there was a change in him—subtle but eloquent. On second reading, it was clear that though his lighthearted, adventurous side had described the battle in light detail, he had also expressed his own deep feelings. Now, more than ever, she longed with a great yearning for his love to welcome her into the secret places of his heart. And he would be home soon, he said.

As night came on, the treetops began to bend and sway with a wind that sprang up out of the north, then the earth suddenly was swept with the hard, driving force of unseen power. It was bitter cold, and the clouds, blacker than the night, spread rapidly over the sky. Then, as if a giant spigot had been turned on, rain began falling in torrents.

Mamba came in and said that the forty-odd slaves who were left were taking refuge in the kitchen. Well, that would do. They could sleep on the brick floor and the two great fireplaces would be kept going as a substitute for blankets.

"I just don't know what we're going to do, Mamba," Elizabeth said as the old woman spread her nightgown on the bed. "Maybe it's the rain, but I feel more discouraged tonight than I ever have before."

"Hit's a dreary time, and you is had enough to disencourage you. Git yo' clo'es off and let me bresh yo' hair. Dat soothe you."

"I don't want to move. Brush it now, I'll undress afterward."

"Mist' James say he comin' back soon, doan forgit. You'll feel bettah once he gits heah an' knows 'bout ouah troubles. Mens jes' nacherly knows what to do 'bout things."

"Yes, maybe he'll know. I don't." But suddenly she realized what a comfort it would be to lay her burdens on his shoulders, even just to have him home. She leaned back and closed her eyes, and the firm strokes of Mamba's brush made her sleepy.

The rain was a heavy monotone on the roof, and at first she thought she was dreaming when the sound of the bell at the river landing came over the noise of the storm. She sat up, wide-eyed. Mamba had heard it, too, for the brush was suspended motionless in her hand. They listened for a second gong, but none came, and this somehow made the first more urgent.

Elizabeth cupped her hands and peered out the window. There was nothing but wet blackness until she saw the feeble glow of Sergeant Anson's lantern with the rain slanting through it, making its way toward the landing.

She ran down the stairs and out on the gallery. An icy wind struck her, but she felt a strange need to follow the sergeant. She went back and rummaged hurriedly for a wrap in the closet under the stairs. The first thing her hand touched was a Continental officer's greatcoat which James had left behind. She threw it around her shoulders and ducked out into the rain. The glow from the lantern guided her down the walk and across the grass to the river's edge where Anson was bent over a still figure lying halfway up the muddy bank.

"What is it, Sergeant? Here, turn your light this way." She stooped and gently turned the head so that the face was in the light, and stopped the gasp that rose in her throat. She ran her eyes swiftly over the rest of the body and realized with a shock that the uniform was that of a colonial officer. Thank God for that! Even if Anson had ever known John Richardson, he would not have recognized him tonight as a member of Cornwallis' staff he undoubtedly still was, and she knew it was not because of any change in his convictions that he had appeared in the Continental uniform.

Quickly she slipped out of the coat and wrapped it over the unconscious body.

"You're gonna take a chill, Mis' Richar'son."

"No, I'm all right. We must get this man to the house. He's badly wounded." There was a dirty, bloodstained bandage around his head, and one sleeve of his jacket was stiff with blood.

"Here, Sergeant, lift him up. I can carry his feet."

"Shucks, I can carry him." Anson lifted him as easily as he might a child.

Finally in the house, with Mamba and Tip-toe bustling about for hot water, blankets, and brandy, the question arose as to where to lay his bed. She must find a secret place for him. If James came and found him here . . .

"That will be all, thank you, Sergeant Anson," she said, terrified lest the Negroes recognize John and speak before him. "We can take care of him now."

"We'll have to put him in your room in the attic, Tip," she said when Anson had taken his muddy boots and dripping lantern out the door.

Mamba gave her a quick look. "Dat's Mist' Jawn, ain't it?"

"Yes, it is, and I don't know any more about it than that. We mustn't let anyone know who he is or even that he's here, do you understand? Not even Mr. James."

"Suttinly not Mist' James," said Mamba sagaciously.

At length they had him on his cot, wrapped in blankets and fresh bandages. Elizabeth sat down beside him, laying the back of her hand gently against his cheek. He was burning with fever. The deep-set eyes were closed, but occasionally his lips moved in a faint, mumbled attempt at speech. Weak and unconscious as he was, his presence, she realized looking down at him, was a comfort. She felt the admiration she had always held for him well up at the sight of his sweetly stern face.

Tip-toe stood against the door. "Mis Lizbuth, you bettah git to baid. Ah'll watch ovah 'im."

"All right," she answered, "I'm wet and cold and must change. But don't you let *any*body in here but Mamba and me. And call me if he wakes."

But it was many days before he was conscious again. Days fraught with anxiety over the raging fever, the fear of his presence becoming known. She spent every moment of her spare time beside his bed, as if she would force some of her own vitality into him and have him out and gone from the danger threatening them both by his being here.

If anyone heard of her harboring an aide of Lord Cornwallis . . . But what else could she do? She could not have left him to die down by the river! Anyway, as an aide his probable duties were only to trail around after the general, write his reports, and help him make up his mind. At most he was only an unimportant enemy. As soon as he was able she would allow his escape. She had to depend on the fact that Anson was not a talkative fellow and would not be likely to tell of the strange man he had carried into the house. That was a chance she must take, for his suspicions would be immediately aroused if she told him not to speak of it. It was certainly not unusual to be caring for a wounded soldier.

So ran her thoughts as she went about her work. The half-burned looms had to be repaired and rerigged, new spinning wheels made, and these housed in what remained of the laundry. The slaves' quarters had to be built again, and at this outlandish time of the year, Matt Rowan arrived to pay good gold money for the lumber left over.

She hugged the treasure from this unexpected windfall against her breast and hurried back to the house. Anson stood on the steps waiting to tell her that he and his men were going downriver and might be gone a day or two. Though he had not been about when she had needed his protection, it was the first time she was glad to see him go. Relieved at the thought of being for a little while unworried by fear of his mentioning John's presence, and so elated over her lumber sale, she decided to lengthen his stay by giving him a commission. From the folds of her shawl she took ten pounds from the money Rowan had paid her and counted it into his palm.

"Please take this to Wilmington and give it to the Committee of Safety—give it to Mr. Harnett if he's there—and tell him that Colonel Richardson sent it for the purchase of medicines."

Anson lifted his wide eyes and looked at her with admiration. "I think that's mighty good of you when you need it so bad yourself. How is the sick man?"

"Doing nicely," she said, thinking that on his return she could tell him John was gone, and there'd be no more danger of his talking.

When she turned, she saw Tip-toe standing in the door beckoning excitedly. "He woken, an' he talkin'. You bettah come."

She took John's hand and tried to utter soothing words, but his eyes stared at her without recognition as he struggled to rise from his cot.

"I've got to hurry. I can't sleep any longer. I've got to go—"

"Where, John? Where do you have to go?"

His answer was unintelligible.

"Now, lie down, John. Please be quiet."

"But I've got reports. I've got to get through the lines."

Her eyes fixed on his face with terrible intentness. She had a fleeting vision of the muddy colonial uniform he had worn on the night they found him. Of course. That explained his delirious talk, and she realized that this had been in the back of her mind all the time.

"Tip, hand me the water." She sponged his face, bending every effort to rouse him to give out more information. "What lines, John?"

"The lines!" He only repeated. "I've got to take it to Cornwallis. The defenses there don't mean a thing. They—"

"Where? What defenses? Oh, don't go to sleep!"

But he had drifted off again, and for the first time seemed comfortable and relaxed. All night long she sat by the bed. At midnight the fever broke, and by morning he was awake and rational. All night long she fought a battle between devotion to him and devotion to the country. Whatever information he had must not be allowed to go through, but neither could she bear to hand him over to the inevitable fate of a spy.

Dawn came gray and cold through the window. When his eyes opened, he looked up at her as if he could not believe them. "Elizabeth!"

"Yes, John, how do you feel?" she asked softly.

"Better. Where are we—in heaven?"

"No, we are certainly not in heaven! This is James' plantation and you came here sick and wounded."

"I came as soon as I could."

She pulled her hand away from his. What *was* he talking about? Was this the fever again?

"Where is James?"

"The last I heard, at King's Mountain, but he is coming home soon and, oh, John, you must be gone before he does. If only you can get strong enough? Why did you come here?"

"I came to find you. When Cornwallis wanted some special information I volunteered for the job of getting it. He wanted to find out, among other things, whether the people along the Cape Fear were disposed to be friendly to the British, how many loyalists we could count on, and I knew the journey would bring me along here. I knew, too, that few in this part of the country knew me and thought I'd be reasonably safe. I didn't count on being shot at by a band of ruffians. But I had to see you. When I heard the details of your marriage I was horrified. If only I hadn't left you in Wilmington alone!"

"No, John, you don't—"

"Ah, yes, I understand! He is breaking your heart, as I

knew he would." He tried to raise himself on an elbow but fell back. "Where are my clothes?"

"I had them burned," she said innocently. That seemed to satisfy him. "And listen, John, you have been very ill. You must give yourself every chance to get well quickly, because you are in the greatest danger here. The house is constantly visited by officers from our army, but no one will come up here if you keep perfectly quiet. Will you promise not to try to get up until I can be sure it's safe?"

"Safe for whom?" he asked with a smile.

"For me, of course!" She forced the old teasing look into her eyes, then sobered. "What do you think would happen if word got about that I, the wife of a colonel in the United States army, had a loyalist hidden in the attic?"

"Why *are* you doing it? I know, it proves your love for me. No, don't deny it. I can see in your eyes the unhappiness you've had. But I'll take you away from here as soon as we end this war." He grasped her hand in a surprisingly strong grip.

"John, I believe you are delirious again," she said, gently disengaging her hand. "You must not excite yourself so. Lie back now, and I'll get you some breakfast. Tip-toe will sit with you."

Once out of his room, she realized she was no nearer a solution as to what to do than she was before. He had read her like an open page, and though this alone was enough to unsettle her mind, she felt a rush of guilt at the feeling of warm security the knowledge of his love had always given her. She could sense, too, a subtle change in him. He was bolder now, with more poise and confidence, ill though he was, as if, once away from his old life, he had discovered within himself a strength and assurance he had not known before. Could she turn him over to the patriots, this man whose love was so enduring, who was so fine and good? But against this, could she allow the enemy the advantage of the information he carried? Dumb with misery, she started down the stairs, stopping at the landing window, and stared out at the leafless trees.

Why, when she had so much on her mind already, must he come and claim her protection, disturb her by reading her heart. That he misread the signs of her unhappiness, he did not know, but his sympathy was comforting just the same. Still, she could not allow him to deliver any word against the meager defenses of the Americans even if she had to turn him over to a certain death. The very thought stopped her heart.

Then suddenly she had an idea, and wondered why she had not thought of it before. The only tangible evidence of his acting as a spy she could destroy by burning his clothes, as she had already told him she had done, and no one could prove *what* he had worn. She could turn him in as a prisoner of war only. This would spare his life and at the same time secure whatever information he had for Cornwallis. Once in a prison camp, he would have no opportunity to make contact with those awaiting his report. He would be safe himself, yet harmless to the American army. Swiftly, she went down and found Tip-toe.

"Tip, I want you to guard Mr. John. Don't, under any circumstances, allow him to leave the room. Use force if you have to. He's too weak to try it, but don't depend on it."

Tip-toe was astonished, but Elizabeth's expression admitted of no questions. He murmured a meek "Yas'm," and went upstairs.

Hurriedly, she went to the closet under the stair where the uniform John had worn was rolled in a bundle. If there was anything in writing in the pockets, she preferred not to know of it.

She rode to the sawmill where a hot fire consumed the sawdust, and watched until the last remnants of cloth had dissolved into ashes.

CHAPTER 16

The sergeant and his men returned earlier than expected, bringing a letter of grateful acknowledgment from Cornelius Hartnett for the money Elizabeth had sent. She took the missive into the house at once, giving Anson no chance to ask questions.

John was much improved. He was propped up on his cot and already becoming restive at his inactivity. Elizabeth kept out of the room except for the briefest possible visits, for she did not want to expose her decision to further protestations of his love, or to any of his questions that might call for answers that could betray her plans for him.

But it was on one of these trips to the attic several days later that she found him sitting up by the window, wearing a dark suit of James' she had found for him to put on. It did very well except for the coat's being a bit loose across the shoulders.

It had been one of those days, bright but cool, with the feeling of false spring in the air, that sometimes comes in the winter. Elizabeth felt it with a small lifting of spirits, and she brought John a fine supper of fried pork, porridge made from some of the precious cornmeal, and a cup of warm milk.

He got to his feet as she came in and smiled. "I think I shall ask you to see if the coast is clear tomorrow. Your patient is ready to leave you. But it won't be long before I'll come back for you."

"Oh, John," she wavered, "do sit down. You are not as strong as you think." She set the tray down, pushing the hair back from her face.

"The flesh is willing enough"—he smiled—"but this time it is the spirit that is weak. Only a thing greater than our own hearts would make me leave you, even for a little while—the heart of the British Empire. But soon—"

"Hush, John, you mustn't talk so." She turned away toward the window, and the light from the sunset fell on the faded pink flowers in her dress.

"I have asked few questions, my dear," he said gently, "but your eyes have answered them all and more."

She whirled and faced him. There was no anger, only a fiercely held pride and loyalty in her voice. "I hate to hurt you, John, but I love James. I love him more than anything in the world. My unhappiness comes from work and worry and the loss of everything I've worked for so hard." Now anger came. "My tobacco, which I was depending on, was ready when that damned Britisher Tarleton came and burned it along with practically everything else on the place."

But he was still not convinced. He reached for her hand, but she went out quickly and closed the door.

Back in her bedroom, Mamba confronted her sternly, her yellow-turbaned head on one side. "You actin' lak a bird wid a cat 'roun' its nes', Mis Lizbuth. What's de mattah wid you? Folks what bottles up dey feelin's 'splodes soonah o' latah, an' Ah doan want none o' yo' pieces flyin' in mah face."

Surprisingly, Elizabeth laughed, but there was hysteria rather than mirth in the sound. She laughed until she had to cling to the tall bedpost. Mamba shook her none too gently. "Now you stop dat! Ah ain't never seed you ack lak dis befo'."

At her touch, the lines between laughter and tears became too fine, and she buried her face on the old woman's bosom and sobbed as if she could never stop. The crooked old hands caressed her hair, and she could hear the soothing words beneath her ear. "All right, now, dat's enough. Les' lay yo' troubles out in a row an' see is dey bad as dey looks. Come on, dry yo' eyes an' speak up."

Words came tumbling out, then: all the pent-up anxiety and uncertainty, the disappointments, the heartaches.

"You were right, Mamba. Everything I did was wrong! James doesn't love me. I thought once we were married he would, but he doesn't." She pushed away from the comforting breast and began to walk up and down the room. "He took a woman into the army with him and—"

"Lawd, chile, dat ain't nuthin' to hole 'gainst a man! Yo' uncle Robert, he had a Injun woman oncet—"

"Oh, I don't care what Uncle Robert had! Don't you see, it

proves he doesn't love me, and there is John, who has never stopped caring though he's been miles away. And he's not— not flippant about it either. He is safe and comforting and steady—"

Mamba's eyes narrowed to pinpoints. "Is you bin up dere lettin' Mist' Jawn talk love to you?"

"No. I couldn't help it if he told me he loved me, could I? He said he's going to come back and take me away with him when the war's over. And I've got to turn him in as a prisoner."

"Why is you got to do dat?"

"Because he's got information for the British that I'm not going to allow them to have."

Mamba was nonplussed. "Who is you gwine give him to?"

"Sergeant Anson can take him to Wilmington to headquarters there," she answered firmly, then melted. "Oh, don't you see how hard it is for me to do it? But I've got to! He has knowledge for Cornwallis that could wreck our whole army and make us lose the war!"

"Well'm, Ah guess you has to, then."

Tip-toe came to the door and said that Mist' Jawn was acting like he was going to leave. This stiffened her resolve. She went to the drawer in the armoir and lifted out a pistol that James had left carefully loaded when he went away.

"Lawd Gawd, honey, you ain't gonna kill 'im?"

"Of course I'm not!"

She climbed the narrow stairs and opened the door to the attic room. John was standing beside a little table, hastily stuffing into his pockets the small effects which had been removed from his clothes the night he came.

He whirled, startled, as the door opened, and for a tense moment neither spoke. Then he strode toward her.

"Don't come a step nearer," she quavered, pointing the gun.

He was shocked. It had never occurred to him that, although she was married to James, she had renounced her loyalty to the crown, or that she might have understood his mission too well. He sought for some word that would lighten the situation and give him a chance to talk her into allowing him to leave.

"All right." He smiled, thinking how like a beautiful child she was, standing there with the big pistol in her hand. "I am your prisoner. What are you going to do with me?"

"I am going to send you to Wilmington under guard to the Committee of Safety," she said in a small voice.

"But why, my darling?"

"Because you have information—"

"How do you know that?" he asked quickly.

"You talked about it when you had fever, and you told me some of it. You know our strength and our weakness and—"

"Oh," he said, his mouth in a tight, stern line. "But why are you so concerned? The last time we talked you seemed to have no particular love for the patriots."

"I am one of them now," she said in a steady voice. "The last time we talked I had no real feeling one way or the other, except what concerned my friends and my own affairs. But now, John, I understand the things America is fighting for. I like the way of life they are trying to build and—"

It was the first time she had put her thoughts into words, and they crystallized in her own mind as she talked. "For the first time in my life I've learned that everybody is really the same when you know and understand them. Oh, it's not only the English, though few people now would admit it. It's only that they represent something—something we don't believe in anymore. No, don't speak. I want you to know why I have to do this thing to you. I married James because I loved him."

"But does he love you?" he burst out, unable longer to keep silent, disregarding her attempt to convince him of her very genuine patriotism.

"Don't interrupt me."

"Ah, I see you will not answer. I knew—"

"That is all beside the point. When he went away to the army, I gave my love and my loyalty to his house and his land. You can't work and put so much of yourself into something and not become part of it. It is *my* land now, in a peculiar way. I have worked over it—sweated and cried over it! Don't you see, I haven't any choice but to defend it and the country it's part of? I will not have the British take it from me! And I won't let you take them a word that might allow them to do it." Her hand holding the gun was shaking now, and her face was flushed with the effort of putting her heart into words.

He stood looking down at her with a strange expression, then gently reached out and grasped the wrist that held the pistol.

"All right, my dear," he said, drawing her into his arms. "You need not be afraid. I will not overpower you and escape, though I could easily do so. As long as you are in this room I won't try to get away. Nor will I allow one acre of your ground to be touched when we have won this war, as we certainly will. But I'll make my escape somehow. Death has as little attraction for me as the next man!"

"Oh, I know, John." She clung to him as a steady pillar of strength in a whirling world and because her heart ached so at its own compulsion to surrender him to Sergeant Anson. His word was good. He would not try to leave as long as she was with him, and it was so heavenly just for a moment to be held in arms that loved her so. For an instant there was a fleeting doubt as to whether anything was worth the sacrifice of the quiet peacefulness of John. She felt the roughness of his cheeks, his lips upon her hair, then the sudden hard tensing of his muscles.

Abruptly, he tilted her head back and looked into her face. His own was white and strained, and just as she gathered strength to tear herself away, the door was flung open and James stood on the threshold.

"Well!" he said after the shocked interval in which the three stood staring silently. Then his mouth twisted into a crooked, mocking smile. "I go to fight a war and return to find the enemy invading my home."

For the first time, he seemed to be without his accustomed composure. There was a strange look in his eyes. Elizabeth ran to him.

"Oh, James, I was going to turn him over as a prisoner! He came here sick and wounded and we took him in—we—" Her speech died away as he saw the futility of an explanation.

James moved slightly, recovering his cool assurance, and leaned against the door in the old manner he had of implying a lack of interest.

"He was going to leave and I came to stop him," she tried again to find words that would make sense to him, but knowing that nothing could explain away the picture his eyes had seen.

The pistol was still clutched in her hand, dangling with dangerous carelessness at her side. He reached out and took it from her. "Apparently, my dear, your gun was superfluous in holding your man. It surprises me that you felt you had to resort to such tactics."

John spoke for the first time. "What Elizabeth says is true. I was going to leave and she held me with the gun until she could convince me that in surrendering me to the rebel authorities she was only doing what she thought was right. After all, I am a loyalist soldier. But I gave her my promise that I wouldn't try to escape as long as she was in the room, and offered her sympathy and comfort in having to hand over a friend to his possible death. You wouldn't understand such tender emotions."

"Perhaps I understand more than you think of tender emotions," James said, and again Elizabeth caught that strange look in his eyes.

If only she could make him understand! But with a shrug of his shoulders he turned and called down the stair to Tiptoe, who was shaking in his shoes on the bottom step.

"Come here, Tip." And when the boy came to the door, he said coldly, "Guard this man. If you let him get away I'll take it out of your hide."

She followed him into their bedroom, speechless with anguish. When he turned to face her, she saw that the strange expression on his face was like that of a hurt little boy, but it was quickly gone.

"Oh, James," she burst out, "what you think is not true! I went to John's room because I knew he was well enough to leave; then, when he promised, I was so relieved and so frightened and confused at having to treat him so, and having to give him up to . . . and everything was so uncertain . . . and you were gone and—"

"And so you turned to other arms for comfort!"

"Oh, no! Please understand."

"I understand that I've been a fool," he said bitterly, anger taking the place of the hurt look. "I rode hard all last night and all day to tell you that I loved you—*loved* you, do you hear?" He grasped her arms and looked straight into her eyes. "Then at the ferry I met Abigail, who told me you were nursing some soldier. I would have thought little of that because it's being done every day, if she had not added that Fanning had been here and insinuated that he had been paying his respects to you. Then I arrive to find you and John—"

"Oh, it's a wicked lie," she cried, choking with fury.

He said he was coming to tell her he loved her! What she had wanted more than anything in the world, and it had to be like this!

"I never believed much in the fidelity of women," he went on, "until I got the crazy idea that you might be different."

"Oh, don't, James—don't! I love you."

"Love! What a snare!"

"I loved you from the beginning. I tried to make you know—I tried to make this home for us, but you wouldn't let me be—you made me be—"

"Not I, my love, it was my absence that made a wench out of you," he said with a low stab of a laugh that seemed to cut him as deeply as it did her. He could not stop the bitter rush of his words, the terrible castigation of them both. He had expected her to explain Fanning's visit, for he more than half-suspected the truth of anything Abigail had to say, but when he had arrived to find that John was the sick man and Elizabeth in his arms, it was too much. The long miles he had ridden, picturing the happiness that awaited him at the end! He was ashamed, too, of his feeling of weakness toward John when, at first sight of him, his basic love for his brother had risen within him. But all of these mixed emotions, his dashed hopes, only whipped his fury to a higher pitch and he poured the scalding caldron over Elizabeth—miserable himself, yet unable to stop.

The color drained from her face, then rushed back with her own sudden hot fury. It rose above the hurt and the disappointment, and her eyes were blue slits between her lashes as she sought for words with which to stab back.

"All right, that will do! I have told you the truth and you don't believe me. Now you can think whatever you like, but I fail to understand why you have the presumption to question my fidelity when everyone knows you bought a bound girl to take to the army with you."

"Oh, that," he said with a peculiar, surprised laugh.

"Yes, that! And I vow if I didn't care so terribly about the war and the country, I'd see to it that John escaped. He is worth a dozen of you." She stared at him, hoping to see she had inflicted a hurt as great as her own.

But instead there was only anger and the well-remembered look of desire. Suddenly, his arms were ruthless, as if they would crush her into a mold of his own making.

"By God, if you've forgotten who you're married to...."

Morning brought the sounds of preparation for the trip downriver. She could hear James' voice giving clipped orders for making the boat ready that would take them to Wilmington. They would have to go by boat since the carriage had been burned in the barn, and Elizabeth knew they would take no chance in trusting the prisoner to a horse of his own however well he was guarded. Her body ached with a dull heaviness; her heart felt as if Tarleton's fire had swept through it, too, and crumbled it to ashes. She had not slept except for a few fitful moments before dawn, but she got up and began to dress quickly.

Downstairs, she found Anson and his men on the gallery waiting for orders to go up after John. James said an almost courteous "Good morning," but her spirits rose not at all.

"All right, men," James said finally, but broke off at the sound of approaching horses. "Wait, we'll see who this is."

She saw Abigail, Lieutenant Randolph, and Adam Boyd riding up the avenue. There was a stiff wind blowing that set the plumes of Abigail's hat bobbing and her dark-red skirts blowing back from over her slender ankles. Elizabeth's hands were clenched in outrage that the girl would dare to come here after her lies to James, her insinuations that had added to the painful situation, but she said nothing. Adam and Randolph wore looks of anxiety.

James wore the same face, but his was paler. "I'm just leaving for Wilmington," he told them, "but come in. A few more minutes won't—"

"No, there is no time," Adam informed him. "We've just had a dispatch that Major Craig is on his way from Charleston to take Wilmington, or try to, so you'd better hurry and finish your business down there."

"When did you learn that?"

"Just now. The lieutenant here was sent to spread the warning. We are to get all the recruits possible from the surrounding country and—"

"When did he leave Charleston?" James asked.

"They don't seem to be sure. It could have been any time."

As they turned their horses to leave, the wind, catching a corner of the lieutenant's cape, tore it from his hand and blew it across the head of Abigail's horse. The frightened animal reared and plunged, so that she was caught off guard and thrown. They hurried her into the house and laid her on the sofa.

"Oh, God, is she hurt?" Randolph asked, fluttering over her.

"Naw, just got the wind knocked out of her," drawled the big soldier called Buck. "Missus Richar'son, 'spose you open up her bodice. It's uncommon tight."

Elizabeth did as he said, and allowed the neck of the dress to fall open, though she would gladly have tightened it.

HARMONY HALL

As the ruffles fell back from her throat, a letter slipped out and to the floor. Elizabeth stepped back, looking down at it, but James stooped, picked it up, glanced at the address, and slipped it into his pocket. He darted a quick glance at Adam and Randolph, who were working over the girl, unaware of anything else.

Mamba came in with a bottle of smelling salts, and presently Abigail's eyelids fluttered open. For a moment she stared about her, dazed. Involuntarily, her hand moved up to the bosom of her habit, clutching the folds together, then her eyes focused and her swift fingers began to search.

"Are you all right, my dear?" Adam and the lieutenant asked in a breath.

"Yes." She sat up. Her lips had gone white. "Where is my letter? Who opened my bodice?"

"What letter, Miss Abigail? Are you sure you know what you are saying, dear?" Randolph asked.

"Of course, you fool! Oh, where is it?"

The eyes of Elizabeth, of Anson, and of the two other soldiers turned to James. He half-sat on the edge of a table, watching the scene with a lazy, half-amused smile, though his eyes were keenly stern. "Is this your letter, Abigail?" he asked, drawing it from his pocket.

"Oh, yes. Oh, thank you, James. I was frightened." She put out her hand with a smile into which she poured all the allure she could muster.

"Just a moment," he said, getting to his feet, and his expression was no longer one of amusement. "This is addressed to a certain colonel in the British army in New York. I'll have to ask you to explain it."

Adam, who had appeared merely bewildered, showed shocked disbelief.

"That's simple," Abigail said easily, though the knuckles of her twisted hands were white as she glanced at her uncle. "I have many friends among the English in New York. As you know, it's my home."

The lieutenant chewed his lip.

James said, "In that case, I'm afraid I'll have to crave your pardon and read it."

"Oh, no!" She flew across the room and tried to take the packet out of his hand, but he held it high over his head. "Please, James, it's only a poor little billet-doux," she wheedled, "I shall just die if you read it!"

"More than likely," he observed dryly.

"Oh, Miss Abigail," cried the betrayed Randolph.

"Read the letter and get it over with," Elizabeth said suddenly. "I understand now what should have been clear from the first. Always riding the roads and—"

Every eye in the room was upon James as he turned toward the window and broke the seal. Abigail made a lunge for the letter, and her nails raked his cheek.

"Hold her, Anson," he said without looking up. "My God, there's enough in this to hang her!"

Lieutenant Randolph came out of his shock with his patriotism above his emotions, and the hand he lent the sergeant was not amorous. Adam crossed to James, his face suddenly white and crumpled, and read over his shoulder. The letter was written in her own hand, composed of information gleaned from soldiers, militiamen, Fanning, anyone with whom she could make conversation on her rides about the country, and the officers who had been entertained at the Browns' home. There was even her humorous account of Tarleton's raids and the destruction he had wrought on certain plantations. It was plain now why he had spared Oakland.

"Uncle Adam," she cried wildly, "are you going to stand there and—"

But though Adam was regarding her as a viper in his bosom, he could hardly believe even yet what he had read. Elizabeth felt a great pity for the broken old man, with his gray and stricken face.

James finished the letter and put it back in his pocket. "Take her to the boat. Randolph, you and Anson go up after the man upstairs. The black woman will show you the way." He turned to Adam, who had dropped into a chair and laid a steadying, sympathetic hand on his shoulder. There was nothing he could say of comfort.

The men came down with John between them, his hands tied behind his back. He gave Elizabeth a wan smile, quiet and fearless, but his face was drawn and pale. James looked at him levelly as they entered the room.

"It seems that we have caught two spies to hand over to the Committee of Safety." He turned to Elizabeth and looked at her as if she were only a small part of an inconvenient situation. "Now that we have a female prisoner, I suppose we'll have to take you along."

"I intended to go anyway," she answered coldly, with a lift of her chin.

A court-martial was being held in the big assembly room on the north side of the courthouse, and it was cold as a barn. Only the man back of the judge's bench, a man Elizabeth had never seen before, had a bag of hot salt to rest his feet on. She pulled her cloak tighter about her and huddled in the chair.

The proceedings seemed interminable. A Negro was convicted for stealing a horse, and led away. A woman was ordered to the pillory for failing to render up a store of cornmeal to the quartermaster.

As Abigail was called to the stand, Elizabeth saw that Adam had come in quietly. His face was haggard, but with the reading aloud of her letter, it was obvious that he had no intention of trying to save his niece. The only sign of his sorrow was a twitching at the corner of his mouth as he identified her handwriting, and when she was pronounced guilty of being a spy against the United States, his head dropped into his cupped hands. She was sent to jail to await sentence of banishment.

As judgment was passed, a man behind Elizabeth spoke in a disgusted whisper, "Gawd damn! Used to be they'd hang a woman quick as a man. Country's gittin' soft," and a stream of tobacco juice struck the wall.

At last the clerk called in an inflectionless voice, "John Richardson, captured at the plantation Harmony Hall by his brother's wife, to the stand."

She watched him mount the platform, saw the defeated droop of his shoulders under the sagging coat, and a great sorrow and pity that almost created regret rose in her.

"What is your name?"

"Jonathan Abner Richardson."

"Nationality?"

"American." Hisses and catcalls demanded the rap of the gavel.

"But you are in the British army?"

"I am." There was pride in the words and a defiant jerk to his chin.

"Rank?"

"Lieutenant-Colonel, Lord Cornwallis' staff."

Whistles sounded through the room, and a man in the back laughed. "Bagged a big 'un, didn't she?"

"James Richardson to the stand."

"Is this man your brother?"

"Yes."

"Were you at home on the night of his capture, Colonel?"

"No, I was not. I was with our army in South Carolina."

"Thank you, sir, that will be all."

"Mrs. Richardson, please."

"Elizabeth Purdie Richardson," she said quietly, quickly removing her hand from the Bible. God would forgive her, since she had only touched it lightly.

She turned her troubled blue eyes on John. "He is John Richardson. He came to the river landing at my plantation wounded and unconscious."

"You took him in?"

"Yes."

"Please tell the court the circumstances of the capture. You must have had help."

"Yes—yes, I did," she said, suddenly terrified at the thought of a testimony from Anson.

"Who was with you?"

"Sergeant Anson, of the commissary department, stationed on the place."

"Thank you, Mrs. Richardson."

She regained her seat, glancing at James, but his face was a mask.

"Sergeant Anson to the stand."

The sergeant went forward with alacrity, eager to take his first part in legal business.

"Sergeant Zed Anson, department of the quartermaster," he said proudly.

"Do you swear that the testimony of Mrs. Richardson is the truth?"

"I do, sir." He turned toward Elizabeth with a pleased expression as if he intended to say something more which would increase the importance of her capture, then looked back at the judge. "Can I tell some more, sir?"

"You may."

"It seems like I kinder remember a rulin' that says a man is a spy if he's caught in enemy territory without his uniform on."

"That is true. Proceed."

Elizabeth's breath caught and held. There it was! She might have known. The man was a dolt and a fool for not consulting her. But even as she thought thus, she knew that he was only being literal about the oath: " . . . the whole truth, and . . ."

"Well," he continued, drawing out his words, enjoying the

feeling of importance it gave him to speak in the courthouse, where only the mighty had stood before, "when I went down to the river that night and turned my lantern on this man he was wearing one o' our uniforms!"

A low murmur went through the assembly.

In the midst of it, Elizabeth rose suddenly, gripping the back of the chair in front of her. "Oh, no," she said breathlessly. "No, you are mistaken."

"Mrs. Richardson," the bench recognized.

Swiftly, she made her way back to the stand and stood with her hand resting on the rail beside Anson. She looked with a brief smile into the hawk eyes of the judge, then with a kindly glance at the sergeant. "You must not make such a mistake, Sergeant Anson. We don't want to get a man hanged just because he is an enemy when he is guiltless of being more!"

The walk of a cat would have been loud in the courtroom. She took a quick look at James. He was sitting forward, a twist to his mouth, a strained anger in his eyes. What she was doing by her false testimony in John's defense, when he was bound to know it was false, to the remnants of their relationship, she was perfectly aware—this would be proof to him even more eloquent than what he had seen. But their marriage was rent to shreds already. Allowing John to lose his life would not mend it.

"The sergeant," she went on hurriedly, in a steady tone, "has mistaken the cloak I threw over Colonel Richardson that night for his own. It was a greatcoat belonging to my husband's uniform. The night was cold and raining, and I snatched it up as I went down to the landing. Don't you remember, Sergeant, when I took off the coat and wrapped it around him you said I'd catch a chill?"

"Yes'n, I do, but—" Anson scratched his head.

"Of course you do! And I remember thinking how he might resent being forced to wear a coat belonging to a colonial. I even laughed to myself a little about it."

John's eyes spoke his gratitude and his admiration. He knew she was lying for him, and it gave him hope.

"Where are the clothes he wore, Mrs. Richardson?" asked the judge.

"Oh, we had to cut them off him, sir. They were covered with mud and blood and—and vermin. I just threw them into the fire!"

She went back to her seat as the presiding officer dismissed

Anson from the stand, and began to address the jury. He was lauding her virtues, making unquestionable her words, telling of her patriotic works, her gifts of money and produce to the army, and the loyalty she had shown in keeping her husband's brother under guard.

Her cheeks burned with embarrassment, her heart with anguish.

The gentlemen of the military jury cleared John of espionage, and he was led away to the heavily guarded camp as a prisoner of war.

Adam moved to her side as they went down the courthouse steps. "That was a fine thing you did, Elizabeth. Sparing a man's life, when, but for your courage in speaking, he might have lost it. It would have been too bad to have more innocent blood on our hands than is necessary in times like these. You are a partisan with a cool head. A splendid thing to be."

She was too distraught and too unhappy to enlighten him or to disavow a virtue he believed her to possess. His knowing the truth would help no one and would only create one more disappointment for him.

"I'm sorry about Abigail," she said simply.

"All I can say is that I'm glad she was among friends when she was detected. Now we will never mention her name again."

Adam had decided to go back up the river with them so that he could break the sad news to Mary. He sat in the bow of the longboat beside James, and both thought they understood the other's gloom. Each was wrapped in his own thoughts, and they sat and stared at the water in silence.

Elizabeth had taken her place in the stern with her own relieved but miserable thoughts. Sergeant Anson sat at her feet, and it seemed that he, too, was uneasy and depressed. She watched the forward, backward movement of the oars in the hands of the slaves. The trees on the banks slid by, and there was no sound except the swish of disturbed water.

Anson changed his position and looked at her, his wide-apart eyes full of concern. "Missus Richar'son, I'm awful sorry I almost spilled the beans this mornin'. I thought I had hold of something that would give you a little—a little glory—you've worked so hard and helped us all so much. I clean forgot Colonel Richar'son sure wouldn't want his brother hanged as a spy. Why I wouldn't hurt him fur nuthin'. You sure fixed it all right, though."

Elizabeth dragged her attention back from her own problems, "What did you say, Sergeant—what about hurting my husband?"

"I said I wouldn't—not for the world. You see, I didn't know till this mornin' that our wounded man was his brother, and so, when I got on that stand, I kinder was confused I reckon."

"Oh, it's all right. Colonel John is safe now." She turned her head away, hoping to discourage further conversation, but the sergeant insisted on making himself clear.

"No, ma'am, it ain't. I ought to of thought better. Mister Richardson done the biggest thing for me any man ever done, and I shore didn't aim to repay him in no such way. Yes, sir, he bought my girl from Lal Dorsey for me and let her march—"

She whirled around to face him so suddenly he was startled.

"He *what?*"

"Oh, it didn't cost him much, ma'am, and she *was* bad treated at the tavern. I'll pay him back when—"

She felt the peculiar rising hysteria again as she had had the night Mamba had shaken her out of it. A low laugh escaped her, but she took a tight grip on the tears. "I didn't mean to frighten you, Sergeant Anson. The money doesn't matter, really it doesn't. What's your girl's name?"

"Name's Susan," he said, bashful as a boy.

"And where is she now?"

"I left her with a nice old lady up close to Camden. She's well took care of up there." He looked up with a shy smile. "We aim to git married soon's I git my land."

Before she had time to remember that it didn't matter anymore, she felt a joyous relief. Susan, James had bought for Anson—not for himself, as she had been led to believe!

"I hope you'll be very happy," she said almost gaily. Then lifting her eyes to the boat's bow, to James' long, lithe figure, her heart fell. His gaze was fixed on the upriver distance so that she couldn't see his face. Only the jutting line of the jaw, and the set of his shoulders was eloquent of cold bitterness. A dull apathy went through her.

They reached the plantation in the late afternoon. A blue haze drifted over the hills and fields, and the setting sun threw a last arrow of flame on the treetops and the red-brick chimneys.

James did not come to the house immediately, but went with Bill to inspect the damage Tarleton had done. He had arrived late last night and left for Wilmington early, and so had only a meager idea of what had happened. His face was grim as they rode over the crusty, frozen ground, but he had to keep dragging his mind back to the devastation of his property. He snapped monosyllabic answers to Bill's questions and statements until the overseer began to think he blamed him for the foray.

"I was sure sorry for Mrs. Richardson when them barns burned," he said. "She had set quite a store by the tobacco, which ain't surprising when you think how she worked with it. Like as if she was a overseer, she rode the rows every day, a-watching every leaf, seein' the niggers didn't miss nothin'."

They rode till dark, then James dismissed him. Bad company though they were, he wanted his own thoughts, and they were a boiling potage. For the first time in his life he had had strange ingredients ladled into his emotional stew, and the fact that he was helpless to extract them only stirred the mess with a long-handled spoon.

Finally, he dropped the reins at the block and went in to supper—a meager meal with only pork and sweet potatoes. A meal with a man and a woman at the table, and between them an acute and agonizing silence.

They hardly tasted their food. Elizabeth thought, If he would only *say* something, anything! Throw things, shout! Anything was better than this awful silence, his cold, still anger. Once she lifted her eyes. He was looking at her, and for a moment their glances held just as they used to. But instead of the merriment that had always followed, they both glanced away. She had a wild desire to go around the table and throw herself into his arms, but pride held her back. She could not beg.

Finally, he laid down his knife and fork, leaned back in his chair, and spoke, "I saw Matt Rowan today. The schooner you so handsomely paid for is ready for launching. Perhaps 'tis as well you made the ill-advised purchase."

"What—what do you mean?"

"I mean it'll be worth the thousand pounds you paid for it to be rid of you," he said shortly. "If the British fleet will hold off for a few days, you'll be packed and headed for Jamaica."

This was not really what he wanted to say. He wanted to speak the words that might give them both some opening into a conversation to set everything right. But his arrogance and his pride held them back. Anyway, he wasn't sure that Elizabeth would care to respond to a peace proposal. After her defense of John, when things had happened as they had, she had proved where her heart lay. His vanity was injured. His vanity, and something more—his own heart—and he could not bear the thought of exposing them to another attack.

After the whirling blackness that enveloped Elizabeth at his decision, only anger emerged. She bit her tongue until she could control it.

"Yes, I suppose you are right. That's where I belong. Not here, not running your plantation, not working for a man who has no idea of the meaning of anything."

They left the table. He went to the secretary and got out the account books. She stood hesitantly for a moment, then spoke to him in a small, uncertain voice. "Do you want any explanation of my bookkeeping?"

"No. I can read."

Upstairs in the bedroom, she sent Mamba away and got out the only nightgown she had left that was still pretty. He would have to come up *sometime*. She would read until he did, propped up on the pillows with her hair falling loose in the way he liked. Her thoughts revolved like a waterwheel. Everything was wrong. Wrong and crazy. Maybe when he came up to bed, maybe in the darkness she could put off her pride and tell him again of her love, *make* him understand. Maybe his need of her would sweep away these false, nightmarish persuasions and she could convince him. Out of all the turmoil there were a few crumbs of hope: he had said he loved her, had ridden all night to come to her and tell her so; Susan had not been bought for himself at all; and the British fleet was headed for Wilmington!

Suddenly, against all thoughts of possible consequences, all patriotism, she prayed for the arrival of Craig and his ships. Let them close the port, lock it solid with English men-of-war! Let that schooner stay on the ways forever!

At length she heard his step in the hall. The familiar, loved sound of his boots on the stair made a painful shortness of breath, and she felt his presence in the room before she raised her eyes.

He went to the clothes press and took down his dressing gown. Her heart racing, she swept her eyes back to the book. He paused at the foot of the bed. There was the old mocking, disparaging smile on his lips, the indifferent set of his shoulders as he regarded her, but there was no laughter in his eyes.

"You've quite an accomplishment there, in being able to read with your book upside down," he said, and crossed the hall to his own room, closing the door behind him.

CHAPTER 17

Daylight was just striking the river when there came a terrific pounding on the avenue door, followed by the sound of Tiptoe's heavy feet striking only at wide intervals on his way up the stairs.

"Mist' James! Mist' James! Mist' Podge heah! Say de British is comin'!"

Elizabeth flew to her door as James' head appeared from his.

"When? Where are they?"

By this time Podge was up the stairs himself. "They're a-comin'! Rider jest come across and shouted it to me and rid on. Craig's fleet landed in the night, and they're a-headin' thisaway. I kep' the ferry on this side, and I ain't gonna take it back over till you're out and gone, James Rich'son!"

In a very short time, as if the news had traveled by wind, Adam Boyd arrived in company with the Browns' overseer, some slaves, now mounted and armed, and several other men he had gathered on his way, and this time he himself carried a gun.

It was all over in so short a time. The men rode away to the north in a rapid retreat before Elizabeth had time to realize that she was being saved from being sent away. James had not even said good-bye. In fact, after the word came, he had seemed unaware of anything except the frenzied preparations for departure. There were not enough of them to make a stand and fight, for every man knew himself to be too valuable to take a chance on sacrificing his life. All they could do was to ride toward reinforcements.

Elizabeth climbed on the gate at the foot of the avenue and watched them disappear up the river road. The whole group together. Sergeant Anson and his men, and even a few of their own slaves who had somehow been supplied with weapons and mounts, joined the exodus—amazingly swift, silent, grim, before the expected onslaught of the British forces.

She hurried back to the house and helped Mamba and Tip-toe pack all the silver to be hidden in the woods garden.

By late afternoon, the first enemy troops began to pass, and all night long the rumble of artillery and wagons, and the muffled sound of many men marching, talking, and singing drifted up to the house on the still, cold air.

Next morning they discovered the horse-pond road, and the haystacks Sergeant Anson had gathered with such labor and pride disappeared into the ravenous maws of British horses. In their haste they made no attempt to lay waste the plantations, possibly thinking they would be useful after they had won the war.

But the hospitality to English officers began to be forced on the household. Elizabeth would not sit at table with them until it occurred to her that perhaps she was behaving foolishly. One might arrive who resented her attitude and burn the house down over her head. Perhaps she would do better to be more gracious if it meant protection. And so she forced down her food while listening to their boastful talk and their expressed contempt for the Americans and their army. If only General Greene could do something to make them change their minds!

Avid for news, she began to spend some time down at the gate at the avenue's end, talking to the troops whenever there was an opportunity. She couldn't ride. They couldn't even plow for, even though only the crippled Bill Lipman and a few slaves were left, they had no horses. So she had to depend on the soldiers for news. And news flew thick and fast. But since it was entirely from the British point of view, it was horribly depressing. The Tories were having their innings at last, and it was but natural that they should exaggerate the greatness of their victories. The Cape Fear was swept as clean of colonials as the back of one's hand, and the condition of the Whigs in the whole section of the country began to be deplorable.

Bands of outlaws seized the opportunity to plunder and murder, and this, she learned with shame, was not confined to the loyalists. It was the chance for the low of both sides to do some fine looting under the cloak of war. Camp followers in droves followed every detachment of the king's men, and

HARMONY HALL

the inhabitants suffered more from their insults and thievery than from the troops themselves. Sarah Brown's horse came back to Oakland and was recognized under a wench who had formerly been the recipient of the Browns' charity; and by the light fingers of half a dozen other such creatures, upheld by armed escorts, she was reduced to the dress she wore. They had even stripped the sheets from her beds and curtains from the windows.

This story Elizabeth heard from the laughing lips of a British officer who sat at her table complaining of the food. Her anger flared, but her small white teeth drew blood in holding back a shouting spate of furious words.

But when such a mob finally arrived at Harmony Hall, the procedure was slightly different from what she had expected. A small party of men and women, half-drunk, laughing hilariously, clattered into the horse-pond road, and at their head rode David Fanning. She went to the gallery with stormy eyes and shaking, tightly clenched hands. Fanning dismounted, saluting with an exaggerated gallantry that sent the women into gales of mirth.

"Have you heard the latest news, Miss Elizabeth?" he asked, smiling.

"I am Mrs. Richardson to you, and I don't care to hear anything you have to say."

"I think you will *this!* General Morgan licked the pants off Tarleton at Cowpens, and the fat boy, Colonel Washington, nicked the fancy Britisher with the point of his sword nigh enough to spoil his pretty face!"

"I wouldn't think that cause for your rejoicing," she said, secretly delighted over both the colonials' victory and Tarleton's injury.

"Oh, anything is cause for my rejoicing today! When Craig took Wilmington, he liberated all the prisoners—yes, even your Colonel John Richardson. Miss Abigail is sailing on a packet for New York and I'll sail along with her. I've been given a commission in Lord Howe's army, but once back in civilization, I'll ditch the fighting and settle down to enjoy my profits." He was immaculately dressed and groomed, and as he stepped up closer to her, Elizabeth caught the sickening scent of the pomade he used.

"Suppose you take your—these creatures off my premises," she said, moving back.

But he grasped her wrist and pulled her up to him. "Oh, the girls are just looking for a few pretties, or," he whispered, "have you decided I might give you some pleasant protection?"

"Don't you dare touch me," she cried, fighting him off.

"All right, girls, I don't think Mrs. Richardson will object to your coming in for a spot of tea or brandy or whatever you can find."

At this, the women slid to the ground and swarmed past her into the house, followed by several men. With a single movement, Fanning lifted her and carried her through the door. "Want to change your mind?"

She fought him like a small wild thing, pushing, scratching, her heart hammering with fear as he made for the sofa. Over all she could hear the altercation from upstairs that meant Mamba and Tip-toe were trying valiantly to defend whatever was portable.

He held his lips to hers and kicked the library door shut. With one hand he held her down, while the other fumbled at his belt. Then suddenly, with a look of having remembered something, he let go of her, opened the door, and made for the stairs himself. Swiftly, shakily, but realizing it was her jewelry he had remembered, she followed.

In her bedroom, the women gabbled and rummaged through her clothes, which they pulled out and fought over. Mamba looked at her for an intense moment, then started backing toward the chest of drawers. The man in the door with the gun did not notice. He was amusedly watching the women, and Fanning had gone to her desk on a search of his own.

Inch by inch, Mamba reached the chest and silently slid a drawer open, then moved slowly back and stood quietly by the window.

After emptying the drawers of the desk, Fanning turned. "Get out, girls! I've got some business of my own here."

They giggled with lewd and knowing looks and trooped toward the door—all but one, who stood staring at Mamba. "What's the black 'oman got in 'er 'and?"

"I'm sure I don't know, Susan," he said, his bright eyes sparkling now that he knew the women had not found the jewels. "Shall I have a look?" He glanced at Elizabeth, who was staring at the girl. "Oh, yes, my dear, I forgot to introduce you. This is the girl your husband bought." And he crossed to where Mamba stood, her hands behind her. "What have you got?" he demanded.

"Nuthin' you wants an' nuthin' you's gwine tech. Get away fum me, man!"

"Just give him what you have, Mamba, there's nothing we can do," Elizabeth said dispiritedly.

"That's right, we don't want any trouble." Fanning laughed as he reached for Mamba's arm.

Mamba saw that he meant to have what she held, but she was not powerless to prevent it. With a single thrust the hand holding the jewels went through the windowpane, dropping the chamois bag, but the other shot out and threw its contents of red pepper mixed with lye full in Fanning's face.

Fanning screamed with pain and stumbled, running blind, trying to find the staircase. Tip-toe caught him in the upstairs hall, dragged him down the steps, and threw him out among the gang's horses. "That'll teach you to 'noy Miss Lizbuth!"

Meanwhile, Mamba had raised the window and was yelling for Bill, Beezie, anybody, to come down there quick. But by the time they discovered where she desired their presence, the women and the other men had got there—and they had guns.

Elizabeth had stood silently, tense and helpless, during the whole affair. Her head was spinning and a queer nausea began to rise in waves through her stomach. She sat down on the side of the bed, holding on to the post, forehead resting on her arm and her eyes fixed on the floor. Everything became quiet then. Seeing what Tip-toe had done to Fanning, with no visible weapon, those horrible people had ridden rapidly away, and after a while Mamba came back with something in her hand beside the bandage where the glass had cut. She saw the bottom of her skirt first where it came into her line of vision, covered with bits of dead grass. She raised her head.

The old slave was holding out to her the little shell necklace James had given her so long ago in Nassau. "Dis here's all you got lef', honey," she croaked.

Elizabeth tried to answer; she reached out and took the precious little trinket, gripping it in her hand, but the nausea had come back and she dropped her head quickly back to her arm again.

Mamba smoothed her hair. "As ain't aimed to worry you, baby. You lay back on de baid and Ah'll git you a drink. Dem womens was enough t'make a pig sick!" She helped her up to the pillow, and Elizabeth closed her eyes gratefully.

But when she came back with a little glass of brandy, Mamba stood looking down at her with a new and speculative intensity. Dark circles lay deep under her lashes, and the dress was pulled tight over almost imperceptively enlarged breasts. "How you feel now, baby?" she asked, carefully watching every sign.

"Better." Elizabeth smiled up into the wrinkled face. Now that the dizziness was gone again, nothing else seemed to matter very much.

"Miz Lizbuth, you is pregnant. That's what you is!"

"Oh!" She sat up abruptly and immediately dropped back again, shutting her eyes against another wave of reeling blackness. "Oh, no!"

For a week, she allowed herself to be pampered and waited on, nursed and coddled. She scarcely touched the trays of food the servants tried so hard to make appetizing, and hardly a word escaped her lips. She lay and stared at the ceiling in a dull, melancholy resentment of this fate which had overtaken her.

At first, she had dreamed of the happiness it would give her if James wanted a child. But now, now that she was going to have one, the idea filled her with bitterness. He didn't even want *her!* And babies were for people who loved each other, not for a house divided and a world torn by war. No, not that. The war would not have mattered. How proudly she would have taught her son that his birth year was the same as his country's—how loyal and devoted he must be to this nation that had come into being with him. Crazy, slippery thoughts! Who knew when the war would end, or if a new nation would come into being at all? Maybe I'm delirious, she thought. But she knew she was not. There was no fever, and she was not even dizzy anymore.

She was just lying there in a stupefying turmoil that got nowhere at all. If James found out about her pregnancy he would undoubtedly keep her here and they would go on and on for the rest of their lives like they were that last night at dinner—silent and hating. No. She could not take such slow poison as that. Better one swift stroke that would cut her out of his life. Better go back to Jamaica somehow, on her own before he came home again.

With this idea, she could not stay in bed any longer, and when Mamba came in, she was putting on her clothes. "We are going back to Jamaica," she said.

"Mis Lizbuth, is you plumb crazy?"

"No. I think for the first time I've got some sense. Oh, I

don't mean right away. We've got to wait for a chance. I just thought I'd tell you so you wouldn't be so shocked when the time came."

"Now looka heah, honey, you git rat back into dat baid!"

"No, I'm not. I'm tired of acting like a goose. Having a baby isn't anything much."

"Thas all you knows 'bout it!"

"Well, suppose it is terrible, a good many people go on doing it year after year."

"How is you plannin' to take keer of a chile 'thoughten no pa fo' it?"

"Mr. John said he'd come back for me after he wins the war. I guess—I guess he'd take care of us."

Mamba regarded her stiffly. "Mis Lizbuth, folks what has babies cain't think jes' 'bout theyselfs."

This was a new idea and an extremely disturbing one. That Mamba should consider anyone before her piqued her. "Seems like nobody wants me anymore," she said dolefully.

"Lawd, honey, soon's Mist' James fine out he wouldn't paht wid you fo' nuthin'."

"Oh, I don't want it to be like that! I won't stay here and just be tolerated. He said he was going to send me back to Jamaica, and he'd have done it, too, if the British fleet hadn't bottled up the port."

"Well," Mamba grumbled, "hit's a good thing de wah lak hit is an' you couldn't git outta dis country ef you try. Ah'd sho' hate t'think yo' friens 'roun heah'd know, afteh all yo' good works, dat you'd tuhn yo' back on dis country jes' cause things got a little hahd!" She turned without a backward glance and stalked out of the room.

A few days later, Elizabeth came hurrying back from the avenue gate with the news of a skirmish at McCowan's Ford between Davidson and Cornwallis, so disastrous to the Americans that even the scattered, retreating forces were caught at Tarrant's farm and destroyed. The purveyor of this information was delighted at reporting the battle, and in his eagerness further to impress the pretty little lady hanging over the palings, he had gone on to tell her that Cornwallis and his generals intended to push the colonials out of the Carolinas and all the way to the North, where they would smash the life out of them.

She seemed to realize for the first time that actually, in spite of everything, England was going to keep her colonies.

Everybody's sacrifices would be in vain, their homes lost and all their work and lives would go for nothing.

"You is bettah off not to know dem things," Mamba said darkly. "An' you is got to quit talkin' to dem sojers. It ain't 'spectable. You stay in de house now an' ack lak a lady what's delicate."

"Oh, that's crazy," Elizabeth broke in. "Nobody in the world could tell."

"Mebbe dey cain't an' mebbe dey can. But hit ain't proper either way. You oughtn' t' leave dis house."

"Imagine! And me with only twenty-seven slaves to start the spring work!"

"You ain't walkin' dem fiel's!"

"I'm doing everything I can to feed us all. Baby or no baby, it's got to be done!"

In March, Bill began the plowing in earnest. She had decided it would be useless to put in tobacco this year at all. With Craig in possession of Wilmington, there would be no market and no outlet even if they were fortunate enough to make a crop and lucky enough to keep it from raiders. She would start early and plant corn everywhere, except in the field nearest the house, and that would be given over to vegetables, especially those that would keep well for winter or would not perish too quickly in army commissaries.

The spinning wheels had long been silent for lack of material, and she decided to try a little cotton where the indigo had been before. There was no longer any hope of securing wool.

"I'll get all this started," she said to herself as she stood in her bedraggled skirts at the edge of a field and watched the heavy, wooden plows bite deep into the loam. Bill had only one old spavined mule now, which had wandered in and which no one had claimed, and the slaves were taking turns driving each other.

She turned away from the miserable sight, then stopped to watch a noisy wedge of geese flying high overhead. She was conscious only of interest in whatever it was that made wild things behave with such wisdom—knowing when the time came to go—and suddenly tears were streaming down her face. She fought them back, but great sobs rose in her throat. She turned, blindly groping into the horse-pond road, so intent on her own thoughts that the rider in the redcoat was upon her before she saw him.

"Elizabeth!"

"John! Oh, John!"

He threw himself off his horse in a glitter of gold braid and gleam of shirt ruffles, ran one hand through the bridle, and took her in his arms. "Oh, my dear, what is the matter?"

"Nothing," she replied, wiping her eyes on her sleeve and looking up at him with a tremulous smile, "I was just—just watching some geese go over—"

"But you are crying! I can't bear to see you cry." He pulled a fine linen handkerchief from his cuff and offered it to her. "Dry your eyes, darling. You are through with tears now! At last we have the situation in hand, and I'm going to take care of you. You can't imagine what I have suffered, thinking of you here after I left!"

His arm was around her waist, and she leaned back against him as they made their way toward the house. When she could trust herself to speak, she stopped in the road and faced him.

"John, now that you are here, now that the British have Wilmington, could you get me a passage to Jamaica?"

"Why, my dearest, you don't want to go back there. I can and will arrange to take you with me while we finish up this business in the South, then we will go back to our own land in Connecticut. A marriage can be dissolved, thank God. It won't be long, then you and I can settle down to a life of happiness and peace."

Was this what she wanted, after all? Maybe so—she was so tired and sick at heart it was hard to be sure. "But, John, I—I'm—"

"You're only doubtful because you're so unhappy." He pressed her hand and smiled indulgently. "I knew where your heart really lay when you spoke up and saved me from being shot!"

Gravely, she handed back his handkerchief.

"Better now? Sure you are," he said, a loving sparkle in his eyes. "I haven't had much time for thinking, as you can imagine, since Craig's landing, but all the time I did have was spent on you. And I understand much that I didn't understand before. In Wilmington I heard all the details of your marriage. You are a loyal woman, and I appreciate that, but I never did believe you were really in love with James, no matter what you said. Then when you lied to him and all the others to save my life, after trying to convince me of your patriotism, I knew. Oh, my dear, I knew you loved me."

"John, you don't know that—you don't—"

"Let's not talk about it now. I wanted to tell you that Lord Cornwallis and some of our officers are following me here, and we shall want to impose on your hospitality for a day or two."

"Oh, no! Who?"

"There'll be, besides the general and myself, Colonel Stedman and Colonel Tarleton."

"Tarleton! I won't have him in my house!"

"Oh, I assure you, he can be a most delightful guest. He fancies himself quite a lady-killer."

"There's no doubt he's a killer! He came here once before and destroyed everything he could. If it hadn't been for Tiptoe—"

"Yes, I believe I remember hearing of it, and I'm sorry he has to come with us. But I'm sure he will apologize beautifully."

"That will not rebuild my barns or restore my crops."

"No, but then you won't have use for them much longer anyway. James can build them back himself—if he gets back and if this property is not confiscated to pay for what he helped to take away from some of our loyal citizens."

Elizabeth sighed, but did not answer. There was no use arguing. She was too tired, and she doubted if it were worthwhile to refuse the hospitality of her house. They would only come anyway.

And as for going away with John, she would decide nothing now—not until she could think about it longer—and when the time came, she could tell him she was going to have a baby and couldn't stand the rigors of travel. Then if she did decide to go, at least he would know about it. She could not help clinging to one more hope of a reconciliation with James, and in the meantime she would work and slave in the fields if necessary to keep the plantation going and to get food and whatever else she could spare to the army. The thought of Harmony Hall given up to some loyalist stabbed her. Perhaps John was overly sanguine about the end's being so near and the British successful. But in any event, even if all was lost and she did go to Connecticut, she would have the comfort of knowing she had done everything she could to help save the country, the plantation, and her marriage.

The officers, with their mounted grooms, arrived before supper time. The general was very tall, big-boned, and heavy—middle-aged. He had a large nose and a high forehead above dark, piercing eyes, and he held his thin lips compressed and drawn down at the corners as if he were continuously harassed, and bad-tempered because of it.

Banastre Tarleton came now as a guest, but before he was presented, his handsome mouth twisted to emit a vulgarly appreciative whistle at the sight of Elizabeth's beauty. Her eyebrow rose with the lift of her chin, and she stared at him without saying a word.

Colonel Stedman was a merry, bouncing little member of the staff in charge of commissaries. He had a fiery crop of red hair and twinkling blue eyes, and he seemed constantly to be getting on Cornwallis' nerves. Every time he spoke, the general's face expressed distaste and his fingers plucked at his cuff laces.

Elizabeth was gratified to see that, indeed, what Fanning had said of the wound on Tarleton's face was true. But, contrary to the report, it did not at all "spoil his pretty face." A saber cut, healed into a still-livid line running from forehead to cheek across the bridge of his nose, it merely added a masculine interest to an almost feminine beauty. His eyelashes were as long as a girl's. But the eyes blazed with spirit, and his well-molded mouth had a set to it suggestive of cruelty.

Lord Cornwallis gave her only a stiff shadow of a bow that implied he was doing her a favor by condescending to come into her house. She left John to entertain them, went upstairs to dress. But coming down again, she paused on the bottom step, hearing him say, "She is the granddaughter of Sir George DeRossett!"

"Indeed?" answered Cornwallis with interest, and when she came into the room, he had changed his manner to one of extreme deference.

Never in her life having been patronized, she had remained coolly aloof at his first greeting. Now she was filled with scorn as the reason for his change of manner became apparent. One of her grandfathers had made a second marriage into the family of the man whose wife was Lord Germaine's favorite sister, and Lord Germaine was the minister in charge of military operations in America!

What a sycophant and beastly snob, she thought. She well knew how far beneath them the English considered all Americans, and what they had lost by snubbing even the loyalists. With a proud lift of her head, she ignored his proffered arm and went into the dining room chatting pleasantly with John.

And the more she held him coldly at a distance, the more urgently he sought to win her friendship.

At table, the conversation turned to various incidents of the war, and to Tarleton's discomfort, they fell to discussing the battle of Cowpens. Cornwallis blamed Tarleton for so precipitate an action as attacking Morgan just when he did, thereby losing the day.

"Well, I expected reinforcements which didn't arrive," he answered with an accusing look at Cornwallis, "though they had plenty of time in which to have done so."

"Morgan had his back to the Broad River," the general said, making an effort to control his temper. "One could not possibly have thought you needed them."

Tarleton turned the subject. "And very ill-advised of him, too, though he gave the very sound reason that if there were no possibility of a retreat, his troops would be forced to sell their lives dearly."

"Colonel Washington's cavalry apparently needed no such incentive," the general said, looking smilingly at Elizabeth.

But Tarleton was determined to remain in good humor, more than likely to impress his pretty hostess. "True," he said. "I should like to know the fellow. He is a skilled commander, I'm forced to admit, though they do tell me he can neither read nor write. Can you fancy that?"

Elizabeth allowed her eyes, for a silent moment, to run slowly over the scar bisecting his face, then remarked pointedly, "That may or may not be true, Colonel Tarleton, but you must admit he knows how to make his mark adroitly enough!"

She had the pleasure of seeing the dreaded raider flush scarlet and hearing the uproarious laughter of the others. The general reached over and grasped her hand. "Mistress Richardson, I'd give you my stripes for that!"

After supper, the men went to give the grooms orders for stabling and feeding their horses, but they found the facilities most unsatifactory and forced the slaves out of their makeshift quarters, leading the horses in and scattering hay and grain all over the Negroes' scanty belongings.

Elizabeth started to remonstrate, when John privately apologized. There was nothing he could do, he said, and indeed there was not, as Cornwallis ranked him by several notches.

"We shall want paper and quills, ink and candles, and your guarantee that we are undisturbed," he told her.

"Very well, John." There was no doubt that he loved her

deeply and devotedly, but still he would pursue his course of duty first and last, regardless of anything. Well, she had a purpose and a duty, too, and an idea had suddenly taken form in her mind.

But before she could give it much thought, she must first attend to the wants of her unwelcome guests. There was a small quantity of paper Uncle Adam had given her months ago, and a few quills picked up from the floor after Fanning had rifled her desk. The stock of candles was low and she was glad. She would give them saucers of hog fat with wicks in the middle that would furnish a good but uncomfortably malodorous light. Tip-toe went out to old Lulu, despot of the dye pots, for something to use for ink.

"What's all this for, John?" Elizabeth asked when he came to her alone for the supplies.

"You may as well know," he answered quietly, "since it concerns your future happiness and well-being. We are planning the final thrust that will crush Greene's forces and allow the thousands of loyalists to flock back to our standards, as they will the minute the pressure of these autocratic rebels upon them is relieved. I must get my farms back, too, before you and I can begin to build our future—and that means winning the war first!" He smiled down at her, and she saw that, along with a newfound poise and assurance in his manner, there was a twinkle of gaiety in his eye, as if he had discovered that life could be exciting and—fun.

Still, she was sorry for him. He didn't understand the many emotions involved in causing her to save him—he didn't understand at all. He had misunderstood everything she had done. It was too bad, and she would have given much to convince him of her love for James so that he need not hope for too much, even if she finally decided to go away with him. She knew he had paid little attention to her, too, when she had tried to tell him how she felt about the colonists' cause. Indeed, she doubted if he believed her, for her subsequent actions, she had to admit, did not fully reflect her convictions—letting a known spy get away! But now—now she must try to glean from this conference something, some word of information, that might help the patriots, and to do this she must still all his fears.

"There is a desk in the room Lord Cornwallis will occupy," she told him. "Have your talks in there, and Tip-toe can bring additional supplies if you need them. Do you have to take part?"

"Oh, yes. The information I have will be a large part of the basis for our plans. We've already got Greene on the run, now we've got to figure out a way to get in between his divisions and prevent their joining. I'll try not to be too long. If you'll wait up for me, I'll come back and we can talk. There's a lot to be said, you know!" He pulled her to him and kissed her gently.

The other men came in and she climbed the stairs beside him, turning into her own room at the top and wishing them all good night. But once inside, she waited only long enough to hear Tip-toe come out, having delivered the desired articles, shutting the door behind him. She whispered something to Mamba, who saw that protestations were useless, and slipped downstairs again.

The night was black as good black velvet, and a wind had sprung up, bringing a fine mist that rapidly threatened to turn into rain. But she knew every inch of the passage through the sally port connecting the little room she had given Bill Lipman after his own quarters were burned. There was an outside stairway running up beside it to a small landing beneath a window in the room where the officers were holding their parley. Bill had told her that that room had belonged to one of the Parker boys whose nocturnal prowlings had been better served by a private entrance, and that, after his death, his father had left it as built by the boy's own hand.

Gathering up her skirts and slipping out of her shoes, she began to climb the rickety, rotted steps. She could hear voices above her, and she quickened her climb so as not to miss a single word that might be important. The window was up a few inches and the light from the smoking saucers of lard came through chinks in the shutters. She was out of breath from a fearful excitement and a faint unaccustomed feeling in her body. Her heart pounded in fear of discovery. What would they do to John if they believed him to have led them here only to betray their plans?

On the last step before the landing, a board gave way suddenly beneath her foot, and she threw herself against the wall to keep from falling. Abruptly, the talk in the room ceased. Terrified, she flattened herself against the house in the blackness, as one of the men hurried to the window, threw open the shutters, and stuck his head out. The light streamed across the empty landing, and in its glow she could see Stedman's fiery head against the dark.

He seemed to stand there an eon listening, and she thought

surely he could hear her breathing. She could have touched him without moving an inch.

At last he withdrew his head. "Wind, I suppose," she heard him say as he closed the shutters. "There's a stairway out there. Could be a loose plank blowing."

"A stairway!" came the harassed voice of Cornwallis. "Well, for God's sake, go down and make sure nobody is on it."

"The wood looks too old and too rotten to hold anybody up, my lord. I don't like to risk it."

"You'll have to risk it. Or do you consider your own fat neck of more value than a king's colony? Wait. Take a flare."

Elizabeth heard a piece of the valued paper torn and twisted into a spill. It gave her a small margin of time. She stumbled down the steps and reached the shelter of the blacker than black shadows on the other side of Bill's room as the shutter was flung open again and Stedman climbed out. He turned his head back and forth, holding his paper torch high, peering around, then came down the stair gingerly and reentered the house by way of the sally port. Evidently no king's province was worth a second trip on those steps.

She gave him time to get back, then entered the house herself. Standing in the hall, she heard the company moving into the adjoining room and chairs being pushed about. For a moment she was at a loss, then she remembered that the room they now occupied was just below Tip-toe's little attic space. The ceiling there was not thick because of the protection of this third floor—perhaps she could catch a few words by listening from above. Her shoes lay where she had left them in her flight. It was a wonder Stedman hadn't stumbled over them.

She crept up the stairs and on up the narrow, steep flight to the attic, cautiously making her way past the astonished Tip-toe to the center of his room. She shook her head at him with a finger to her lips. Then, on her hands and knees, with an ear against the floor, every word spoken in the room below was plainly audible.

John was saying, "I told you, m'lord, that the defenses of Wilmington were nothing, and I was right. Craig took it with little resistance. Now, I can't understand why you don't believe me when I tell you that you are making a mistake by heading for Salisbury."

"You don't know everything, Colonel Richardson. Greene has chosen that route, and we shall close in on him before his reinforcements can join him. Besides, it puts me in control of the river sources."

"Yes, but don't you see that Greene can retreat and cross the Dan and into Virginia and slip out of your reach like water?"

"I will, however," Cornwallis answered, "control the road to Wilmington, which I must do to keep in communication with my supplies."

"You'll find it too far, sir."

Someone unfolded a map with much crackling. "Here," he continued, "we will make our march along this route, gathering up loyalists who are but waiting for us—"

"I think, sir, you mistake there. You have been misinformed as to the number of people disposed to be friendly."

"You talk like a traitor, Colonel Tarleton. They flocked to us readily enough in the south, or would you prefer not to remember the south too well," he asked in heavy sarcasm.

"Lord Cornwallis, I am tired of your harping on my rout at Cowpens. 'Twas your own fault, I assure you, that the day was lost."

Elizabeth's knees were cramped beneath her, and with her head bent to the floor the retarded circulation of blood throbbed and ached in her hot cheeks. But she listened to every word, words that were cut deep in her memory with the stylus of intense concentration. There was no need to write down what was said. Every plan and argument, suggestion and possibility, as well as the newly settled line of march, was carved in her mind in letters of fire.

"Be silent," Cornwallis roared at Tarleton, then dropped his voice to a sinister low pitch, "I'll have your stripes, sir! I am still your commander-in-chief!"

"And Clinton is yours, m'lord, don't forget," answered the impudent Tarleton, "and if I mistake not, his express orders to you were not to separate yourself too far from your bases. 'Twas his policy to send predatory expeditions into the country, but refrain from endangering his main force while gradually wearing the rebels out."

"Nothing but tobacco stealing," scoffed Cornwallis. "The ministry is tiring of his timid ways. What is needed is a man who can take hold of this country's neck and wring the life out of it quickly."

She heard Stedman speak for the first time. "But, sir, this plan of yours leaves the commissary department at a loss to be of any assistance to you."

"Stedman, I will not be questioned by my subordinates. Besides, how could General Greene possibly know how far I'll be from supplies? We'll strike quickly—"

"But," John interrupted, "Greene has had the foresight to provide himself with boats in which he can cross these rivers and so make your possession of their sources valueless. If we don't move soon, we ourselves can't cross them. The spring rains—"

"Don't believe all you hear, Richardson."

"You evidently believed all you heard about the loyalists being unable to wait all over the country until they could join us, but you saw what happened to Ferguson at King's Mountain," said the irrepressible Tarleton. "He didn't pick up a handful of recruits."

"General Washington has sent a force under Steuben," John went on as if he had not been interrupted, "to prevent Arnold's coming down to reinforce us from the northeast, and if you insist upon invading this colony again, we are as like to be crushed between Greene's twin divisions as we are to destroy him. You run the risk, sir, of having your communications cut and of leaving yourself in hostile territory without provisions."

"And how do you propose to make such a march with all your heavy baggage?" asked Stedman. "We can't possibly support the army that far from the nearest base!"

"You can't cross swollen streams with such stuff!"

"We'll burn the baggage," declared Cornwallis.

"Oh, for God's sake!" ejaculated Tarleton. "If you strike now, before giving Greene a chance to retreat, you won't have to do that. How do you expect to keep your forces going without the heavy stuff? You've got everything your own way now, but, mark my words, if you let him get away, you've lost him. It's as plain as the nose on your face, sir." Tarleton had dropped his voice to a tone almost of entreaty.

"My nose, sir," said Cornwallis irritably, "is not, praise God, a matter for your consideration. Enough of this bickering. This is our line of march, and we will wait until—"

"My lord," John said quietly, "Greene is now in temporary camp on Hick's Creek, which joins the Peedee a little below Cheraw. One thrust at him there before he can unite his commands, and the war is over."

"Not so simple as it sounds, Colonel. Every delay strengthens us and weakens him. They've not the spirit or the equipment for long delaying."

"Then don't let *us* delay, sir," Tarleton cried.

"No!" Cornwallis' hand came down hard on the table. "I propose to take North Carolina in my own way. Perhaps you gentlemen don't know that I have a commission from Lord Germaine himself giving me full authority to direct this campaign according to my own judgment. We will take the Salisbury route and force Greene into battle at a time of least convenience to him."

"Well, you're running the show," Tarleton said in disgust.

But Elizabeth waited to hear no more. She slipped out to Bill Lipman's room, waked him, and told him he would have to ride to Hick's Creek with a message for General Greene.

"This time o' night?" he asked sleepily.

"Of course this time of night! It's urgent!"

"On what? We don't have a horse."

"There are horses here."

"Them British nags and the house full o' Britishers, and me takin' a message to Greene! No, ma'am. They'd catch me and skin me alive."

He was right, of course. There was no chance of stealing one of their well-guarded mounts. She bit her lip as an idea came that might not work—but it *had* to!"

"All right, Bill. I'll go myself. Give me your boots and a pair of your breeches! And if anyone questions you, say that I've gone to see a sick friend. Not a word to anyone about what I've said, you understand?"

"Yes'm. But—"

She picked up her shoes and the borrowed garments and ran to the house, where she threw a long cloak over Bill's garb. She took no care this time to be quiet going up the stairway. The men had been so engrossed in their talk that they could likely be fooled into thinking they had missed the sound of her footsteps.

As she approached their door, the talking stopped, but she knocked quickly, urgently, and called to John. It was not difficult to put on an air of anxiety, and as he opened the door and looked out, she was standing with her eyes wide, her hands twisting together.

"Oh, John, Sarah Brown is very sick! I've got to go to her."

"When? How do you know?"

"Mary Boyd sent one of the slaves to Podge to tell me to come as quick as I could," she lied. "Come on! You've got to take me! I've got to have a horse."

"Oh, Elizabeth, I can't possibly go until—"

"You must. She may be dying!"

By now Cornwallis was at the door. Quickly she dabbed at her eyes and swept her lashes up at him beseechingly. Fear was in her face, drops of sweat appeared on her forehead. "Oh, Lord Cornwallis," she wailed.

"Now, now, Mrs. Richardson, what can we do for you?"

"I've got to get to Oakland, to Sarah Brown. She's—she's dying, and Mary is blind and I haven't got a horse."

"Now, now," he said again, "you may have my own horse."

She could hardly believe her ears. The monstrous humor, the ridiculous drollery of using his own mount! "Oh, thank you, sir. I'll send him right back."

"But, Elizabeth," John protested, "you can't ride through—"

"Just what I was thinking," Cornwallis broke in. "The least we can do after your hospitality is to have you escorted."

"Oh, I'm not afraid," she said quickly, her heart sinking.

"Indeed, no, madam, my own groom shall take you."

It was the best she could do. At Oakland maybe she could get another horse or figure out something.

It was better that John didn't come, she thought, as, followed by Cornwallis' groom, she rode through the dark forest, because Sarah herself might answer the door.

And she did, holding a candle high, peering out. Elizabeth pushed in, threw her arms around her, and whispered something. And Sarah's pale voice came louder than she had ever heard it. "Oh, thank God you're here!"

She thanked the groom over her shoulder and saw him go off down the avenue at a fast trot, leading the general's horse. By this time Mary was feeling her way down the stairs. Elizabeth poured out her story and the need for haste.

"We've only a broken-down old cob we were plowing with."

"Well, he'll have to do. Sarah, you've got to go to bed and stay there and pretend to be as sick as I told them you were. And, Mary, you'll have to stay down here night and day in case anybody comes. Make it real even to the slaves. If John comes asking for me, say I'm upstairs nursing Sarah; she's got—got the smallpox, anything that would keep him from coming to her door and trying to see me. You know how to handle it. Now let's go get the horse."

"But you don't mean now—you can't go out in the middle of the night alone," Sarah cried.

"She's got to," Mary said quietly.

At the ferry she pounded on Podge's door, but out of the light sleep of the old, he answered instantly. "Take me across, Podge." He did not argue. His nightcap bobbed along ahead down to the landing, as she told him what she was doing and his own fabricated part in the scheme. When the horse had been coaxed aboard, he began to give her instructions for reaching the Cheraw country.

When he had done, she laughed. "Podge, you are wonderful! You and Mary Boyd are the only two people on earth who wouldn't have tried to stop me!"

" 'N' I like to see you go off alone less'n anybuddy. But I give up on tryin' to persuade women a long time ago, and anyhow, I know you got to go. You got any money on you?"

"No, I—" She had not even thought of money.

"Here." He took a small bag from around his neck, heavy with pennies. "I ain't goin' nowhere." He pulled the ferry up on the opposite bank with a bump. "Take keer of yourself, ma'am."

CHAPTER 18

The horse was even worse than Sarah had thought. A starved, dispirited creature, stringhalted and slow. The night was black and cold; the mist of earlier evening had turned to frozen, stinging particles, and suddenly Elizabeth was more frightened than she had ever been in her life. In the excitement and hurry to get away, she had given no thought as to how it would be, riding alone through the darkness, through strange forests with their thousand stealthy night sounds—utterly alone, and on a horse that only wanted to lie down and die. She was afraid to stop and get down for a branch to beat him with. All she could do was to kick at his side with the heel of the too-big boots.

At length she came out of the long wood into a clearing, and a watery moon showed intermittently between fast-moving clouds. She was thankful for the dim light, the cessation of the freezing mist. Would morning never come? A terrible thirst began to torment her and pangs of hunger that was almost nausea. She had had no food since dinner, and had only picked at that. When daylight came, she would have to find some place to stop and eat or she'd never have the strength to get to Greene's camp. And this brought another question. She didn't know this part of the country. What would she say to anyone, either loyalist or patriot, kind enough to take her in for a meal? Everybody was suspicious these days. How would she know which side a householder was on? She must fight off the weariness and the sleep she knew would overcome her sooner or later and think what to say.

Woods closed around the road again, and darkness and ominous shadows. A fox leaped suddenly out of a thicket and frightened the horse so that he stumbled and fell. She slid off in panic, reached down and broke off a branch whip, lashed him until he got up, and scrambled back onto the saddle, continuing the blows until he started off again.

For hours the road wound on, the slow clumping hooves making a ragged, soporific rhythm. Burning pains darted through her legs, her shoulders, her back. But above all was the burning necessity to reach Greene in time.

Around an abrupt turn she was challenged by a sentry. The horse stopped gratefully as a man stepped up with a lantern that revealed a scarlet jacket.

Gradually the night had begun to dissolve. Shadows became gray and trunks of trees gray-black. Lightly frozen ruts in the road became visible, and overhead a few sleepy chirps announced the birds' awakening.

"And where might you be going, miss, all by yourself in the dark?"

She forced every ounce of willpower to stop the trembling of her icy hands and lips, which, had she thought about it, made her story more convincing. "Oh, sir, I'm trying to get to my sister. She's sick. She's—she's having a baby—or she was a few days ago. By now—"

The light grew and the soldier opened the lantern and blew out the flame. Afraid of his next question, she asked, "Where am I? It's been so long—"

"You're at Angel's Creek, about six miles from a plantation called Huntley—" He stopped suddenly, fearing perhaps he had spoken ineptly, not waiting for a more thorough questioning, and his eye fell on the old horse.

But Elizabeth followed his glance, "Damned colonials took my mare," she told him, "and I've got to—"

"Well, now, lady, you look awful tired," he said, relieved. "We got some coffee goin' and breakfast pretty soon. You come rest and eat. A few minutes more won't hurt, and you'll be more good to your sister when you get there."

She dismounted, forcing a smile, her lashes lifting to display trusting blue eyes. "It's very kind of you. I *am* tired."

He took her arm, leading her to a seat on a stump in front of a campfire, and brought her a cup of coffee. Never had anything tasted so good! The hot brew took the chill out of her bones and the cramps from her muscles. She looked around at the men assembling about the cook fires, trying to estimate their numbers. Might as well take General Greene all the information she could.

The sentry, having had himself relieved of duty, now brought her a plate of food. Others came around and stared at her, but she took only a mouthful and handed the plate back. "I'm too tired, too anxious—"

"Yes, ma'am, but you must eat."

She tried again and this time managed to get down some of the cornmeal mush and the bacon. (She could have wolfed it all!) But she was terrified of staying longer on account of possible questions and a weakening of her story of haste. But the coffee and the food had brought back a measure of strength and some amusement at her situation, and she began almost to enjoy it.

Had she passed any colonial encampments on the road? What was the condition of the Whigs where she came from? And, by the way, where *did* she come from? The questions flew back and forth.

She made a vague gesture and answered that she had ridden for two days, from away on the other side of the Cape Fear River. The condition of the Whigs was terrible—"Sometimes I almost feel sorry for them," she said, "really I almost do!"

When she rose to go, the man who had brought her in asked where she was going. This gave her pause for a moment, then she turned a wan smile on him and voiced the first idea that came into her head. "I'm going to the Huntley plantation. I didn't realize it was so near."

"Well, now, ma'am, I'll ride along with you. You don't look like you—"

"Oh, no," she said, her heart beginning to pound, "it isn't necessary at all. I was only confused by the dark and being so—"

"Indeed I'll go! Somebody's got to patrol the road. I'll be glad to."

She drew her cloak around her and mounted the old horse again. There was nothing to do but let him come along with her, but her thoughts were going round and round with fear of what would happen when they got there. Suppose the Huntleys were loyalists and he knew it! She had not an excuse in the world to go there. It seemed that some of the king's men were always wanting to escort her! Well, she'd just have to think what to do when they arrived, but she was so nervous that she answered him only in monosyllables when he spoke and, fortunately, he attributed this to anxiety over her sister.

They rode through a long pine forest, then came out at the edge of a field of blackened stumps—newly cleared land, glistening with frost in the early sun. Beyond stood a white house.

Then the soldier said, pulling up, "Oh, ma'am, I'm afraid you are too late!"

She saw that in the yard there were several saddled horses, one or two gigs, and a wagon draped in black. A festoon of black cloth also adorned the front door. With all her strength, all her ability for acting, she pressed the back of her hand to her mouth. Fear so filled her that there were real tears in her eyes as she turned to him, "Oh, do leave me now! I—I want to go on from here alone." She had almost begun to believe her own story.

With a deferential touch to his cap, he turned his horse. "I understand, ma'am. And I'm—I'm awful sorry."

When he was out of sight down the road, she skirted the field slowly—slowly of necessity on the old horse that was now about done for—and came out back of the house. She was as alert now as a fox, but there was no one in the backyard. She dismounted, having made up a story of being a neighbor or a passerby—whichever was most convincing at the time if anyone questioned. In time of death, no one considered it odd that strangers were present.

A doleful singing was beginning inside the house. Then a slave who did not look too intelligent came out of the stable. She rushed toward him.

"Hurry," she cried, "take the saddle off this worn-out nag and put it on a good one. Quick! There's no time to lose!" She depended on his confusion over the emergency that must have existed in the house for some time and on the fact that he was accustomed to do what he was told.

In less than five minutes, he led a spirited bay out of the stable, and she was away and gone before the bemused darky could ask a question.

Having lost too much time already, she pushed the horse to a gallop. But about noon she became really tired. The pounding hooves, the saddle aches, lack of sleep, the cold, made a weariness so vast that it seemed there was nothing else in the whole world. A little spring beside the road gave some refreshment. She broke the thin covering of ice, drank from cupped hands, splashed the water over her face, and let the horse have his fill. While she waited, a young man in nondescript clothes rode up on a fresh-looking mount, himself to make use of the spring. He looked at her curiously as she questioned him as to the surrounding territory.

"Can you tell me how far it is to Hick's Creek?" she asked.

"Whadda you want to know for?" he asked suspiciously.

She held her temper. "I have an errand over that way. My sister—is sick," she faltered. Having just seen her funeral, the sister did not seem so real as before, and for the first time the charm of the blue eyes and dimples failed.

"A likely story," he replied coldly, leaning against his saddle while the horse drank.

She stamped her foot. "What's the matter with you? I've ridden all night and all day today trying to get there!"

He was not convinced, but his expression changed to one of cunning. "All right. Keep on this road till you come to a shallow stream. Ford it and go on about a mile to a fork in the road. Take the right hand and you'll find Hick's Creek right ahead." He remounted and dashed off in the direction he had described, out of sight before she could climb back on her own saddle.

She wondered at his manner as the road unrolled before her. It occurred to her that the man might have given her wrong directions, that he might be sending her into a trap where he could make an attack on her. But if he had intended to harm her, he could easily have overpowered her at the spring.

Presently, there was the stream, then the fork in the road, just as he had said, and it came to her suddenly that if this were the way to Hick's Creek, he was probably an outpost. In that case, Greene had not moved and she would be in time. This horse, too, was winded now, but she lashed him to a run, and as they topped a rise, she saw the tents spread haphazardly over a field. Men were moving about and cook fires going.

A sentry stepped out in front of her, and accompanying him was the man she had met at the spring, hostility plain on both their faces.

Exhaustion had finally overtaken her, but she slid from the saddle and demanded urgently to be taken to General Greene.

"Thought you was going to see your sister."

"No. I have a message for the general. I—I didn't know who you were!"

They questioned her for valuable minutes until finally she lost her temper. Then she started to laugh at the thought of the way the British had helped her on her way, when here were the patriots treating her with the greatest suspicion.

"I got away on Lord Cornwallis' own horse," she said. "And I had breakfast with one of his detachments on Angel's Creek. Now are you convinced?" She stopped laughing and fixed them with a hard blue stare, her brow lifted. "You'd better take me to the general at once or I vow you'll be sorry!"

The man from the spring glanced at the sentry and took her arm. "All right, we'll see."

He hurried her across to one of the tents and pushed her ahead of him through the flap. "Someone to see you, General."

She was left swaying on her feet before a man seated behind an old box and writing busily. There was the stub of a candle at his elbow which gave only a flickering glow inside the dim tent.

"General Greene," she said in a shaking voice, "I have—"

He looked up at once, shocked at the sight of a woman, and quickly came around his makeshift table. She looked very young and small, and at a glance he took in her weariness and her disheveled appearance.

"My dear miss! You are ill! Here, sit down." His stern tones were overlaid with gentleness. He poured brandy into a cup and handed it to her.

She sank onto a low cot, breathing rapidly, trying to focus her tired eyes, and sipped at the drink. She saw that he had a powerful face, heavily lined, with a full, well-shaped mouth, hazel eyes that were almost brown, and surprisingly, there was a dimple in his left cheek. So this was the man who had been chosen to tackle a superhuman job. To bring order out of the chaos of General Gates' making and build an army out of the scattered, ragged regiments of the Southern Division. Her heart warmed to him at once, and presently the brandy warmed her body and loosened her tongue. But she glanced at the man still standing by the tent opening, and seeming to understand, the general dismissed him.

As she talked, his only interruption was a question now and again, a grim smile, a nod of agreement. Elizabeth poured out the discussion between the British officers exactly as she had heard it, gave him Cornwallis' plan to force him into battle before he should have withdrawn from his present position and been joined by reinforcements. She told him of the British general's plan to reach first the upper waterways and of the weakness of the plan from the lips of his own staff. Everything, word for word. At the end she sank back helplessly and closed her eyes. Sharp, bright pains were shooting through her entire body. She still felt the motion of the horse and the cramp in her right leg from its position on the saddle.

Then, through the dimness, she heard Greene call for his orderly to send the doctor, and she tried to struggle up. With an effort she opened her eyes. "I'm all right, sir, just a long ride and—"

He spread a blanket over her. "Do lie still, ma'am. Don't try to talk any more now."

Several men came in, and she heard the orders to strike camp, heard the clipped orders and the excitement of the officers as Greene conveyed her information to them. They went out and the doctor came in. She was perfectly conscious, but her muscles refused to move. She felt a hand on her wrist, felt a weight beside her on the cot, the pull of a thumb opening her eyelids, then the upswing of the cot as the doctor rose.

"Just cold and exhaustion, sir, I think—"

"I've got to go home," she said feebly.

"Where do you live, miss?" Greene asked.

"On the Cape Fear."

"Who are you? What is your name?" he persisted, but she pretended a greater drowsiness and did not answer.

He repeated the question and added, "You see, I want to believe your story, but unless I know, I can't be sure that I am to credit it."

This roused her instantly. He must believe her! Her chin quivered, and she opened tear filled eyes, "I am Colonel James Richardson's wife, and I live at Harmony Hall on the Cape Fear River some miles above Wilmington."

Relief flooded the general's voice. "You could have been some loyalist, you know, giving me wrong information."

"Oh, no!"

"Well, now, you rest a bit. The doctor here will see what he can do for you. We can't let you go that far back without being sure you're all right."

"But I've got to go. I'm—I'm going to have a baby and—"

"Great Jehovah," the doctor exploded. "And you rode all night and all day!"

"What'll we do?" The general who would one day outmaneuver the best British military minds was plainly at a loss.

"Do? I don't know!" The doctor was equally bewildered.

"We can't let her go back through that Tory-infested country. She wouldn't stand a chance, and certainly not on a horse. I guess we'll have to take her with us, and we've got to leave here in a few minutes."

Elizabeth fought off the drowsiness. This was impossible. She could not go with the army, for she knew that Greene, in taking advantage of her report, would gather every patriot force in the country on his march to beat Cornwallis to the upper rivers. James would certainly join him from wherever he was. They would tell him she was along, and the doctor would tell him about the baby.

She sat up shakily and tried to stand. "I *can't* go—I just want to go home!"

"Mistress Richardson, you can't do that without an armed escort, and I can't spare a man now if we're to use the information you so bravely brought us. Please don't ask it of me, for I feel that after what you've done you deserve anything you want."

"I came alone," she persisted.

"Yes, but you slipped away, and the Lord was with you! You couldn't possibly get back without being caught. And in your condition! Why, the whole country is no doubt searching for you by now."

At last, against all her arguments and pleadings, they made a bed for her in one of the baggage wagons, and the long retreat was begun.

The retreat to the northern part of North Carolina: through rain and spring thunder and sudden hailstorms; through hot sun and cold nights; over the swollen rivers on rafts and barges and boats—the boats Lord Cornwallis had not believed Greene could gather; in hunger sometimes and weariness always, the ragged army wound its way northward. The red-clay roads were quagmires. The heavy, sticky mud gathered and clung to foot and wheel and hoof. Sometimes the pursuing army of Cornwallis was so near at night that the British campfires could be seen twinkling through the trees; sometimes a day or two separated them. Once the rear guard of the American forces forded a river quite easily through shallow water, but the next day when the enemy arrived, freshets from the mountains had come down and Cornwallis was stranded on the other side. The patriots slapped one another on the back and said it was like Moses at the Red Sea.

Always north by east they moved. Sometimes a day was

punctuated by the addition of joyously welcomed recruits, and sometimes throughout the long hours there was nothing except the same plodding columns, and nothing to hear but the rumbling, creaking wagons, the jingle of harness, the indistinct murmuring roll of an army on the march.

After a deep sleep of many hours and several days of lying listlessly in the wagon bed, Elizabeth began to watch for the sight of James' tall figure on some incoming saddle, but if he came, she did not see him. At first she stayed to herself as much as possible, though the general invited her to a meal with him whenever he had anything to eat and time to think of it. Then she would go over the conversation she had overheard in the attic again, and Greene would sit in contemplation, nodding his head while he kept her talking. It seemed to ease him, to be soothing to nerves keyed too high, and he searched her words for any small detail he might have missed. She made him laugh by telling him how Cornwallis came to be so kindly disposed to her that he offered her his own horse and his own groom to escort her as she rode away that night, of how the British detachment she had encountered had entertained her at breakfast, and of the funeral at the Huntley plantation furnishing her a fresh horse.

Often in a section through which they passed, there were families so terrified of being abandoned to the oncoming British that they would fall in behind the army and follow. Some had wagons piled with household goods, and some had cows and a few chickens.

Elizabeth took special interest in the women who had babies or small children. Occasionally she could buy milk and bits of fresh food for them with the pennies from Podge's bag, and one grateful mother gave her a clean dress from her own supply.

In camp, when the army rested, the relieving cessation of motion was usually enough to send her straight into sleep, but if at times she lay awake, nothing seemed to worry her greatly. Even the thought of Mamba's anxiety over her prolonged absence was not too disquieting, and that the incompetent Bill was having to attend to everything at the plantation bothered her very little. The hardships of the journey she accepted stoically. She had a strange feeling that she had been living like this forever, and really it mattered not at all.

"It's a trick of nature," said the doctor one evening in answer to an anxious question of Greene's, "just a trick of nature to guard the happiness of an unborn child before she throws it out into a world of trouble. Don't worry, your patient is well enough." But the general fretted just the same. He worried over the possible effects of the long march and the fear that the girl was not getting the proper food. But there was little he could do under the circumstances except to share with her what fresh produce his men could scrounge from the countryside.

So the days passed. Riders dashed by with dispatches for the general, and the messages they carried swept backward through the snakelike train. Cornwallis was at Salisbury; Cornwallis was at Halifax; at Hillsboro; he had crossed the Yadkin; he had received fresh troops. . . .

But Greene had now crossed the Dan River and, to the hilarious rejoicing of his army, had beaten his adversary to his own goal, reversed their positions, and himself held control of the upper waterways. He could retire into Virginia if he liked, or he could advance and force Cornwallis into battle.

He decided in favor of battle. But first he crossed over and went into camp at the old ironworks on Troublesome Creek. Here he could rest his forces for a few days after the strenuous retreat and hope for additional recruits.

The sick and wounded were placed in a small building that had to do for a hospital. Elizabeth, with the other women and the children, was given an old log cabin nearby where they spread what they could find for beds, and cooked what could be found to eat in an iron pot in the yard.

Messengers and scouts rushed in and out of the camp, bringing reports of the enemy's positions, taking dispatches from the general to any and all who might send him reinforcements.

Then, one day, there was a quickening in the atmosphere as fresh troops began to converge on the site. Colonel Campbell brought in four hundred Continentals; next there came two brigades of North Carolina militia; and later, sixteen hundred Virginia rifles and two companies of seasoned veterans from Maryland. It was almost beyond anything Greene could have hoped for, bringing his numbers up to nearly three thousand men against Cornwallis' reported nineteen hundred. But the British troops were well-disciplined, well-trained soldiers, and Greene knew that not long could he count on his own militia, what with their short-term enlistments constantly expiring and with the many new, inexperienced recruits. He must force a battle while at least he had the advantage of superior numbers and of choosing his own ground. Added to this was a trump card: the fact that he had drawn Cornwallis far, very far from his base. Now was the time to strike.

He had already chosen his location. Spring was beginning to swell the buds on the trees and wild flowers to paint the land as the little group of women, children, and disabled men watched the army move out on the road to Guilford Courthouse a few miles away.

James and William Washington were just finishing a supper of meat broiled over open coals when a rider dashed into their camp with the general's orders. Their detachment of cavalry had been out for weeks, harassing the enemy outposts, shutting off their communications and foraging parties, and there had been a good many sharp skirmishes. Both men were tired, and their men and horses were weakened from hunger and the chill of the early-spring nights. But word from Greene ordering them to join him as soon as possible at Guilford Courthouse lifted their spirits.

"Looks like a battle at last," Washington said.

"Let us hope so. You can't keep recruits hanging around long in their present condition."

They were traveling light, and within a few minutes were on the Salisbury road going north. A slow, dreary rain was falling and mud made a slippery footing for the horses so that their progress was slow. James huddled in his coat as the hours passed, his hat pulled low over his eyes, his chin sunk in his collar. As usual, ever since his last departure from the plantation, his thoughts turned to Elizabeth. At first, after his shameful conduct toward her, he had comforted himself with the promise of going back the moment there was a lull in the fighting to tell her again that he loved her, to apologize, to try to win her back. But there had been no lull. Instead, every passing day had increased his responsibilities and brought continuous orders sending him farther and farther away. He had suffered tortures remembering her hurt, reproachful eyes. They had haunted him on the long marches, through the long nights, even in the heat of battle.

It was not as if he had not known deep down that all was as it should be, though at the time he had believed the worst. It was his pride and his disappointment that had caused that. When, suddenly, after the battle at King's Mountain he had realized that what he had been feeling for her all the time was an overwhelming love and that he had wasted some valuable months in not knowing it, the compulsion to get back to her had been irresistible, and he had ridden long and hard toward a dream of reunion that had been as the proverbial pillars of cloud and fire. Along the way, little things kept coming back to him that proved her love as real as his own. What a fool he had been not to have seen it before! In his laughing elation over the discovery, he had shouted in his heart, "To hell with the war for a few days!" And, strangely enough, this had startled him with the realization that now the war was more important than ever. Now America had to be free! Free, so that a man and a woman might love and build their homes and their lives on ground that was firm beneath their feet; so that their sons might face the world proud and unafraid. Their sons! What beautiful children Elizabeth would have! Has ever a man known such happiness, he had asked himself, his eagerness increasing with every mile.

But his arrival had been so different from his picture of it. Reaching Harmony Hall only to find her in John's arms had cast him headlong out of the paradise he had woven around his homecoming. He was proud, impetuous, quick to anger, and it had been too much. He had behaved horribly, but at the time he had been unable to help himself. Morning might have brought some measure of apology and reconciliation if things had not happened so fast or if he had made some gesture that might have bridged the way.

Now, looking back, he saw that she had been far more patient with him than one would have expected of her. Then, finally, when her anger did come, it had only intensified his own. The last straw had been her defense of John. It had seemed proof that she was willing to save him at any cost, that it was John she really loved and had only married him, James, out of expediency. The passion inside him had risen to a peak of love and hate so near the same color he could not differentiate between them—and he had told her he was sending her away. Snakes crawled in his belly at the memory!

Slogging through the rain, he wondered in agony if he had killed her love, if he could ever make amends. And on top of all was a constant anxiety as to what might be happening to her at the plantation with only the slaves and Bill to protect her and the British in possession of all that country.

There was nothing of cheer or comfort in his own surroundings either that might have helped to ease the gnawing inside him. His company, as indeed most of the army, was without rum, often without food, and the condition of the soldiers was enough to keep any man in tears. But the thought of the coming rendezvous with Greene gave him a small hope.

The message had been urgent. Perhaps the general was at last ready to fight, and if all went well they might end this miserable conflict. He spurred his horse, already sliding and slipping in the mud, to a faster pace.

At dawn, they were but a few miles from Guilford. The rain had stopped sometime during the long night, and as the sun rose, they saw smoke rising from the top of the hill where the courthouse stood. The road passed through a narrow defile beyond which was a clearing surrounded by a zigzag rail fence. Around it, on both sides and beyond were dense woods, and back of that rose the hill. James gave a low whistle and turned to Washington, riding just behind him. There was a grin on his face—the first Washington had seen there in a long time.

"Looks like the old man has picked himself a location," he said.

As they approached, they were astonished at the number of reinforcements, and hastily pushed on to headquarters.

The general looked up with a relieved smile as they came in. He and his staff and a number of other officers were busily planning the placement of troops. As he shook hands with James, Greene started to say something, but turned at a quick question from someone, and whatever it was was lost in the hurried and intense preparations for battle. There was a great deal of rushing in and out, explanations, instructions, orders. Then it seemed but a moment before the companies were moving down toward their charted stations.

It was the fifteenth of March, and the day was cool, without a cloud in the sky. The general had placed the North Carolina militia recruits on the near side of the clearing back of the forward rail fence, with Washington's cavalry flanking them on the right and Lee's dragoons on the left. Some three hundred yards back, he put the Virginia militia under Stevens and Lawson, straddling the road, behind another rail fence that ran almost parallel to the other. Singleton's guns were in the center, and the Virginia Continentals, the Maryland rifles under Huger and Williams, defended the base of the courthouse in the rear. With this arrangement he was ready for anything Cornwallis might have to offer.

About noon Greene walked along in front of the first line

of militia. "Keep your guns rested and steady on the rail," he shouted, "and aim with precision at the officers. Don't be in a hurry. Hold your fire until you're sure of a mark. Just give me two rounds, boys, then you can fall back."

At one-thirty the men in front could see down the narrow cut the red and white uniforms and sun-flashing steel of the British vanguard approaching. The general had chosen his ground well, for the enemy had to pass not only through the defile, but through the open clearing before coming into musket range, while the dead-shot rifles had the longer reach and were steadied as well on the fence rails.

Yet on they came, deploying rapidly, spreading out as they entered the clearing. There was tenseness on every face as the red line moved forward like a gash of blood. There was no sound except a distant ruffle of drums, and somewhere back in the woods a bird called.

Then at a signal the rifles flared. The red line wavered and great chunks of it lay on the ground, but like molten metal it reformed and flowed forward.

The rifles spoke again, and again the enemy was flung back. But by now the rear lines were pushing forward to fill the gaps. At musket range they stopped and fired, and the first American militia, having delivered its two volleys, took to its heels and the woods. The cavalry companies came into action, and the guns in the center, the big six-pounders, poured destruction into the Yagers, Webster's Fusiliers, and the Highlanders.

Now the British guns were moving up. The carnage on both sides mounted. There were the screams of men and horses, thunder of guns, the rattle of rifle and musket, shouted orders of officers trying desperately to reform their lines.

James, in the midst of men and horses, felt a vicious need to victory. His blade glittered over his head as he swung and cut and thrust. The British lines were falling into confusion as were the Americans' in the close hand-to-hand combat. It was then that Cornwallis gave his ugly order for a round of grapeshot to be fired into the melee. Even though it meant killing his own men as well as the patriots, he must give his lines a chance to reform. The results were frightful, but the Americans fell back and he got his disciplined troops back in line—what was left of them. They began to push the Americans backward, only to be met by the withering rifles behind the second fence. Then they were beyond the clearing and fighting in the woods. This was more to the patriots' liking as they took refuge and aim from behind treetrunks. The Hessians had never fought this way, and their white crossbelts and gaiters made terrible targets. But the Highlanders kept pushing back a portion of the Virginia militia until they were behind the line, and James took his horsemen to cover their retreat. It was then that he saw the loyalist officer on the ground whom he recognized in the flashing instant as his brother. But there was no time to stop. He could only whirl his horse around to avoid the prone figure, and rush on to overtake his men, who were protecting the Virginians.

It was an afternoon of smoke and thunder—smoke that obscured the daylight; thunder of guns, yells and screams, running men, rearing, plunging horses. There was the rattle of grape and the clash of steel as bayonets thrust and sabers swung; there was wild excitement and fury, with every human soul caught up in the primitive frenzy of battle. One country fought to keep its possessions; the other fought for its life.

Impossible as it seemed to those engaged, it was after only two and a half hours that Greene sent out orders to stop the fighting. He ordered retreat. But Washington and Richardson and Campbell were locked in combat with the Hessians, and the American Continentals were hammering so at Webster's Fusiliers that not a man of them could leave the field until Tarleton was sent by Cornwallis to attack the American flanks and withdraw his men.

The lord general claimed the field, but he knew he was beaten. Both sides were ready to retire and lick their wounds.

Greene waited beyond the courthouse until he had his army reassembled. He had been true to his resolve to save it, for he knew that once lost there would be scant chance of putting together another. He knew he had crippled Cornwallis badly, and he could still clutch to his breast the cheering knowledge that the British bases were far, very far away. He ordered then a general retreat, back to the camp on Troublesome Creek.

The first man to return to Troublesome was the man named Buck who had been with Sergeant Anson at Harmony Hall. He had been with the first militia line and had run with the rest as soon as the second volley was fired. Finding himself back of the lines in comparative safety, he had stayed, awaiting orders, until the general's intentions were conveyed to him; then he was sent ahead to report the battle and to advise those still in camp of the returning army.

Elizabeth was sitting on the steps of the cabin in the late-afternoon sunlight when she saw him coming. She ran to meet him.

"Why, Missus Richardson, what in hell are you doin' here?"

"I've been here for quite a while," she said with a twisted little smile. "Tell me quickly, what happened!"

"The general is retreating, bringing the whole army back here."

"Retreating? Is the battle lost then?"

Buck looked at her white face. "You better come set," he said, wiping the sweat from his own face on a ragged sleeve. "He ain't retreatin' fur. Didn't you ever hear about the feller that fights and runs away'll live to fight another day? No, ma'am, he ain't licked, but I calc'late them Britishers has had about enough."

"Oh," she said, relieved. "Are you with Sergeant Anson?"

"No, ma'am, not anymore. He's dead."

"Dead!"

"Killed with a musket ball in the first charge. Shore hated it." He ducked his head quickly and chuckled with a queer fondness in his voice. "Had some mighty fine plans for hisself, too."

Elizabeth did not answer. She was thinking of the wide-apart gray eyes, and Anson's plans for the legislature, the marriage with Susan. Poor soul. But perhaps it was just as well that he didn't live to know the disappointments that would have been in store for him. Susan surely was not what thought now amid all the democratic talk of the day.

They sat on the steps talking of the battle and of the war he had hoped for, and it would be many a year before men of his station reached the seats of the mighty, whatever they in general, and just before dark Greene rode up. He smiled at her gently, but with the sadness of a commander who has seen the faces of dead friends on the field.

"Mrs. Richardson, I wonder if you know what you've done for your country. It will always owe you a debt of gratitude for our strategic victory today. Thanks to your bravery and your courage we may soon all be able to live in peace again. And I must apologize for not having time to tell James you were with us. He joined us just before the battle when there was much confusion. But if you will wait for a little while, I'll send him to you. He has fought a gallant fight today."

She forced a smile. "I'm happy over the victory, sir. Is—is my husband well?"

"Fit as a young recruit!" He turned to Buck. "Tell Colonel Richardson to report to me as soon as he comes in, soldier."

Buck saluted. "Yes, sir!"

But as Greene rode off, a sergeant came by calling the militia to assembly for roll call, and Buck, perforce, went to answer.

Elizabeth's first impulse was to leave the place at once. Go anywhere to avoid seeing James. She could not bear again that look in his eyes that had been there last time, or hear the chafing remarks he might make upon her presence. But, on second thought, she would have to face him sometime. Perhaps he might arrange some way to send her home or, better still, take her there himself. Maybe during these long days and nights he had thought of her, had realized that the things she had told him were true, that she was not false. Surely, if he really loved her, he could not stop just on account of appearances.

She sat on in the gathering dusk, refusing to leave long enough even to partake of the scanty meal the other women had cooked. James was a long time coming. Maybe he would not come at all. Her thoughts spun. She was afraid to see him, and so terribly afraid not to! She tried to be calm, but the minutes were slipping into hours, fear and disappointment were slipping in with them. Over beyond the creek she heard the soldiers singing around the campfires.

Huddled into a little ball of dejection, she closed her eyes. When she awakened, the night was still and quiet. She was stiff and cramped from sleeping in the cold, and at first too bemused to remember where she was or why. Then it came to her in a flood of misery. She had waited half through the night and he had not come. He had not changed, then. He had meant it when he said he wanted to be rid of her.

She was hungry and so weary that when she rose to her feet the blessed lethargy spread through her brain like a fog. There was but one clear thought on top of the vast misery: she must get home. Slowly, she went down the steps and turned with instinctive sense of direction back down the road over which she had passed with the army days ago, and from which someone had pointed out to her the junction of the highway leading down the Cape Fear.

She plodded on, concentrating only on keeping to the road. Her footsteps resounded on the planking of a bridge over a small run. She remembered crossing it before in the lumbering wagon. Then around a turn there was a campfire and two men sitting beside it. Had she made a circle and arrived back at the camp on Troublesome after all the hours of walking?

The men caught sight of her and got up quickly, suspiciously. Then she saw that they wore the kilts of Highlanders, but somehow it didn't matter now into whose hands she fell. She could not see their faces against the firelight, though hers was brightly revealed to them, and a voice said suddenly, wonderingly, "Mistress Elizabeth!" She stumbled forward, and Gordon Denny caught her in his arms.

They spread a blanket by the fire for her and, when she was rested, gave her hot tea and a thick gruel. Gordon sat down beside her. He did not ask how she happened to be here, for from his past knowledge of her courage as well as her capriciousness, he was little surprised. But he did ask where she was going. News of her marriage to James had reached him months ago, and so he was not surprised either at her obvious condition—in the dress made for an earlier waistline.

"I'm going home," she said, "to the plantation on the Cape Fear."

"Then I can take you there, mum, for we are carrying our wounded down to Wilmington. McLeod, here, and I were given char-rge of the wagons. My enlistment is up, but I dinna mind helping the puir lads."

McLeod got up at a call from one of the wagons, and Gordon said hastily, "Say nothing before him, Mistress Elizabeth. He only knows you are my friend and will ask no questions."

When the man came back, Gordon was saying, "John Richardson is along with us. Not badly wounded, but uncomfortable and feverish."

She sat up. "Oh, Gordon, when can I see him?" The old feeling of security and comfort came over her that she had always had in knowing John was near. "Why—why don't you leave him with us at the plantation? We can take care of him, and it will—will be much better for him than the army hospital in town!" It seemed as if fate had ordered this. She would nurse John back to health, then go away with him—back to Connecticut—when the war was over.

"A gude idea. 'Twould pleasure Lord Cornwallis for him to be well-cared-for. You can see him in a little while. We tr-ry to let them sleep until daybreak if they can. The jolting is har-rd on them."

Presently a pale-gray band appeared in the east, and a dawn wind rustled the trees overhead. McLeod had gone to the creek for water. Gordon got up, knocked out his pipe, and stretched. "We'll give them breakfast now," he said. "Stay where you are, Mis' Elizabeth, and rest until we are ready."

John did not understand Elizabeth's presence. He thought perhaps he was wavering between lucidity and delirium. It seemed that whenever he was sick and wounded, she appeared. But she whispered something to him, and a foggy notion of what might have happened came to him. He smiled and raised her hand to his lips.

"You are going back to the plantation, John," she said gently. "We are going to take care of you there."

Then Gordon made a place for her beside him on his wagon, a bullwhip cracked, and the plodding oxen moved out into the road. He was not given to much talk, and after a silence he said, "We should be at Cross Creeks by evening." He turned to her, his boyish face in a wide grin.

"Oh, that was your home, wasn't it?"

"Yes. And more than ever-r now that my Lucy's there!"

"Gordon, I didn't know!"

"You dinna? Oh, yes. It's been a long time, hasn't it? I wasna' so bad wounded as they thought, and I escaped from their hospital when our troops landed doon at Brunswick. Our army took Robert Howe's plantation, and I took Lucy! We were mar-ried then and I brought her home to bide with my family. Decided love was never-r a matter of politics, and 'tis happy we are when we've had time to be."

"Oh, I'm so glad. Remember when you left Mrs. Bell's house that night dressed up like a Negro?" And though Elizabeth would never have believed she could laugh again, she did, as they fell to reminiscing. But she was very sleepy now, and presently the steady swaying and lurching of the wagon made her drowsy. She slept until late afternoon, until the little train of wounded pulled into the Denny plantation near Cross Creeks.

It was good to see Lucy again. The girl had gained enough weight to make her cheeks plump and pink, and there was that glow in her eyes of a woman in love. She was in Gordon's arms before Elizabeth could climb down from her seat.

The sick and wounded, the foot soldiers sent along as

guards, were all fed from the great kitchen, and dinner in the house would have been a gala meal if Elizabeth's heart had been less heavy. Even as it was, her spirits were lifted by the pleasant company and the sight of Lucy and Gordon's happiness. To all who had been away with the armies, the nourishing, palatable food was a minor miracle.

After dinner she left the family to itself and went out to talk for a while with John. "Are you feeling better?" she asked.

He pulled a corner of his blanket around to cover the blood-soaked bandage on his shoulder. "Yes, my dear little Elizabeth." He looked at her, a strangely sad smile in his eyes, yet there was love there, too. "You are going to have a child."

"Yes," she murmured, her lashes black fans on her cheeks. Two great tears rolled from under them, and she brushed at them angrily.

"Aren't you happy about it?"

"No. Oh, John, you were right—you told me how it would be—but I didn't listen. James didn't love me."

"Do you love him, Elizabeth?"

She looked down at him. "More than anything in the world, but can't you see— Oh, John, please take me with you to—"

"No." The word was tenderly spoken, but firm. "Your child has a right to its inheritance. To a home and its own father." He paused, shifted his position, and winced at a jerk of pain. "I was wrong, very wrong, not to have believed you when you told me before. I would not accept the fact because I loved you so much myself. Selfish of me, but I was afraid of your being hurt. Now I know, my dear, that no one can be protected from that kind of pain; there is always some kind of suffering mixed in with love. Perhaps that's what makes it so precious." He studied the starry sky for a moment, then looked at her. "Give James another chance, Elizabeth. I believe you will find him much changed."

She pushed back her hair impatiently. "What makes you think so? You haven't seen him since I have—except one awful day, and night!"

"Yes, I saw him not many hours ago."

"Oh, where?"

"First, during the battle at Guilford Courthouse when my horse was shot from under me and I got this ball through the shoulder. I was on the ground squarely in his path when he wheeled his mount to avoid running over me. It was impossible for him to stop at that moment, but later, he came back." There was a little chuckle in his voice. "He came back and got down beside me. Did what he could, and sat with me all night talking. Then, when he saw our stretcher-bearers coming, he ducked into the trees. Wanted to be sure somebody picked me up! You know we had to leave many of our wounded on the field, not being able to care for them."

Elizabeth said nothing. She sat staring down at her skirt where her shaking fingers were making little pleats in the fabric—nettled at his quick refusal of her. He and James had reached some sort of reconciliation, she supposed. Now neither of them seemed to want her, and she felt like a child pushed out into the dark.

"War is a miserable business, my dear," John went on, "but it has the effect of making people grow up emotionally rather more quickly than they might in ordinary times. I was so smugly set in my own self-righteousness I failed to see any side of a question but mine—an adolescent attitude! James, for all his seeming irresponsibility, was already much farther along the road. And you, my dear, have outdistanced us both."

This was not true, she thought with a little sting of shame. Willful and headstrong she was—the very mark of a child— she had always been that way. And it was still so. Selfishly, she had expected John, out of his love for her, to do anything she asked, giving him nothing in return; and selfishly, her purpose was still strong to get herself out of a painful situation, not thinking of her baby at all. Mamba's words came back, "People what has babies cain't think jes' 'bout deyselfs."

"No," she said slowly, "you are wrong. I—"

"I think not. I've not asked you why you are so far from home, but thinking on it, I have an idea it has to do with those patriotic convictions you tried to convey to me. People aren't traveling for pleasure these days! No, darling, don't slip backward. Go home and have your baby, your husband, and make a real home for you all. Remember, we always have to pay some sort of price for loving, but I have a feeling yours won't be too high."

She looked at him with a tremulous smile and started to speak, but he interrupted her, "I won't stop at the plantation, Elizabeth, though I thank you for the invitation. It's better this way. We'll say good-bye here, tonight."

"Yes," she said softly, and leaned toward him.

Gently, he kissed her forehead. "Good-bye, my—my little sister."

There were tears on her lashes. The starlight touched them with silver.

CHAPTER 19

Elizabeth lay in her bed luxuriating in the feel of the smooth sheet beneath her and the wonderful quiescence of a house. After a whole day and night of deep, unbroken sleep, she felt almost herself again, and in spite of all Mamba's excited, dark prophecies when Gordon had escorted her in, she had not lost her baby.

"Ah b'lieves you is paht Injun," she said. Her voice carried disgust, but the old eyes were twinkling. " 'Tain't decent fo' a lady to go gallivantin' all ovah de country wid a ahmy an' ridin' a hawse an' still keep a baby. Ah reckons dat's yo' O'Neal blood. Hit ain't DeRossett!"

"Then it's good, strong blood, and I'm proud of it." She had forced herself to reply in the same jesting tone, but a struggle was still going on in her mind. John's advice fought with her own inclinations. The little O'Neal hoyden was dying hard.

Mamba became serious then. "Is we still gonna leave heah?"

"Oh, I don't know. I don't know what to do about anything." She rolled over and hid her face in the pillow. "Mr. John won't take us and—"

"Dat's *good*," Mamba stated firmly, then changed quickly to a more placating tone. "Ah heahs tell it's mougbty cole up dah wha' he live at. 'Tain't good fo' babies."

Everybody seemed to think of nothing but this baby—not about her at all. If only she could just lie here and never have to think or talk again!

But that had too shortly proved to be impossible. Mary Boyd and Sarah Brown arrived in the afternoon and must be told all about her experiences. They must tell her, too, how well they had carried out her orders on that fearsome night.

"We made it so real that after I had stayed in bed for the next few weeks I began to think I really *had* the smallpox!" Sarah laughed.

"And when Adam came home, the house servants wouldn't even let *him* upstairs! We had to make a bed for him in the library!" Mary had to wipe the tears of laughter from her sightless eyes. "He said to tell you you were as wonderful as he always thought you were! He was sent home from Halifax too ill to join General Greene, and he would have come with us today but he's still in bed."

They went on to report the frightful things that had happened in Wilmington after the occupation of the British. Cornelius Harnett had been captured at a plantation in Onslow County where he lay on a sickbed, and brought to town thrown carelessly across the back of a horse, and the last they heard, he was still hovering between life and death. Mrs. Bell's house was used for British headquarters, and the men were stabling their horses in Reverend Will's church. Everything was in a perfectly deplorable condition, but somehow everybody felt a renewed hope after the battle at Guilford.

Tales of Elizabeth's heroism had not taken long to be repeated in patriot homes up and down the river, and they were all as proud of her as if they had had a hand themselves in the business of tricking the British.

When Mary and Sarah had gone, Grandma Love arrived with an enormous bowl of calf's-foot jelly, and a torrent of abuse against the enemy. It was her nearest approach to an apology, and she left with a fervently expressed hope that Elizabeth would not die in childbirth.

She was tired and depressed by their stories, but Grandma's tactlessness brought a smile to her lips. She got out of bed and put her clothes on, enjoying the feel of fresh, fragrant linen and the swish of her own skirts.

She wandered slowly and none too steadily out into the garden. It had had no care for a long time. The paths were littered with twigs and dead leaves, but here and there a tulip and a few daffodils had struggled up through the debris and the forsythia was flaming like dazzling sunlight everywhere. She felt a warm and sudden glow of love for these little flowers that answered the call of spring, according to their natures, and tried to cover with their beauty a country devastated by war. Sitting down on a stone bench, she looked back at the house—at Harmony Hall—and smiled, remembering the day, now peculiarly happy in retrospect, when she had named it.

Podge, having heard she was back, came up the avenue, saw her sitting there, and hurried over. "Missus Richar'son! By God, I been worried about you. But you done it, all right! 'N' I got news! Cornwallis is retreatin' down the river on his way to Yorktown. I'll cross 'em gladly this time! Looks like, from what I hear, we've about broke their backs!"

"Oh, really, Podge?"

"I'm a-tellin' you, ain't I? O' course the great Lord Cornwallis claimed the field at Guilford, but he said another victory like that would ruin him. Golly be to Moses, I hope he gets it!"

When he was leaving, Bill Lipman came up and asked if she felt like walking to the edge of the first field to see what he had done.

"I—I think so, Bill."

He held her arm as they walked around the house and down the horse-pond road. And there beyond she saw long straight rows of young cotton, their little leaves already glistening in the sun.

"I planted some tobacco, too, even though we hadn't planned on it. Just put it in. I figured after Guilford we wouldn't be bothered with no more raiders and we might make a good crop. Be good to have a little money comin' in."

"Oh, yes. Bill, how did you do it?"

"Well, we scrounged around a little. Found an old mule, and the field hands helped a lot—the few that's left."

He showed her the vegetable garden next to the house. Beans were beginning to reach their tendrils toward the stakes, and the broad leaves of squash and pumpkin were already stretching to shade their little blossoms.

"It's beautiful, Bill. You've done so well I don't believe you need me anymore!"

Bill blushed with pleasure. "We'll always need you, ma'am. When's Mr. Richardson comin' home?"

"Soon, I—I hope."

The next afternoon saw the approach on the river road of the vanguard of the enemy's retreat. Their forces were pitifully shrunken now, and there was no singing, no loud shouting—nothing but the roll of a few wagons, the soft thud of dispirited feet.

Elizabeth, who had been sitting in the sun—in the garden

again—watched the distant, moving figures with mingled emotions. She was glad, of course, that they were retreating, that they had failed in their plans to take the South, but she could not help feeling sorry for them. Gordon had told her how they had gone into battle at Guilford on empty stomachs after a twelve-mile march, with no supplies near enough to be available. He had told her, too, how the surgeons in the king's army had gone back to the field after the battle and had divided impartially, as had the Americans, their scanty medical goods with each other. When people were basically so kind, it was a great pity their differences couldn't be settled without war—without all the destruction, the suffering, the heartache, that went with it.

She sighed, remembering her own heartache, the problem still belaboring her mind. Then the thought came suddenly that she herself was about to retreat: she was about to run away, robbing James of his child and the child of its birthright. For the first time she felt a great love well up in her for the little creature distorting her body, and she realized that even if the rest of her life must be spent without ecstasy, she would not leave. This was home. This was her baby's home—she would stand and fight!

She got up slowly, feeling older somehow, and started up the brick-bordered path toward the house. The April dusk was gathering in a soft, blue fragrance. Wind murmured in the magnolias down the avenue.

Having made her decision, she felt strangely lighthearted. She would go in and tell Mamba that they were staying. But she stopped at the sound of rapid hooves in the horse-pond road. She stood motionless until the rider came into view, dismounted hurriedly at the block. James!

The sudden racing of her heart swept away any thought that might have slowed her steps, and she gathered up her skirts and flew down the path into his open arms.

There was no need for words. He held her close, so close and so long that Mamba, watching from the window upstairs, thought he would never let her go.

Beaming, she called to Tip-toe, handing him her big ring of keys. "Mix de rum punch! An' tell Beezie Ah wants a dinner on dat table tonight. We's got three to eat!" Then she added sternly, though her eyes were shining, "An' looka heah, boy, Ah wants it served proper. You walk sof' 'roun' dat table lak you bin taught."

ABOUT THE AUTHOR

Mrs. Meredith is a native Texan, educated in Washington and the University of Texas. She was given the basic plot and facts of this award-winning first novel by her great-grandmother, who was born in Harmony Hall and whose great-grandmother is the heroine of the story.

The research for the book was extensive, reaching over most of the original thirteen colonies and the history of England during the reign of George III. Description of historical characters, costumes, architecture, etc., were taken from portraits in Independence Hall in Philadelphia, Williamsburg, Va., and in homes and libraries, wherever found, that displayed anything pertinent to the period.

She currently lives in Florida.

More Big Bestsellers from SIGNET

- ☐ **TORCH SONG by Anne Roiphe.** (#J7901—$1.95)
- ☐ **OPERATION URANIUM SHIP by Dennis Eisenberg, Eli Landau, and Menahem Portugale.** (#E8001—$1.75)
- ☐ **NIXON VS. NIXON by Dr. David Abrahamsen.** (#E7902—$2.25)
- ☐ **ISLAND OF THE WINDS by Althena Dallas-Damis.** (#J7905—$1.95)
- ☐ **CARRIE by Stephen King.** (#J7280—$1.95)
- ☐ **'SALEM'S LOT by Stephen King.** (#E8000—$2.25)
- ☐ **THE SHINING by Stephen King.** (#E7872—$2.50)
- ☐ **SLEEP POSITIONS: The Night Language of the Body by Dr. Samuel Dunkell.** (#E7875—$2.25)
- ☐ **OAKHURST by Walter Reed Johnson.** (#J7874—$1.95)
- ☐ **FRENCH KISS by Mark Logan.** (#J7876—$1.95)
- ☐ **COMA by Robin Cook.** (#E8202—$2.50)
- ☐ **THE YEAR OF THE INTERN by Robin Cook.** (#E7674—$1.75)
- ☐ **MISTRESS OF DARKNESS by Christopher Nicole.** (#J7782—$1.95)
- ☐ **SOHO SQUARE by Clare Rayner.** (#J7783—$1.95)
- ☐ **CALDO LARGO by Earl Thompson.** (#E7737—$2.25)

THE NEW AMERICAN LIBRARY, INC.,
P.O. Box 999, Bergenfield, New Jersey 07621

Please send me the books I have checked above. I am enclosing $_____$ (check or money order—no currency or C.O.D.'s). Prices and numbers are subject to change without notice. Please include the list price plus the following amounts for postage and handling: 35¢ for Signets, Signet Classics, and Mentors; 50¢ for Plumes, Meridians, and Abrams.

Name_____